REBELS AND RUNAWAYS

EDEN ACADEMY BOOK ONE

GRACE MCGINTY

ALSO BY GRACE MCGINTY

Hell's Redemption Series

The Redeemable/The Unrepentant/The Fallen

The Azar Nazemi Trilogy

Smoke and Smolder/Burn and Blaze/Rage and Ruin

Dark River Days Series

Newly Undead In Dark River/Happily Undead In Dark River/Pleasantly Undead in Dark River

Black Mountain Mates

Hunting Isla

Eden Academy Series

The Lost and the Hunted (Prequel)

Heart of the Hounded (Prequel)

Stand Alone Novels and Novellas

Bright Lights From A Hurricane

The Last Note

Castle of Carnal Desires

For my readers. Every single one of you.
But especially the ones who don't even blink when I say I
want to write a story about a detachable dick.
You guys are seriously the best.
G x

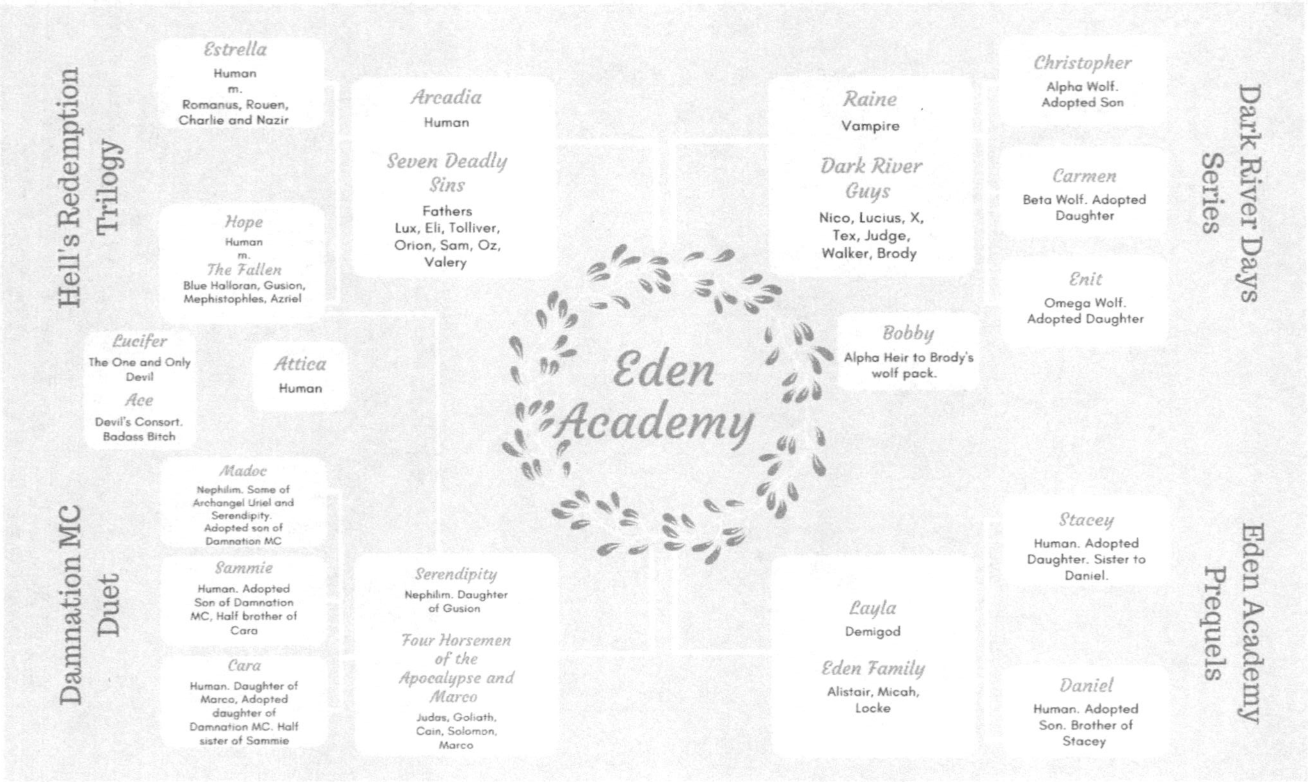
Eden Academy
Hell's Redemption Trilogy
Estrella
Human
m.
Romanus, Rouen, Charlie and Nazir
Hope
Human
m.
The Fallen
Blue Halloran, Gusion, Mephistophles, Azriel
Lucifer
The One and Only Devil
Ace
Devil's Consort. Badass Bitch
Attica
Human
Arcadia
Human
Seven Deadly Sins
Fathers
Lux, Eli, Tolliver, Orion, Sam, Oz, Valery
Damnation MC Duet
Madoc
Nephilim. Some of Archangel Uriel and Serendipity. Adopted son of Damnation MC
Sammie
Human. Adopted Son of Damnation MC, Half brother of Cara
Cara
Human. Daughter of Marco, Adopted daughter of Damnation MC. Half sister of Sammie
Serendipity
Nephilim. Daughter of Gusion
Four Horsemen of the Apocalypse and Marco
Judas, Goliath, Cain, Solomon, Marco
Dark River Days Series
Raine
Vampire
Dark River Guys
Nico, Lucius, X, Tex, Judge, Walker, Brody
Bobby
Alpha Heir to Brody's wolf pack.
Christopher
Alpha Wolf. Adopted Son
Carmen
Beta Wolf. Adopted Daughter
Enit
Omega Wolf. Adopted Daughter
Eden Academy Prequels
Layla
Demigod
Eden Family
Alistair, Micah, Locke
Stacey
Human. Adopted Daughter. Sister to Daniel.
Daniel
Human. Adopted Son. Brother of Stacey

PROLOGUE
CARMEN

Bobby was lookin' at me with a frown again. I didn't know why he was here. Not like he was my boss or anything. He was only four years older than me, but whenever me or my littermates, Christopher and Enit, got in trouble, they'd always call Bobby. No, not Enit. She never got into trouble.

It wasn't like us and Bobby were related, but it probably had something to do with Pack politics, and the fact that Bobby was the next Alpha of the Nîso Pack. So here he sat beside me on the hard plastic chairs out the front of Principal Pea's office.

I swung my legs in the air like I didn't have a care in the world. I was still short for twelve, and no one let me forget it.

"Why'd you do it, Mouse?"

I screwed up my nose. I wished he wouldn't call me that like I was still a baby. "He deserved it."

"But why? You know what Miss Pea said about fighting. It's instant suspension." Yeah, Bobby was worried. I didn't think Miss Pea would kick me out though.

I turned and looked at Bobby's dark eyes, and my chest felt funny, but I wasn't sure if it was because my hand still ached from punching Josh in the face, or because I enjoyed the way the blood spurted from his nose, or because Bobby had the darkest, prettiest eyes I've ever seen.

Yeah, it was probably the bloody nose.

Bobby did that thing where he waited for me to answer with a patient look on his face. I liked to think of it as his future Alpha face. It'd stopped working on me years ago though.

"Josh squeezed my boob. I hit him in the face. Seemed fair at the time."

Bobby's whole body went rigid. "He did what?" The growl in his voice made me want to whimper, but I ducked my head, looking over at him from beneath my lashes. I didn't respond though, because just then the door opened and my dad stepped in.

Well, one of my dads. I had, like seven, and none of them were actually my real dad. But I loved them anyway, and they loved me.

I breathed a sigh of relief, and then my face stretched into a grin. It was Lucius. Thank God.

Bobby stood and strode over to Lucius, his body still held tightly. He'd had a growth spurt a year ago, and now he was nearly as tall as Lucius. He murmured something in a low voice, and I strained to hear.

Whatever Bobby whispered made Lucius' lip curl, and he thumped Bobby on the back. "You'll take care of it?"

"Yes, Sir."

Lucius nodded once. "Good."

With that, he strode toward me, a small smile on his face. His pointed teeth shone in the stark fluorescent lights. Did I mention most of my parents were vampires? Not me though, I was a wolf shifter. It was complicated.

"What mischief are you up to now, Carmen?" He didn't say it like mischief was a bad thing.

"I punched a boy in the face."

"Did you make him bleed?"

I grinned. "Yep."

He frowned slightly, his eyes boring into mine. "Did hurting him make you feel better?"

I shrugged. Lucius wouldn't judge me if the answer was yes. He was the most bloodthirsty of my dads, and his reputation was enough to make the most powerful beings fear him. Not that I'd ever seen it firsthand. My mom, Raine, would kick his ass if he so much as swore bad around us.

He appraised me for a little longer, then stood straight. "Okay. Let us go talk to your Principal."

As if summoned, the door to the Principal's office opened, and Miss Pea stepped out. She looked at Lucius and her whole body went on high alert. Yeah, Lucius had that effect.

"Lucius, I didn't realize it would be you coming down today."

Yeah, Lucius terrified the hell out of Miss Pea. I mean, I guess I got it. He wasn't exactly sane. But he loved Raine with something bordering on obsession, and by extension, he loved the rest of us too. He would protect us with a violence that was probably terrifying to others, but it was the only reason I ever slept at night.

"Unfortunately, everyone else is occupied. They decided I could handle one school visit without killing anyone," he joked, but even his jokes held a hint of death. Miss Pea's face was pale and I pressed my lips together to hold back a grin. Bet she wished she'd just given me detention now.

I saw the moment Miss Pea steeled her spine because she pasted a polite smile on her face. "Please, come in. I'm sure this will be quick."

Yeah, because no one wants to spend too long in a closed room with an ancient vampire. The Principal's office was a large, well-lit room, and the furniture was light and modern. Lucius waited for me to sit, and then sat down in the chair next to mine.

Miss Pea took a deep breath. "Carmen physically assaulted another student in the playground today, and under the rules of the Academy, she will need to be suspended."

I swallowed hard and looked at Lucius. The only sign he'd even heard her was a tiny crease between his brows. "I see. And for the other child? The one who touched *my daughter* without her permission? What will he get?"

The suggestion that he should definitely get some kind of punishment, or instead he'd get death, hung heavily in the air. I resisted the urge to smirk. The color had drained again from Miss Pea's face. Her eyes shot to mine.

"Is this true?"

I shrugged. "I handled it. You guys are the ones making a big deal out of it."

Miss Pea pinched the bridge of her nose. "Look, in light of the circumstances, I'm willing to let Carmen off with a warning. I will also talk to the other student." She met Lucius' eyes, which was really brave of her. I generally respected Miss Pea. She took no shit. "There will be no need for further action by yourself, Sir." Aw, no death and destruction for dear old Dad today. Miss Pea's eyes slid back to me. "Carmen, please, if it happens again, let one of the teaching staff know. It will not be tolerated in any situation, but neither will violence. Are we clear?"

I nodded, because I was pretty sure everyone in this room would know I was lying when I said, "Yep."

She shook her head at me. Yeah, the problem with Miss Pea? She was a telepath. I mentally apologized, and stood. Lucius let me leave the office first and then walked me down to the doors of the Academy building.

"You should head back to class. I will see you at home this evening. I believe that X is cooking some kind of roast beef thing. We'll have a talk about your propensity for violence later. I have pointers."

I smiled. "Thanks for coming and having my back," I said softly and I did something I rarely do. I stepped forward and hugged him. He stood stiffly, because Lucius wasn't a hugger, but eventually, he squeezed me back tightly.

"Always."

1

CARMEN - SIX YEARS LATER

I rested my chin on my hand as I sat at the long counter at Bert and Beatrice's Diner. Enit was making origami swans out of her napkin and Christopher was talking about some grunge rock band with one of our dads, Tex. Tex was blind, but he had a real affinity for music. He'd taught both me and my siblings how to play guitar and piano by the time we were eight.

My other dad, X, was trying to outfold Enit in origami, but all his swans ended up looking like roadkill. He could kill a man in the blink of an eye, or perform surgery, but folding paper was beyond him, apparently.

Beatrice bustled over with the largest plate of fries I'd ever seen, and I perked up. She smiled widely at us, and I couldn't help but smile back.

"How are my sweet little *bairns* today? Hungry, I hope? Bert is out back frying up some of those tomahawk steaks he saw on that cooking show, just for you three."

Huge ass steaks? Yeah, that was enough to perk up any girl, but especially a wolf shifter. Enit gave her a sweet smile, and I rolled my eyes. I loved Enit. I would lay down my life and tear out the throat of any person who so much as hurt her feelings. Because she was an Omega shifter, it was almost bred into my DNA to protect her.

But sometimes, she was too perfect, and living in the shadow of my Alpha brother and my Omega sister was like being suffocated on both sides. I was just a boring old beta. We didn't even get capitalization. A default setting. Run of the mill, everyday, nothin' special, beta.

I grabbed a handful of fries and stuffed them in my mouth. Beatrice kissed Enit's cheek and ran a hand down my smooth brown hair. If we had a grandmother, Beatrice would be it. Even my parents stepped carefully around Beatrice.

"Are you three excited to start the Academy this year?"

I was old enough to remember when Eden Academy was first built. I would have only been six, but Enit, Christopher and I were some of their first elementary pupils. We were definitely part of the first class to go through our entire schooling at the Academy.

It was a pretty cool set up really. It was your normal K-12 school, teaching the average school subjects, spelling, math, science. Shit that everyone needed to know, whether you were preternatural or just a human.

But once you graduated senior year, you went on to do an extra four years at the Academy. This was where they taught you what you needed to know as a supernatural in a world filled with humans and every variety of preternatural known to the Moon Goddess. From vampires and shapeshifters like my parents, to humans with extra senses and abilities. To actual freaking demi-gods like the co-founders of the school, Locke and Layla. They were called Offspring, and they were half *god*. Like actual deity. That shit blew my mind every time I thought about it.

Enit grinned at Beatrice. "Well, I'm certainly excited."

I snorted, and Christopher nudged me with his elbow. "Four more years of school? Of course, sign me up."

X chuckled from the other side of the table, snagging a handful of fries and somehow inhaling them. "Learning supernatural politics at the Academy will save your ass. Ask your mother, you don't want to stumble around in that cesspool blind. Not everything can be solved with your fists."

Now it was Tex's turn to snort. "Sure thing, Executioner."

Oh yeah, so two of my dads used to be part of the most feared mercenary team in vampire society. They were the ones who put down rabid vampires. How they ended up here being a doctor and a deputy sheriff still blew my mind.

But I knew that X was referring to my secret. The one that not even my littermates knew. Hell, only Lucius and X knew, and that was because Lucius had tattled on me all those years ago, and they'd decided that if I wanted to be a bloodthirsty psycho, at least I was going to be a properly trained bloodthirsty psycho.

The front door of the diner opened, and the room went silent.

"Who the fuck..." Christopher whispered, and I snapped my head around.

So, Dark River didn't get a whole lot of visitors, given the fact we were in the middle of fucking nowhere. And we definitely didn't get any visitors like the ones standing in the doorway now.

Unease tickled down my spine as I tried to take them all in, my gaze flying back to my dads. Tex was tense, his head tilted slightly to the side, as if he was trying to read the room using only his hearing. Tex was blind, but you wouldn't know it.

If you looked at X though, he seemed completely relaxed, the smug grin on his face resting there like he didn't have a care in the world. But I knew him well enough to know that he was poised to leap the table and rain down pain.

I turned back around, tucking Enit tighter between me and Christopher. A beautiful woman with golden hair was surrounded by four men. No, they weren't men, they were fucking bikers. Their patches read Damnation MC around a stylized horse head. There was another guy at the back, his dark eyes taking in everything, light streaks of grey coming from his temple. He looked a little older than the other guys, but hey, I wouldn't mind calling him Daddy.

Ensconced between them all was a girl who had to be my age, her looks so similar to the older guy, she had to be his daughter. She had long dark hair, dark eyes, and a smile that said she meant absolutely nothing good.

I liked her instantly.

They stepped toward the counter, their bodies tense. A huge fucking guy covered in tattoos was watching the whole room like he could kill us all if we made one wrong move. X stood, stepping from the booth and straightening to his full height.

Oh shit.

I went to stand, to run and get Lucius or Walker or Judge or someone who could talk sense into X before he got into a fight with a guy who literally turned my blood to ice.

I climbed to my feet, but then they glued to the floor. Because when the pretty girl moved, behind her was a guy.

Holy fuck.

Like holy bad boy, wet dream, take me now 'cause I am done, fuckness. I may have whined, and Christopher growled.

I dropped my eyes, and the head of every one of those strangers turned toward me. Including the hot bad boy with the panty-dropping pout.

Another huge fucker stepped forward, I swear this one was as big, maybe bigger than the tattooed guy, his eyes running between me and Christopher. He frowned. Did he think Christopher was chastising me?

I looked up, gave him a wink, and grinned.

Beatrice, bless her, stepped from around the counter, and my eyes went back to the hottie with a body.

I watched him as he watched the room. He was young, maybe Bobby's age? Definitely a little older than me. I could see tattoos peeking out from beneath the sleeve of his leather jacket, and his black shirt bore the same insignia as the biker's cuts.

I tuned back into the convo when the woman spoke. "Just stopping for something to eat on the way to the Academy."

I perked up. They were going to the Academy?

Well, the next four years just got more exciting, though the guy looked too old to be enrolling.

Beatrice nodded, her face friendly. "Of course. Come on, I'll show you to one of the booths at the back."

They all stepped in, and I realized that they hadn't been all hunkered around the girl. No, they'd all been standing around another kid, younger than us all.

And he was...

Shit, I think he was...

"An Angel," Enit whispered.

The kid with the flaming red hair had fucking wings. Big white and blue wings. "Holy Jesus," I whispered as he walked past, and the kid—I swear he must have been thirteen at most—looked over at me and winked. "It's Madoc actually." The hottie shook his head, and nudged him on, but Madoc wasn't done. He waggled his eyebrows. "And he's Sammie. In case you wanted to know." He gave me a cheesy grin, and I tipped an imaginary hat at him in thanks.

Yeah, I'll be seeing you around, Sammie.

The big, tattooed guy walked past X, and the whole room held its breath. They sized each other up, and I shook myself out of my lust filled thoughts to get ready to run for help again.

Their stare off ended when X grinned. "Like your tatts, mate."

The big guy dragged his eyes down X's body slowly,

admiring his tattoos as well. At least, I think it was his tattoos. When he looked back up, he quirked an eyebrow. "It's Goliath."

X ran his eyes quickly down the other guy's body too. "I bet it is."

Um, were they fucking flirting right now?

A man with an honest-to-god eyepatch whistled, and this, uh Goliath? Maybe? Winked and walked away.

What the hell was happening here? I took in that whole group, and when I looked at Christopher and Enit, I realized I wasn't the only one. I didn't know who these guys were, but they were going to shake shit up.

I could hardly wait.

2

The wilds of fucking Canada were eerily loud. I mean, I was used to being in isolated, rural locations, but this Academy took shit to the next level. I could hear bird cries and kids yelling, and the sound of the wind through the trees was almost deafening.

I turned away from the window and looked around at all the boxes. Cara was playing on her phone, and Madoc had somehow found his gaming console in all this crap and plugged it into the TV.

This house was going to be our home away from home for the next five years. I was already having fucking regrets. I could have been in the city, patching into Damnation. Trigger would be laughing his ass off if he realized I gave up being a Prospect to babysit for half a decade.

Still, I knew in my gut I wouldn't have been able to rest easy thinking they were up here by themselves. Cara would've had them all fucking leading a coup against the administration in a month.

Thank god our best friend, and lion Alpha, Bohdie was arriving tonight to help maintain my sanity and mitigate some of Cara's more impulsive behaviors. He was flying up, but his flight wouldn't arrive until late.

"We should get this shit put away," I grumbled, and Cara sighed, dropping her phone onto the coffee table. The parentals had just left, and Cara already looked like she was plotting ways to take full advantage of her freedom.

Fuck me.

"Madoc." The little shit ignored me. "Madoc, I'm serious. Get your ass over here and help. They'll be here soon."

Yeah, that had him leaping up. "When are they arriving?"

As if we summoned them, three Angels appeared, as well as my Aunt Hope and my cousin Attica. Not by blood, but they were family. Family was what you made, not the blood that ran through your veins.

They had a weird story, but you'd be surprised how quickly Angels and the Devil became a mundane part of your life. Mephistopheles made a great potato salad, and Gusion always cried a little if he got too drunk.

They were just part of the family, but granted, they had wings, could read your mind, and would drag you to the very bowels of Hell if you pissed them off.

Hope smiled, coming over to hug us all, starting with me. I couldn't help the goofy smile that I gave her back. Aunt Hope was like that, she made you feel happy without even trying. And Attica? She was basically a miniature version.

"Sammie!" she squealed, dragging me into a hug.

"Hey, kid." I ruffled her red hair as she climbed all over Cara. She was the sweetest little thing, with such a pure heart, and I would stomp any little fucker who hurt her.

Azriel, the former Angel of Death, huffed. "As well you should. We are trusting you with our heart." The mind reading bit was a real bitch sometimes.

So, no pressure or anything. Attica looked over at Azriel and rolled her eyes. "Dad. I will be fine. Besides, you guys, and Great-Uncle Luc are literally, like, a thought away. You're suffocating me." She rolled her eyes, and I swear to god, I stood there biting my tongue so I didn't laugh. She had them wrapped around her little finger. Three of Hell's Fallen Angels, literal Princes of the Underworld, and she put them in their place.

See, how could you not love that kid?

"I promise I'll take care of her, Sirs."

"We know you will, Sammie. We wouldn't leave her here if we had doubts," Gusion, the least intimidating of Hope's husbands, laughed. He was also Madoc's grandfather. Yeah, it was confusing. It was a whole thing. I guess that happened when you lived a really long time—your story had so many twists and turns that sometimes, it twisted right back around on itself.

Mephistopheles crossed his arms and frowned. "I voted for homeschooling."

Hope laughed, hugging Madoc tight. "You'll look after Attica, won't you Madoc? They both need an opportunity to live like normal children, and this is the perfect place. Sammie and Cara will care for them, and they'll have each other."

After some more grumbling, they got Attica sorted, popping in and out with stuff for her room. Handy damn trick. We'd driven up in the SUV, hauling all the stuff we'd need to live here comfortably.

Hope was right though. We'd gotten lucky. Eden Academy had given us our own house, so the kids didn't have to stay in the dorms and I didn't have to stay offsite in that creepy as fuck town.

Well, most of it had been creepy. Except for that girl. She hadn't been creepy at all. She'd been goddamn beautiful. Long dark brown hair, eyes so damn blue I swear it was like she could cut me with them like lasers. She'd smirked at me like she knew all my secrets, and hell, maybe she did.

When the guy next to her, her boyfriend or brother or whoever the fuck he was had growled at her, I was so close to walking over there and shoving my gun between his teeth until he apologized. Cain too. If there was one thing we didn't stand for in Damnation MC, and in our family, it was women being beaten down, physically or verbally.

Then she'd smirked and winked at Cain and my chest had done this weird thump. And so had my dick.

Someone cleared their throat, and I looked up and stared straight into the inky blackness of Mephistopheles' eyes. Shit, I needed to remember the company I was keeping.

Gusion laughed again, and elbowed Mephistopheles. "Leave him alone, Memphis. He's allowed to fantasize about pretty girls."

My cheeks flushed, and I picked up a moving box and shoved it in the master bedroom. One thing I had learned as a human in a supernatural world, was that I was always going to be at the bottom of the food chain, but screw it. It wasn't a competition to the top. Against Angels and immortal beings, there was no winning. All you could do was stand your ground, trust your instincts and know when to cut and run.

Speaking of running, I was dying right now. I threw on a pair of sweats and a tank, lacing on my Nikes.

The house was blissfully quiet as everyone got down to work. I ducked my head into Attica's room.

Somehow, it was already zen as hell, and she'd barely moved in. That kid was like a walking tranquilizer.

"Hey, Aunt Hope? I'm just going for a run while you're here to take care of all... this." I indicated the room, but I meant more than that. I meant Madoc two rooms over, and Cara downstairs.

She nodded, her normal small smile in place on her face. "Sure thing, Sammie. Actually, let me walk with you downstairs."

I stepped back so she could go down the stairs first. When I met her at the bottom, she stilled me with a touch on my elbow. "Look, Sammie, I know this is a lot of responsibility, and despite what the guys say, it isn't all on you. You are allowed to have a life. You are their guardian for the next however many years, not their jailer. And they aren't your jailers either. Have fun too, okay? They are teens not toddlers; they are capable of being alone for a few hours unsupervised on the Academy grounds. Besides, they're good kids. They won't get up to too much mischief." We both looked at Cara's door. "Well, most of them anyway. But you have as much chance of controlling that one as a snowflake's chance in Hell."

I chuckled because she wasn't wrong. Cara had always had a mind of her own, and I'd learned a long time ago that I couldn't keep her caged. I could only mitigate the damage.

"I got it, Aunt Hope."

She squeezed me to her side like I didn't stand a full foot taller than her. "Go run while I still feel guilty for offloading two preteens onto you."

I shook my head and stepped outside my terrace door. The Eden Academy compound was pretty cool, really. The huge building at the center was basically an impenetrable fortress. It must have cost a fortune, but it was a weird mixture of stone and reflective glass that made it blend so easily with the landscape. The houses were all situated under towering trees that must have been hundreds of years old, though how they'd managed to build the houses without damaging tree roots or trunks was beyond me.

The only sign that this place was inhabited at all was a giant mansion looking house in the corner, though even that was ruggedly rich. A massive log cabin with a wrap around porch and two stories. Insanity.

Stretching a little, I took off at a slow jog down the driveway, but I quickly turned off onto a path that headed into the trees. It was little more than a wildlife trail but I liked the tranquility of it.

I let myself get lost in the run, taking in different parts of the compound but not focusing on anything. Off to the right seemed to be a large sports field and beside that was what appeared to be a full working farm, complete with different types of crops and livestock.

I ran along the fence line, taking in a grizzled old horse that chuffed at me from where it chewed nonchalantly. I saluted it and ran back toward the woods.

I ran the perimeter, because I liked to know where the boundary line was. I noted that in the corner of each part of the fenceline was a small watchtower, complete with guards inside. These guys took their security seriously. I saluted one of the guards and he eyed me long and hard before he waved back.

I faltered on the track when I spotted another runner up in front of me. He must have been a hundred yards away, but he stopped, cocking his head to the side in a significantly animalistic move, and then turned until he spotted me. I continued running, because I didn't want to seem suspicious. He was definitely a supe of some kind then.

I wanted to mentally slap myself. They were all supes here. I was the odd one out for once. I was the human in a compound of *other*. As I got closer, I felt the power coming off this guy, even as a human.

I'd grown up around supes. Sera, my mother for lack of a better title, was Nephilim—half Angel, half human. Judas, Cain, Solomon and Goliath were the freaking Four Horsemen of the Apocalypse. The Devil himself built a fort in our backyard. Supernatural shit didn't scare me, but for a human, I had a pretty good sense for it. This guy was powerful, but his mannerisms were animalistic. My bet was shifter, Alpha definitely. My best friends were lion and bear shifters, so I knew the taste of their power.

He looked me up and down. "You're new."

I slowed my steps until I was standing across from him. A safe distance away, but not far enough to be offensive. I met his eyes and dropped them quickly, a shifter protocol drummed into me by a bear Alpha who didn't give a shit about formalities but still made sure we all knew them.

"Yep."

"Not supernatural. Human with an extra ability?"

"Nope. Just a regular human."

He frowned. "That can't be right. We don't enroll *Normals*."

I shrugged. I didn't correct him that I wasn't exactly enrolled. I kind of came as a package deal, because Cara hadn't wanted Madoc to come alone, and Cara got what Cara wanted. My dad couldn't trust Cara not to burn this place to the ground, because she was who she was, so they made a deal. Azriel had visited the Academy's administration personally to ensure that both Cara and I enrolled with Attica, and who said no to the former Angel of Death?

No one.

I was too old for their Academy program, so I'd

made myself more profitable by insisting I could do weapons training tutoring. And I could. What I didn't know about a gun, or a sword, didn't really need to be known. I could kill a man just as easily with a ballpoint pen as I could with a switchblade.

My parents had made sure I knew how, but then ensured I'd never had to use my knowledge. I appreciated that. Cara and me, we'd seen enough. I'd patch into Damnation eventually, and then maybe I'd be able to use my talents. Until then, I'd teach preternaturals with claws how to use a knife. Seemed redundant but whatever.

The guy in front of me stuck out a hand. "Fair enough. Hey, I'm Bobby. Alpha-Heir to the Nîso Pack."

"Sammie Richards, designated guardian of a whole bunch of punk kids."

Bobby laughed. "I get that feeling. You run pretty fast for a human. You track back wherever you came from?"

I grinned. "Nah, spent my time racing a lion Alpha growing up. Makes you fast."

The guy grinned. He looked about my age, maybe a year or so older. He had a nice face, but appraising eyes. Definitely an Alpha.

"Oh yeah? Wanna race?" His grin thought this would be easy, and in all likelihood, it would be.

But I didn't shy away from a challenge. I was a lot like my sister in that way.

"Sure." I looked the guy over. He was fit, that much was obvious. He wasn't bulky, but you could tell he worked out. I'd bet my favorite kicks that he ran like the wind. But still, I could never say no to a challenge.

"Like what you see, Sammie Richards?" Bobby laughed, like I should be embarrassed I was checking him out.

I wasn't. I had a healthy appreciation for the physical form, and the gender of the person really didn't matter much to me. It definitely didn't make me less of a man. I dared anyone to tell my dads, Goliath and Judas, that because they loved each other as much as they loved Serendipity, that it made them less.

There wouldn't be anything left for the authorities to find.

So I couldn't resist the small smug smile on my face as I looked him dead in the eye and said, "Yeah, I do." Then I took off toward the main Academy building, trying not to laugh at his gaping expression. "Your reflexes suck, Alpha. Are we racing or what?" I yelled over my shoulder, but I was already fifty yards away. Like I said, I was quick.

I'd gone off the path, but it didn't matter. The undergrowth was clear and well maintained, and I was used to running through the woods. It wasn't long until Bobby was hot on my heels, and when we reached the sports field, I put my head down and sprinted until my lungs burned and my heart felt like it would beat out of my chest.

Still, Bobby overtook me within the last ten yards, spinning to run backwards as he slowed. "You weren't kidding, human. You are fast," he laughed.

I grinned, feeling the expression stretch my face. Yeah, this Academy might be alright after all.

3

CARMEN

The best part of graduating from Eden High to the Academy was that I no longer had to wear the uniform. I mean, I got the purpose of them. The junior school wore a forest green, and the senior school wore grey, and for a variety of kids with differing aging rates, being able to quickly identify where they were meant to be was a godsend. But when you joined the Academy, you got to wear whatever you liked, as long as you were wearing the Academy blazer. And I'm not going to lie—my ripped black jeans, Doc Martens and this blazer was a definite style.

We rolled into the parking lot thirty minutes before school started, Christopher at the wheel and Enit actually looking excited for the first day. For three people born in the very same litter, we would struggle to be more different. Sure, Christopher and I had similar styles, jeans and tees, though his were bands and mine were just whatever graphic tees I liked.

Today was a Harley Davidson tank that I'd tied just above my belly button. I wore dark lipstick, and eyeliner as black as my heart, but both made my blue eyes look electric. My dark hair ran down my back in a wild tangle of waves. Shit yeah, I was feeling myself today.

Enit though, was my polar opposite. She had a long flowing skirt, a beautifully embroidered blouse and soft pink lipstick that set off her pale skin and white-blond hair.

Like night and day. Winter and summer.

As she bounced around me, I couldn't help but pull her into my side. "Calm down, Enit. You'd think we hadn't spent the last twelve freaking years here."

She squeezed me tightly, her Omega vibes washing over me. "I know, but I get to finally focus on my Omega talents, and pick a career path, and there'll be all sorts of new people to meet!"

I rolled my eyes but gave her a squeeze. I loved the fuck out of her, every sweet part of her nature.

I had no sweetness. I was all bitterness, the type you tasted before you died from poisoning.

As if to prove her point, the kids from the diner the other day all bustled out of one of the group homes, along with a couple of extras. One was a girl with the same red hair as Madoc, the kid with the wings. She had eyes too big for her face and a smile so wide, it was a wonder it didn't touch her ears.

The other one was a golden-haired boy, and he was big. I put my hand on Enit's arm, stopping her. The golden-haired boy stopped too, his head snapping around to look at us. Christopher stepped in front of us both, a low growl rumbling on the air.

The golden-haired boy raised his lip, holding Christopher's eyes.

Shit, another Alpha. I mean, there were a few of them here. Maybe five or so, but every single time a new one was introduced, there were fights. Bobby and Christopher were fine, I guess because they were introduced when they were so young, before they had all these fucking pheromones rolling around.

Christopher looked over his shoulder at us. "Stay behind me."

I snorted and he threw me his Alpha look. I rolled my eyes, but didn't move.

The golden kid stepped toward us, and I could feel his Alpha juju from here. Fuck, he was powerful. More so than Christopher? I couldn't tell unless they fought, but they were pretty well matched. It would be a rough fight.

"You have an Omega?" The blond guy growled, and this time my hackles raised.

I pushed Enit behind me a bit more. "What's it to you?" I shouted, and the girl was stepping up to him.

"Bohdie, enough. You're gonna start a fight on the first day."

Too right he was, especially if he didn't stop looking at my Enit like that. Because Christopher was going to punch his teeth in. Eesh, I didn't want to get expelled on the first day, but I still did what I always did. Ran in first and stressed Christopher right out. I slipped out of my blazer and handed it to my sister.

"Watch Enit," I whispered to Christopher, and then jogged around him.

"Fucking hell, Carmen. Get your ass back here."

I gave him the finger and slid to a stop in front of the new kids. I smiled pleasantly at the group. This close, I could tell the guy was some kind of feline. Jaguar maybe? Possibly lion? Definitely big cat. "Bohdie, is it? I'd prefer if you kept your Alpha eyes off my sister."

The guy grinned down at me. He was pretty, if you were into that Alpha bullshit. I had enough of that in my life, thank you very much. "Or what?"

Oh, I was so glad he asked.

I pulled back my fist and punched him straight in the face. I heard the satisfying crack of his nose. Honestly, I think I was addicted to that sound. His head snapped back, and the shock on his face was just as satisfying.

"You fucking bitch," he spluttered, launching for

me, and I fell into my fighter's stance. Oh yeah. Let's do this shit.

I swung again, but before it could connect, a hand grabbed my wrist and an arm wrapped around my waist from the back, spinning me away.

I tried wiggling out of the hold, kicking my legs forward to try and get some momentum but the guy's arms were like vices. "Enough, Bohdie," a voice growled, and I looked up at the chin of Sammie.

I stopped struggling so hard. I could appreciate being pressed against a hot guy for a few more seconds.

Then Christopher was there, in Sammie's face. "Get your fucking hands off her."

Sammie released me immediately, and I stepped away, looking over my shoulder and winking at him. That was until I heard the low rumble in the air. Oh shit. Lion shifter for sure.

I spun back around, and saw Enit there, right in front of Bohdie, the motherfucking lion. Fuck. "Enit, stop!"

But she just rested her hand on his chest, and the rumble dropped to a low purr. Still, I was by her side in a single step, wrenching her hand away, and when the lion shifter's golden eyes snapped to mine, I bared my teeth.

"Fuck off," I growled back. "Enit, stop touching the pussy."

Enit rolled her eyes, but stepped back to my side. But she smiled up at the huge ass Alpha. "Nice to meet you, Bohdie. I'm Enit."

Bohdie dipped his head low, a sign of respect. "Omega."

I huffed. At least he had chosen the right manners. In shifter society, feelings about Omegas fell one of two ways. They were revered or reviled. There was never any in-between. There'd been an incident in junior high with another wolf Alpha that had ended badly. Which was why Christopher and I were always extra protective when it came to other shifters.

Enit reached out to touch his arm again, and I whacked her fingers. Bohdie looked up and growled. "Yeah, yeah, pussy. I get it. You big bad Alpha. I'm lowly beta. Fuck off."

I grabbed her arm, spinning on my heel to drag her away and slamming straight into a chest. Ah fuck. That scent I knew too well. Busted.

I pasted on a wide, smug smile, giving my best impression of innocence. "Hi, Bobby. When did you get here?"

"Mouse, what the hell is going on here?"

Uh oh. Definitely busted. "Would you believe I'm making friends?"

Bobby's eyes travelled to the bleeding lion Alpha, the scared-looking thirteen-year-olds, and Christopher and Sammie who were looking as if they were going to throw down. Actually, when I looked closer, maybe it was Christopher and the girl who were about to come to blows.

His eyes travelled back to me. "No. I wouldn't. Christopher," he said, not yelling, but the Alpha in his voice vibrated like a wave. Both the lion Alpha and Christopher shuddered, but Christopher turned his back on Sammie and the girl.

She glared at his back. "I'll be seeing you, Chris," she muttered.

"Not if I see you first. And it's Christopher." With that, he walked toward us, herding us into the Academy building. I let him, because he looked really close to wolfing out on the first day. I looked over my shoulder one more time, noticing Bobby and Sammie standing close together, talking softly, but their eyes on me.

I turned back around, grinning to myself, and maybe putting an extra little sway into my hips. Enit shook her head, handing me back my blazer. "You're really something, Carmen," she whispered.

"Amazing? Fearless?"

She grinned. "I was thinking psycho."

I threw back my head and laughed. "You know what, I'll take it."

. . .

THE FIRST CLASS of the day had been shifter politics, and given who my parents were, that had been as boring as batshit. Honestly, my family tree was like the who's who of supernatural politics. I was good.

But I'd been dying for lunch, to get back outside into the sun. We grabbed our food from the cafeteria, Christopher holding the tray that contained all our lunches. Enit chatted softly about her class in herbology with Professor Ramer, and I tuned her out a little. The shifter girls watched Christopher hungrily, and I resisted the urge to gag. It had always been like that. Shifters responded to Alphas like cats all over catnip. I swear to god, I'd been fending off girls for him since elementary school.

No Cindy-Lou, he doesn't want to be your boyfriend.

What they seemed to forget was that while Christopher might be an Alpha, he absolutely hated everyone except a handful of people. He loved even less than that. He indicated our spot, which was empty despite the fact that the whole Academy seemed to be outside today.

I laid down on the bench seat, and waited. I didn't have to wait long as a shadow blocked out my sun. I didn't even have to open my eyes to know who it was. "Sup, Bobby? You're in my sun."

"Up, Mouse. We need to go for a walk."

I opened one eye. "It's done, Bobby. Let it go."

"Now, Carmen, or so help me, I'll..."

Uh-oh. He'd used my real name.

I opened both eyes and grinned up at his flustered face. "You'll what? Spank me? No offense, Bobby, but you aren't my father." I quirked my eyebrow. "But I'll call you Daddy if you want me to."

Christopher choked on whatever he was eating and Enit gasped. Bobby let out a frustrated sound, bending down and dragging me into his arms, dumping me over his shoulder like a sack of potatoes.

Then he marched me out of the courtyard like I was an errant child. I lifted my head to ask Christopher for help, but instead spotted Sammie talking to one of the teachers in an archway. He raised both eyebrows, and even from here, I could see his smug grin. I gave him the finger, and flopped my head down.

Ugh. Me and my mouth.

4

BOBBY

She was the most infuriating, frustrating, violent, beautiful girl I'd ever met. I didn't know how those things could even add up to someone who made me hard, but it did. She cursed me, wiggling around, and I resisted the urge to take a bite out of her ass. All I'd have to do was turn my head. Hell, maybe I'd spank her like she taunted me about.

Finally, when we were in the woods, I dumped her to her feet before I gave into my baser instincts.

"What the hell was that this morning?"

She stretched, straightening out her blazer that did nothing but hug her curves. "I was diverting an Alpha fight. You can thank me now."

I blinked. That was a purely Carmen thing to say. "You broke someone's nose to stop a fight? You're going to have to explain that to me."

She stepped closer. She reached out, putting her hands on my lapels. "Well, you see, it's like dogs and cats. Well, it is essentially dogs and cats. Christopher and that new Alpha? They're pretty evenly matched. If it came down to a fight, one of them was leaving in an ambulance. So what did I do? I threw my inoffensive beta ass at them in tribute. You're welcome."

When she was this close, smelling the way she did, it made it hard for me to remember that she was part of my Pack. I was going to be her Alpha one day. It was hard to remember her as that damaged little kid who'd followed me around like I hung the moon.

It was hard for me to remember when she turned from an annoying kid that I had to look after, to something else.

Probably when she hit Josh that time. I'd only been fifteen, but I felt responsible for them even back then. But when she punched Josh for touching her without her permission, I'd seen red. I'd beaten the shit out of Josh, and let's just say, he probably asked for written consent from women now. But from that point on, she went from a kid to something more precious that needed to be protected. To something I couldn't lose.

She was still rubbing the material of my lapels between her fingers, and I put my hands over hers, stilling the movement. Her hands pressed flat against my chest, and that was even more distracting.

"You can't do that, Carmen. You can't jump in with your fists, especially with an Alpha."

She frowned, stepping away and taking her hands with her. I wanted to howl at the loss of the touch, but I pushed that feeling down. Way, way, way down.

"Why? Because I'm a beta? Because I'm a woman?" The fire in her eyes was captivating.

"Because it is my job to protect you!"

She snorted. "Why? I'm barely your Pack. You don't have an obligation to me. You don't need to keep stepping in."

It was on the tip of my tongue to tell her why. I wanted to scream it out.

Because you're my mate!

I swallowed hard. I didn't say it. "How long has it been since your last fight?"

Her face shuttered, but she couldn't hide that fire from me. "Three weeks. There's another one this weekend."

My heart thumped in my chest. I hated those damn fights. Hated that she hopped into a bloodstained ring with men bigger than her, stronger than her, and let them beat her up. But I also knew she needed it. Needed to inflict the pain. Whatever was broken in her when she was a kid needed the violence to feel centered.

We all knew the story. Lucius had given Enit to

their mother, Raine, as a courting gift, after buying the wolf pup at the black market. Because he was a crazy bastard.

But Raine, their mother? She was the best person in the world. She'd made him go back and get the rest of her litter. But the shit that Carmen and Christopher had seen in that time between Enit being taken and Lucius murdering everyone to save them had damaged them both. She'd been mute for years afterwards.

So I did what any good secret mate would do. I hovered. I protected. I pissed her the hell off by always being around.

"I'll take you."

She huffed. "I don't need a chaperone, Bobby. I'm there because I can take care of myself. If I wanted someone to loom beside me like an overprotective menace, I'd take Christopher or one of my dads." She actually shuddered at the thought. I didn't blame her. The only ones that knew she fought, according to her, were Lucius and X.

I folded my arms over my chest. "I said I'll take you."

She rolled her eyes, straightening her shirt again. "Fine, Bobby. Whatever. You can take me to my fight if you're going to be such a bitch about it."

I bit my bottom lip, because the urge to pick her up in my arms, slam her against the tree, and kiss the brat out of her was almost overwhelming. She must have seen something in my expression, because she tilted her head and took a single step forward until she was back in my space.

She looked up at me, her eyes hooded. "You know what? Maybe I should invite Sammie. He's hot and I'm pretty sure he'd let me work off my post-workout endorphins on his body, you know."

Jealousy that was all-consuming washed over my body. "I'm pretty sure he's gay. He was checking me out yesterday on my run."

She let out a low, seductive chuckle. "Nah, he's definitely not gay. But if he thinks you're hot too? Even better." She wet her lower lip, her eyes glazing over with whatever she was thinking about, and the scent of her arousal—her arousal over someone else—made something inside me snap.

I grabbed her hips roughly, lifting her into my arms and slamming my lips onto hers. She tasted like heaven. Like spice, the kind that burns so good that you just can't stop. But there was sweetness in her too. The way her soft curves wrapped around my hard edges was glorious.

I spun her until I had her pressed against a tree and she kissed me back with just as much ferocity. Her long legs were wrapped around my waist, pinning me to her body so I couldn't escape, even if I wanted to. Which I didn't.

She kissed just how I'd dreamed she would. Fuck, no, she kissed better. She kissed how she lived. With no inhibitions, no second guessing. She kissed like she was fighting and it was heady as hell. My tongue slid into her mouth, tangling with hers, as we fought for control of that kiss.

I buried my hands in her hair, gripping it tight, holding her still so I could devour her. She moaned and ground her body on my dick, and I froze.

I dropped her to her feet, and she wobbled on shaky legs before I caught her. Then I leapt away like she was on fire.

We were both panting and her eyes were too wide, their sparkling blue depths wild like a storm.

I swallowed hard, taking another step back.

"I'll pick you up at ten on Saturday night."

Then I turned and ran away like the little bitch she accused me of being.

I jogged all the way to my next class. I took the stairs down to the second subterranean level of the Academy. There was one floor above ground level, and two more below. There were also several underground tunnels that would lead you up to the surface in the woods behind the Academy. Sometimes the Academy's roots as a refuge for preternaturals really shone through. Though, they hadn't had an incursion in the decade it had been open, from what I was aware.

Just my luck that my next class was weapons

training with the new guy. When I walked in, I noticed Sammie Richards over by the weapons cupboard, his grey tank top fitting snugly to his body, the Eden logo on the front.

All of his arms were covered in tattoos, and nice ones at that. He was damn good-looking, and I had to give it to Carmen, she had great fucking taste. Still, I wanted to put my fist through his face.

I sucked in a deep breath. She was my mate, but she didn't really know that. Sammie was human. He wouldn't know that either. Wouldn't know that she was even into him. How did humans exist with such shitty senses?

He must have felt my eyes because he turned, lifting his chin. "How's it going, Bobby?"

I strolled over, trying to keep my emotions in check. "It's... been an interesting day. How are you finding all the equipment?"

Sammie let out a low whistle. "It's all beautiful stuff. This sword?" He lifted down a long sword and did an elegant pattern with the blade. "She's just gorgeous."

He spoke about the weapon like it was a woman. Hmm, maybe Carmen was wrong about this one. I breathed out my tension.

"Can I ask you a question?"

Sammie lowered the sword. "Sure, but I might not answer it."

"Are you gay?"

His eyebrows shot up, and his eyes flicked up and down my body again, like he was trying to decide if I was gay and coming onto him.

His eyes met mine again. "Guess it depends why you're asking? Are we going to have a problem about it?"

I snorted, shaking my head. "Nah, man. Love whoever the hell you want." *As long as it isn't Carmen.*

He chewed his lower lip, and I noticed that there was a slight bump on his nose, like he'd had it broken before. We didn't get that as shifters. We healed too well. I kinda liked it though.

"Are you asking because you're interested in me? Because I gotta say, man, I don't know what the Academy's rules are on fraternization with students." He grinned and I rolled my eyes.

"What are you, like, twenty?"

"I'm twenty-one."

I shook my head. "I'm twenty-two. This is my final year of the Academy. So if anyone would be taking advantage…"

Sammie threw back his head and laughed. "So you are interested?" he murmured in a low voice.

Well, fuck. Was I? This wasn't what I was coming over here for, not why I wanted to know. The supernatural world had different ideals about relationships in

general, from how many people should be in a relationship, to relations between men.

Generally speaking, in the old days, we bonded for
strength. Oh sure, there were fated mates, like Carmen
was with me—

My brain stuttered at how lucky I was once more.
To have met my fated mate. It was a statistical impossi-
bility but there she was, all fire and sass and perfection.

Anyway, you mated for strength. Women who had
the strength to bear you offspring. Men who were
strong enough to hunt with you in a Pack. Whether
you made love to them all, or not, was entirely up to
you. As it should be.

So when I met his eyes and said, "Maybe," it was
the total truth. There was something about Sammie
Richards that was appealing. I could see why Carmen
wanted him.

"Well, in that case, I should warn you I'm not gay."
He shrugged. "I am bi, though."

With his words, I remembered why I was over here.
"In that case, about Carmen…"

He raised an eyebrow as other students began to
wander in. "You like her."

I nodded, because I wasn't about to explain that
she was my mate to a stranger, even if he was attractive.

He nodded again. "I can see why. She's something
else. Beautiful. Fiery. She screams trouble."

I snorted. "You've got that right."

He gave me a wide grin that made my dick begin to harden. "Sounds like a handful. And you know what they say? Four hands are better than two."

With that, he turned away and began to address the class, splitting them into skill levels, while I stood at the back trying to come to terms with what the fuck just happened.

Sneaking out when your parents were all vampires and the town came alive at night was simultaneously easier and harder. Easier because everyone was at work, except Tex and Brody. Harder, because everyone was out in the streets. So I'd developed a foolproof system. I walked out the back door, through the backyard and into the woods behind the house. Then I'd run to the main road just outside the town limits and Bobby would pick me up.

All I had to do was pretend I wasn't sneaking around. It was like stealing shit; if you put on a high-vis vest, no one asked questions.

I stood on the side of the road at our designated pick up spot. We'd gotten it down to a fine art since the first time we'd done this two years ago. Bobby had worked out pretty quick that I was up to something, and basically nagged me until I told him what it was. He'd threatened to tell my parents if I didn't let him come.

So I had, and secretly, I was glad he was there. He gave me a certain peace of mind that I wouldn't have had otherwise. He was strong and powerful and I felt secure with him in a way I rarely felt with anyone outside my parents and Christopher.

Bobby's beat up pickup truck pulled up, and I climbed in before it even came to a complete stop. I hadn't seen Bobby all week. Not since that kiss.

But man, I'd thought about that kiss every single second of every single day since then. Still, I needed to play it cool.

"Hey, stranger. Thanks for the ride."

Bobby gave me a weird look, but just nodded. "Who are you fighting tonight?"

I shrugged. "Dunno, Rat didn't say. Just that he had some new contenders come up from the States if I wanted to fight."

Bobby's frown deepened. "From the States?"

"Uh huh." I put my feet up on his dash, my worn high tops leaving dust prints on the plastic.

Bobby reached over and pushed my ankles down. "If we crash, the airbag will shove your knees into your eye sockets and destroy your face."

I rolled my eyes at him, but dropped my feet into

the footwell. "Wouldn't you love me if my face was all mangled?"

He was silent and I huffed. Not going to lie, I was a little hurt too. "It was a joke, Bobby. We kissed, I don't expect a confession of undying love. I've forgotten about it already."

Lie. Lie. Lie.

Bobby was still silent, but his fingers gripped the steering wheel in a white-knuckled grip. I looked out the window for the rest of the trip, ignoring the tension in the cabin of the truck.

Despite how much shit I gave him, Bobby was my best friend. Sure, we had our moments. We fought as often as we laughed, but Bobby? He'd had my back since I was five. So the sooner we got over this kiss weirdness, the better.

I needed Bobby.

Luckily the trip was pretty quick, and we drove up to an abandoned storage shed in the middle of nowhere. It sat on the very boundaries of Pack lands, in a sort of grey area. The Nîso Pack Enforcers didn't patrol it, but it was still technically part of the greater Nîso lands. I think that was the only reason Bobby let me come to these things, because even though he was twenty-two, and not all the people in attendance were Pack, he still had a little bit of authority. We pulled up under a tree, and I slammed out of the pickup, dragging my gear behind me. It was bare knuckle fighting, so I didn't really need a lot, but I had a lot of first aid crap in here just in case, including a mouthguard. I could heal most things, but I couldn't regrow teeth.

I waited patiently by the door until Bobby rounded the hood, and then he walked us in. Metal music played from huge speakers in the corners of the room and people writhed as they danced. It was packed here tonight, lots of familiar faces, but a lot of strangers too. It put me on alert.

Outsiders were never good, but I was itching for a fight. Bobby looked tense, his shoulders bunched as we walked through the crowd. The ones I knew as Pack moved aside, but a lot had no fucking idea. He stared them down until they dropped their eyes, but some of them weren't shifters and blatantly held his gaze.

There were no fancy change rooms or any shit like that, but Bobby led me to my usual corner. It was beside a window, away from where the booze was, and he could shove me in a corner where he didn't have to watch both my back and my front. It was fine with me. I wasn't here to mingle. I was here to bleed.

Rat appeared from the darkness, his grin lifting the edges of his scar. He wasn't as old as he looked, but he wasn't young either. Apparently too much liquor and blow could age even a shifter.

"Pretty girl! Glad you showed tonight," he shouted, and Bobby gritted his teeth. He didn't like Rat. I didn't want to be his best friend either, but he was a means to an end.

I rolled my shoulders. "Nowhere I'd rather be."

Rat nodded repeatedly. "You're opening with a kid from this new bunch. It'll be a good fight, but watch his hands. They go up like the Fourth of July," he giggled as he wandered off. Yeah, Rat was off his face already.

I pulled my earbuds out of my duffle and put them in my ears, blocking out the crowd as the sounds of Marilyn Manson's *Sweet Dreams* pumped into my ears. I strapped my fists, swaying to the music in the earphones. Bobby grabbed my right hand and strapped it properly. I looked up at him from under my lashes, my eyes snagging on his lips. Memories of how they felt beneath mine, how his body felt between my thighs, swam up unbidden, and I pushed them back down. I needed to be focused.

I kicked my shoes off, and shrugged out of my oversized hoodie. I'd stolen it ages ago from Bobby, and he let me keep it. It was my lucky hoodie; I hadn't died in it yet.

I bounced on the balls of my feet, stretching quickly, warming up my muscles. One of Rat's enforcers appeared, dipping his head respectfully at Bobby. He met my eyes, tilting his head at the ring.

I appreciated the fact he was big and silent. I couldn't have heard him anyway. I nodded, rolling my shoulders a few more times. I tore my earbuds from my ears and the sound of some screaming metal band made me wince.

I stepped forward, and Bobby walked with me. There was no octagon at this fight. It was rudimentary, underground fighting at its best. There was a ring in the dirt. Rat made it clear that if anyone stepped into the ring during the fight, he cancelled all bets, kept the money, and the pissed off crowd would tear apart the offender.

It was barbaric, but it worked. You could use your supernatural strength and speed, but no shifting to animals. If people wanted to see a dog fight, they'd just go see a dog fight.

I took a deep breath, shaking my wrists, and stepped over the white, painted line.

On the other side of the clearing, a kid stepped into the ring too. He had to be my age, maybe a year or so older judging by his build.

And the guy was built. He was tight. His muscles looked hard as rocks beneath his pale skin, and the V of his obliques were cut like the damn Grand Canyon. Scars criss-crossed his entire body and I swallowed hard. He was in tight shorts, and he had these weird metal bands on his wrists. That shit would hurt if it connected, but I wasn't going to be a wuss and complain to Rat about it.

When my eyes climbed to his face, it was to see a mouthguard flashing back at me as he grinned. I turned back to Bobby, who slipped mine into my mouth.

Bobby looked like he wanted to drag me out of here, so I stepped further into the center ring. There were no referees, just a high-as-fuck Rat.

I stood beside him, bouncing gently on my feet to stay warm. "Ladies and gentlemen, we have a real Lady and the Tramp matchup for you today. Our hometown girl versus our newcomer for the night—Flint, is it?"

The guy gave a sharp nod. Flint. It suited him, like his parents had named him after the dark grey color of his eyes.

"You know the rules. Fight goes until someone's unconscious or dead. No tap outs."

Flint quirked an eyebrow, but nodded. I lifted my chin. I knew the rules by now.

Rat stumbled out of the ring. I drifted back to the edge as the crowd muttered, placing bets and getting drinks before the fight.

I watched the kid in front of me. He held himself tight, despite the casual swing of his arms as he moved around. Flint was ready for a fight, no matter what direction it came from. "You're kind of cute," he yelled over the jeers of the crowd, his voice muffled from his mouthguard, but years of fighting meant I was used to conversing with mouthguards in. "Too pretty for the ring, anyway."

I grinned, and I could feel the feral stretch of it.

"Not too pretty to kick your ass. Are you going to be a talker? 'Cause I really only like that in the bedroom."

I lunged forward and he danced away with a laugh. "Oh, it's like that, hey? Just so you know, I can't go easy on you."

I frowned a bit at his words. I mean, I'd heard it all before, but usually it was *won't*, not *can't*. He lunged forward and jabbed at my face, and I cursed myself for my distraction. It just grazed my chin, enough to hurt but not enough to do any damage.

I reset myself, watching him move. He was fast and strong. He fought like he'd been doing it forever, his body relaxed like this was just another day at the office. But he had to be like eighteen. How could an eighteen-year-old move like a career fighter?

I feinted left, and then delivered a sharp jab to his ribs. He moved with the hit, minimizing the damage.

Definitely a pro.

I danced out of the range of his arms, but he was taller than me, with a longer reach. I was going to have to be smarter if I didn't want to die tonight. And despite the fact I needed these fights like I needed to breathe, I didn't want to die while I did it.

Flint laughed. "Pretty and fast. Not gonna lie, Sugar Plum, I think I might be in love."

The noise of the crowd faded into the background as we measured each other up. I moved without thinking. I let my body do the work, flowing around him to come up behind him and slam a fist into his kidneys. When he let all his weight drop backwards, I launched myself onto his back and twisted, aiming a few blows to his temple.

But as my back brushed the dirt, I realized I'd made a fatal error in judgement. I'd been too fixated on how fast he'd been, but despite his lean muscles, he was heavier than me too.

Just before I hit the dirt with a thud, he twisted, locking his legs in mine and getting under my guard. He grinned. "Sorry, Sugar Plum."

Then his fist hurtled toward my face. KO. Lights out.

Damn, she was fucking gorgeous. She was still pressed under my body, and for a second, I imagined it was pleasure that put her in this position, not pain. Someone called the fight, and then a hand was wrapping around my throat and dragging me off.

The big guy she'd come with was there, glaring down at me. I grinned, letting my power trickle into my hands. "It was a love tap. She'll be up in a minute, but she'll have a hell of a headache."

I'd pulled my punch, which meant I was going to get my ass kicked, but it was better than making her bleed. I hadn't drawn the fight out for long enough either, and that meant nothin' good.

I climbed to my feet and tried not to meet Rook's

gaze in the crowd. I could feel his eyes on me as I dusted myself off. The big guy picked up the girl, cradling her in his arms like she was a breakable doll and not a fighter.

"What's her name?" I asked in a lowered voice. Last thing I needed was to show too much interest in anyone.

"None of your damn business," the guy growled.

I gritted my teeth. "She fought well. I just want to put a name to the fists." I pointed to where a bruise was blossoming on my gut.

The guy hesitated. "Carmen."

Hmm, it suited her. Pretty, but tough. "If you like her half as much as you seem to, keep her away from this shit for the next couple of weeks." Until Rook was gone. Until I was gone.

The guy snorted and made his way out of the ring. She still hadn't woken up, but I wasn't worried. I hadn't hit her hard enough to do any real damage.

I made my way out of the ring, but no one cheered, no one slapped me on the back. I was basically a junk-yard dog, trained to tear out throats and get kicked around without biting back. I made my way to my shit in the corner, pulling on my boots and my hoodie. I fought barefoot, but I knew better than to walk around venues like this with no shoes. Only had to step on one dirty needle to learn that lesson. The next contenders got into the ring, both big bastards, and I knew from their faces that one of them was going to die tonight.

I needed to get the fuck out of here. The smell of these things was always godawful, like piss and cigarettes. And sweat. I pushed through the back of the crowd and out the back door. I walked past a couple fucking in the bushes, and tuned out the sounds of the grunting. There was a dirty trailer in the woods that Rat had put there for our crew. And I mean, it was filthy. There were cockroaches and fleas, suspicious stains and smears. The floor of the ring would probably be cleaner. But I'd slept in worse places, and that said something about my life.

There were three of us in here, but the other two guys weren't back yet. I rested my head against the door of the trailer, probably the cleanest part of the whole thing because the paint was peeling from the force of the weather. I didn't want to be in there yet either.

I got so little time alone, I was going to enjoy it for once.

"Kid."

My body stiffened of its own accord, but I forced it to relax. I turned, my usual sneer across my face. I was met with a fist.

It slammed across my face with bone-crunching force. Something shattered and I could only hope it healed right. I hit the ground hard, but scrambled to my feet because once Rook started laying in the boots, I'd be in for a world of pain.

"You bitch out of a fight like that again, I'll show you what I do to bitches."

Fear made my muscle tense and my heart race. I nodded sharply, not daring to so much as breathe in case he took it as an insult.

He backhanded me once more, making my head slam against the trailer wall, and then turned and melted back into the darkness. I stayed still until he was gone, and then I sucked in a deep, panicked breath.

I stared at the cuffs on my wrists, the ones that marked me as what I was. A slave. A half-blood Djinn with enough juice to make the illegal cuffs work, enough to have Anadari bracelets bind me to Rook as my master.

Sure, the Djinn Council had banned them years ago after the battle of New York, destroying every pair they could find, but still, on the odd occasion they popped up on the black market.

You know what else popped up on the black market? Orphaned Djinn kids.

Some days, I wanted to cut off my hands to be free of them, other days I knew I only had to survive another 86 years, and they'd come off of their own accord.

The bitter laugh that bubbled from my throat echoed around the woods, and I distracted myself from my morbid reality with thoughts of the girl from tonight. Carmen. So fucking fierce.

I went to the back of the trailer and slid down the side. I didn't feel the cold, and sleeping under the trailer was more agreeable than sleeping inside it with the guys. Eric was a straight up psycho who would murder me for my teeth, and Silar never slept anyway. I'd appreciated that over the years. Silar was a good guy with a shit past, which is how he ended up fighting for Rook. He'd taken care of me as a kid, but he was getting old and slow. I knew, deep down, that one day he wouldn't win his fight.

He'd be dead and buried in an unmarked grave like so many before him. And then it would be my job to take care of the younger ones. To make sure the predators in Rook's crew didn't make their lives any more miserable.

I slid beneath the trailer, looking up at the underside. But in front of me weren't wheel bearings and crankshafts. In front of me was a pretty girl with flashing blue eyes. And I wasn't a slave, I was her equal. Maybe we went to high school together. She'd wear my jacket like we were in fucking Riverdale and I was Archie and she was Veronica or some bullshit. I'd kiss her full red lips, and she'd gaze up at me with those wide eyes set in thick lashes as she wrapped those perfect cupid's bow lips around my cock.

I popped a boner in my shorts, and I wished I'd slipped into my sweats before getting under here. Still, I reached in and grabbed my cock. There was rarely a moment that I was alone, and honestly, some of the shit I'd seen had killed my sex drive.

But apparently it only took one pouty little brunette to bring it back. I imagined her soft curves beneath my body when I took her to the ground. I imagined what her husky voice would sound like as she whispered my name. She was fit and I bet she would be glorious naked. I pulled my dick, imagining her mouth around it. She'd be rough, but I'd love it. I'd slide my dick inside her tight body and I'd fuck her until she was screaming my name over and over.

I pulled my cock harder, more roughly. Jesus, I was going to come like I'd never touched myself before. I rolled to my side, and I imagined her lips on mine, laying her head on my chest and telling me her hopes and dreams. I imagined being in a position that I could help her achieve them. I imagined her whispering 'I love you' into my ear as she rode my dick.

I came all over the grass, and I mentally apologized to all the bugs that had just drowned in my gunk.

Panting loudly in the silence, I rolled onto my back. I tucked my dick back into my pants before Eric came home and saw me with my dick out as an invitation. I shuddered.

Hopefully, this was as close as I'd ever get to Carmen. Hopefully that big fucker would keep her away.

Because I meant nothing but pain and death for her and anyone I got close to.

My head throbbed. I'd woken in the front seat of Bobby's truck, and the hard set of his jaw warned me against small talk. I'd snuck back into the house, and slid beneath the covers just before dawn. Three hours of sleep didn't help my raging headache at all.

It didn't help that every time I closed my eyes, I pictured a fire-haired, scarred guy with a wicked grin. And if I wasn't thinking about him? I was thinking about that fucking kiss with Bobby. Sensing either my shitty mood, or the fact I was in pain, my siblings stuck to me tighter than glue. Enit had her hand in mine, and Christopher hovered closer than Peter Pan's shadow.

Luckily, by the time I'd woken up in the morning, the bruise had faded enough that it was easily covered by makeup, and if anyone noticed I caked it on a little thicker than usual, no one had mentioned it.

I drowned my pain in a cup of coffee so big that I could have actually drowned in it. Luckily for us all, we hadn't had any more run-ins with Bohdie the golden lion, or the rest of the group. I had found out that the girl who looked so much like Sammie was his sister, Cara. Madoc with the wings was their adopted younger brother and the red-headed girl with the soft face was their cousin.

Something had happened between Christopher and the girl Cara, so now apparently we hated her. I snorted. I liked seeing Christopher rattled. I also liked to see him rattled by a woman. Shifter society was still wildly patriarchal, so power to a girl who could bring an Alpha to his knees without being naked on a bed at the same time.

But still, family loyalty meant I'd probably have to kick her ass at some point.

I was going to need a diagram or something. That was the thing about the supernatural world. It was all about the bloodlines.

I had combat class this morning, and I'd heard through the grapevine that Sammie was tutoring it, as well as running the weapons class. It was interesting really, considering he was a human and young. What could he have possibly done in his short life to be considered a viable option as a combat tutor at a school for the preternatural?

There was a depth to Sammie, and I was going to explore it. Preferably with my tongue.

Enit had her Omega class, and Christopher his Alpha Leadership seminar, so I was by myself in combat. Well, there were a bunch of other first years here too, including all the beta bitches who normally hung off Christopher, but right now were making moonstruck eyes at Sammie.

I growled low in my throat, and several looked over at me. I lifted my lip in a snarl and Teesha smirked. I hated that wench.

Honestly, I wouldn't even call her a bitch, because that would be an insult to my kind. She was like pond scum. Pond scum that had broken my brother's heart in the seventh grade and was all over Bobby like a rash at all the Pack's social events.

I wanted to kick her ass out of principle, but I resisted. We were adults now, and when you were an adult, you didn't just hit girls in the face because they pissed you off.

I strode over to the bleachers on the other side of the gym, already in my tight shorts and sports bra. I was looking forward to kicking some Academy-sanctioned ass.

The room started to fill up when the door opened, and Cara Richards swished her way in. Half her body was tattooed in brightly colored ink, and I envied her. She was wearing an outfit similar to mine, though she had a tied up shirt over her sports bra.

The whole room stopped speaking as she strode in, and my gaze drifted to Sammie in the corner. He rolled his eyes, but looked at his sister fondly.

They didn't acknowledge each other, and that was fair enough. Everyone knew they were related, but at least she wasn't going to try and coast through this class. When she stopped beside me, I raised an eyebrow. She stuck out a hand and I looked at it.

"I'm Cara."

I shrugged, shaking her hand like we were fucking businessmen. "Carmen."

A frown folded her pretty face. "Hm, that's a bit close to Cara. I'm not sure we can be friends."

I snorted. Dammit, I kinda liked her. "Well, that and the fact my brother hates your guts."

Cara curled her lip. "The feeling is mutual." She sighed heavily and slumped onto the bench beside me, despite her declaration that we couldn't be friends. "It's a pity though. I know your kind."

"Wolf shifter?"

She grinned and shook her head. "Nah, trouble. With a capital T."

I threw back my head and laughed, because somehow, in two short interactions, she had me pegged.

"Like knows like, I guess," I said, smirking back.

"Fine, for this class, we'll be friends. But outside, I'm going to have to hate you. Sorry. Family first." I shrugged like that statement made total sense, and judging by the way she was nodding seriously, she got it. "By the way, my friends call me Mouse."

Someone cleared their throat, and I looked up at Sammie. "I'm not sure if I like what's going on here," he murmured softly, his eyes bouncing between me and his sister. "This? It can only mean trouble."

Cara snorted and I laughed again. She rolled her eyes at her brother. "Relax, Sammie. We're mortal enemies. The Montagues and the Capulets. The Angels and the Fallen. Coke and Pepsi. Ne'er shall the two combine."

Yeah, Sammie didn't look convinced. He eyeballed his sister and mouthed, "Behave," as the other instructors walked in. I watched his ass as he walked away, and let's face it, so did half of the class.

He was in a tank, all his ink on display and he was glorious. I look over at Cara in time to see her scrunch up her face. "Jesus, not you too. I kind of hoped you were into girls so we could be friends."

I lifted a finger. "One, don't assume."

She looked genuinely gleeful for a moment. "You're a lesbian?"

I scoffed. "No. Unfortunately. I'm all about the dick."

Cara sighed heavily. "Yeah, me too. But it would

have been nice to have one female friend who didn't want to ride my brother like he was a white stallion and there was a sunset waiting on the other side of his twin bed."

I blinked. And then I blinked again. "Okay... I'm not going to unpack all that. That shit is for your human therapist. Though, if you want to meet a white stallion shifter to ride, I know a guy." I leaned in closer. "But I've heard that he doesn't share all those horse traits, if you know what I mean."

Cara snorted loudly, drawing the attention of the other half of the class. The ones that weren't looking at Sammie's impressive guns. She gave a fake pout. "Well, that's disappointing. So what was point number two?"

I cleared my throat. "I wasn't checking out your brother, I was admiring his artwork. Yours too. You have some beautiful ink."

The grin that lit up her face was radiant, and for a moment I was enraptured. She was human, I knew that without a shadow of a doubt, but right then, I could have been convinced she was a siren. "Thanks. My parents own a tattoo parlor, and my dad is one hell of an artist. So's Sammie." She held out her arm and I had a quick look at the sleeve that ran from the center of her hand, up over her arm and disappeared under the sleeve of her tee. It was dark. There was a dying tree with a snake wrapped around its base, and that led up to Death, who was directly below a woman in a black mourning veil with a blue and white feather between her teeth.

The exact blue and white of Madoc's wings. This tattoo meant something, and I didn't know Cara well enough to pry. But one thing I was certain of though was that the artistry of it was unbelievable.

"Did your dad do this?"

Cara looked at it and shook her head. "No, this one was Sammie. He designed it, drew it and tattooed it."

My eyes shot back to the man himself. He was talking to John, the combat trainer, his brows drawn together as he concentrated on what the other man was saying. From here, I could see that his tattoo was similar to Cara's. They both had a crying woman, though his one was holding a gun to her temple. Death was kissing La Catrina, below wings either side of a sword.

Below that was a rotted apple. The style was a little different, and you could tell a different artist had inked it.

John's voice boomed around the room. "Alright, people. Pair up so I can see everyone's base skills."

"Wanna fight me, Not-A-Lesbian Carmen?" Cara asked, and I was in the middle of nodding when Sammie reappeared.

"Oh, hell no. Neither of you has an off switch. One of you would be bleeding on the floor in seconds. Cara, go pair up with Teesha."

She screwed up her face. "Who the fuck is Teesha?"

"The blonde with a face like a smashed crab."

Teesha spun on her heel and glared at me. I just grinned and waved. "Fuck you, bitch," she screeched and I waved her away.

"No thanks, Teesh. I've seen where you've been."

She smirked. "All over your brother's cock."

I rolled my eyes, and flipped her the finger. "You say that like it's a complicated feat. You just have to have tits and spring-loaded thighs."

I turned back to Cara and she was shooting daggers at Teesha. On my behalf? Or because she'd mentioned screwing Christopher? Oh goodie, can someone say sexual tension?

She strode over, and Sammie sighed. "You know where the first aid kit is here?"

I pointed at the corner of the room, where we had a kit that rivalled an entire first aid tent at a music festival.

Everyone else had paired off, and I was the odd one out. John looked over at us. "Mouse, you go with Sammie."

"Sir, I don't—" Sammie protested, but John had already walked away. John was Pack and knew that I was trained in MMA. He knew that I was damn good at it too. Did he know that I fought underground? Maybe, maybe not, but if he did he hadn't told on me yet.

Sammie frowned again, but moved toward an open

section of mat. "I hold a significant height and weight advantage on you, but then you're a tiny thing so most of your opponents will have that. I'm going to come at you, and I want you to show me how you'd evade me."

I held in the smug smirk that wanted to spread across my face. "Okay. I'll try."

He lumbered toward me, almost hesitantly. I let him grab me, and for a microsecond, I appreciated the strength of his body as it encased me.

But you know what's better than a hot body?

Vindication.

I slipped my foot between his legs, and then stepped into him rather than trying to wiggle away. He went down and I went down with him, but then I had him in an arm bar in exactly eight seconds from the moment he touched me to the moment he tapped out.

He looked up at me, my grin manic and wild as it stretched across my face. "So, not a beginner, huh?"

I let go and helped him to his feet. "Not quite. I have seven overprotective fathers and a thirst for pain."

He tilted his head at me. "Yours or someone else's?" I might have imagined his voice dropping, or the note of lust that colored his question.

I bit my lip, and his eyes followed the gesture. "Does it matter?"

He was silent for a long time, his eyes just taking in my face, the frown still there despite the desire I could see. Finally, he shook his head. "No, it doesn't matter.

Just don't forget to tap out if you need to." He cleared his throat, and nodded back at the mats. "Alright, let's go again. I won't underestimate you this time."

I nodded and sucked down some water, before climbing on the mats. He might seem impervious, but I'd seen him adjusting his hard dick in those sweats.

Sammie Richards wanted me as much as I wanted him, and I was pretty sure that when I had him—and I would have him—he would make it hurt so good.

8

ome of the older Academy kids had invited me to a party on Friday night, and I couldn't seem to find a reason to say no. Cara was in a rare mood, someone had definitely pissed in her Cheerios because when I asked if she was going, she all but threw a punch at my face. Whatever, she could stay behind and watch the kids.

Bohdie was dressed in a white t-shirt, and it set off the golden hues of his skin perfectly. Bohdie was beautiful, but straight as an arrow. It was a bit of a shame really. We made a matching pair, me with my black tee and tight ripped jeans. Black and gold. I checked on the kids, and pulled a few beers from the fridge.

Bohdie's room was on the ground floor beside Cara's, which would normally worry me, but Bohdie and Cara had grown up together. To say they had zero interest in each other was an understatement. I was waiting for that Hallmark moment when they realized that they were both attractive and single, but I was beginning to think it was never coming. I was fine with that. They were both too similar, too stubborn and wild, that they would burn too hot and break each other in the end.

We wandered toward the back of the compound, and I could see the glow of the bonfire from here. They weren't trying to be quiet, so I had to assume the faculty knew what they were doing. But I guess, if they were all old enough to drive, to vote, to die in a war, then they were old enough to drink flammable liquids around a roaring fire.

Bohdie's eyes tracked the shadows for threats, and I left him to it. Sure, I was always on alert; I was raised by killers after all. But Bohdie would pick up any threats long before my human ears caught up. I trusted Bohdie with my life. We'd been friends since we'd moved to Black Mountain when I was eight. He was a good guy who believed in family above all else.

There were very few people I trusted in this world, and I knew that it probably had something to do with how I grew up, pre-Damnation anyway. I was rich. Hell, I was still rich. The only son of a ruthless businessman, who'd smiled for the camera by day, and sold women for a clandestine cartel at night. He beat me, beat my mom, and was just an all-around shit human being. I wouldn't feel bad for my mother though. When she'd had Cara, she'd neglected her so badly that even my fragile two-year-old brain had known that if I didn't feed her and care for her, my little sister would die. They'd both 'accidentally' died in prison, and not a soul in the whole world mourned them.

We hit the outer ring of the crowd, and there had to be fifty or so people here, and I shook thoughts of the past from my mind. I recognized some faces from the combat and weapons classes, but I didn't know them well enough to chat to them casually yet.

Making friends didn't come easily to me. Bohdie, however? He was as congenial as they got. He cracked a beer and passed it to me, and we found an empty place near the fire. There were a couple of tigers lying around in front of the fire, and I didn't know if they were two-natured shifters, or shapeshifters like Bobby. There was a difference apparently, and I was a little envious of Cara, who'd be able to learn all this stuff without actually being one of them. She'd be less of an outsider.

"It's weird being so far from home," Bohdie murmured, and I nodded. It really was. Black Mountain and Damnation MC had been home for so long, they were basically a safety blanket. The shifters of the

Mountain had taken us in without too much trouble, once they realized that my parents didn't want to destroy the place. Cara and I had gone to school with the bear shifters and Bohdie. We'd all gone to high school among the humans. But this? Preternaturals of every shape and variety, just lazing around and being friendly? They'd created something special here, and I wasn't even sure if anyone would know just how special for years to come.

"Not going to lie, Teach, I didn't think you'd show your face at one of these parties," a voice said behind me, and I couldn't help the smile that curled my lips, even before I turned around. "Aren't you a little old for parties with students?"

I snorted, looking down at Carmen. She was average height, but in her heels, she could almost look in my eyes without craning her neck. She was wearing a short leather skirt and a torn crop top with a band I'd never heard of branded across the front. She had on her signature dark lipstick and her winged eyeliner again, and she looked fierce and infinitely fuckable. God help me. "I'm younger than some of the students here."

She held a bottle of Jack in her hand and a grin on her face. "Touché. Guess there's no living out my naughty schoolgirl/dirty professor fantasies with you then."

Her pale-haired sister gasped and smacked her on the arm. "Carmen!"

"Come on, Enit. You know I'm kidding," she soothed, but I didn't miss the wink she threw me.

I couldn't help my boom of laughter. Damn, this girl was something.

There was a deep rumble, and Bohdie was bowing his head at Enit. "Omega."

Enit reached out, putting a hand on his bicep. I watched Carmen tense, like she was ready to throw down with Bohdie again if he made one wrong move. Bohdie was tense too, but the way he watched the Omega, I mean Enit, was with pure reverence.

"Tonight is a party, Alpha. You can relax," Enit grinned, but I saw something in her face that wasn't entirely teasing when she looked at Bohdie.

Interesting. I mean, I got it. Bohdie was handsome as hell, and Enit was beautiful in an ethereal kind of way that made you want to care for her. She wasn't my type—I liked my girls a little more kickass—but for a lion Alpha like Bohdie? She was catnip.

It got too much for Carmen, who grabbed Enit and pulled her away. "I think I hear Christopher calling. We should go before he gets mauled by she-wolves again."

She looked over her shoulder, her eyes travelling over my body before biting her lip. My dick got hard just watching her ass sway away.

"Brother, you are fucked. You should see your face right now."

I dragged my eyes away from her departing back, and turned to Bohdie. "Oh, you can talk? Omegaaaaa," I mocked, and Bohdie snorted.

"I did not do that."

I cocked an eyebrow, but didn't get time to say anything further when he was surrounded by a group of women. Well, more accurately I guess, we were surrounded by a group of women. While Bohdie soaked it up like a lion soaked up the sun, it made me uncomfortable as hell. Especially when Teesha from my combat class stood way too close. I took a step backwards, but she mirrored the move.

She pasted a smile on her Barbie pink lips and I grimaced back. "So, Mr. Richards, how are you settling in? Has anyone shown you all that Eden has to offer?" she purred.

Woah, that was about as subtle as a two-by-four to the temple. "Yes, thank you. The orientation was very comprehensive."

I wondered if she was a shark shifter, because the smile she gave me next was a hundred percent predatory. "What about the extracurricular... activities?"

"Jesus fucking Christ, Teesha. Have some self-respect, or at least a little less cheesiness," Carmen said from behind her, and I almost audibly sighed with relief.

Teesha whirled on her heels, her hair slapping me in the face. Well, that was embarrassing. "What self respect could you have, Trash? Your own Pack didn't even want you. They sold you to fucking skin dealers for drug money or something. Why don't you, and your prick of a brother, go back to Deadsville where you belong. Even better, go back to the gutter, slut."

Woah. I wasn't quick enough to catch Carmen before the first hit connected—okay that was a lie, but the little bitch deserved it—but I did manage to catch her before she landed a second strike.

Bohdie caught the other girl around the waist as I dragged Carmen away, and I faintly heard Bohdie using his Alpha voice to get the girl to stop coming after Carmen.

I did not sign up for girl fights.

It didn't help that everyone within a ten yard radius had heard Teesha's comments and was watching Carmen like she was a bomb waiting to explode. I took her into the shadows beyond the glow of the bonfire and set her on her feet.

Her big blue eyes were all fire and fury, but beneath that, they were slightly shinier than they normally were. She paced back and forward, her hands clenching and releasing, as she wrangled her anger.

She stopped and looked up at me. Her eyes were

huge and my mouth bypassed my brain. "Come here," I whispered.

When she stepped into my arms, it felt so fucking right. I barely knew this girl, but when she buried her face in my chest and screamed, I knew that this moment, right here? This was what I wanted. I wanted to be this girl's rock. Her anchor. I stroked her back as she got all the frustrated anger out.

Finally, she dragged herself away and took a shaky breath. Then she launched herself into my arms.

I let out a little oomph as I caught her, and then her lips were on mine. Her legs wrapped around my waist and her arms around my neck, and I didn't stop to think. I kissed her back with as much possessive desire as she was throwing at me. She tasted like Jack Daniels and cherry lip gloss. I wanted to feast on her mouth forever.

I dragged my lips away from hers, and wrapped the smooth waterfall of her hair around my fist. I pulled her head back, and she mewled, which made my dick achingly hard. I kissed her jaw, the column of her throat and she moaned.

"What the fuck is going on here?"

She froze against my body, her eyes going wide again. I looked around her shoulder at Bobby. The pain on his face was raw, but by the time I'd slid Carmen to her feet, he'd hidden it behind a mask of fury.

As she looked up at me, I watched her drop her own feelings behind a nonchalant mask, and she spun on her high heel to look at Bobby. "I don't know, Bobby, looks like two consenting adults making out, but I'm willing to try it again, you know, for science."

"Cute, Mouse. Get the fuck back out with the crowd."

She stepped up into his space, and I leaned back against the tree behind me. My hard-on was raging, and the unfulfilled lust between these two wasn't helping. "Or what, Bobby? You aren't my boyfriend or my father. You get no fucking say on what, or who, I do."

Ah, I didn't imagine the pain in that statement, and I doubted Bobby missed it either. "I'm your Alpha."

Eesh, wrong thing to say. Her whole body tensed. "Not yet, you aren't. Run along, *Alpha*. I can take care of myself."

"Dammit, Mouse," he growled, and she threw a punch at his face. He dodged. The dude had good reflexes.

He cut her off with a kiss. I went to step in, to pull him off her if she didn't want it, but when her body curved into his the way it had into mine a moment ago, I stopped. They kissed like it was an extension of their argument, all rough hands and clashing teeth.

I was going to blow my load in my pants. When his hand slid down over the curve of her back, only to slide up under her skirt and grip her ass, I grabbed my crotch and squeezed, trying to maneuver my dick somewhere comfortable or give myself some kind of relief; I didn't know which lie I was going with.

When I saw she was wearing a lace thong, I groaned, and it seemed to break them from their trance. Bobby looked straight at me, his gaze defiant like he expected me to be some kind of jealous mess. Honestly, that was the hottest thing I'd ever seen and one day, I wanted to see us all naked and doing this exact same thing together.

So I held his gaze, held up my hands, and grinned. "Four hands, brother. Four hands."

His eyes bounced between me and Carmen, and then back again. Then he stepped around us both, shifting into a large black wolf between one blink and the next, before taking off into the woods. Carmen stared after him, and the look on her face broke my heart a little.

"You love him?"

She bit her lip and shrugged. "Since the year I turned fourteen and found out he beat up Josh Stanmore for touching my boob in the seventh grade." She shook her head. "But he's not for me." She pasted a smile on her face, and grabbed my hand. "Come on, let's go back to the fire and you can tell me all about who Sammie Richards is and how he came to be one of the only humans in a school for the inhuman."

I shook my head at them both. She might want the

Alpha, but that kiss we shared? It was something. It wasn't just hot, it was perfection, and I wasn't going to give up without a fight.

And if it meant I had to share her with a hot Alpha with an angst problem?

Perfection.

9

CARMEN

The following Saturday rolled around, and I'd successfully avoided both Bobby and Sammie all week. I needed a medal or a gold star or something. The Ostrich Award. Still, I was kind of surprised that when I stood in our meeting place before the fight on Saturday, Bobby didn't show.

I swore under my breath and trudged back into town. The closer to home I got though, the madder I became. What, did he think I needed him? He was wrong. I could take care of myself, with my fists if I could, but with my teeth if I had to.

I crept back through the house, grabbing the keys to Christopher's car. Technically it belonged to the three of us, but Christopher was a typical Alpha control freak, so he always drove whenever we went anywhere. And we always did everything together. We were three parts to a whole, even more than normal littermates. What happened when we were five...

I slammed the wall down on that thought.

I breathed a sigh of relief that he'd only parked in the driveway and hadn't garaged it for the night. It started nearly silently—hooray for Teslas—and I rolled out of the driveway. I took the quickest way out of town, knowing that if Christopher woke up and realized both me and the car were gone, he'd flip.

I turned on the radio, listening to the weird old emo music Christopher liked. It suited my mood anyway. I was fuming, but the drive was over quickly. I might have been speeding a little.

It was a bumper night at the warehouse, and whoever Flint belonged to had brought in the crowds. That usually meant one thing. They were ready to fight to the death.

My chest constricted at the idea that Flint wasn't fighting with me tonight. Would he be fighting with one of the others, maybe one that was willing to snap his neck for the bonus? Rat only ever paired me with people he knew would hold back from killing me, probably because he didn't want to end up with his heart crushed in Lucius' fist. Or maybe they made that decision themselves, if they were smart enough.

I parked Christopher's car under a light, close to the back doors of the building. I tucked the keys in a spot under the dash and hoped everyone would be too drunk to try and steal the car. I grabbed my gear, getting changed in the car because I didn't want to be vulnerable inside without Bobby watching my back.

Fuck him. I didn't need him.

I strapped my hands myself, tearing at the stiff tape with my teeth. Then I did the other hand. It wasn't perfect but it would do. I pulled off my hoodie, but left on my boots. I looked like GI Jane with my workout shorts and crop top. I kind of missed the armor of Bobby's hoodie, but I didn't need any reminders of that fucking fiasco right now. I needed my head in the fight.

I stepped through the back doors and kept to the edges of the crowd. There was already fighting, and I could hear the dull thuds of fists hitting flesh. I moved toward my spot at the back, avoiding eye contact but keeping my head high. If they sensed weakness, they'd pounce. But they were used to me being with Bobby, and so far the predators hadn't realized I was alone. Let's hope it stayed that way.

I was almost to my spot when a hand reached out and grabbed me. I whirled around on a snarl, ready to throw a punch, but stopped myself inches away from Sammie's face.

He looked furious. "What the hell are you doing here, Mouse?"

His eyes ran down my body, and his fury doubled down as he made the logical connections. Lust tinged his gaze too, but he squashed it quickly. Mad it was, then.

"I think the more interesting question is, what are you doing here, Sammie?"

His face shuttered, and his shoulders tensed. "I like to watch the fights."

I frowned, because what did I really know about Sammie? "Illegal underground fights? With supernaturals?"

He shook his head. "No, normally I just watch normal, run of the mill humans beat the shit out of each other."

"You know they fight to the death here, right?"

"And... you... no!" His face grew even stormier, and he reached to grab me.

I danced away. "You even so much as think about manhandling me in here, I will chop your balls off, shift, and then let my wolf eat them, you hear me? I don't care who you are, but right here, right now, you are in my domain, so keep that he-man shit to yourself," I whisper-shouted furiously. If he carried me out of here like an errant child? I would lose all the credibility I'd gained over the last few years.

I strode off toward my corner, but I felt his presence behind me. To my left, some guy was getting his face turned to mush, as if to prove my point. The deaths, although they were truly few and far between considering most of us healed like supernaturals, no longer made that big of an impact on me.

I was broken, and I accepted that.

The guy in the ring would live if the guy on top of him stopped now. But given the manic set to his jaw, that wasn't going to happen. Sammie watched on, and when he realized no one was going to call a stop to the fight, went to step in.

I grabbed his arm this time, tugging him into the corner with me. "Are you trying to die?" I hissed. "You step in that ring and interfere, and they'll tear you apart like the cinnamon roll you are."

He lifted up his jacket and flashed a gun. And a knife. I mean, I wasn't surprised considering he was our weapons tutor.

I pointed at the gun. "That won't save you here. You need to leave, before I fight." Because I could just tell he was the kind of asshole who'd flip out about it and do something stupid. He already had that look on his face.

They dragged the limp body of the last guy out of the ring, and Rat stepped in. He looked a little less high today, which boded badly for us all. He deserved his name. He was a conniving motherfucker.

"Next up we have the new kid, Flint, and a hometown favorite, Monster. This is sure to be a good fight. Get your bets in now."

Oh no.

No.

I swayed on my feet, and Sammie grabbed my arms. "Carmen, are you okay?" he whispered, but I couldn't drag my eyes away. Monster deserved his name. Even in a world of animals, he was a savage. Brutal. He liked to torture his opponents before he snapped their necks. It was barbaric, and usually I liked to fight before he came on so I could go home before I had to watch.

He couldn't fight Flint.

The two fighters stepped into the ring. Monster first, huge and scarred, one side of his body burnt. Rumor had it, his Pack had been so horrified by his actions, they'd burned him at the stake. But he'd managed to get free, and murdered them all. No one could prove it, and at this stage it was probably more likely to be an urban legend.

"A Djinn?" Sammie whispered, and I whipped my eyes to the other side of the ring to Flint. Was that what he was?

"How can you tell?"

"The things on his wrists, they're slave cuffs. They're illegal, but they were once used to bind Djinn to their masters for a hundred years."

The actual hell? There were several things wrong with this whole thing.

No one should be a slave, and Flint was what, like eighteen or nineteen? He had over eighty years to go being a slave. The second thing was how did Sammie, a human, know more about Djinn than I did?

I knew deep down in my gut I couldn't let the inevitable end of this fight happen. I'd figure out a way to get him out of this.

The fight started, and Flint weighed up his opponent. Monster just stared at him with dead eyes.

Flint's hands went up in flames and I gasped. Monster flinched slightly, but his posture didn't change at all.

Rat knew what he was doing, the sick bastard. Put the burned monster against the kid with flames for hands.

Monster was still loose and ready for whatever Flint threw at him. So when Flint stepped forward, his flaming fist swinging at Monster's face, the big guy sidestepped it easy. Then his face morphed, and his teeth elongated, antlers growing from his head as he partially shifted.

"What the fuck..." Sammie whispered behind me, and I looked at him with wide eyes.

"Monster is a Wendigo."

Flint reared back, his other hand coming up to protect his face. He dodged Monster's fist, and laid a decent hit to the other creature's stomach. But he wasn't quick enough. Monster got inside Flint's guard and snapped two quick punches to his face, sending him to the floor.

"Get up, get up," I whispered, but the force behind Monster's punch must have rattled his brain, because as he struggled to his knees, he wasn't fast enough to avoid a kick to the ribs. I heard them crack and my heart cracked with it.

I looked over at Sammie, and he must have seen what I was thinking, because he nodded, his hand going to his gun. Monster was on top of Flint, his huge boulder-sized fists slamming into his face with those long, jagged teeth bared.

He was going to tear out his throat, then put his hand in Flint's chest and eat his heart. It was his signature move, and the crowd was almost giddy with excitement.

I couldn't let this happen.

I shoved my way through the crowd, and dived into the ring. I hit Monster with my entire body weight, and it was enough to push him off balance and topple him to the side.

The crowd howled its outrage. I didn't dare take my eyes off Monster, aiming a punch at his face that he caught easily. He was still partially shifted, his antlers sharp and pink, soaked with the blood of people he'd killed in the past.

But he just held my fist, not trying to snap it like he could have done so easily. He just stared up at me with the saddest eyes I'd ever seen. Looking into his black depths was like looking into an abyss of despair, and I was dying inside with him.

"Carmen!" Sammie yelled.

It snapped us both out of the trance, and he threw me off. I skidded into Flint's body, as he struggled to his knees once more.

The crowd was surging closer. Fuck, we were going to be torn apart. I pulled Flint to his feet, but I couldn't hold him steady. If I shifted I'd be vulnerable too long. Fuck, we were going to have to fight and flee.

Sammie fired above everyone's head. "No one fucking move."

But they were above logic. They were screaming like animals and the noise was terrifying. As if the mob made up its mind as one, they charged. I braced myself. I didn't have regrets, this had been the right thing to do.

Suddenly, there was a body in front of me. Rat's enforcer.

He looked over his shoulder at me. "Pack first," he yelled, and I noticed there were other shapeshifters in the fray, fighting against the crowd. Shit, this was turning into a brawl. There was a bloodcurdling roar and I turned to see that Monster had turned full Wendigo.

I wanted to vomit and piss myself. He was fucking terrifying. So thin he was almost skeletal, his face was elongated like the skull of a buck, huge pointed antlers sticking from his head. He was easily seven feet and his body was hunched in on itself, basically melted down one side.

I was too scared to move. We were dead.

Dead.

When he turned and charged into the enraged mob rather than at us, I was momentarily shocked into stillness.

Rat's enforcer—fuck, I couldn't remember his name—turned to us. "Get the fuck out of here," he growled, his fist caving the face of a guy with a knife. He pulled his own Bowie knife, the thing big enough to gut a bear.

Flint moaned, and I looked at him curled in pain. "He's calling me. I can't resist it." He lifted his wrists. His face was wild with fear, and I knew it matched mine. "Go. Get out of here."

Fuck that. I'd made enough of an impression now. I wasn't going to waste this chance. "Come with us. Flint. Come with us! You'll be safe."

Even as he nodded, he was moving away from me. "I can't stop it. The cuffs make me obey."

So I did the only thing I could think of. I reached out and punched him in the temple. He went down like a sack, and I grabbed his waist. Even though I was strong, carrying a guy as tall as Flint was hard.

"Sammie!" I shouted, and he took one look at me and another at Flint, tossed me his gun and hefted the unconscious Djinn over his shoulder. "Go out the back exit!"

I nodded my head at the large double doors at the rear of the building, firing my gun at people who came after me. And I was shooting to kill. Most of these guys would survive a bullet wound, but if you got one in the chest, you were down for a while. If you got one in the heart? Well, not all of us were lucky enough to be immortal.

I grabbed a second gun from the waistband of Sammie's pants, and when I stepped out of the ring, I realized that they didn't know we'd left. It was a frenzy, and I could already see the blood soaking into the dirt of the ring.

We burst through the back doors, and I pointed to Christopher's car. "Let's get the hell out of here."

Sammie threw Flint in the backseat and scrambled in behind him. I climbed into the driver's seat, grabbing the keys. I jammed them into the ignition, silently chanting "Fuck, fuck, fuck," as the engine roared to life.

"Go!"

I floored it and skidded out of that clearing, knowing I could never return. I'd made the right choice, but when I looked at the unconscious guy in the back seat, his face black and blue, I didn't think that this was the end of the story at all.

I woke up handcuffed to a bed. Not going to lie, it wasn't the first time. Judging by the ceiling, I was probably in someone's basement. Again, not the first time.

Though it was the first time for the combination of both. I tested the cuffs, and they clinked against the metal bed frame.

The burning ache in my gut told me that Rook was trying to summon me back, though for some reason it was muted. Normally, the pain was so intense it felt like my insides were on fire and the compulsion was overwhelming.

Wherever I was, it was blocking the power of the Anadari bracelets.

"Sorry about the cuffs. Sammie said you kept trying to sleepwalk out of the house."

I looked over and saw Carmen sitting on the washing machine in the corner. She was in black skinny jeans, high tops and a black blazer with an insignia on the breast pocket. I couldn't make it out from here, but it looked like a uniform.

Well, now I remembered why my head ached. "Good left hook you've got."

She grinned, and it was the perfect blend of joy and mischievousness. "Sorry about that. But I don't think that was my fault."

I raised an eyebrow, but my face ached. I remembered the giant *thing* with antlers coated in gore and fists like freight trains. "What the hell was that thing?"

Carmen's face lost its happiness. "Monster the Wendigo."

I shook my head, and I swear I heard it slosh. "Aptly named." My face grew solemn as I remembered the rest of the night. "You have to take me back. Rook isn't someone to fuck around with. He will kill you."

She snorted. Actually damn snorted. "I'm not worried. You're in Eden now."

Well, she'd lost her damn mind. Rook was not to be messed with. I'd seen him skin a guy he considered a traitor to his organization.

Carmen jumped off the washing machine and walked over to me, wiggling a handcuff key from her pocket. She looked down at me from beside the bed, and I had the most vivid fantasy about her climbing on top of my hips and making me beg.

She smirked as if she sensed the direction of my thoughts. "If I let you go, are you going to go running back to your master?"

It was a valid question, but I still hated the word master. Rook was a psychopath who'd bought me as a child and kept me trapped with him since. So I gritted my teeth and shook my head. "I don't think so. The urge to return is there but it isn't strong. If I'm awake, I can fight it."

To her credit, she didn't question me. She just unlocked the cuffs and stepped away. They'd been wrapped around my slave cuffs, which was probably the only reason I hadn't burned them off in my sleep. My wrists ached where the magic pulsed uselessly against my skin.

She swung the cuffs around her finger before slipping them into her back pocket. "Where'd you get the cuffs from anyway?" I said, raising an eyebrow. "Your dad a cop?"

"Yeah, actually. But the cuffs are mine." She winked and I knew it then. I was definitely in love.

I wondered if I could kiss her or if she'd punch me in the face again. I also wondered why that thought turned me on so much.

I took a shuddering breath. "So now you have me

trapped in the basement, what are you going to do with me?"

She sat on the bed beside me, and I marvelled at her balls. I mean, I was basically a stranger, a stranger with a known taste for violence. Where was that big bastard from the other night? Why was no one down here making sure I wasn't a psycho who would attack women and rape them on conveniently located beds?

Because I'd met those kinds of psychos. Shared meals with those people. And I wasn't convinced that they hadn't tainted me with that level of evil. Because you couldn't grow up in the darkness without taking a bit of it into your soul.

I should just leave. Yeah, that would be the right thing to do. Maybe I could take whatever magic-blocking tech was hiding in this basement and head to New York, try and find the Djinn Council. Get them to take these things off my wrists so I could be free.

"Flint?" I turned back to the girl, my accidental savior. "I know that look. But you don't need to run. I've got you, okay?"

"You don't understand."

She stood, slipping off her jacket and unbuttoning her jeans. I gaped. I wanted to say something witty or sexy, but I just stared like a teenage boy seeing boobs for the first time. But when she pulled down the waistband of her jeans at the back, I saw the red scarred numbers.

Lot numbers. She'd been sold in the black market before.

She redid up her button and turned back to me. "I understand better than you think. This is the beginning of freedom for you, I just need you to hold strong while we navigate your way out."

There was a thumping overhead, and then the door at the top of the stairs wrenched open. A boy with blue and white wings half leapt, half fell down the stairs.

"Mouse, Cara said I had to race down here and tell you—"

Carmen gripped the kid by the shoulders. "Tell me what?"

The voice at the top of the stairs had a gentle British lilt. "Tell you that we're here."

She looked up at the top of the stairs, and two huge guys walked down the stairs. "Ah crap," Carmen muttered, and I was pretty sure the one built like a Mack truck chuckled. She stepped in front of me a little, like she could hide me behind her tiny frame. Still, hiding behind people wasn't my style, so I stepped up beside her.

The one at the front, with thick framed glasses and gold eyes tilted his head to the side. "Really, Carmen? You didn't think we'd know when there was a stranger on the property?"

She shrugged and gave them a megawatt smile. Honestly, it was blinding and I couldn't look away. She was so fucking beautiful, how were they even breathing?

"I was kinda hoping I'd have more time to come up with a good argument, but here we are." She turned to me. "Flint, meet Alistair and Locke, two of the founders of Eden. Did I mention how wonderful and magnanimous they are, and that Eden was originally started to provide refuge for poor, lost, supernatural souls just like yourself?"

Alistair rolled his eyes, and Locke coughed to hide a laugh. "Carmen, this is why you send Enit when you want something. Schmoozing does not come naturally to you."

Carmen pouted and crossed her arms over her chest. "I didn't think I could win a fist fight with Locke, so I was trying diplomacy. Aren't you the one always telling me I should talk through my problems?" she said to Alistair, and the dude literally shook his head.

He turned those yellow eyes to me, and they were freaky as hell. They looked ancient, like he could see into my soul, and had me weighed and measured in seconds.

Locke stepped forward and put out a hand. I took it tentatively, and when I say his huge hand engulfed mine, I mean it. I felt like a toddler.

When he frowned and gripped it, showing my slave cuff to the other guy, Alistair, I tried to pull away.

Alistair looked at me, a frown on his face. "I

thought they outlawed these. Probably explains the magic bouncing off the wards though." He looked between Carmen and me. "Let's go to my office. Pea has already called your parents, and Mr. Richards has been pulled from his class."

I noticed the kid with the wings was still standing there, looking at us all like he was watching a trainwreck.

Locke looked over his shoulder. "Head to class, Madoc," he said softly, and the kid took off up the stairs like his feathers were on fire.

Carmen looked like she wanted to do the same. "Sirs, this had nothing to do with Sammie, this was all my idea. You shouldn't punish him."

Locke let out a booming laugh. "This is very much a Carmen-style idea, there was never any doubt. I bet your captive didn't even have a choice in the matter, am I right?" We were both stubbornly silent and he chuckled. "Yeah, that was what I thought." He ushered us up the stairs and I went, because fuck tangling with that guy. Besides, my gut said he was okay, and it helped that Carmen didn't really seem scared of them. More peeved at getting caught. I walked through the house for the first time, and it was a nice place. Reasonably modern, it had a spacious kitchen and dining room, and a living room through an open arch. It was clean and bright and I wasn't sure I'd even lived in a place like it in my entire life.

I saw a pretty girl standing at the front door, and she looked like she was ready to pick a fight. Carmen quickly shook her head, and when she walked past, she reached out and squeezed her hand.

The girl looked me up and down. "Not the weirdest thing they've pulled out of Sammie's basement," she murmured. "But definitely the prettiest."

Carmen looked over her shoulder and bared her teeth, but her eyes were laughing. "Eyes off, Cara. This one is mine."

The girl pouted playfully, but nodded.

We stepped out into a beautiful sunny day, which made the stormy-looking dude in front of us seem even more ominous. I recognized him as the guy from our first fight. He stepped up to Carmen and she looked up at him with the same fury, but it was tinged with sadness, her arms crossed against her chest. "What do you want, Bobby?"

"I let you go alone once, and there's a brawl, seventeen of our Pack are injured and there're countless dead bodies that I'm pretty sure Monster has chewed on," he said in a low voice, and Carmen flinched.

But then she steeled her spine and stepped up so they were nose to nose. Or like nose to nipple. "They shouldn't have been there."

"You shouldn't have been there!" Bobby yelled, and I grabbed Carmen's arm and pulled her behind me, my hand lighting up instinctively.

The two big guys were there instantly, Locke blocking us from view, and Alistair speaking to this Bobby in a low voice. Locke looked down at us, his eyes travelling from my flame-covered hand to where I had Carmen tucked behind me.

"Ifrit, hey? I've met a couple of your kind. Quick to anger, but generally cool people. You got that problem, son?"

I shrugged, because I didn't think so, but I'd grown up around psychos. How was I to know what the appropriate level of anger was?

"I'm sensing there's more to this story than I originally thought, and it has something to do with the underground fight ring Ghost messaged us about this morning."

Who the hell was Ghost?

"Ah shit. Shit, shit, shit. I'm in so much trouble now." Carmen stepped around me and looked up at Locke. "Are my parents here already?"

He nodded, and looked over his shoulder. Bobby was still here, but he looked a lot calmer. Alistair lifted his chin, indicating we should continue.

Kids in school uniforms stopped to stare as we walked past, and I got more and more confused. What the fuck was this place?

Oh fuck, I was so screwed. I shuffled along between Bobby and Flint like a prisoner heading to death row. We walked through the Academy building, and I saw Enit and Christopher staring at me. I mouthed that I'd explain later, and Bobby threw a look over his shoulder at me.

That look said a lot.

That look said he was done keeping secrets for me. Christopher would definitely know that I'd been fighting before the day was out. As would my parents. As would all of Nîso, if I was right about my suspicions with Ghost. Uncle Ghost, not that I'd ever call him that to his face, was my dad's best friend. He was mute, and one of the few people who hadn't pressured me to speak when I was a traumatized little kid.

Toward the center of the Academy building, on the

ground floor, were the staff offices. Most of the class-rooms were on the subterranean levels if they weren't outside. I looked between Alistair and Locke as they led us to the conference room. "I'm surprised Micah isn't here. No offense, Locke, but he's usually the bad cop in these situations. You can't do good cop, good cop."

Micah was his packmate. Or a co-husband. Or whatever Lycanthropes called their family groups. It was hard to remember all the different rules and names of the different supernaturals, which I guess was the reason we had to do this last four years at the Academy. So we knew the difference between Washington and a Wendigo. Either way, they were brother-husbands to Layla, the world's nicest person. Even if she didn't have a filter. And wore dresses with things like weiner dogs in hot dog buns printed all over them.

"Layla is days from giving birth and Micah is being... Micah," Locke explained, and I nodded like I knew what the fuck that meant. I assumed it meant he was being crazy protective, because that's what most pack animals did when one was about to give birth. Micah was head of security, so usually he would handle a blip like Flint.

I, for one, was especially glad it wasn't Micah. Micah was a scary mofo. Nice, but he took the security of Eden very seriously.

The door of the conference room opened, and I

saw X standing there. Thank fuck. I mean, he'd still be mad I was in a brawl, but him and Lucius? They were cool with a little bloodletting. They knew the need to make someone bleed to appease the darkness inside. I stepped into the room and froze when I saw the rest of the people here. Ah shit.

I stepped up beside a frozen Flint. "It's probably a bit soon to play 'meet the parents', but here we go. Flint, meet my mother, Raine."

Not that she looked like my mother. Well, she wasn't really. In fact, we basically looked the same age. She was turned into a vampire when she was a year older than me now. Eventually, she'd look like my kid, and that simultaneously made me want to laugh and cry. "Beside her are my dads, Nico and Walker," I pointed to them, Walker still in his Sheriff's uniform.

Flint leaned close. "Is that the one you stole the cuffs from?"

"I believe that would be me," X said from behind me, plucking the cuffs from my back pocket. He pointed a finger at me. "You, stay out of the stash unless you want to be traumatized. I'm too poor for the therapy it would take to make you better," he said sternly, but his eyes were laughing.

I wanted to tell him it was too late. I'd come home for my gym clothes in the middle of the day once, and let's just say, I'd stuffed that memory down into a tiny little box so I didn't vomit everywhere.

"Uh, no offense Carmen, but all your parents are vampires." Then Brody stood up, his Alpha vibes slapping us all in the face. Flint whistled low. "Except that one. The Eau de Alpha is strong with that one."

"This is my dad, Brody. Alpha of Nîso, and the greater North Western Packs."

Bobby went and stood beside him, and Flint's eyes darted around the room. "Holy shit, how many parents do you have?"

"Eight. Seven dads. One mom."

Flint whistled low. "That must keep your mom very busy."

I mentally facepalmed. Well, it'd been nice knowing him. He was cute while he lasted. Walker curled his lip, showing his fangs, but X just laughed.

"I like him. You should invite him over for dinner."

I narrowed my eyes at the man who had raised me since I was five. He was scary, covered with tattoos and scars he must have gotten as a human, even though apparently he'd been a doctor. I didn't understand it, and he was reluctant to talk about his life before he turned.

"You mean, as a *guest* to dinner, right?"

"For. As. It's all the same, Squeak." He flashed his fangs at Flint, and finally all the color drained from the ballsy Djinn guy's face.

Raine laughed, breaking the tension. "Come and sit before X makes good on his threat." I went over and hugged my mom. I know she'd been young when Lucius had literally dropped us on her doorstep, but she'd stepped up and raised us like we were flesh and blood. Even when people said we'd be better off in Nîso with a shapeshifter family, she'd fought to keep us with her, because that's where we wanted to be, where we felt safest. There was never any doubt that she loved us.

I noticed Sammie on the other side of the huge table. "I'm sorry," I mouthed, and he just shook his head, giving me a tight smile. Yep, got him fired in the first month. That took skills, quite frankly.

Alistair sat down and Flint sat beside him. Yeah, that was probably a safe move at this point.

Nico gave me a soft smile. All my dads had a different role, because they were all really different people, despite most of them being vampires. Nico was the cool one; the one that took us to concerts and plays, who bought us ATV's and came up with crazy games and schemes for us to do as kids. But you would be stupid if you didn't realize the true extent of his power. Nico was ancient and so powerful that it made my inner wolf whine when he was angry.

Not that he was ever angry at us. Not even now. He looked Flint over, his eyes snagging on those decorative metal wristbands. "You're Djinn. Though I believe slave bracelets were outlawed," he said more to the room than to Flint. "Fullblood or half? I know the cuffs don't work as well on anyone of more diluted origins. Or the Unbound."

Flint shrugged. "No idea of the exact ratio. No one ever showed me my pedigree papers. Not a fullblood, but at least half-blood judging from this." He lifted his shirt to show a faded tattoo shaped almost like a sun. "My slave mark."

I leaned in close to Nico. "He was bought on the black market. Like us."

Nico's body tensed, and if anything was going to get my parents onside, it was the idea of the skin trade and people selling children.

My mother looked at him like she wanted to adopt him too, but I was definitely going to take issue with that. "If he can't stay here, he can come back to Dark River with us. He will not be going back to wherever my daughter rescued him from."

And that was that. My dads were never able to say no to Raine. She had them all wrapped around her little finger. "She pulled him out of an illegal underground fighting ring," Brody told her. "A fight ring that she'd participated in. A fight ring, if we are judging by all the shallow graves around the area, that condoned fighting to the death."

Raine gasped, her eyes finding mine. There was real terror in her expression, and coupled with the straight out disapproval of Brody, it made me feel guilty as fuck. There was a reason I'd hidden it from them for years. I knew they'd be disappointed in me, but I couldn't help it. It gave me something I needed.

Walker, who had been silent up until this point, laid a hand on Raine's arm. "We'll talk about that at home. Let us talk about the more pressing problem. Raine is correct—we can't send the kid back to the ring, and he has to lose the cuffs. Do we know anyone from the Djinn Council who could remove them?"

Alistair nodded. "Micah does. He met the Councilor for the Unbound a few years ago, back when she was a half-blood on the run from the Council itself. He'll be able to get her to come up here and destroy those things. Break the contract between you and your abductor." He directed that last part at Flint, and we all saw him flinch. But there was such raw hopefulness in his eyes that it made my chest ache.

"And where will the boy stay?"

Even I knew this was a rhetorical question. Eden had been a refuge first and foremost, and Flint? He was the poster child for who they saved. Alistair quirked an eyebrow. "Of course he can stay here. It was why we were built, after all, and our wards are the best in Canada. Until a member of the Djinn Council appears, he's safest here." He looked at Flint. "If that's what you want. Once you are free from your bindings, you are welcome to stay or leave. If you stay, I suggest you do so as a student of the Academy. When were you given into your servitude?"

"I was four."

Raine gasped again and Brody was frowning. "I didn't think the cuffs even worked until you were eighteen?"

Flint just shrugged, and I got it. Where was he going to go when he was four? I ached for the childhood he missed out on. There'd been no Lucius there to save him from his fate. I clenched my back teeth as emotions threatened to creep up and make me do something embarrassing like cry.

"Fine, let's move on. Carmen and Mr. Richards broke the rules by sneaking an unapproved supernatural onto Eden grounds," Alistair said, his piercing golden eyes nailing me to the spot. "We have a duty of care to every individual who lives in these walls, Miss Baxter, and you created a possible situation that could have had dire consequences. We are lucky that your friend Flint has strong mental shields. If his master had been a little stronger, or Flint a little weaker, he could have burned this entire institution down while we slept." Ah, shit. He was right, and I felt guilty, but what was I supposed to do? Leave him there to be torn apart? I opened my mouth to say as much, but Alistair held up a hand. "I know what you are about to say, Miss Baxter. I do. No, you couldn't have left him in the situation that he was in. But you could have come to us instead of hiding him in Mr. Richards' basement like a feral kitten."

Locke laughed, before swallowing the sound back down. "We aren't your parents, Carmen. While I don't approve of your pastimes, it isn't my job to police your life outside of these walls. If you'd brought him to us, we would have only asked the questions we needed to know to keep all our charges safe." He paused. "Would we have told your parents that you found him at an underground fight ring? Probably. But they found out anyway, and here you are, neck deep in shit. Not only that, you dragged Sammie into it with you."

Sammie went to say something, probably something noble like to insist it was all his idea, because that's the kind of guy he was. But Locke stopped him. "We all know it was Carmen's idea to stash him in the basement. We've known Carmen since she was six. This whole scheme has her name plastered across it in neon lights."

He sounded amused, and I frowned. What did he mean by that? "I'm a damn angel, and you know it!"

Bobby snorted and even X laughed. Assholes.

I crossed my arms over my chest and waited for my punishment. Alistair didn't keep me in suspense. "You have to do the junior orientations for the rest of the year," he said, and I gritted my teeth. Ugh. Great. "Plus, you have to help Mr. McKintock with the farm animals for the month." Wonderful. Scooping shit for a month. Still, at least they didn't suspend me and send Flint packing. I could take shit for that.

They looked at Sammie. "Mr. Richards, consider this your first warning. You understand the nature of your position here at the school is that of an authority figure. If you cannot abide by the rules, there's no place for you. Do you understand?"

Sammie gave a stiff nod, and I felt even guiltier. I'd really fucked it up for him, and the sad thing was, I wouldn't have done anything differently.

Alistair looked at Flint, his expression serious yet somehow reassuring. "You're welcome and safe here. Anything you need, you can ask for, and we'll find a way. My door is always open. Off you go." He flicked his eyes to me. "Show the newest member of Eden around, then take him down to Admin to get him set up. I want to speak to your parents in a more official capacity."

I stood like my tail was on fire. Raine was a member of the supernatural governing body, the Convocation, so I wasn't overly surprised that they wanted to talk without us here. Bobby and Sammie were right behind me, and I gave X a quick side hug on my way past his sentinel spot by the door.

I gripped Flint's hand and dragged him along behind me as I all but ran from the conference room, just in case they changed their minds. Sammie and Bobby seemed to follow along as well, and I heard Sammie murmur, "Well, I guess six is better than four."

What the hell did that mean?

You didn't know fear until you were sitting at a table being stared down by men whose combined age was older than Christianity. The terrifying five. The twins Lucius and Nico, each a millennia old. Judge and X—more widely known as The Executioner—the most feared assassination duo in vampire society. Walker, Sheriff of Dark River. Actually, we were less terrified of Walker. He was a good guy. Young for a vampire, and he still had his old world manners. The shapeshifters still whispered their names, even with Raine being our Alpha Mate for over a decade.

On top of that, and almost worse, were the waves of disapproval pouring off my Alpha, Brody.

Carmen must have forgotten her previous anger at me, because she was gripping my hand beneath the table like I was her only lifeline. It made the ass whooping I was about to get totally worth it.

Walker tapped his fingers on the table, human-slow. It was disconcerting as hell. "Remind me again, how long have you been taking her to a place where she could possibly have died, behind our back, totally betraying our trust?"

Carmen bristled beside me. "Dad, it's not—"

Walker raised his hand. "We are all fully aware that if Bobby hadn't taken you, that you would have done this stupidly reckless thing all by yourself."

I looked to Christopher for some kind of support, but he was giving me an equally steely look. The only person who was showing me any compassion was Enit. Enit knew her sister better than anyone else in this room,

"We should be thankful that she thought to take him at all," Raine said, throwing me something that might have been pity, but equally might have been a desire to kick my ass.

Judge cleared his throat. "I think we should place the blame where it so rightfully belongs. On X and Lucius."

X slapped a hand across his chest. "What did I do?"

"Oh, she needs to know how to fight, Judge. It'll be good for her to work out her demons, Judge," Judge mimicked in a high-pitched, bad Cockney accent. I pressed my lips tighter so I didn't laugh.

"Feck off, mate. That was Lucius' idea. He's the one who liked the idea of having a bloodthirsty little protegé."

Everyone's eyes moved to the ancient vampire in question. He smirked and shrugged. "She's still alive. I trained her well. I do not see what the big deal is?"

Carmen's last father, Tex, arguably the one she was closest with, nodded his head. "As crazy as it sounds, I agree with Lucius on this one." He cocked his head, his eyes unseeing in his human form. "As much as I disapprove of her voluntarily putting herself in danger, we still see her as a child. But she's not. She is almost as old as Raine was when she was turned. I'm glad she can defend herself."

They started to bicker among themselves again, and I could almost breathe.

Except for the piercing gaze of the Alpha. "You betrayed my trust."

I shook my head, even though my inner shifter was quavering under his glare. I was the future Alpha. I respected him, but as Alphas, our power was almost matched. Outside of Pack politics, I respected the hell out of Brody. I loved him.

"No. I was not betraying Carmen's trust."

He frowned. "And her trust, her respect, was more important than mine?"

I swallowed hard. Fuck. I took a deep breath, and

held his eye no matter how much the urge to dip my head rode me. "Yes."

The room went silent. I was back under the scrutiny of every person in the room, waiting to see how Brody would react. He pinned me to the spot with a stare that would have made a lesser man wet himself, but I held steady. I could see on his face that he knew what I meant. Knew what this meant.

Mouse's hand was gripping me so tightly that I was fairly sure there'd be crescent-shaped wounds in my palm.

Finally, Brody nodded, and I sucked in the air that I needed as inconspicuously as possible. "So be it." He switched his gaze to Mouse. "You're grounded. You're either at school or at home. Got it?" She nodded, even though I could sense her need to protest. "Good. Get to school."

Just like that, we were dismissed.

Did I just get tentative approval from my Alpha to date his daughter? I didn't want to let myself hope, but considering he hadn't taken me out and let Lucius skin me, I was taking that as a win. None of us stuck around, though Mouse went and hugged each of her parents before we left.

I stepped out the front door and straight into a fist. I'd kind of expected it really, but it still hurt like a bitch.

Christopher wrenched back, getting one more

good one to my nose, and then Carmen was there, dragging him away, while Enit whispered something to him. I struggled back to my feet, sucking my split and swollen lip into my mouth.

Christopher looked pissed. His eyes flashed and I could tell he was close to shifting. I was glad we were doing this here, and not at school where we'd get suspended. "It was one thing not telling our parents, but you should have told *me,*" he growled and I nodded my head. He was right, though he wouldn't understand the way that Brody had. Wouldn't understand that she was my fated mate and I would do anything for her, including keep her secrets.

I inclined my head. In his position, I would be fucking pissed too. So I'd take his wrath and know deep down I wouldn't have changed a damn thing.

Mouse made a frustrated sound in the back of her throat, and I thought that perhaps she was pretty close to wolfing out as well. "I'll ride to school with Bobby. You can drive Enit," she growled at Christopher. For a beta, she didn't take any shit. The three of them, Christopher, Carmen and Enit, were so damn different. Their trauma had warped them, but I wasn't complaining. They were three of my favorite people in the whole world.

Enit was whispering to Christopher. "Come on, Christopher. I don't want to be late to class. Besides, the lion Alpha keeps looking at me."

I held back my snort as Christopher and Carmen's eyes shot to their Omega sister. They were obsessive about her safety, but Enit was a wiley little she-wolf. She had them wrapped around her finger, and sometimes she played them like a fiddle. Never vindictively though. More like she maneuvered them for their own good. Enit had the sweetest heart. As an Alpha, I probably should have been pursuing her, but fortunately, my heart led me in the direction of her fiery sister, who was currently dragging me toward my pickup.

She opened the driver's door and stuffed me in. Maybe I should have chosen Enit, who would at least have pretended like she needed me. Instead, my Princess didn't need me at all, because she was a fucking Queen. She didn't need a white knight. She needed someone who would fight at her back.

She threw her backpack in the cab and climbed in after it. "Let's go before they change their minds and decide to keep me locked in my room."

I peeled out of the driveway, then out of Dark River, waving to the residents I knew. It hadn't been that long ago that the only shapeshifter who would come to Dark River was Brody, as the emissary for Nîso. But now, my cousin Everly worked at the cupcake shop, Mouse and her siblings lived here and growing up, I basically came and went from their house like it was a second home. Our two communities were so intertwined now that the old fears were mostly gone.

· "Are you just going to give me the silent treatment forever?"

I flicked my eyes from the road to her stubborn face. "Maybe."

"That's stupid. You can't give me the silent treatment everytime I do something you don't like."

I wrenched the car over onto the shoulder of the road, glad that Christopher was in front of us. "Yes I fucking can. I can get mad at you when you put yourself in danger. I can get mad at you when you put everyone else in danger too. I can get mad when the possibility of losing you forever to some bloodthirsty fucking Wendigo almost became a reality. I can do all those things because you mean so fucking much to me that I think my chest is about to burst and my balls are sprouting more grey hair than Martin Scorcese's eyebrows!"

She just sat there, gaping at me. "Who the hell is Martin Scorcese?"

I growled low, unclipping her belt and dragging her onto my lap in the space of a heartbeat. I kissed her hard, channelling every ounce of frustration from my lips to hers. She kissed me back just as hard, and I had a premonition that it would always be this way. It will always be a tug o' war for control, a challenge that I so desperately needed.

She bit my lip and ripped open my shirt, her hands finding my chest and she moaned into my mouth. Fuck she felt good, and my cock was so damn hard where it was constricted in my jeans. She let her short denim skirt ride up, so when I slipped my hands up her thighs, I didn't stop until I got to the firm globes of her ass.

I grunted and ground up, like my dick had a mind of its own. I should stop, but then her fingernails scraped across my nipple, and I tore my mouth away so I could throw my head back with pleasure.

Seeing I liked it, she got the wickedest look on her face, one I knew meant nothing but trouble. But then she was kissing down my neck, sucking on my throat like she was part vampire. My hands squeezed her ass cheeks of their own accord and it was perfect. The best ass in the world. Hell, maybe in the universe.

Her lips were on my chest before I realized what she was going to do. "Mouse!" I gasped as she sucked my nipple into her mouth, scraping it between her teeth. I was a fucking goner. I spread her cheeks apart and ground her down on my dick, and she let out a whimpering moan.

It was the sweetest thing I'd ever heard.

This was out of control. I gripped her head, pulling her mouth from my nipple and dragging her lips back to mine. I banded my arm around her waist, holding her to me tightly, restricting her movements.

I pulled away from the kiss. "We need to stop."

She launched back at my face, kissing me so hard

our teeth clacked. Then she pulled away, her cheeks flushed, her hair a little mussed. She'd never been more beautiful to me than she was in that moment. "You're right. We should stop."

Despite the fact that I'd literally said the same thing only moments ago, my heart lurched a little. But then she leaned in, and kissed my cheek. "For now."

She climbed back onto her seat, wiggling her skirt down over her creamy thighs. I wanted to rest my head between those thighs and never reemerge.

I told my boner to relent, just a little, so driving wouldn't be torture, but the asshole wasn't listening. I pulled back onto the road, and she pulled down the visor to redo her lipstick in the mirror.

"This changes things, Mouse."

She slid her eyes to me. "How so?"

"It means we are together now."

She snorted. "It was a kiss, Bobby. Not a mating ceremony." She turned and looked at me. "I like you, Bobby. Liked you since I was a kid. We both know it, so let's not pretend any different. But you're gonna be Alpha one day, and the pressure will be on you to marry a nice shapeshifter girl, not some trash heap wolf shifter."

I gave her a furious look. She was not a trash heap anything. But before I could open my mouth, she was continuing. "I'm selfish, or a masochist or something, because I want you despite knowing that it can't go anywhere. But I also want to keep my options open. Sammie makes my heart race. And Flint... I don't know. There's something about his darkness that speaks to mine." She fell silent, her eyes unfocused as she thought deeply. She shook her head and looked back at me. "I can't give you my whole heart, Bobby, because I know eventually you'll break it."

We pulled into the Academy parking lot, and I yanked on the brake. "You're wrong." She gave me a sad expression and I knew that no matter what I said, she wasn't going to believe me. "I'll prove it to you." I got out of the truck, racing around to open her door for her. I lifted her out of the cab of my pickup and pressed her against the side. "Exhibit A? I have no problem with you pursuing Flint and Sammie. You're it for me, Mouse. Whether you believe me or not." I kissed her softly, until she was curling into my body. "But if they hurt you, I will grind them down into so much dust, that not even their ancestors will be able to find them in the afterlife."

I grabbed her backpack and slung it over my shoulder. I saw Christopher watching us with heated eyes. Ah yeah. I was definitely getting my ass kicked again today. "Let's go, beautiful. My beating awaits."

13

Fortunately for both Bobby and Christopher, I'd dragged my brother away before he'd thrown himself at Bobby like some rabid pitbull. Then he went back to glaring at me and giving me the silent treatment, which was only slightly better than Enit's forlorn looks, like she didn't know what she'd done wrong to make me keep a secret like this.

I was doing what I did best, and ignoring the whole thing. While I was ignoring shit, I was also purposefully not listening to the whispered gossip that seemed to follow me through the hallways. A little bit about the fight ring, a little bit about Bobby kissing me like he wanted to eat me whole. But a lot of it was about the guy behind the door in front of me.

Room 167. Flint's room.

I knocked on the door, and the man in question swung it open. Shirtless.

Holy shit. I mean, he'd fought shirtless, so I'd seen the washboard abs, and the criss-crossing scars, and that deep V...

A throat cleared, and I dragged my eyes back up to his face. Busted. Instead of being embarrassed, I marched into his room.

"Why aren't you dressed? We've got class in like, ten minutes."

He scrunched up his face, which somehow made him look somewhere between James Dean and one of those rolly dogs that were so incredibly ugly they were cute.

"I don't think I want to go," he said in a quiet voice, and it was my turn to frown. I looked at his face, trying to read his frown like a fortune teller reads a palm, but let's face it, guys were a mystery. He could be solving cold fusion or needing to take a dump, and it would all look the same to me.

So I shrugged. "Okay."

I threw my bag on the ground near his bed, and flopped down. Grabbing the remote from the night-stand, I switched on the TV. "Gotta tell you though, my parents expect me to ace all these damn courses, and when they ask why I didn't, I'm going to say that I was keeping you company in your bedroom. You haven't met my dad Lucius yet. He's fucking crazy. I heard he once skinned and then julienned another vampire for daring to lay a finger on Raine."

Flint paled, and I grinned. It was all teeth.

"Fine." He turned toward the drawers and pulled out a pair of gym shorts. He shucked out of his sweats, and I realized he didn't have any underwear on. Also, he had an ass sculpted by the gods. I couldn't look away, even when he bent over and gave me a full view of his sack. Great balls of fire. Well, at least I knew he wasn't dying his hair to match his ring persona.

He pulled on a t-shirt with the Eden logo on the chest, and I eyed him up. "You look like the poster boy for healthy living and a good education here at Eden Academy," I said in my best telesales voice. "When you get those things off, I'll take you into Dark River and hook you up."

I rolled off his bed and grabbed my backpack. "Fair warning though, you're the talk of the Academy. Also, I'm kind of dating Bobby now, so I'm going to walk along holding your hand so they really have something to talk about, you know?"

This got a laugh out of him, finally. "You're trouble."

I winked at him and dragged him into the hall. A couple of the junior kids saw us and scuttled away. "Normally, we could hit up the cafeteria and get coffee, but as it is, someone decided to sleep in. So you're going to have to wait until lunch."

He groaned and as I jogged along, he was forced to keep up. But I did pull out a protein bar from my blazer pocket and handed him the thermos of iced coffee that Enit made for me every day. She really was amazing. Cooking was her thing and holy shit she did it well.

He slid to a stop, holding the food and coffee in front of him. A quick look at my watch told me we were going to be late for Mrs. Ferrentes' Ethics and Morality class, and lets just say, Mrs. Ferrentes was a bitch. That would definitely land me back in Alistair's office and I didn't want to push my luck.

"Hey, what's up?"

He was looking between his thermos and the protein bar, frowning. "Nothing." He twisted the cap off the thermos and took a deep gulp. His eyes lit up like he'd ingested unicorn jizz and not Enit's iced coffee. "This is amazing!"

I couldn't keep the grin from my face. Yeah, it was. I didn't know what she put in there, but there was an argument that it was probably crack. "Yep. Now feel that caffeination in your veins because we have to book it if we aren't going to end up in detention on your first day."

I took off at a jog and tried not to think too hard

about the wounded look in his eyes when I casually gave him food. Like he'd never had enough. Never been given food for free.

That shit hurt my heart.

Despite my best efforts, we were still late for Ethics class. Mrs. Ferrentes looked like she wanted to tear me a new one, so I did something completely uncharacteristic of me and threw Flint under the bus. Pushing him into the room in front of me, I smiled my most winning smile at the telekinetic human.

"Sorry I'm late, ma'am, just showing our new class member where to go." I mentally apologized to Flint for the fact that every person in that class turned to stare.

Mrs. Ferrentes gave me a look that said she'd like to skin me without ever lifting a finger, but my butter-wouldn't-melt expression remained stoically on my face.

"This is your only chance, Miss Baxter. I will not have a repeat of last year, or you are out. Good luck passing the Academy if you fail first year Ethics."

Fucking old cow. I was briefly happy she was telekinetic and not telepathic because there's no way I'd have been able to keep that shit to myself. "I understand, ma'am."

She gave me the stink eye and tipped her chin toward the back of the class where Enit already sat. I gripped Flint's hand and dragged him along behind me. "That goes for you too. I don't care if you're new," Mrs. Ferrentes said to a slightly stunned Flint. I stuffed him down at a free desk Enit had been keeping for us, and then flopped in beside him.

Enit leaned over. She gave him a gentle smile, like she could see the trauma of his past painted across his skin. Maybe she could. I'd trusted her judgement and empathy for a long time. "Hello. You must be Flint. I'm Mouse's sister, Enit." Her voice was soft like she was speaking to an injured horse and not a six and a half foot fiery ball of muscle.

I watched his face. While he softened when she spoke, he didn't look at her with anything that I construed as desire, and trust me, I was well-versed in seeing that. Enit was beautiful, her pale white hair and blue eyes, creamy skin and pink lips, it all made her look somewhere between a doll and Marilyn Monroe. Add to that the fact she was an Omega, and she was like catnip for assholes. I'd nailed more guys in the nuts defending her than I'd had Christmas dinners. While she was sweet and trusting, she was also a crazy pacifist. Christopher's and my own trauma had made me turn to violence and pain, but hers had manifested itself in avoiding confrontation at all costs. I'd once caught a guy feeling her up in the bathrooms in the ninth grade, and she had been absolutely paralyzed with fear.

I'd nearly put that kid in a coma.

Christopher had finished the job. He'd never returned.

But Flint just looked at my sister like she was something too pure for this world, like you would a kitten in a den of wolves. Nothing like the way he looked at me.

I breathed a sigh of relief, not just because I wouldn't have to fight Flint if he got all weird, but also a bit of relief for myself too.

Where every guy and his dog had fawned over Enit, I'd been on like four first dates in my life. That was it. Four first dates. They never got to second dates, and honestly, I got it.

I wasn't an Omega. I was just a run-of-the-mill beta.

I wasn't a damsel that needed saving. I could handle my own shit.

I came from a family of psychos. One look at my dads was a deterrent for any man with two brain cells to rub together. Christopher just rounded them out nicely.

But Flint? He seemed to like that. I saw the heat in his eyes when he fought against me. I saw the way he looked at me when I'd been lying on his bed this morning. He wanted me.

Mrs. Ferrentes cleared her throat loudly and started her lecture, and I zoned the hell out. There was nothing wrong with my ethics or morality, although I'm sure that Mrs. Ferrentes would strongly disagree.

Aside from Flint, I hadn't stepped in to save any of the people in the ring when I fought, but I'd never taken a life. Should I have told someone so they'd shut it down? Eh, probably.

Ferrentes liked to pretend that the world was black and white, but it wasn't. It was all shades of grey with splashes of red.

Still, I wrote notes so when the pop quiz came around, I could pretend that if I found my former Alpha, the one that sold us, I wouldn't spend days and days chopping him into tiny pieces. I would pretend that if anyone laid a single hand on my sister in violence, that I wouldn't remove that hand perfectly.

There wasn't a problem with my ethics or morality. I lived by a strong code. The problem was that code wasn't particularly socially acceptable.

I looked over at Flint's notebook and realized he hadn't written anything. He was looking down at his hands, his jaw tense.

"What's wrong?"

"Nothing," he mumbled, but his fingers curled into a fist. Yeah, that didn't look like nothing. I slid my hand into his and squeezed it in support. This shit was weird for him; I knew that. But I had his back. He just didn't know it yet.

I got through the rest of the class, but only just. Ferrentes was so monotonous, I bet she did it with Mr.

Ferrentes lights off, nightgown still on, bathed in lube. I gagged a little even as I thought about it.

Flint slammed his notebook shut, but not so fast that I missed the fact he hadn't written a single thing. I frowned at him.

"You didn't write any notes. Ferrentes wasn't joking. She will fail you."

Flint stepped closer. "I can't read or write," he said in a low voice, and I could tell that it pained him.

However, he mustn't have said it low enough, because Mrs. Ferrentes turned to look at us, her eyebrows arched high on her face. "You can't read or write? I suggest you get a tutor because I am *not* baby stepping you through this class," she barked incredulously. Every eye in the room turned toward us.

I wondered if I'd get expelled for hitting a teacher. Because at that moment, I wanted to shatter her face more than any other person's on the planet. Enit was there, grabbing my arm and putting a hand on a mortified Flint's back and propelling us both from the room.

I was barely in the hall when I aimed a kick at the water fountain.

"That crusty, good for nothing, mother fuck—"

"Carmen," Enit chastised. She looked at Flint. "It's no big deal. Tex, our dad, is blind, so when they made an agreement with the Pack to use this land for the Academy, our family made sure that the school would be accessible to everyone. There are ways to sit your exams and do tests without literacy." When she said it, it really did sound like no big deal. Like it was just something that happened, which it totally was. "Carmen and I will help you study; it'll be good for us too. And if you want to learn to read or write, we can help you with that too. Bobby as well. Totally up to you." She gave him a smile that was full of love and purity, and I hugged her.

She gave me a squeeze and then shoved me away. "Go. I have permaculture and you have combat with the new combat instructor," she teased, waggling her eyebrows as she flounced off.

Flint watched her go, frowning. "I like your sister. She's sweet. I'm not used to people who are just so damn... nice?"

I laughed, even though the black ball of insecurity was heavy in my stomach. "She's the best. But if you're interested in her, I'm going to have to castrate you first."

He whipped his head towards me, frowning. "She's nice, but not my type. I like my women with fire as well as good hearts."

"Oh?" I squeaked out, moving along the corridors now there were more people.

He nodded, his long legs easily keeping up with me. "Yep. I like a girl who will fight for those she considers friends. Who will risk their life for a stranger." I didn't say anything, because if I spoke I'd probably say something super embarrassing.

"Carmen," he said, reaching out and grabbing my hand. He tugged me back and slammed his mouth into mine.

His lips were like fire. They branded as they moved across mine, and I was helpless to move. I moaned a little and he slid his tongue past my teeth, flicking it pornographically inside my mouth.

Suddenly, he was wrenched away. Behind him were three of the future Pack Enforcers. They were all dumb as rocks and huge as houses. They scowled down at Flint. "Hands off what doesn't belong to you, shitstain."

Ugh. Here we go. "And who do I belong to, numb-nuts?" I snarked back.

"The Alpha-Heir," he said slowly, like I was the stupid one.

I slapped a hand on my heart. "I do? Why didn't anyone tell me?" I let the fake shock drop. "You guys have no say in what I do or who I kiss, so fuck off."

Then Tweedle-Dee, Tweedle-Dumb, and Tweedle-Douche crowded around me in something that might have resembled intimidation if they weren't such a fucking joke.

"Listen here, you little whore. You'll be faithful to the Alpha-Heir, or I'll fuck the slut out of you myself," Tweedle-Douche growled.

I looked over at Flint and he raised an eyebrow. I

shrugged my shoulders, spun, and headbutted fucker number one in the face. It hurt like a bitch, but it was worth it.

Flint jumped in, and it was on. Fists flew, blood splattered. My lips were still tingling from Flint's kiss.

It was a good fucking day to be alive.

14

FLINT

Miss Pea pinched the bridge of her nose and sighed. She looked at Carmen, who just grinned back. "I'm thinking about getting you your own commemorative bench for this room. What do you think?"

Carmen steepled her fingers and rested her chin on them. "Are we talking vinyl cushions or a throne made out of swords?"

Miss Pea just shook her head, working hard to maintain her dour face. I didn't have any such problems, openly grinning at Carmen.

We'd been hauled to the Principal's office, and it wasn't the first impression I wanted to make. But Miss Pea, she insisted I call her Pea, like the vegetable not the human waste, seemed to be fond of Carmen so that was okay.

She flicked her eyes to me. "You've got that right. I feel like Carmen was hauled in here every second day for fighting. Well, up until a few years ago, and now we all know why that was." Yeah, I guess the fact we'd both been hauled in from illegal fighting had gotten around the gossip grapevine.

Actually, I didn't think I'd even spoken yet. I frowned, looking between Pea and Carmen. "She's telepathic. Gird your thoughts, laddie," Carmen said in a truly terrible Scottish accent. I mean, it was genuinely awful.

Oh shit. She was telepathic. Dammit, had I thought about Carmen's tits when I walked in here? I definitely thought about her ass. I mean, her legs were— No, fuck stop it, Flint. Think about those pricks standing over Carmen, intimidating her like she would be scared of those overgrown neck muscles on legs. My girl was fearless. And beautiful. So fucking beautiful. Did I mention her ass? It was—

"Ugh. I swear. Teenage boys haven't changed in a hundred years." She turned from me. "Carmen, you can't hit every person who pisses you off, no matter how overbearing they're being. You've both got detention for a week."

Carmen screwed up her nose. "Can you even give me detention now that I'm in the Academy?"

Miss Pea raised both brows. "It's that or blacklist you from the coffee cart."

"I'll take the detention," Carmen said, jumping to her feet.

Pea snorted. "I figured. I'll talk to Mrs. Ferrentes about being a 'bitch ass crust bucket', and if you need a tutor, Flint, just let us know." She turned to Carmen again. "Also, you should pick up some extra combat lessons from the new teacher, Mr. Richards. I know that with the ring now gone, you'll be back in here every five minutes if you don't have an outlet for all that pent up rage. Put it down as your extracurricular, and I'll make it count toward your final grade."

Carmen smoothed down her skirt and stepped toward the door. "Thanks, Pea."

The woman lifted her chin and then pinned me to the spot with her eyes. "I hear everything. One misstep, and I'm coming for your ass. Do you hear me?"

I didn't think she was talking academically. She was warning me to tread carefully with Carmen. I'd been right, Miss Pea was fond of Carmen.

"Got it."

With a nod, Pea picked up a pen and shooed us out of the room. "Go. I have shit to do."

I didn't need to be asked twice. Carmen grabbed my hand and pulled me out into the hall.

When we stepped out though, the big guy from the fight ring the other night was leaning against the wall. He had a big aura, filled with power. He looked from me, to Carmen, and then to our joined hands.

I tensed, ready to receive a fist in the face. Instead, he leaned forward and kissed Carmen. "I heard you had a run in with someone trying to protect my honor." He looked at me. "I heard you had her back. I'm Bobby."

"Flint."

I'd normally have shaken his hand, but Carmen had a death grip on my fingers.

Carmen frowned, turning to walk down the hall, but she still hadn't let go of my hand. I looked at it, trying to work out if it meant something. Was she claiming me? She said her and this guy were together now.

Women were confusing.

"You need to get rid of those jackasses, Bobby. I wouldn't trust them to watch a Twinkie, let alone your back."

He stepped up to her other side, wrapping his arms around her shoulders and pulling her into his side so he could kiss her temple. "Are you offering to take their place?"

She snorted. "I'd be as effective as all three of those dropkicks combined. But you know the Elders would have a fit."

Bobby shrugged. "There's a precedent already. I handled your friends though. They are no longer considered as future Enforcers." His face grew solemn. "You're right. I can't trust them with my back." He looked over her head, his eyes appraising me quickly, but his face was neutral. Was I found wanting? "How are you finding Eden?"

"It's been... interesting. Most of the people seem nice."

Carmen snorted. "We had Ferrentes and then your blockheads. Flint hasn't had time to appreciate the true joys of Eden."

Bobby grinned, his eyes drifting to where Carmen seemed to be unconsciously holding my fingers now. "I think it's because he's skipped to the best part, Mouse."

I'D BEEN at this Academy for three days, and I think that Bobby had been right. Carmen was the best part of this place. Don't get me wrong, most of the rest of the students were nice enough. I still felt the gazes of those dicks from my first day staring daggers at my back, but I wasn't letting it bother me. I was used to watching my back, even when the threat was invisible.

Carmen, or Mouse as apparently everyone called her, slotted me seamlessly into her social group. Which basically consisted of her siblings, the sweet Enit and the perpetually scowling Christopher. Christopher—it was always Christopher and never Chris apparently—wasn't mad at me though, for which I was thankful. I had enough on my plate without going head to head with an Alpha whose sister I wanted to make love to.

No, his ire was directed toward a pretty girl who looked exactly like Sammie. Quite frankly, the sexual tension between those two would kill a horse. Whatever. Not my business.

What was my business was the fact that Bobby, and a group of his hangers-on, always sat with us at lunch. I liked Bobby, but I didn't particularly trust any of his friends. I didn't think he did either. It must be lonely to be the Alpha-Heir, always surrounded by people jockeying for position. Except Carmen.

She sat on his lap, or on mine if she was feeling particularly torturous that day. She'd give him shit, tease him, argue with him just as often as she'd kiss him. You just had to take one look at the guy to realize he was head over heels in love with the girl, and I got it. I truly did.

I'd stolen half a dozen more kisses, and my body grew rock hard every time I thought about them. My body wanted to be inside hers as soon as possible, but I was willing to take it slow. Plus, a part of me didn't want to sully her with the evil that was my body attached to these bracelets.

Ever present in the back of my brain was Rook, trying to call me back to him. I'd learned to ignore it like a low level headache, but I'd still asked Carmen to 'reborrow' her dad's handcuffs and secured myself to the headboard of my bed every night. Just in case.

I discovered that Flint was very motivated to learn when rewarded with kisses. Enit had taught Flint the basic phonetic sounds and how to write the alphabet already. She had better patience. I just provided positive reinforcement in the form of French kissing.

Did we teach him to write using swear words? Fuck yeah.

A is for Asshole.

B is for Ballsack.

C is for... you get the idea.

But once Enit left for another class, the heat of Flint's kisses were melting my brain so bad I was pretty sure I was actually losing brain cells. All conscious thought was shifting lower, to a place that only wanted one thing. But with everything with me and Bobby so new, I was sticking to kissing for now.

Who said I was impulsive and irresponsible?

I walked across the center courtyard, my hand wrapped in Flint's, toward the other paramour of my errant vagina. We'd missed our last combat session because of the fight with Bobby's former slut-shaming Enforcer-Dicks, but Miss Pea had come through with the private lessons for both Flint and I.

I pushed open the door to the empty gym. I could hear the dull thumping of fists against a bag, and as I headed further into the dimly lit room, my feet stuttered to a standstill. Sammie was in the back of the gym, his fists pounding into a punching bag. Shirtless.

Sweat slid along the intricate artwork down his spine, and his body moved like it was made of liquid. I must have moaned, because Flint stared down at me, an eyebrow raised.

"This one too? I mean, I get it. His form is good." He grinned. "His fighting style, I mean, not his body."

I flushed, but when I looked over at Flint, his eyes were watching Sammie hungrily.

Surely no. Surely, I hadn't been that good in a past life that the Fates would grant me three bisexual boyfriends. Three hot bi boyfriends who also thought the other ones were hot.

No one was that lucky.

Sammie must have finally heard us talking,

because he looked over his shoulder and smiled. "Fuck," Flint whispered.

"Amen to that." Because Sammie, sweaty and half-naked with that smile? It was like kryptonite to my ovaries and it made my stomach do flip-flops with an emotion I really didn't want to examine.

Sammie wandered towards us, his body a slow swagger that was entirely human. I can't explain it. Supernaturals walked with ease, like the restrictions of humanity meant little to us. Which, let's face it, they don't. But the way Sammie moved was raw, like he'd conquered those restrictions and made them his bitch.

I bet he was fucking amazing in bed.

He bit his full lower lip when he stopped in front of me. Leaning forward, he kissed my cheek in a way that was both chaste and completely perverted. "Hey, Mouse." He slid his eyes to Flint, his eyebrows raised. "Flint. Good to see you again, not handcuffed in my basement."

Flint grinned, and I marvelled that in all his years of fighting, he still had all his perfect teeth. "I've got time if you want to remedy that right now?"

I definitely forgot to breathe. Thank you Moon Goddess. Thank you horny Greek deities. Thank you Fates. I don't think Jesus had much to do with this one. It definitely came from someone with a vagina.

How did I suggest that they both get naked and

start making out, you know, without sounding desperate?

Sammie shook his head, and walked toward the bench seats that ran around the edges of the room. He picked up his shirt and slipped it over his head, then gulped from his bottle of water. I wanted to pout, but I held it together.

All in good time, Carmen.

"I thought we'd catch up on some hand to hand combat techniques, and then do some sparring. Just pound out our aggression on each other until we all feel better."

I choked on my saliva, and even Flint's mouth fell open.

Sammie grinned, reaching out to press a finger beneath Flint's chin and snapping his mouth closed. "In the ring. Don't get any ideas."

Too freaking late. I had all the ideas. Or were they fantasies?

Sammie made us warm up by running laps of the gym, and then talked through some of the general principles of Muay Thai. We practiced some moves on each other until we were all equally sweaty and my lady parts had hit five thousand degrees.

Sammie helped Flint from the ground after he'd demonstrated an arm bar. "You fight well. Untrained but ruthless."

Flint shrugged, pulling off his shirt and wiping his

face with it. I saw his scars, pink and raised, and I wondered what he'd been tortured with that could cause such damage on a nearly immortal being. I let my gaze skip over them, because I didn't want him to think I pitied him. That was the last thing I felt for Flint right now, while he was all sweaty and shirtless.

"Let's spar. Street fighting style, no extra abilities," Sammie offered, and I resisted the urge to squeal and jump up and down like a kid on Christmas morning.

They climbed into the ring, and Sammie threw off his shirt too. Not going to lie, this was going in the spank bank already. They circled each other slowly, and both looked like predators.

Sammie lunged, giving a half-hearted jab at Flint's gut, then dancing away. Oh, it was on.

One would think that, being human, Sammie would be at a disadvantage, but he moved like he was magic. His training came through, and hell he must have been training from a kid, because he saw each of Flint's jabs coming, blocking most and dodging a few.

But Flint moved with unparalleled rage. He fought like his body was possessed, and for every hit he took, he gave back another.

It was fucking beautiful.

They traded blows until Sammie got him on the ground. I noted that the ground was Flint's weakness, because they were more evenly matched there. They rolled for dominance, and I was simultaneously absorbed in the fight, and completely distracted by the eroticness that was happening before me. My brain filled in the blanks, and instead of violence, their movements became seductive. I groaned as my nipples hardened and my pussy throbbed. When Sammie got behind Flint, locking his legs around Flint's and restraining his arms against the mat, the fight was over.

Flint tapped out, and Sammie let him go, rolling onto his back and panting on the mats. I stood, intending to go over there and rub myself on one of them until I came, but then Flint was crawling across the mats and over Sammie's body.

He kissed him, and it was just as much of a punishing blow as his fists had been a moment ago. Sammie's hand crept up until he could curl his fingers in the bright red strands of Flint's hair, kissing him back, and the fight was on again. But their bodies were now the weapons and I was torn between watching and throwing myself in the ring.

In the end, I held back, needing to see everything in this moment. The way Flint climbed over Sammie, sliding one knee between his thighs, their sweat-soaked skin moving against each other. Flint ground against him, and I slid one of my own hands between my thighs, watching them like they were live action porn. I was swollen and wet, and just brushing my fingers across the seam of my workout shorts had me moaning.

Like a gunshot, the noise that burst from my throat had them whipping their heads toward me. Sammie gently rolled Flint from his body, and stood, adjusting his dick in his shorts.

He cleared his throat, his cheeks flushed red. "You guys should get to class."

With that, he walked through the back into the locker rooms, the door slamming shut behind him.

Both Flint and I watched him go with equal looks of confusion. What the hell had just happened?

I looked over at Flint as he climbed to his feet, my gaze traveling from his frown to his dick tenting his pants, and then back to his eyes. "I guess we better go to class? Unless you need to do something with that?" I purred like I was a cat shifter and not a freaking wolf.

"You offering?"

I stepped close to him, and he bent down, kissing me softly. Nothing like the way he'd kissed Sammie moments earlier. It might have been my imagination, but I was sure I could taste Sammie on his lips, and it just made me wetter. I pulled away just enough that my lips brushed against his as I spoke. "I could be persuaded."

He threw back his head and laughed. He pulled me tight to his body. "When I persuade you onto my cock, it won't be in some sweaty ass gym." He kissed me once more, and I was strongly considering protesting that gym mats were just fine, but he was stepping away and dragging me toward the exit.

"Come on, we have Supernatural Politics and I want to grill the teacher about the Djinn Council."

He was pretending he was okay, but I knew he was worried about the Djinn Council official who was coming up to remove his slave cuffs. Alistair had said she would be here tomorrow, but that was about it. The whole thing made me anxious, and I hope everyone realized that there was no way Flint was going anywhere without me. If some Djinn bigwig decided he needed to go back to New York with them, then I was going too, kicking and screaming.

I knew it had only been a week, but I was kind of attached to the guy. Nico used to tell me a Chinese proverb that went something like if you save a life, then you're responsible for that life. I wouldn't go that far, but I did feel extra attached to Flint, like somehow our lives were inextricably entwined now.

Fate had handed me Flint, and I wasn't letting him go.

SAMMIE

Fuck. Shit. Fuckshit!

After getting my proverbial ass kicked the other day by Alistair and Locke, I'd convinced myself that I was going to keep my head down, follow the rules. Did I think I could stay away from Carmen? No. But I had a feeling that the guys knew that Carmen was a force of nature and that most mere mortal men would be completely helpless to resist.

But Flint, now that was a whole other fucking problem. Because while they might overlook me falling ass over heels in love with Carmen, seducing a kid who had just come to the Academy after being rescued from a seriously traumatic life would be a whole other matter. Even when I thought about it like that, I wanted to punch myself in the dick.

But the way Carmen and Flint moved together was

really something else. Watching them try the different moves, directing their bodies like they were mine to control, it was heady stuff.

And then I sparred with Flint and the way he was watching me, with those hooded bedroom eyes filled with fire...

I growled and punched the closest wall. I was in so much damn trouble. Bohdie rounded the corner, his eyebrows already raised. "You know, I heard that wall was talking shit about your mama. You beat its ass."

I scowled at him and he laughed. His face looked kind of punchable right now. It was lucky I loved him like a brother.

"Do you want to talk about it?" he cooed like I was a baby, and then I did punch him in the arm.

"No."

"Does it have anything to do with the Omega's pretty sister? The one that eyefucks you like a cheap two dollar hooker every time she's in touching distance?"

I bared my teeth and he held up both hands. "Okay, okay. But if you want my advice, you should go for it. She obviously wants you, though the gossip is she's dating the Alpha-Heir of the local shapeshifter Pack. Hopefully he isn't the territorial type."

Alphas generally were. Bohdie was definitely the territorial type. I'd seen him sniffing around Carmen's sister, and when she wasn't looking, he beat the shit out of anyone who said so much as an unkind word about her. Or ogled her in any way. I don't know what his endgame was, but I could tell he was one hundred percent obsessed with Enit.

I walked into the kitchen of our little townhouse, and grabbed a frozen pizza from the freezer. I was enjoying the cafeteria, but today I just wanted to hide in my fortress of solitude. The kids both came and left, and their joy at being independent was cute as hell.

Cara strode into the house about four in the afternoon, looked between me and Bohdie sitting on the couch playing video games and eating pizza, and growled at us.

"Men fucking suck. Screw you all. I'm becoming a lesbian and stealing your girl," she said, pointing at me. "You've been warned."

With that, she stormed up the stairs to her bedroom, slamming the door so hard it reverberated around the house. Both Bohdie and I stared at the ceiling, where we could still hear her stomping around.

"Do you think I need to beat someone up?" he asked, and I shrugged.

I always thought Cara was a bird that I had to set free so she could fly, but as I got older, I realized that if she was a bird, it wasn't a delicate little bluebird. No, she was a damn bird of prey, a falcon that would score out your eyes if you crossed her. She didn't need me to fight her battles, but if she asked me to do it, I would tear down the world for her.

Of all the people in this world, I loved my sister the most. It was closely followed by Madoc and our parents, but I'd raised Cara since before I recognized the difference between dolls and living, breathing humans.

Bohdie kicked my ass in Madden for a bit, and then I began to feel restless. It was about five, so most of the day students should be gone for the day, including Carmen. I could quit being a coward, leave my hidey-hole and go for a run. Work off some of this pent up frustration. More so than I did in the showers this afternoon. As soon as I'd heard the doors to the gym close, I'd walked into the shower, set it to cold and pulled my dick until my release splattered the tiles.

I threw the console controller onto the couch and stood. "I'm going for a run." I walked out the back door and put on my shoes. I didn't need music to muddy my thoughts. I'd run through my problems until I came up with a solution or passed out from exhaustion. Which-ever came first.

I set off on the path I took the first day here, running the perimeter of the compound. I didn't see Bobby this time, he was probably with Carmen some-where, but I did run across a big guy with a stern face and slightly greying temples. He wasn't faculty, and I slowed and eyeballed him.

Human, definitely. He had dark eyes, tattoos and a hard face that told me he'd seen and done things. I gave him a wide berth, but I watched him.

"What are you looking at, kid?" he growled.

I straightened my spine. "You're human. Just making sure you belong. You aren't faculty."

The guy threw back his head and laughed. "Can't argue with that. You must be the new tutor Celeste was telling me about. Name's Lincoln. I live there." He pointed to a large house in the corner of the compound, still inside the fence. It was a sprawling thing with a wrap around porch, a fenced off yard, and half a dozen small children running around. They screamed like banshees, and hell, did one of them just turn into a kitten?

"They all your kids?"

The guy's face softened. "Most of them." He looked back at me, his face firming up again. "Come over for dinner one night. There aren't many vanilla humans up here, and I know it can be daunting at the beginning."

This time it was my turn to laugh. "My parents are a Nephilim and the Four Horseman of the Apocalypse. Trust me when I say you don't know daunting."

The guy stared at me for a moment, his mouth swinging open. "Fair enough. Come for dinner anyway. Bring your family."

I nodded, and watched as Lincoln continued on his

run. Shaking my head, I finished my circuit, running across the sports field, back toward the houses. I slowed when I saw a body lying in the middle of the field.

Skirting closer, I canvassed the area in case it was dead. Sensing no threats, I stepped closer, and recognized the hue of red hair. Flint.

I knew I should leave. Run away as fast as my tired legs could carry me. Instead, I stepped forward, blocking the sun over his face with my shadow. "You okay?"

He smiled up at me and it was like a punch in the gut. "Yeah, just enjoying the sky. You don't really appreciate the sunshine until you've lived only in the dark, you know?"

I did know. But I'd been living in the sunshine for a lot longer than this guy before me. He patted the grass beside him. "Come hang out with me. I could use the distraction from my own thoughts." His soft smile becomes a shit eating grin. "Unless you want to run away again?"

I felt my face fold into a grimace, but I sat down beside him. "What I did this afternoon was inappropriate."

Flint snorted, sliding his eyes to me. "One, I'm pretty sure I'm the one that kissed you. Two, I haven't been some blushing innocent in a really long time.

What happened in the gym was completely and utterly consensual."

I huffed out a breath. "Consensual or not, it wasn't particularly professional of me. So I apologize."

He rolled his eyes, before staring back at the sun. "Apology unnecessary but accepted." He rolled onto his side and watched me. "So, you like Carmen too, or are you strictly dickly?"

I thought of the way her blue eyes burned, and her body moved like it was not of this earth. Of the way she fiercely protected her sister, and even Flint.

The guy in question snorted. "You don't have to answer. I can see it in your face. Though, I think even if you were gay, Carmen might be the exception."

I leaned back on my arms, realizing that I might be two or three years older than Flint, but the life he'd lived? I doubt he'd ever been a child. "Are you adjusting okay?"

Flint shrugged. "I'll be better when these come off." He pointed at the metal bands around his wrists. I looked at their intricate design. They were beautiful, but looking at them made a cold shiver run down my spine.

"I know they're slave cuffs, used to control Djinn, but I don't know much more than that."

"Anadari bracelets. They were made to enslave my kind for one hundred years of servitude. For a half-caste like myself, that's the majority of my life. That's if

I got to a hundred in the ring. I would've been really fucking surprised." His face turned hard, and I was once again eternally grateful that Bobby had asked me to go and watch over Carmen that night.

We hadn't told her that I wasn't at that fight by chance, though underground fighting was something that went on a lot in Damnation. It was a way to make money, settle disputes, and generally speaking, everyone was there voluntarily.

Not so much in Flint's case. He continued and his voice was flat, like he wasn't involved in his life, like he was narrating someone else's captivity. "The Anadari bracelets are illegal now, Djinn-kind has moved on from the slavery bullshit. But they are still in the underground, and if you know the right people, you can still use them."

I nodded, because what the hell could I say? "But you're safe from that shit in Eden, right?"

He rolled onto his back again, going back to staring at the sun. "It's still there, and it's getting stronger, especially when my mental guards are down and I'm asleep. I've been handcuffing myself to the bed. Last night, I managed to uncuff myself and was halfway down the hall by the time I woke up. Rook is getting desperate and I'm running out of time. But the Djinn rep arrives tomorrow, so tonight I just won't sleep."

I shuddered at that level of violation, of someone crawling around inside his head, luring him out as he slept. I didn't think, I just spoke. "Come over to my place. We'll play videogames and drink coffee until the sun comes up and your official arrives."

He gave me a grin that was pure sin. "I'm sure there are better ways we can pass a night."

My dick hardened, and I forced out a laugh that was strangled. "I don't think so. Caffeine and Call of Duty is all I can offer."

He sat up, springing to his feet like a cat. "I'll take it."

I'd messaged Bobby last night to see if he could pick me up at the asscrack of dawn. I wanted to be there when the Djinn rep came to visit Flint. I wasn't going to miss it just because Christopher slept late and Enit couldn't decide which pair of sparkly slippers to wear. Obviously, Bobby was still enamoured by the idea of being my boyfriend, because he pulled up in front of my house just as the sun was lightening the sky. Primo parent home time, like they weren't already watching me like a hawk, and I kissed Raine and Nico as they walked through the front door.

When Walker strolled up a few moments later, he stopped and gave me a side hug. He was still dressed in his Sheriff's uniform, but he had his hat tucked under his arm. "You're off early? Something to do with the Djinn kid?"

I nodded. "The Djinn are sending a rep to undo his slave cuffs today. I wanted to be there for support."

Walker frowned. "Djinn politics are tricky. Dangerous even. I'd prefer if you stayed away while they were there." I opened my mouth to protest and he raised a hand. "But considering you are you, and I assume you really like the kid?" It was a question as much as a statement, and I gave another tight nod. "Then I'm just going to advise you to be careful. Take Bobby in with you, watch what you say. They get really easily offended." He paused. "And bring this Flint to dinner tonight."

I narrowed my eyes at him. "Are you guys going to grill him about his intentions, or something equally as archaic and patriarchal?"

Walker lifted a single brow. "Maybe I just want to know who has my kid up at the crack of dawn. Who made her want to risk her life to save him. That's not so hard to believe, right?"

I copied his expression, raising my eyebrow as Bobby rolled up. He laughed and ruffled my hair. "Okay, okay. I'll make sure everyone is on their best behavior."

I shook my head but I couldn't help the smile that curved my face. We had a shitty start to life, but I was eternally grateful for what I had now. It was gloriously mundane. Well, as mundane as a family filled with powerful supernaturals could be.

Bobby waved at Walker, and he flapped his hat back. "Come to dinner tonight," he yelled and gave me a loaded look that told me he knew exactly how much my relationship with Bobby had changed. Walker was observant like that, dammit.

Because Bobby was a smart guy, he knew that it was an order and not a request. "Sure thing. See you tonight, Sir."

I rolled my eyes at him and slammed the door shut behind me. Belting myself in, we peeled out of town and onto the mountain road that led to the Academy. "I think my parents know you're my boyfriend now."

Bobby reached over and put his hand on my knee, and I tucked it tightly between my thighs. He squeezed it gently, but didn't try to move his hand upwards. It was both sweet and insanely frustrating. But before we took that step, I'd have to talk to all three of them about, well, each other. That was going to be a little awkward for sure.

I shot off a quick text to Flint. *Omw. Meet me in the cafeteria for coffee?* We'd set up his phone to read him his texts. Sure, I could call him, but who calls anymore? Psychopaths, that's who.

His message came back almost immediately. It was just an emoji of a coffee cup and two guys. Sometimes it was like learning Egyptian hieroglyphs. I was going to just take that as a yes and meet him in the cafeteria.

The compound was basically dead this time of the

day, except for the hardcore fitness freaks and the naturally nocturnal coming in to rest for the day. There weren't many of them though. Bobby got out of the cab and raced around to open my door like he forgot who the hell I was. Still, although I'd never admit it, my heart thudded extra loud as he held open the door, holding out a hand to steady me as I jumped out of the pickup. Like I hadn't crawled inside it drunk off my face one too many times.

But, I forgot that Bobby wasn't all sweetness and chivalry. Once both my feet were on the ground, he backed me up against his truck and kissed me like he hadn't seen me in years. I opened for his tongue, letting it stroke against mine in a long, languid exploration. He reached down to palm my ass, and I briefly cursed that I was wearing jeans and not my leather skirt.

Still, he ground against me, and I was literally between a cock and a hard place. Wait. That's not how the saying went. Someone whistled, and Bobby finally tore himself away, while I gasped in air. My body felt flushed all over, like my skin was on fire. He grinned down at me, his chocolate brown eyes bright, and his grin smug. He was so fucking handsome that I'd never stood a chance.

"One day you're going to kiss me like that in a bedroom, Bobby, and we're going to see just how good you really are."

He grabbed my chin, kissing me almost chastely, before running his lips along my jaw to my ear. "I can barely wait."

Then he turned and walked away, and I felt like I no longer had sensation in my legs. Locking my knees, I strode after him like I was completely unaffected by his kisses, though I doubted anyone would believe me.

Like the rest of the campus, there weren't many people in the cafeteria. Mostly early birds who wanted to beat the morning rush. I saw Flint, and surprisingly, beside him was Sammie.

Well, now, that was interesting. I looked between the two of them, as different as night and day. Flint looking incandescent with his fiery golden hair glinting beneath the high windows, and Sammie like a dark avenger, his inked arms and dark hair making him look like the kind of man who old ladies would cross the street to avoid, and who young ladies would crawl beneath the sheets with for one night only.

Bobby dropped his hand to my lower back, his palm warm and possessive without being overbearing. He was laying a subtle claim to me, making sure everyone knew I was his, including the two men in front of us. We were all animals here, and body language mattered. Sammie's eyes flicked to where Bobby's hand sat just above impropriety, and raised an eyebrow.

"The rumors are true, then? You two are an item?"

I frowned a little, trying to pick up the odd note in his voice. Jealousy? Frustration? Maybe a dash of longing? Hell, maybe it was none of those things and I was just hearing what I wanted to hear.

"Yep. We are officially a thing. But you know, it doesn't stop me doing this." I stepped into his space and planted a firm kiss on his lips. He stood still, probably out of shock. I pulled away, and his eyes ping-ponged from me to Bobby and back again.

He was probably making sure Bobby wasn't about to pummel him into the ground. He wouldn't though.

I was pretty sure.

The cafeteria was starting to fill up now, as the kids coming in from training arrived and the on campus students rolled out of bed.

I heard someone whisper "whore" though I couldn't be sure which direction it was from, but Bobby snapped his gaze towards the door, pinpointing the culprit immediately.

I shouldn't have been surprised that it was Douche-face's lackey. This should be interesting.

First, let me say that I didn't need a guy to fight my battles, obviously. But watching Bobby stride across the room with complete ease, his Alpha power spreading through the room like a thick blanket until some of the lesser shifters bowed their heads, was pretty awesome. What was better though, was the force he pummelled Butt-Canoe with. Derek. I think his name was Derek.

"I'm sorry. I think I missed that. What did you call my girlfriend?" Bobby asked, outwardly congenially. To someone like Sammie, who was pretty immune to Alpha power, it would almost sound pleasant.

At least until Derek dropped to his knees at Bobby's feet. "Alpha-Heir..." he whined, and one side of my mouth curled up in a smirk.

Bobby waved a hand. "No, please. I insist. What did you call my girlfriend? Say the word." He took his power and used it like a leash, every word binding Derek tighter and tighter in his power until Derek was curled on the floor and helpless to resist his next command.

"I said, what did you call Carmen?" he boomed, and even I had to resist the urge to show my throat.

"A whore," Derek whispered, and there was an audible gasp in the room from people who had more than two braincells.

Suddenly, the Alpha power relaxed, releasing the room from its grip. "Hmm. That's what I thought you said. Get to your feet, Derek."

Derek took a deep, shuddering breath, slowly getting to his feet. Once he was back to his full height, Bobby slapped him on the shoulder.

"You should respect her. She is worth a thousand of you and your ilk. You aren't fit to lick her boots. If I didn't think it would disgust her, I would make you crawl on your knees and do just that." His tone was still amiable, and he was totally correct. Random dumbass saliva on my pretty Doc's would gross me out. Bobby continued. "She is your Alpha's daughter."

Derek curled his nose. "She's a stray." He said it like a curse word, every syllable dripping with disdain.

Oh, this bitch had done it now. Bobby nodded, his brows drawn together in understanding. Then he whipped back his fist and plowed it into Derek's face, flattening him to his back. I heard the crack of bones from across the cafeteria.

"She is mine. Disrespect her again, and I will fucking make you wish you'd never taken your first breath. I don't care if she sleeps with the entire senior class, you will never refer to her as anything other than Queen. Do you understand me?"

Bobby's voice was now so low it was basically a growl, and it raised the hair on my arms in both primordial fear and some seriously extreme arousal.

This was the best foreplay ever. Did that make me a psycho?

While Bobby may have spoken the words to Derek, I knew he wanted the whole cafeteria to hear.

"Am I the only one who thought that was hot as fuck? I'm hard as a rock," Flint murmured to me from the side of his mouth. Okay, so maybe we were both psychos.

Derek crawled away, and Bobby turned his back on him. The ultimate insult in a world filled with predators. He was telling the entire room that he considered Derek prey.

I took a leap and threw myself into his arms, kissing him like I could fuck him right here on the long tables for the whole world to see. Honestly, it was tempting, especially when he gripped my ass tight and I could feel the hardening bulge in his jeans.

We might have gotten there too, if there wasn't a loud clearing of a throat.

"Sorry to interrupt, but the Djinn rep has arrived." I scrambled out of Bobby's arms and looked up into the face of the third head of Eden, Micah.

If Alistair was the level-headed one, and Locke was the fun one, then Micah was the one that made you want to piss your pants. "Micah! Okay. We'll be right there."

He raised a single eyebrow, his golden Lycanthrope eyes somewhere between amused and annoyed. I got that look a lot. "I wasn't aware that you were invited, Miss Baxter."

I stuck my hands on my hips. "Where Flint goes, I go. I've adopted him. He's mine now."

I may have seen Micah's lip quirk, but it might have been a trick of the sun. "Fine. Let's go."

I looked over my shoulder at Flint, and Sammie was saying something into his ear. Actually, he was kind of pressed close and his fingertips were brushing against Flint's. Hmm, maybe I should have asked what they'd been up to that they were both in the cafeteria this early in the morning.

I smelled forbidden lust, and it was going to be delicious.

"Behave yourself," Bobby growled against my hair, like I was going to be bad in a room filled with powerful beings. What was I? Insane?

Don't answer that.

I didn't tell Bobby that Walker had ordered him to come. I didn't need a keeper, dammit. So I threaded my fingers through Flint's and kept my mouth shut until Micah had led us away from the cafeteria and into the halls that would lead to the public conference rooms.

"How's Layla? Has the baby come yet?"

Micah looked across at me, his face softening slightly as he thought of his mate. "Not yet, but both Alistair and Stacey agree that it will probably be within the next day or two. The baby is beginning to turn and prepare."

I shook my head at the mention of Stacey. Stacey was their adopted kid—yeah, adoption happened a lot in a society as tumultuous as the supernatural world—but that girl was insanely smart. She was a year younger than me, but she didn't even attend the Academy. She was doing her Doctorate in Astrophysics back when I was still trying to master my multiplication tables. She was like, genius-level smart. Her brain was scary and amazing all at once. Plus, she was nice as hell, if a little aloof.

Micah opened the door, and I quickly catalogued everyone in the room. Alistair and Locke were both here as well, so whoever the Djinn had sent, they'd decided it was worth having all three of them present. That was a lot of supernatural firepower.

There was a woman in the room, she was tall with beautiful golden skin and long dark hair. The guy next to her made me want to run. I squeezed Flint's hand until I heard the bones creak.

Alistair looked at us. "Flint, may I introduce you to Azar Nazemi, Councilor for the Unbound. This is her consort, Donovan."

Run, run, run.

I swallowed hard, curling my fingers into my fists, until the woman elbowed him in the ribs. "Tone it down. They're just kids."

All of a sudden, I could breathe again.

What the hell had we just stepped into?

"Apologies. Donovan is half-Shaitan. They inspire a fear response in most beings."

I looked at the guy, and I was pretty sure he'd be scary as fuck as a human too. He was covered head to toe in tattoos, from his nail beds to the sharp line of his jaw. He wore a leather vest and leather pants, displaying his ink like it was art.

Next to him, the woman should have looked plain, but she was beautiful. Long, brown hair was pulled back into a tight braid, and her tank and jeans clung to her body. She looked at me softly and I tore my eyes away.

Carmen's hand was squeezing mine with supernatural force, and I realized she was trying not to shake in fear in front of these strangers. I pulled her against my body, fortifying her with my strength. Carmen sucked in a deep breath and a romantic part of me, that I'd thought was long dead, wanted to believe she was sucking in my scent to steady herself. See? What in the dime store romance bullshit was that?

I watched as the ferocious angel beside me straightened her shoulders, her spine going ramrod stiff and her chin lifting.

Could a man fall in love in a week? Or was that some kind of teenage Hollywood bullshit? The woman, this Azar, walked over and shook my hand, and then she surprised the shit out of me by shaking Carmen's hand too. The Shaitan just lifted his chin from across the room and I was totally fine with that.

I didn't miss the look of revulsion on her face when she caught a glimpse of my slave cuffs though. I could tell she didn't even like being in the same room as them. While the cuffs themselves were not inherently bad, the person on the other end of my strings was, and the traditional purpose of Anadari bracelets had been unethical at best. Torturous at worst.

Azar reached into her pocket and pulled out a small key, about the size of a handcuff key. I raised both eyebrows and coughed. "You're kidding me right? All this time I could have removed them with a universal handcuff key?"

The Shaitan snorted. "You wish."

Carmen chuckled. "Wish. Because you're genies, right?"

We all looked at her at once, and Carmen swallowed hard. Azar though, she laughed softly along with her. "Not quite. Humanity has bastardized our origins, much like that of the werewolf." She cast a look between Micah and Alistair, and then back to Carmen. "None of you are what Hollywood would portray as a werewolf now, are you?"

She made a good point, but I didn't expect Disney to get anything right. They were fairy tales for kids, and my life? It had been so far from a fairytale, it was practically a slasher flick.

Azar beckoned me over, and I went hesitantly. She wasn't inherently powerful in the physical sense, at least not from what I could tell, but she held a lot of sway. Getting on her bad side would be just as detrimental as walking out of these gates with the Anadari bracelets still on.

"To answer your question, Flint, no this isn't just an ordinary handcuff key. A magical contract is used to bind Djinn to their masters, and a magical contract has to unbind them too. You know what none of us wanted to do? Transport around a crusty, seven hundred year old Marid to make magical contracts for us." A Marid was a rare, long-lived type of Djinn with an affinity to the sea. Just because I hadn't grown up in their society, didn't mean that I hadn't quizzed every amiable supe I'd come across about them. Maybe somewhere in the back of my mind, I'd been planning to escape Rook's tender, loving care and ask them for help.

One day.

Azar was still talking, and I dragged myself away from my spiralling thoughts. "So we needed something that would sever the magical tie. Quite frankly, a handcuff key is both symbolic and conveniently travel-sized." She grinned and then tapped my cuffs, murmuring under her breath.

The cuffs fell off with a clatter, and for a moment, I was frozen. I stared down at my wrists, nearly too thin and pale from where they'd been trapped during my formative years. I stared at the chunks of metal on the ground, a leash turned into a noose that had been slowly killing me for years.

The force in my head was gone, and I sunk to my knees with relief.

"I'm free." I looked at my wrists, and then up at the empathetic faces around me. "I'm actually... I don't..."

I couldn't explain this feeling. It was like the steady hum of the fridge, suddenly turning off. You thought the room was silent before, but it turned out that you never knew what true silence was until the motor switched off.

Azar looked down at me sadly, though there wasn't pity on her face, only empathy with more than a hint of anger on my behalf. "Yeah, you are. You belong to no one but yourself. What you do now is entirely up to you."

I hadn't realized that Carmen was on the ground with me until she wrapped her arms around my chest and squeezed me tightly, anchoring me to the moment. It was surreal.

Alistair cleared his throat. "We've offered Flint a place here at Eden, if he wants it."

"You are welcome in New York, as well. We can provide a home for you, a career if you wish it. We will give you an allowance for up to a year, so you would have the means to make decisions."

I looked past Azar and at the scary looking dude behind her. He had one eyebrow raised and was shaking his head at her, but I didn't know why.

"I'd appreciate that. Just until I get on my feet. I have nothing." It burned my tongue to say those words, and part of me wanted to flinch away from Carmen's touch.

I was free, but I was still shackled by my past. I had no money. No support system that wasn't provided by charity. I had no family, no friends.

Carmen made a rude noise and bumped me with her shoulder. "Stop that shit." I frowned at her, giving her my scariest glare, and she laughed in my face. "Sorry, Flint. But next to that guy? You look like an angry kitten."

Donovan spat a laugh, and I couldn't stop my lips from curling. "I resent that."

I climbed to my feet, and we all just stood there. I realized they were waiting for my decision. Carmen slipped her hand into mine, and I realized there was no choice. "I'll stay at Eden, get some kind of education if it's not too late."

Alistair gave me a full, white smile, like he was proud of me or some shit. It made my chest feel uncomfortable. "It's never too late. You are more than welcome here, Flint. I have a feeling that you would have caused quite the protest if you'd decided to leave." He raised an eyebrow at Carmen, who shrugged.

"I have no shame."

Azar laughed. "I really like her." She turned back to Alistair and Micah. "We will pay his tuition."

Micah waved a hand. "Eden is a refuge first and foremost. There is no fee to stay here."

Azar waved a hand. "Please, consider it a donation then. The freaking Djinn Council has so much fucking money and they can use some of it to right the wrongs that occurred while they sat around with their thumbs up their asses, while hundreds of us were enslaved by fucking psychopaths."

We all blinked and her boyfriend just outright laughed. A small flush colored her cheeks. "Consider it, and your monthly income, restitution."

I shrugged. Money was money, and it was one less worry in a world filled with them. "Thanks?"

"You're welcome. We should go. I'm going to meet my consort in his old stomping grounds. A weekend away from the kids. Preteens are the real demons." She let out a huff, and held out a business card. "If you need anything, call me. Or if you ever want to explore your Ifrit abilities more." She flicked her fingers and a tiny flame danced along her knuckles. "Do you have an Ifrit form?"

"A what?"

She grinned, and it was pure mischief. "We have time for a quick lesson, don't we, Donovan?"

He shrugged again, and his leather pants slipped a little lower. Carmen squeaked, and I realized you could almost see his dick. Almost, but not quite. "Jack will wait. We have time."

Azar clapped her hands. "Excellent. We're going to want to do this outside."

19

CARMEN

We'd headed out to the fields behind the Academy, and I'd been marginally surprised by the fact that Sammie and Bobby had been waiting for us outside the conference rooms. They didn't ask when they joined our group, and despite the side-eye Donovan gave them, no one protested their presence.

Once we were directly in the middle of the field, Azar nodded. "Yep. This will work." She rolled her shoulders. "Okay, kid. Light it up and show me what you can do."

Flint frowned, but he lit his hands on fire, and it was fucking impressive. He made the fire into a ball and threw it at Azar, who caught it easily and extinguished it. "Nice! Is that all you've tried to do?"

Flint shrugged, but the wariness was back in his

eyes. Every time I thought about the moment when his cuffs hit the floor and the pure relief on his face, I wanted to cry. I was kind of glad he'd been distracted at that moment, because I did cry. Hot tears had run down my face, Alistair seeing them before I could wipe them away.

Watching Flint so closely, I'd spotted the moment when doubt set in. I wouldn't have it. He'd gone on despite being so miserable for his entire life—he was so fucking strong, and I would not let him think of himself as anything but a fucking warrior.

An arm wrapped around my waist and I looked up at Bobby as Sammie bracketed me on the other side. "How'd it go?" Sammie whispered.

"He's free, and he's staying."

Sammie let out a relieved breath, and I turned my head so I could watch both him and Flint. "You want to tell me what you and Flint got up to last night?" It was just a suspicion, but why else would they be together at the asscrack of dawn?

"Why would that be any of your business?" he whispered back, an eyebrow raised challengingly.

I sucked my teeth, giving Sammie my full attention. "Because I'd like for you to both be mine. If you guys are going to get together, then I kind of want a front row ticket to watch."

My body was pressed right along Bobby's and I let my senses gather for any hint of tension, but so far he seemed completely chilled by the idea of sharing me, and the idea of Flint and Sammie having sex.

I'd always had my suspicions that Bobby liked guys too, but since Sammie's arrival, I was almost positive. I felt like doing a fist pump in the air, but you know, I resisted so I didn't have to explain.

Sammie looked me dead in the eye, his deep brown irises so soft I wanted to drown in them. "He was having trouble with sleepwalking. I said I'd keep him company until these guys got here." He lifted his chin toward Azar and Donovan.

"By handcuffing him to your bed?" Bobby teased, and I swear Sammie flushed.

"Oh my god, did you handcuff him to your bed, Samuel Richards?" At least, I think his name was Samuel. I really needed to get to know these guys better. "Also, you have to come to dinner tonight."

"Tonigh—"

I waved a hand at him. "We'll talk about that later, get back to the handcuffs."

Micah cleared his throat. "Please, for the sweet love of the fucking Moon Goddess, do not go back to the handcuffs." Alistair laughed, murmuring something to him. "I get they're young, Alistair, but I still don't wanna know what they do behind closed doors. Shifter hearing, kids. Shut the fuck up or I'll have to call your dad." He didn't specify which one, but he didn't have to. Any of them would suck.

Still, learning to keep my mouth shut wasn't my forte. "Please. Like you don't have a billion kids. We all know where they come from, Micah."

"Five is hardly a billion, Carmen. Shall we send you back to the first grade?" Alistair teased. "Plus two are only children of our hearts, not of our bodies."

I gagged. "I don't want to think about your bodies doing anything, Alistair. Gross."

They laughed, and we all turned back to where Azar was murmuring instructions to Flint. "Can you feel the fire there, just below the surface? It runs through your veins, under your skin? You just need to let it out. Your hands are a focal point, but the flames can come from anywhere."

"Can I shoot fire from my dick?"

Donovan groaned and wiped a hand over his face. "Fucking teenagers."

Azar cleared her throat. "I... don't know. I don't have a dick. I guess, theoretically? Test that one in the safety of your home though, okay?" She was definitely trying to hold in her laughter. "Okay, as I was saying, feel the flames in your veins, and then push it outwards. Ready?"

Flint frowned, concentrating, and for a second absolutely nothing happened. Then all at once, he went up like an inferno. It was like someone had doused him with gasoline and lit a match.

"Flint!" I jumped forward, but Bobby had me tight around the waist, holding me back.

"Wait, Mouse. Just watch," he whispered.

As he said it, Flint's flames became a bit less intense. He moaned and fell to his knees. "My back," he gasped, and I stopped breathing as he hunched forward.

Azar dropped to her knees in front of him. "Let it out, kid. Embrace your Ifrit, and he will embrace you back."

As if summoned by her words, his whole body shuddered before two huge wings tore from his back on a scream. Bat wings. Two fucking huge bat wings unfurled from his back like petals, dripping fire onto the grass.

Flint was panting, his clothes completely burned off. I gaped at him, at the sheer beauty of his flames as they rolled across his skin, clothing him. I dropped my eyes to his dick. I couldn't really see it, so I guess that gave credence to his dick shooting fire.

Bobby pressed me into Sammie's arms. "I'm going to the gym to grab him some clothes. Don't let her do anything dumb like hug his flaming body," he whispered.

I half-heartedly gave him the finger, but I was mesmerized by Flint. He stretched his wings wide, and I could hear the cartilage cracking. They were perfect.

"Wow," I whispered.

He turned to us, his mouth pulling wide in a grin. "This is amazing." I was smiling so widely at him my face hurt.

"If you exercise these, you can fly."

We both whipped toward Azar and spoke simultaneously.

"I can fly?"

"He can fly?"

She nodded. "It'll take a bit of time, but I'll show you the basics. The rest is just practice."

For the next hour, Azar ran him through all sorts of things his body could do in its Ifrit form. I learned that full-bloods shapeshift their whole bodies, until they looked a little like the human visage of the devil. I was kinda happy Flint was a half-blood, because that shit sounded terrifying.

When Flint's legs started to shake with strain and his wings drooped into the grass, they called it a day.

"You did great. You're a natural. To resume your human form, you want to suck all that fire back into your gut, to that space inside of you that burns red hot. Your Ifrit will recede, but unfortunately your clothes don't come back so when you're ready, I'm going to look over there."

I wondered if you could blush while you were on fire?

I watched as Flint's flames receded back into his body, like a serpent slithering into a hole in the ground. His wings just pulled straight back into his spine. It was cool as hell.

But once he was naked and human again, he collapsed onto shaking knees. I shrugged out of Sammie's arms and ran over to him. "Holy shit, Flint. That was insane!"

Bobby and Sammie were right behind me, and Bobby held out some gym shorts and a tank top. Sammie helped him struggle to his feet, but he could barely lift his feet from the grass. I knelt down, slipping the legs of his shorts over one foot, then the other. I got them to his knees and he reached down and dragged them up the rest of the way, over his cock that was right there in my face.

"Nice dick."

"Thanks, Sugar Plum. You can look at it more later."

Another deep sigh from Micah. "Seriously, if you guys are quite done?"

Shifters had no hang ups about nudity. We were like a naked commune from the get-go. There was nothing inherently sexual about the meat suit you walked around in. However, between two consenting meat suits, the body became a wonderland.

The adults turned back around, and I didn't miss the quick glances at the scars on Flint's back. They made me so angry. The kind of gut-burning, red haze producing, angry. But also frustrated. And sad.

I looked at the adults' faces, because I was eighteen so technically an adult, but what the fuck did I do about an injustice like Flint's?

My eyes flicked to Azar's, and the anger I saw in them reassured me. She met my eyes over his shoulder and nodded. She'd do something. I knew they'd all do something if they could. But they had lives, and in Alistair and Micah's case, literally hundreds of young charges to look after every day. Trust me, we didn't make that shit easy.

No, I had a feeling that if I wanted justice for Flint, I would have to do it myself. I wrapped him in my arms.

"Hey, I know we kinda just met, but do you want to be my boyfriend?"

Bobby groaned, and Sammie still looked kind of stunned. I grinned over my shoulder at them both. "Those two as well. Like one big, happy, slightly psycho quad. Except Bobby. He's the token good guy."

"Hey!"

"Uh, sure?"

Well, he wasn't overly enthusiastic in his response, but it had been a big day. I leaned up and kissed him softly on the lips, and he held me tighter. He'd come around. I would lure him to his doom with soft kisses and softer hands, and then by the time he realized he'd fallen into my trap, he'd love me.

Muah ha ha.

"Good. But also, my dad kinda said you have to come over to dinner tonight, and so does Bobby."

"Which dad?"

Bobby snorted. "Doesn't matter, bro. They are all scary as fuck. Even Tex, and he's blind and like, half human. But he's also the grandson of a dragon, so you know, he's got some cred."

I looked over my shoulder at Sammie. "You too?" It wasn't a demand, more of a hopeful question.

I knew Sammie had obligations here at the Academy. He was a good guy, taking care of his little brother and cousin, but they were teenagers, and probably wanted to be playing video games or underage drinking or something anyway. Plus, this thing with the four of us might be a little more confronting to a human.

Maybe I'd call in a favor with Cara. Lord knows she'd probably need to call in the favor sooner rather than later if her little war with my brother continued.

Sammie smiled and nodded, and I had to give it to the guy. He was willing to throw himself into a den of sharks, just for a chance to... I don't know what. With Bobby and Flint, I had a century. With Sammie? I'd have fifty years if I was lucky, and for most of those I'd look like his daughter and not his mate.

The very nature of Sammie's humanness hit me like a two-by-four. No. That wouldn't do. Not at all. But I had to prioritize.

First, Operation: Retribution For Flint.

Then, Operation: Together Forever.

Yeah, I'd give it a less stalkery name eventually. You know, if it worked out. But as I watched him skim his fingers gently down Flint's arms, and Flint leaning into the touch, I had a sneaking suspicion that this was it.

These three guys? They were mine.

20

BOBBY

The sun set below the horizon, which cast a warm light over the guy in my passenger seat. It made him look like a piece of expressionist art, the sharp lines of his cheekbones and jaw becoming even more pronounced. I noticed a slight bump on his nose, like he'd had it broken at some point. Given what I knew about him, which was a lot because his brother and cousin liked to talk and I had informants all through the school, it seemed reasonable that he'd broken his nose fighting.

"So, you and Flint?"

Sammie slid his eyes toward me. "There isn't really a me and Flint." He tilted his head at me, meeting my eyes despite protocol. I knew he knew the etiquette, but I found the fact he ignored it kind of nice. "So, you and Carmen?"

I let out a sigh, but it was both a sigh of contentment and frustration. That was Mouse in a nutshell. "It's always been me and Mouse. We just added tongue."

Sammie laughed, and it was a warm sound, the kind of laugh that was like a starburst of happiness. How the kid of the Four Horsemen and a mobster ended up with a laugh like that was beyond me. I raised an eyebrow. "You and Mouse?"

This time he couldn't help the smile. "If I was smart, I'd run the opposite direction. I'm on one strike already with the Academy Board. And Carmen, she doesn't seem like the stay-out-of-trouble type."

I barked out a laugh, because he couldn't have been more right. "That's what you don't understand. Trouble follows her and her littermates around like a fourth sibling. But Mouse is the worst. Enit is sweet, but she's a little devilish too, though in a much more subtle way than Mouse. Christopher is an Alpha, and quite a powerful one. Combined with his trauma, it makes him a little volatile."

"Trauma?"

I shook my head. "Not my story to tell." Although it was one that everyone in Dark River and Nîso knew. But still, I'd give Mouse the opportunity.

"Would he hurt my sister?" Ah, I'd heard about the squabble between Cara and Christopher. Something told me that there was a fine line between hate and lust with those two.

Still, I took my eyes off the road so Sammie could see my absolute sincerity when I said, "He would rather die than lay a hand on your sister in violence. I swear on my life, and give you my word as Alpha-Heir of Nîso."

Sammie dipped his chin. "You don't have to use your hands to hurt though, do you?" I didn't answer, and the question must have been rhetorical, because then he asked, "Why do you call her Mouse? I can't think of anything less fitting for her."

Memories of a younger Carmen rushed to the surface, but they were memories colored by a little boy's obsession. "When Carmen and her littermates arrived in Canada, Carmen didn't speak to anyone but Christopher and Enit. Those three used to be able to speak telepathically, I'm not sure if they outgrew it or not. Like it was the magic's defense against their situation, and once it determined they were safe, it just receded." I shrugged because I had no idea. "Anyway, she was completely mute, but she was also stealthy. She would creep around in the shadows, trying to ensure no one saw her, so that she didn't have to interact with people any more than necessary. My Matriarch, before she died, said she was quiet like a mouse shifter. It made her laugh at a time when you never heard a sound pass her lips, so it became a nickname and it stuck." Apart from those few years when she was going from kid to teenager and hated everyone and everything, including the nickname, she'd embraced being Mouse. "Now, it's more like one of those ironic names, because there's nothing timid about her."

We sat in silence for a while, me stuck in my memories and Sammie figuring out whatever it was he needed to figure out. I pulled into Carmen's driveway just as the sun dipped behind the horizon. It wouldn't be full dark for a few more hours, but this time of the day was more comfortable for the newer vampires.

Sammie's eyes seemed to take in everything, and as he leaned over to grab the cake from the center seat, I noticed the hard outline of a gun at his waistband. When he stood, I frowned at him. "You know that won't do you any good here, right? You can't shoot a vampire with normal bullets. It just pisses them off."

He nodded, though I could almost see him mentally filing it away. "I'm here to meet my, uh, girlfriend's parents. I don't want to shoot anyone. I just wear it out of habit." I guess, for a human in a paranormal world, that would make sense. I didn't blame him, but the idea of him trying to shoot Nico or Lucius? Or hell, X? They would tear him apart for the insult.

At least Walker would probably listen to reason. Maybe.

We only just beat Christopher and everyone else home, which would probably grate against his competitive Alpha nature, but fuck it. I smiled smugly as he slid out of the driver's seat and scowled at me.

"Getting slow?" I taunted with a grin, and he gave me the finger.

He looked over at Enit. "Enit was running late from Shamanistic Medicine and Indigenous Treatments class. Had too many questions." He sounded simultaneously indulgent and annoyed, which summed up his relationship with his Omega sister completely. He was harder on Carmen, but that was because Carmen enjoyed winding him up way too much. Speaking of which, she slid out of the car, her fingers twined with Flint's. He looked like he wanted to eat her alive, and it was an expression I knew well. When she got closer, I pulled her from his arms and into mine, kissing her like I owned her. It was a lie. If anyone was conquered, it was me. She owned me heart and soul. But it wouldn't hurt to remind them that I was first among equals.

She moaned against my lips, until Christopher came over and slapped the back of my head. I looked over my shoulder and growled at him. He just rolled his eyes and herded Enit into the house.

Enit waggled her eyebrows at us, and I had a feeling she knew more about everything than she let on. "Come inside. If Brody comes out and catches you guys making out in the street, he'll be pissed."

Yeah, she had a point and I was on thin ice with the Alpha as it was. I walked up to the door and Lucius appeared from nowhere.

Mouse's scariest parent was identical twins with her coolest parent. Lucius and Nico were like night and day, both in personality and in parenting.

Lucius looked between Flint and Sammie, his eyes dropping to the bulge where Sammie's gun was. "The Alpha-Heir is correct, that will do you no good here."

Because he was either brilliant or stupid, I wasn't sure which, Sammie pulled the gun from the holster sitting at his lower back and handed it to Lucius, butt first.

We all froze as Lucius looked from the gun now in his hand, to the very human guy in front of him. "You're human, correct?" Sammie nodded, and Lucius just stared at him appraisingly. Then, surprising each and every one of us, he handed the gun back to Sammie. "Interesting. They are out back grilling meat."

Then he disappeared like he'd never been there at all. "Damn, I think I just pissed myself," Flint whispered, and Mouse snorted.

"He's a marshmallow. Let's go." She tugged Flint

into the house, Sammie close on his heels. When he looked at me, his expression said he knew how close he'd come to death. He'd gambled and it was good, but damn it had some serious potential to go wrong.

Lucius was a psycho. He'd kill Sammie just to watch him bleed red on the lawn. It was a testament to how much he really loved Mouse that Sammie still lived. I herded them all into the house, like leading lambs into the lion's den, and Carmen threw her backpack beside the door.

"Put that away," Tex, her dad, said from somewhere in the house, his sense of hearing more honed in both his human and shifter form.

Flint leaned back toward me. "Do I have to remember all their names?"

I nodded. "Default to Sir. Trust me on this one," I whispered back.

Mouse huffed, picking up her bag and then tossing it through the door of her bedroom. It was a mess of clothes and band posters, but it smelled like her and I wanted to go and roll on her bedsheets like the truly pathetic creature that she'd made me.

We walked through the house which was really a home. There were pictures of Mouse and her siblings all over the walls, pictures of them on holidays, of Raine and all the guys together. There were trophies and awards and all that shit that came with being parents.

Carmen pushed through the back door and I realized everyone had turned out to give Flint the third degree. While I was glad it wasn't me, again, I kind of felt protective of the Ifrit kid, purely for the fact Mouse liked him. Plus, he was kinda funny. And hot.

Their eyes bounced between the three of us; me, Flint and Sammie. "You brought a human for dessert? You shouldn't have, Squeak," X cooed, and Mouse rolled her eyes.

She grabbed Sammie's hand and dragged him to her side. She glared at them all. "Mine. Sammie is mine. Don't give me that, 'we're vampires and can't help ourselves' bullshit either."

X laughed, and ruffled her hair. "You're my favorite."

"Liar. You said Christopher was your favorite yesterday, and Enit was your favorite when she made you pancakes on Sunday."

He shrugged. "I'm fickle."

Liar. He might be a scary psychopath, but he loved these guys equally. Mouse rolled her eyes again and stood in the middle of her parents. "Guys, this is Flint and Sammie. They're my boyfriends."

She stuck out her chin defiantly, as if she was daring them to say something about her having a human and an Ifrit as boyfriends. Though of the two, Flint was probably the easier to accept.

Raine looked over at me, her eyebrow raised. "I thought you were with Bobby?"

Mouse looked over at me, a small, secret smile curling her lips. That smile—no, it was more a smirk—made my heart race.

Sammie looked between us both. "Aren't they fated mates? I mean, I've only ever seen it once, but the way you spoke about her in the car ride over, I just thought —" he cut off as Mouse's head whipped toward him.

"What?"

Sammie seemed to realize he'd fucked up, and I felt the blood drain from my face. "Hey, what the hell do I know? I'm a human. Hey, I brought cake? Where should I put it?" Desperation began to edge his voice.

"Fuck the cake, Sammie. Explain."

He looked at me and my blood started to rush in my ears. Shit. Fuck. His gaze bounced around the rest of them, though only Christopher and Flint seemed to still be confused. Enit just looked worried.

She'd known.

Sammie dragged his eyes back toward Carmen. "I'm no expert. But he's an Alpha, and the way he is with you, the protectiveness, the raw way he looks at you, it's a lot like a bear couple I knew that were fated mates. But I might totally be wrong?"

She dropped his hands and stepped toward me. When we were toe to toe, she looked up at me, her eyes somewhere between angry and tearful.

"Is that true? Am I your fated mate?"

I wanted to lie. To keep things the way they were, because they were finally good. But I couldn't lie to her.

"Yes."

I should have expected the fist she threw at my nose.

21

CARMEN

So many emotions flashed through my body, I didn't know how to catalogue it all. I wanted to melt down on the floor.

Was I happy? Yes. Of course I was. You know how often fated mates meet? Almost never.

Was I glad that I was Bobby's fated mate? More than I could ever express.

Was I angry? Hell motherfucking yes I was. He'd known. He'd known that we were mates and he never said a word.

I stared up at him, my skin alternating from hot to clammy to hot again. "Exactly how long have you known?"

He ground his jaw, but I gave him points for holding my gaze. "The year you turned fourteen.

Forever? I don't really know. You've always been mine, I just didn't realize why for the longest time."

"You've known for *years?*" I screeched.

My dad stepped forward. "You were too young to be thinking about mates at fourteen, fated or not." He was talking as Pack Alpha, not my dad.

I turned to him, and the look on his face spiked my rage too. "You knew too?" I looked around at the rest of my family. Stupid question. Brody would have known, and if Brody knew, then everyone knew. They didn't keep secrets from each other.

But it was Enit's face that hurt me most. "No."

"Carmen," she pleaded.

I was done. I looked at Christopher. "Give me your keys."

He frowned and didn't move. "Carmen..."

I held up a hand and launched myself at him, patting down his pockets until I found his keys. Then I strode back toward Sammie and Flint, not even looking at Bobby. "Let's go."

Bobby stepped forward. "Mouse... Carmen, you can't drive this angry."

Sammie slipped the keys from my hand. "I've got her." I pretended not to see him mouth, "I'm sorry."

Raine stepped forward. "Carmen, sweetheart." I just raised a hand. I didn't want her excuses.

I dragged Flint toward the door, Sammie behind

us. "I'm sorry. Uh, it was nice to meet you," Sammie said over his shoulder.

I stormed through the house, grabbing my phone and stuffing it in my pocket. Christopher would freak out if he couldn't get ahold of me, and judging by the shock on his face, he was the only one who hadn't known.

I don't know at what point Flint became the herder rather than the herded, but he bundled me into the back seat, climbing in after me and then wrapping me in his arms. Sammie hopped into the driver's seat and pulled out of the driveway.

I turned my face into Flint's chest and then screamed. Tears burned my eyes, but I didn't know why I was crying. I hated being lied to, though no one had out and out said that I wasn't Bobby's mate. They'd merely omitted the truth.

"I don't know where I'm going, so I'm just going to drive until you say stop, okay?" Sammie said from the driver's seat, and I sucked in a deep breath, slapped my lady balls and crawled off Flint's lap. He looked up at me with soft eyes, his lip pulled between his teeth.

"I'm okay. Just angry or surprised or something," I mumbled. I looked through the front windshield. "Take a left up here."

I rested my head against the window and tried to unpack my mind the way my parents had taught me when I was a kid. First, I worked out what I was feeling.

Angry. Sad. Cheated somehow. But also so damn hopeful. And scared. There was a little part of my brain that wondered if Bobby didn't tell me I was his mate because he was trying to find a way out of it. Maybe I was too broken, too much stray trash shifter to mate with the next most powerful Alpha of Canada.

Flint gripped my chin, turning my face towards him. "Whatever you are thinking that is making you look so damn sad, I promise you it's not true. Bobby loves you. His face screams it everytime he looks at you."

I wrenched my face away. "Not enough to make a move. If I hadn't kissed him, would he have treated me as a friend forever, until he found a more appropriate mate?"

Sammie must have worked out where I was guiding us, because he pulled into a clearing in front of a small spring-fed waterhole. It was beautiful, green and remote. He shoved the SUV into park and climbed out the car, walking around the hood and coming to my door. He wrenched it open, grabbed me out, and I was forced to clutch his shoulders. He carried me around to the front of the vehicle and rested me on the hood of the car. He took my face in his hands.

"You, Carmen Baxter, are unforgettable. I swear to you, whatever Bobby's reasons for keeping it a secret have everything to do with him and nothing to do with you. You are fierce." He kissed my cheek softly. "Beautiful." His lips moved down to my jaw. "Loyal." He kissed the corner of my lips, his tongue darting into the crease. "And sexy as hell. He wants you so bad, it must have hurt him to be so close to you all these years and not touch you. Torturous even."

Then he kissed me, and the taste of his lips was heady. He kissed me with a ferocity that backed up his words, and I was breathless by the time he pulled away. Flint leaned on the driver's side fender, watching us with heated eyes.

Sammie stepped back, heaving in breaths. "This is not what we're here for. Do you swim, Fireball?"

Flint looked affronted at the very idea. "Um, no." He looked at the spring like it might rise up and eat him. Sammie grinned at me, moving towards Flint faster than I thought would be possible for a human, grabbed him up and ran toward the spring. It was probably pretty cold this time of the year, but I didn't care. I peeled out of my jeans and boots, stuffing them on the passenger seat of the car. Sammie dropped Flint into the water then ran back toward the shore. Flint burst out of the water like an angry salmon, his shirt plastered to his body like a literal wet dream.

"You better run, human!"

Sammie laughed, taking off toward the back of the SUV and my face curled into a smile over their antics, despite my crappy mood.

I stepped between a pissed-off looking Flint and

Sammie, placing a hand on Flint's chest. "Come and swim with me."

His eyes moved away from his prey and back at me. He took in my tight tank that showed off my midriff and the long expanse of my legs. "I can't swim," he said absently.

I heard Sammie curse, but I didn't say anything about it. "That's okay, the water isn't deep. I'll swim and you can stand." I tugged at his sopping wet shirt. "Get these off first though."

He grinned, and there was that mischievousness again. He peeled out of his clothes and it was like the best kind of stripshow. Slow. Torturous. Even Sammie drifted over from the safety of the back of the SUV, pulling his own clothes off as he watched us with hungry eyes. He didn't come closer though, letting me tame the fiery beast.

When Flint was standing before me in tight boxers, I led him into the water, his fingers wrapped in mine. "You won't let me drown, right?" he whispered.

I looked over my shoulder at him. There was real concern in his eyes as we waded out. I stopped and turned, putting my arms around his neck and pulling him close. "Never. I'll be here to keep you afloat for as long as you need me."

"What if it's forever?"

I didn't answer. I just kissed him. The kiss was soft

and sweet and full of the promises that I couldn't say out loud. Not yet at least. "Let's swim."

I looked at the shore, at Sammie in his boxers and nothing else, his warm skin decorated with dark tattoos. Damn, he was so beautiful.

Standing this close to Flint, I could feel the hardness of his cock, hopefully partly because of me, but also partly because of the man on the shore. "Are you coming in?" I yelled.

He nodded, quickly eating the space between us as I grabbed Flint's hand and pulled us in deeper. He gripped my fingers tightly, but followed me anyway. Into the very thing that scared him.

How could a guy who'd been so abused for so long give over his trust to me so easily?

I wondered what he'd be like if he'd never been sold, if he'd grown up with loving Djinn parents. We would have never met, and although a selfish part of me hated that idea, I would give anything for him to have skipped that trauma. I just had to make it up to him, I guess. Make the next hundred years the best ever.

I was about shoulder deep by the time Sammie caught up, and once he was beside Flint, I waded further out. The water in this lake was so clear that I could see the bottom, and it wrapped around my body, cooling my blood. Bobby had never done anything but protect me my whole life. I'd always trusted him implicitly so I probably owed him the benefit of the doubt. I would hear him out.

But if I didn't like his answers, what the hell would I do? I was it for him. His fated mate. He could have other mates, but it wouldn't be the same. I looked between the two men in front of me. What I felt for these guys was different from what I felt for Bobby. He was like an addiction, like fire in my blood. A need in my belly. Some other anatomical, romantic bullshit. It was like our souls had been connected together before I'd even gotten over the idea that boys were gross. I was still getting over that one.

If I didn't like his answers, I would make him grovel like no man had grovelled before him, that was for sure.

I flipped over onto my back and watched the sky turn to a deep azure. The nocturnal animals were starting to rise, and sounds of the forest were soothing. A hand reached out and gripped my ankle, and I was gently towed back between the bodies of my boyfriends. Two of my three boyfriends. Well, maybe three.

Sammie looked down at me, his dark eyes filled with heat. "You look like a mermaid or a water nymph or something."

He slipped his arms around my back and held me up as he bent down and kissed me. It started out gentle, small sipping kisses that got deeper and deeper until I moaned. He yanked me upright out of the water, pressing me against his broad, hard chest. I couldn't help but wrap my legs around his hips.

When Flint moved in behind me, his warmth pressed against my back, I moaned again. Holy shit, this was perfect. Sammie kissed me harder as Flint slid his hands under my tank, peeling it off and flinging it back toward the shore. Then, he was unclipping my bra, and my nipples were pebbled hard in the cool water. My bra went in the same direction as my tank, and then his hands covered my breasts. Our collective groans echoed around the clearing. His hands were amazingly warm despite the cold water, and the dichotomous feelings made my brain short circuit. I could feel the hard press of both of their cocks; Sammie's against my core and Flint's between the cheeks of my ass.

Sammie slid a hand up into my hair, the other one holding my hips still as he ground his cock into my center, making me moan even as my ass rubbed against Flint, making him groan too.

"Jesus Christ," he muttered, kissing and nipping at my neck, and I was pretty sure I'd died and gone to heaven.

Sammie kissed me again, sliding his hand out of my hair to grab my ass. "Best. Ass. Ever."

Then he was lifting me up, helping me float on my back as he hooked his fingers under my panties, sliding them down my thighs and letting them float away. I laid there, floating and bare between them, and the feel of their eyes eating up my flesh made me warm despite the slightly cool wind.

Sammie sunk lower in the water until his shoulders were below the surface and his head was between my knees.

"I'm going to taste you, because I've been dying to know if you're as sweet as you look." His words were confident, and so damn erotic, but his eyes asked permission. I should probably tell them that the only person who'd ever gotten me off was, well, me. Maybe mention to them both that I was a virgin and that this was meant to be some kind of momentous thing. But I didn't.

His lips travelled up my thighs, hot lips pressing against cooling skin, as he hooked my thighs over his shoulders. I felt Flint's hands under my back, holding me in place.

Sammie's kisses turned into nips, and my breathy noises turned into moans as his hot breath slid over my pussy. When he ran his tongue up my slit, I didn't know if I should be embarrassed or turned on, but I think it was the latter because I was pretty sure I was going to explode.

Then he sucked my clit and I knew the answer. I slammed my thighs around his ears with a shout. Hopefully I didn't bust his eardrums.

He must have been okay though because his tongue swirled and sucked in ways I didn't think were possible. Heat rolled up from my gut as my whole body throbbed with the climax that was just out of reach.

Well, out of reach until Flint reached around and tweaked my nipple. "Oh my god," I gasped, my hands somehow wrapped in Sammie's tight curls, holding him where he was as I ground against his face.

Flint bent in half and kissed me, catching my moans with his tongue. But Sammie wasn't done. He slid two fingers inside of me, even as my pussy fluttered around them, curling his fingers against my g-spot and drawing out my orgasm into one long, torturously good moment.

"Uh oh," Flint whispered against my lips.

I sat up, my feet touching the rocky bottom of the lake, and I looked over to see Bobby standing on the shore. He could have been there for seconds or hours. His face was unreadable, his hands thrust tightly into his pockets.

Sammie's eyes ran over my face, trying to figure out what I wanted, probably. I couldn't help him with that. I didn't know what the fuck I wanted.

But I knew I wouldn't find out if I remained hiding here in the depths of the lake. I gave the guys each a soft kiss, and walked toward the shore.

Toward my best friend.

Toward my fated mate.

22

SAMMIE

She was a fucking goddess. She strode out of the water with complete confidence, water sluicing off her pale skin. She stole my breath. Shifters had a different opinion of nudity by necessity, but I knew for a fact that body dysmorphia was just as rampant in the supernatural communities as it was in normal human society. They still looked at the same magazines, followed the same models on social media, got told the same values of what beautiful was.

But Carmen, she didn't even seem remotely bothered as she strode into the cold night air to stand toe to toe with Bobby.

The guy had fucked up. I mean, I'd fucked up too, but I had no idea he'd been denying his mate bond. That was almost impossible. Unless you were a strong Alpha, apparently.

We couldn't hear what he said, but he whipped off his hoodie and dragged it over her head. The cool night air swirled around us with the setting sun, and goosebumps broke out across my skin.

"It's cold, right? Here, let me," Flint whispered, stepping toward me and wrapping his arms around my ribs, pressing his long, tight body into mine. Then he imperceptibly warmed his body, until it was hot and hard against me. It was... amazing.

Our faces were so close that I could have leaned forward an inch and kissed him. I looked into his gray eyes, searching them for something. I didn't know what, so I swallowed the lump that had lodged in my throat. "Cool trick."

"You should see what I can do with a candle and an ice cube." He laughed, looking over at the shore. "Should we go up there?"

Despite the warmth coming from Flint, I was still cold. "It's that, or let my balls freeze off."

Flint laughed, sliding his hand down my abs until it dipped below the water and the waistband of my boxers. He bypassed my still hard dick and cupped my balls. Then he warmed them with his palm. Leaning closer so his lips were beside my ear, he rolled my balls in his hand. "Roasted nuts."

A laugh burst from my chest, and it might have come out more like a moan. He nipped my ear with his teeth, dragging his fingers along my hard cock before pulling his hand out of my shorts altogether.

I was so well and truly, royally, fucked. These two had a grip on me and I was too enraptured to struggle. I moved toward the shore, my head held high. I had to tell myself that I wasn't doing anything wrong. Mouse had claimed me too. I was making love to my girlfriend, not stealing Bobby's mate.

I just had to repeat it to myself when I met his eyes. His face was carefully neutral as he looked between Flint and I, and I didn't know what to do. Let them fight it out? They obviously had shit to work through. But I didn't want Mouse to think I didn't have her back. So I held Bobby's eyes as I walked up to her, running my hand across her back.

"I'll be just over here if you need me," I murmured in a low voice. She gave me a brittle smile, and I resisted the urge to pull her into my arms and drag her away from whatever was causing her pain. In this case, it was Bobby.

Maybe I should kick his ass for her, but she didn't need my help in that department. Flint whispered something in her ear and moved to the back of the SUV with me.

We were only giving them the illusion of privacy. I could hear every word clearly, even with my human ears.

"I'm sorry, Mouse."

"Fuck your apology, Bobby. You lied to me."

I could almost hear him grinding his teeth. "I never lied."

There was the unmissable sound of flesh hitting flesh, and Bobby let out a grunt. "A lie by omission is still a lie. I deserved to know. I've been walking around mooning after you like an idiot, and everyone but me knew that it was because you were my fated mate." She huffed, and then her voice sounded a little closer. "I feel betrayed, even though I shouldn't. I feel like an idiot."

I clenched my fists to stop myself from rounding the back of the SUV and reassuring her.

"If anyone's an idiot, Carmen, it's me."

Flint snorted and I had to agree with them both. Bobby was an idiot. But he was an idiot who was paying for his mistakes now. I pulled on my shirt and jacket, shimmying my jeans over my still damp legs with great hardship. Flint, however, was one hundred percent dry already. Damn fire genies.

Mouse dropped her voice on the other side of the car, and I strained my ears to hear. "What about the other two? If we are fated mates, shouldn't you be going crazy? Maybe you're wrong?"

Okay, rude or not, I needed this fucking answer. I looked through the tinted windows and saw Bobby stepping toward Mouse, taking her into his arms and pulling her to his chest. They looked right together. If he said he wouldn't accept us, could I just go back to being her tutor?

"I'm not wrong about you being my fated mate, Mouse. What I feel for you is buried inside me deeper than my head or my heart. It's like my soul is gasping and you're the only person who can give it air."

Damn, that was pretty romantic.

"As for Flint and Sammie, if I could resist tearing your clothes off and making love to you the minute you turned eighteen, I can resist the more baser urges of the mate bond. I want you, Mouse, any way you'll let me have you." He cleared his throat and spoke a little louder. "Besides, those two guys, they're kinda alright, and maybe they're something special too. Plus they're hot, so I'm not adverse to keeping them around for the view. But if they hurt you, I will tear open their guts and piss on their entrails."

Flint grinned. "That's so romantic, you fucking psycho," he called out.

I guess that was our cue to come out of hiding.

"We all okay?" That was a loaded question with way too many facets. I knew that apparently Mouse and Bobby were okay, but did the Alpha wanna punch me in the throat for outing him like that?

Flint just bounded over to Carmen, picking her up and kissing her, sliding his eyes toward Bobby. That guy was the very definition of asking forgiveness rather than permission. Bobby seemed amused more than jealous and maybe what he'd said to Mouse wasn't just lip service. He tilted his head to the side, a small smile curling his lips. "Six hands, right?"

I finally allowed the tension to ease out of my shoulders. "She'll need it."

Mouse dragged her lips from Flint. "What the hell does that mean?"

We both just laughed.

SOMEHOW, we ended up back on campus, all sitting around in Flint's tiny dorm room. It didn't occur to me to protest, even though I had a perfectly large house that we'd all fit in much better than on Flint's twin bed. But then there would have been Cara and the kids, someone would be asking me what snacks we had, or to help with algebra homework, or something. Here, with these three, it felt more intimate.

I felt guilty for shirking my responsibilities, but I was allowed a night off. We were watching a spy movie with one of my favorite lead actors. That jaw, those eyes, that chest. Honestly, this guy was how I knew that I liked men as well as women.

We were all tangled together on Flint's bed, Carmen lying between Bobby's thighs, resting her back against his chest. But he'd spread his legs wide enough that Flint had managed to slide his wide shoulders in there too so he could rest his head on one of her thighs, and she had the other foot resting on my stomach. Flint had his legs tangled with mine and the whole thing was sort of... nice.

"So, I feel like, given what happened at the lake, I should tell you all a few things."

Bobby made a low, rumbling noise in his chest. "Which part of what happened at the lake?"

My eyes shot to hers, and judging by the flush in her cheeks, I didn't think she meant her fight with Bobby.

"Uh, the part *in* the lake. When, um, Sammie was..."

"Feasting on your pussy like it was a papaya and he was a starving man?" Flint teased unhelpfully, making Mouse flush even more.

It was kind of adorable, which was not an adjective I thought I'd give to Carmen. She was sexy, fierce, and in her own weird, violent way, kind of sweet. But puppies and kittens were adorable, and despite her nickname, there was nothing meek about her. She was a tiger, a predator in her own right.

I cleared my own throat, my eyes hooding at the mere memory of her taste on my tongue, making my cock harden in my jeans. "What about the lake?" I prompted.

She clammed up and I frowned. Finally, she took a deep breath and lifted her chin. "Well, you gotta remember that I've had two overprotective Alphas and seven dads all up in my business forever, okay?" She took a deep breath and met my eyes. "So, I'm kind of a virgin. Which is fucking weird and annoying and I don't want it to be a big deal. Though I'm thinking that maybe I now know why all my dates never progressed to second dates." She glared at Bobby over her shoulder. He shrugged and looked completely unapologetic.

She huffed, and a resoluteness crossed her face, the fierce woman I knew coming back into her eyes. "What I'm saying is that I'd like you guys to divest me of this tool of the patriarchy asap."

Bobby was frowning and Flint looked confused as he mouthed, "Tool of the patriarchy?" to himself, before his eyes shot back to her face. "You want us to have sex *now?*"

Bobby reached down and slapped the back of his head. "No, not now."

Mouse crossed her arms over her chest and glared up at Bobby. "Why not now? Shouldn't it be my choice? It's my virginity."

I watched the tension between them pulse as he huffed so hard that stray bits of her hair flew into her face. "You're my mate. When one of us," he indicated the three of us, which I both appreciated and was terrified by, "makes love to you for the first time, it won't be on a cramped twin bed that hundreds of asses have probably been on, while watching an action flick." His face softened, and he lifted his hand to her cheek, his warm skin contrasting so beautifully with her milky paleness. "I don't care if I'm your first or your fortieth lover. I'd still want our first time together to be special."

Flint groaned. "Told you he was a romantic."

But Bobby was looking past her to me, like I was the most likely candidate to steal her virginity in a janitor's closet or something. "Whatever Carmen wants."

I wasn't stupid. I knew I couldn't deny her a goddamn thing. I'd give her rose petals and candles, or a dirty fuck against a wall.

She had me wrapped up, and I never wanted to get away.

23

CARMEN

Despite my grand announcement in Flint's room last week, none of the guys had tried to deflower me. I snorted. Deflower was such a stupid terminology. If I was a flower, I'd be the pretty kind that lured you in then poisoned you.

Still, I don't know if I was disgruntled or relieved that the guys hadn't made a move. It gave us time to settle into something like a routine and to spend more time both one on one, and as a group. It was... nice.

I rested my head against the passenger window of Christopher's SUV. Enit was a roiling ball of emotions in the back, but I ignored it. Enit and I were currently fighting. No, that wasn't right. Enit didn't fight. But I was pissed off that she'd known for so long that Bobby was my fated mate, and never told me.

Her betrayal cut me the deepest, even more than

Bobby's himself. Enit *knew* how I felt about Bobby. She knew that I'd loved him for years. She knew how much I'd hated seeing him date other girls in Nîso and at the Academy, and yet she'd said nothing.

Christopher heaved out an annoyed sigh. "You two need to get over this shit. You've been giving her the silent treatment for a week, Carmen. You know how much ill feelings affect her. You're being cruel now."

I shot him a glare. Protect the Omega, it was always the way. "You know what affects me, Christopher? Being lied to for years by the person I loved and trusted the most. But doesn't it count, because I'm not a super special Omega, just a regular old beta? Well, guess what? I still have feelings and that shit hurts."

Enit gave a little whimper and I momentarily felt guilty. In all honesty, it was pretty hard to maintain my anger towards her, every instinct in me wanting to soothe her hurts. Shifter biology blew.

"I said I was sorry, Carmen. I didn't know he was your fated mate until very recently. I just knew that he, well, that he loved you. It wasn't my place to tell you. I know these things, but it's incredibly intrusive to inter-fere with someone's emotions like that."

I waved her away. She'd said all this before. While I saw her point, it didn't soothe my anger. I pointed to a mall in town. Not Dark River, but the large town on the other side of Eden. It was our parents' anniversary coming up or maybe the anniversary of our adoption, I didn't know the specifics really. But it was a day we all celebrated together, and we bought each other small gifts. Kind of like Christmas, but when two of your parents were older than Christianity, we didn't really have a big Christmas celebration. Instead, we had Family Day, and every year I loved it.

"Drop me here. Pick me up when you guys are done," I grumbled, and Christopher heaved another sigh.

"If you are going to pout and wander off by yourself, you should have brought your boy toys."

I gave him the middle finger. "I don't need anyone to protect me, Christopher. Not you, and not my boyfriends. I'm more than capable of taking care of myself. Now pull the fuck over or I'll roll out of this fucking car myself."

Christopher swore, swerving to the side of the road to let me out. I slammed out of the car and ignored Enit's tiny whimper.

I would forgive her soon, because it was physically impossible not to, and because I knew my sister. She would never purposefully hurt anyone, least of all me. But she deserved to stew in it for a little while longer.

"So LET me get this straight. You want it to say, 'I just want to drink tea and kill people'?"

I'd broken the girl at the engraving stall.

I gave her my most innocent look. "It's an inside joke."

She still gave me an odd look and took the teacup from me, taking it over to her workbench where she would hand paint on the words.

I looked down at my bags of presents. I'd gotten something for everyone, from pjs with dachshunds for Nico to a framed photo of the family for Mom. It was funny now, because we almost all looked like friends rather than parents and children. Because in a photograph you couldn't see the agelessness of Nico's expression, or the slight creases around Walker's eyes. "I'll just be right back," I said to the girl working on the teacup, walking toward a quiet corner of the mall to call Christopher to come and pick me up. I'd gotten him a shirt from his favorite band, and I'd gotten Enit a delicate crystal lion.

I looked up as someone crowded me, and then fear stilled the breath in my lungs. The man reached out, placing his hands gently on my shoulders, and my whole body went lax. I couldn't move my legs, my arms, my vocal chords. Nothing. I was completely paralyzed.

"Hello, Carmen."

His face was familiar. He had a long face, a patchy beard and several scars littering his cheeks. But it wasn't until I got to his eyes that my brain finally caught up, my heart beginning to thunder in my ears.

I'd seen him at the fights, though I'd never been introduced. But in my gut I knew.

Rook. This was fucking Rook, Flint's former owner. Oh fuck.

"It would only take a little more of my power to paralyze your heart, you know that? I will not, it isn't worth the fucking hassle of dealing with your owners. But I have a message for my property. And you will give it to him and no one else. Blink if you understand."

I blinked rapidly.

"I am taking him back, little wolf, and I will kill everyone you love if you stand in my way, starting with your sweet little Omega sister. Perhaps, I will play with her first though. So few truly submissive Omegas left in the world. I could truly degrade her before I killed her, and she would let me."

My chest started to burn as he stopped my lungs from drawing in air. Blackness began to edge my vision as he leaned in closer until his lips nearly brushed mine. I wanted to gag.

"You tell that little fuck that he better return, or I'm going to kill them off one by one, starting with the youngest. Their blood will be on his hands."

With that, he stepped away and I slid to the floor, sucking in air that felt like acid. Beside me, my phone was shattered when I'd dropped it, but the screen was lit up. I could make out the fragmented picture of Christopher's face.

I answered, my voice cracking. "Christopher. Help."

I must have blacked out, because when I woke up, the girl from the engravement place was standing over me, shaking me awake. "Hey, hey are you okay?"

I blinked as my brain came back online, and then Christopher was there, gently moving the girl out of the way and sliding to his knees in front of me.

"Carmen, what happened?" He sounded frantic and I knew it was probably because he would have been able to feel my fear through our sibling bond. It was something we hadn't used since we were kids, but if I concentrated hard enough, or in times of great stress, it roared to the front.

"We need to get out of here."

I could feel both Christopher and Enit's panic as Christopher hefted me into his arms. Enit was soothing the shop assistant, gathering up my bags. "She gets low blood pressure and sometimes she passes out. She'll be fine. Thank you for caring," she said softly to the shop assistant, who pushed my teacup into her hands.

Christopher strode out of the mall with me in his arms, and for the first time in years I felt like I needed my Alpha brother, like I could hand him all my responsibilities and he would take it onto his shoulders without protest.

I rested my cheek against his chest as he strode to the front doors of the mall, and to his SUV mounting the front steps extremely illegally. He slid me in the back and Enit climbed in after me.

She curled her body around mine, and her very presence soothed me. "Call X so he can check her out," Christopher barked at Enit from the front seat as he roared back into traffic.

I was shaking my head as Enit reached into her back pocket for her phone. "You can't, Christopher."

He looked at me in the rearview mirror, his eyes shifting to the wolf. He was about to lose it. "I felt what you felt, I know who it was. You'll let X check you out and then we'll figure it out, Carmen."

I winced, not realizing I'd projected my panic quite that bad. I looked over at Enit, who was pale and shaky. "I'm sorry."

She squeezed me tightly into her arms, her Omega energy wrapping around me like a fluffy blanket. "Me too. I love you."

"Love you too," I sighed heavily. If they knew, they weren't going to keep it to themselves. "You better call my guys as well. They'll want to hear this."

Enit swallowed hard. "I already messaged Bobby. He's going to get the others and meet us at the house."

Well, I guess I now knew how Bobby turned up every time I was in trouble. He had his own insider. After being faced with the evil of Rook, I didn't have it in me to be mad at her about it though. She did it because she loved me.

I rested my head against her shoulder and tried not to replay that complete and utter helplessness as Rook had kept me paralyzed and pinned to the wall. I tried not to think of his cruel, shadowy face, or the sneer, or the hot feel of his breath against my cheeks. I wanted to pretend I was tough. That I was bulletproof.

But that man? He made me realize I was still a naive little girl who was good with her fists. He made me feel helpless, and I hated it.

Panic flowed through my body like poison. I was jammed between Sammie and Bobby in the pickup as we tore toward Dark River and Carmen's house. Bobby had come and grabbed me from where I was training in the gym, saying nothing except that there was something wrong with Carmen.

I'd busted out my wings and flown the short distance to Sammie's place, bursting through the door and startling the shit out of Sammie's family. It had been the little one—the girl cousin, Attica maybe?— that had grabbed me by the arms, told me to breathe and then called for Sammie.

I needed to work out what that kid's ability was, because while she'd been holding my arms, I'd felt like I'd taken four Xanny with tequila chasers. But when she'd stuffed me out the door, all that fear and panic had roared back.

Bobby had broken several Canadian traffic laws, but in what seemed like the longest minutes of my life, we were roaring to a stop outside of Carmen's house. Bobby didn't even turn the car off before he was out of the driver's seat and through the front door of the house. I leaned across, switching the car off and pulling on the handbrake before scrambling out after Sammie. I pocketed the keys as we ran through the still open door.

Then I skidded to a stop because the level of danger in that room hit me in the face. I'd been in some dangerous situations, obviously. But the sheer level of contained violence in here made me sweat.

Carmen sat on the kitchen island, and the big guy, X, prowled around her with a stethoscope and a little eye flashlight while she rolled her eyes. "I'm fine, X. I promise."

Bobby stood a few feet back, twitching and desperate to get to his mate, but everytime he took a step closer, X snarled at him.

Carmen put her hand on X's arm, squeezing it a little. "I'm okay, Dad."

He seemed to relax a bit, stepping away, and that was all that Bobby needed, beside her in a single jump and pulling her into his arms. She wrapped herself around him and I went over, needing to touch her too.

Sammie seemed frozen, which was probably his human hindbrain saying *danger, danger.* So I grabbed his hand and dragged him in with me until we were all crowded around our girl. I kissed her cheek.

"What happened?" Sammie growled, and I suddenly saw the cold-blooded MC killer in his eyes.

But she found me, reaching out and grabbing my hand, anchoring me to her. "It was Rook."

I felt my knees turn to water and my eyes nearly bug out of my head. "What about Rook?"

I held my breath as she dragged me a little closer, and somehow I knew what she had to say. "He found me at the mall. Told me to give you a message."

I could barely hear her over the panic rushing through my brain. Rook was here. Rook had been close to her. Had touched her.

All over again I was a scared little kid, beaten down until I no longer knew how to fight back. I swallowed repeatedly, like if I could just get the giant lump out of my throat, maybe I could breathe.

I was distantly aware of Carmen nuzzling her face against my throat, but I kept wondering what would have happened if Rook had caught her in some dank alley rather than a crowded mall.

I knew first hand what the paralysis under his hands was like, not being able to escape. Being trapped while Rook—

I hissed as Carmen bit me on the column of my

neck. "Ow."

"Out of your head, Fireball. I'm okay. Stop getting lost in the what-ifs."

"What was the message?" My head whipped around, and I realized that all Carmen's family was here. That question had come from one of her twin dads. I'd forgotten their names, but not the sheer animalistic terror that ran down my spine when I looked them in the eye.

Carmen hesitated, and I could tell Rook was in her head. He excelled at mind games. She looked back at me and sighed. "You're safe and not alone anymore. You're mine. I want you to remember that, okay?" I nodded, but it didn't stop the dread. She took a deep breath. "He said you had to return or he would start killing them off, one by one."

Dark spots danced across my vision. He wouldn't. He wouldn't destroy his merchandise just to spite me, to bring me to heel. I hadn't thought twice about leaving because I didn't think his greed would overrule his pettiness.

Bobby grabbed my face, the pads of his fingers rough on my cheeks. He dragged my eyes towards his, and I got lost in their warm depths. "What is he talking about, Flint?" There was a touch of Alpha in his voice, enough to soothe me.

"He means the Kindergarten." When Bobby looked confused, he continued. "I'm not the only kid Rook has bought from the black market. Like ancient gladiators, he buys us young, and injured or crippled fighters train us. Once a kid's old enough to put on an entertaining fight, he puts them in the ring."

Carmen's mom sucked in a breath. "How many?"

I cast my eyes at my feet. "Fifteen to twenty at a time. Some as young as I was, around four. Some come in older, around twelve. But they push us into the ring not long after that, so those kids usually don't last long."

My tone was flat, emotionless. Like I didn't care about those kids, and to a degree, I didn't anymore. Watching them grow up, only to bury their bodies in darkened burial grounds, had killed off that little part of my soul.

But I wasn't dead enough, and Rook fucking knew it.

"There are fifteen kids being tortured somewhere, and you've been shacking up with my sister and didn't tell anyone?" Christopher yelled, and shame made me numb. He was right. I should have told someone as soon as I was rescued. Should have told Azar, or the Board of Eden, or something. But I didn't because I was scared. Scared that I'd summon Rook like Bloody Mary in a mirror. I wanted to hope that once the cuffs come off, Rook would fuck off back to the States, and I could catch my breath. I would have gone back for them.

I would.

But Christopher was still right. I'd known and said nothing. "Yes."

"You piece of shit—"

Carmen was off the kitchen island and in wolf form before my brain had a chance to catch up. She was fucking beautiful though, tawny brown with golden highlights striped through her fur.

But Christopher shifted just as quickly and he was black. Solid, deathly black.

They fought in the middle of the living room until Bobby stepped toward them and growled, "Enough!"

The feel of his Alpha power permeated the room, and I noticed that not all of Carmen's parents were here. The Alpha with the big energy, and the snake shifter weren't home.

Bobby waded into the middle of them. "Shift back. Now."

Enit disappeared and returned with two robes, and the pair shifted back. But they weren't done fighting apparently.

"You have no fucking right," Carmen growled.

Christopher snarled back. "I have every fucking right. I nearly was one of those kids. Maybe not for Rook, but for some other fucking opportunistic sadist."

"Nearly, Christopher. You were *nearly* one. Lucius saved you, but no one saved Flint, so you don't get to decide how his PTSD manifests, you egotistical fuck! I don't see you out there crusading, and you can't plead ignorance. So get the fuck down from your high horse."

She glared at him, and he shot her a venomous look, before turning on his heel and storming out the door. Naked.

Well, that was awkward. Enit kissed her cheek and handed her sister a robe. "I'll go and soothe him." She looked over at me, nothing but compassion in her eyes. No accusations or pity. "For what it's worth, I'm with Carmen. We all knew it existed, and we didn't do anything about it. This isn't a burden you need to shoulder by yourself."

Somehow, I ended up at the dining table, across from Nico, and he reached out and touched my wrist.

"I think you should tell us what we need to know about Rook and his operation."

I spilled my guts like I had no choice.

THREE HOURS LATER, I was exhausted. Emotionally wrung out. Carmen sat on my lap, her arms around my shoulders and her cheek on top of my head, like she could protect past me from all the hurt that just poured passed my lips.

About halfway through, I realized I was being compelled into unloading everything, and I shored up my mental walls and managed to keep some of my black secrets to myself. The degree to which I'd been used, the things that I'd been forced to do. If Carmen knew, she wouldn't sit in my lap like this. She wouldn't be within ten feet of me.

She looked around the table. "What do we do?"

X sharpened his knife. "*We* do nothing. You four go back to the Academy, continue to learn, and leave it to the Convocation. Leave it to me."

"And me," the pretty one with the Southern accent said. Judge. His name was Judge.

The one that loomed in the corner, that looked like Nico but with way more crazy in his eyes, just smirked and ran a tongue across his fangs. He didn't need to say he would bathe in Rook's blood. His whole aura just screamed massacre.

Carmen tensed on my lap. "We can't just do nothing. We aren't children, we can help. Rook is still out there."

The Sheriff, er Walker, nodded. "She has a point. I think we should talk to the Academy about putting them in the dorms until this whole thing is finished. The wards on the school are impenetrable to nearly all beings, and if Rook had the skills to breach them, he would have walked over them and retrieved Flint himself. He wouldn't have to resort to manipulating schoolkids to be his messengers."

They all nodded as Carmen gaped. "What? No."

However, they'd made up their minds, which is

how we all ended up piled in Bobby's pickup, Carmen spread across mine and Sammie's lap. Sammie had been quiet, not adding much, but he'd been a quiet, steady presence in the background. A rock to hold onto while I caught my breath.

Christopher and Enit were being shipped off too, and Carmen was fuming. "This isn't right. I'm not a child and I'm more than capable of handling myself. This is Flint's revenge, he doesn't need to be shut out of it."

I didn't tell her that a cowardly part of me was glad that someone else was taking care of it. The idea of stepping back into Rook's domain, into the Kindergarten, made cold sweat break out over my body.

As if sensing my thoughts, Sammie twined our fingers where they were pressed between our thighs and squeezed. He stroked his other hand up and down Carmen's hip soothingly.

"Taking down an international human trafficking ring is a bit outside of our pay grade, Mouse," Bobby pointed out, and he was right.

"Besides, they are just trying to keep you safe. You, your siblings, and Flint. He's seen enough violence, don't you think?" Sammie murmured in her ear, and it was like a punch to the gut.

I was steeped in so much violence that it was now a part of me. But I didn't have a thirst for revenge. I was just dying to be happy.

How fucking pathetic was that? Carmen definitely deserved more. She deserved someone who wasn't a piece of shit that let kids die while having the audacity to be so goddamn happy.

Well, Rook got his wish. I wasn't happy anymore.

CARMEN

The Academy students had unisex dorms at the very rear of the main building. Fortunately, there weren't many Academy students who still lived on campus, most preferring to house together off campus for freedom, or because they had their own apartments in Nîso. So when I threw a tantrum and said I wanted to be beside Flint, no one protested. We were adults. If I wanted to sneak into his room every night and fuck him against every surface, that was my business as long as there were no noise complaints.

Sammie had disappeared to check on his family, Flint had slunk back to his room under the guise of taking a shower, and that left just me and Bobby. Bobby watched me pace around my room, stuffing clothes into drawers and unloading stuff from the suit-case of shit I threw together.

"Come here."

I looked over my shoulder at him reclining on my freshly made bed like he owned it, and my lips quirked. Helpless to resist, I crossed the small amount of floor to the bed, crawling up it like I was on the prowl. His intense gaze made me hot, and I still couldn't believe that Bobby was looking at me like that. Like I was something precious and sexy, rather than an annoyance.

When I was finally between his thighs, his hands grabbed at my hips greedily, pulling me into his chest. "I can't help but think what if? What if you hadn't been in the mall? What if he'd decided to take you as a bargaining chip? And I was in Nîso, drinking beer with my dad and talking shit, and I had no idea that you were scared." He let out a shuddering breath. "I think we should seal the bond."

I pulled away in shock. "What? Are you fucking crazy? I'm eighteen."

He gripped my chin. "And my fated mate. I couldn't be more sane about this. I need you more than I need air, Mouse. This isn't some childhood crush. I don't need a ten year engagement to realize I love you."

His words were like a punch in the face. My brain stopped working, my thoughts sluggish and dazed. I reared back, searching his face. He couldn't mean it. It was too soon.

Too soon for you. He's known for years, a petty little voice inside my head taunted. She could fuck off though, because I'd been in love with Bobby for years as well, even when he annoyed the hell out of me. Even when he was being an Alphahole. I'd still loved him.

But I wasn't ready to say the words and I definitely wasn't ready for the bond. I shook my head at him, my shoulders tense. "Not now. Not because you were scared."

He just gave me a crooked smile. "One day then. Sooner rather than later, hey?" He dragged me to his chest and kissed me until I couldn't remember what we were talking about, just nodding agreeably.

At some point, the kisses turned fevered. They weren't sweet and caring anymore, they were hot and needy. I ground my body against his and he groaned, his tongue slipping into my mouth as he deepened the kiss. His hands slid up under my shirt, his huge hands spanning my back easily. He tore his lips from my mouth and slid them along my jaw, nipping and kissing in a way that had me squirming on his lap, making us both moan. I grabbed onto the bottom of his t-shirt and dragged it over his head, baring his golden chest to my eyes and my lips. He was a fucking feast and I was ready to devour him.

I tore at my shirt until I was sitting in front of him

in a pretty bra that I was glad I wore today instead of my normal sports bra.

He kissed down my throat, taking the sensitive skin, that oh so important pulse point between his teeth and pressing down. He'd bite me there for us to become mates, but I trusted Bobby. Hell, I trusted Bobby more than I trusted myself, so I knew when I moaned and pressed my throat closer, that he wouldn't take it as an invitation. Instead, he moved down the column of my throat, kissing along my collarbone until he pushed a nipple from the safety of my bra and sucked it into his mouth.

"Holy fucking shit, Bobby."

Dude. Now I understood all those women in the movies carrying on. I mean, I could touch myself, but I couldn't really suck my own nipples, right? I wasn't that well-endowed in the chest department. But when Bobby scraped his teeth along those hard buds, I almost peeled out of my skin. My moan was so loud it echoed around the room, and Bobby chuckled around the sensitive flesh. Which made me moan more.

My body flushed hot, my hips grinding against the hard line of his dick, looking for some kind of relief. "Bobby," I whined, my voice sounding like a mewling replica of my normal tone.

He slipped a hand between our bodies, tugging at my pants until I sprang off the bed to tear them off.

His eyes were hooded with lust, but he still

searched my face. Considering I was standing there in my bra and underwear, that was pretty impressive.

"We should stop, before this goes further. I don't want to rush you."

I caught my bottom lip between my teeth and worried at it. "Do you not want to?"

He groaned, scrubbing a hand down his face. "So badly, you have no idea how much."

I grinned, my whole body feeling buzzed like the moments before a big fight. "Good. Me too."

Then I dived on the bed and he caught me in his arms. I wanted my mouth to be tasting everything at once, and my hands to touch and memorize every square inch of him.

He chuckled, or maybe it was a groan, and rolled us until he was on top and I was pinned beneath his large body.

"Slow down, little Mouse. I've waited a long, long time for this and I refuse to rush it." He kissed his way down my body, sucking my nipples through the lace of my bra, scraping his teeth along the slight softness of my stomach. His hands came up to wrap around my thighs and he spread them a little wider and shuddered.

"Fuck me, the smell of how much you want me is like crack. It calls to me like a temptation." He looked up at me, his tongue unconsciously wetting his full bottom lip like he could taste me already. "I'm going to eat your pretty pussy until you're screaming my name so loud that even Flint can hear it next door."

All I could do was nod as he bit the curve of my hip and slid his fingers beneath the elastic of my panties. He dragged them down my thighs and I watched his face as he exposed me to the room. His tongue ran along the flesh of my thigh, his hot breath against my core making me moan.

When his tongue ran between my lips, ending on my clit, my body bowed in the middle. I ground my hips against his mouth and he hummed.

"You taste like paradise."

He sucked on my clit and I panted. "Bobby, please."

He just buried his face further between my thighs, though if he went any deeper he'd need a snorkel.

"Please," I moaned again, rolling my hips.

He looked up, his face glistening with my slick. "What do you need, baby?"

Shit, what the fuck did I need? I needed release really fucking bad, but more than that, I needed him inside me. Stat.

I clawed at his shoulders, dragging him up my body. "I want you, inside of me. Now." I winced at how cliché I was being, but it was true. I ached to have Bobby, to have his cock inside me. I was so close to filling this aching pit in my soul that I hadn't even realized was there until now.

He kissed me deeply, and my body burned. He

pulled back, unzipping his jeans and his dick bounced out. It was rock hard and weeping, and my eyes got big as saucers. "Holy shit, Bobby. I didn't realize you were part elephant shifter. The fuck?" I whispered.

I mean, I'd seen Bobby naked. We were shifters and your clothes didn't shift with you. But never hard and never, ever like this. He was definitely a grower. He gave me a crooked smile as he slid on a condom he'd pulled from his back pocket. Alpha boy scout. Always prepared.

He lowered his body back over mine. "You sure about this, Carmen? If you aren't ready, I'm happy to climb back between your thighs and eat you like my favorite sundae for like another two hours."

I gripped both of his cheeks in my hands, pulling his face closer to mine. "You and I are inevitable, Bobby. I want this."

That probably wasn't romantic, but it worked, because I felt the nudge of the head of his cock against my entrance. I was wetter than I could have ever imagined, and his cock slid around a bit before notching against me, making me let out a tiny gasp.

The look of sheer terror on Bobby's face made me reach down and still his hips. "What's wrong? I thought I was the one who meant to look like a terrified virgin. You're stealing my glory, Alpha."

He grimaced, dropping a kiss to my lips. "I don't

want to fuck this up for you. I want it to be so fucking magical and not—"

I gripped his ass and pulled his hips down as I rose mine up to meet them. I sucked in a ragged breath as my body stretched to accommodate his, uncomfortable but not painful. After a few moments, it felt right. No, it felt perfect.

Bobby's mouth hung open, either in shock or in pleasure. "You're something perfect, Carmen Baxter, and I love you."

I gave him a tremulous smile as I swallowed hard. "Good. Now move your ass."

He buried his face in my throat and licked. "Yes, Alpha," he chuckled, and then rolled his hips.

Oh.

Oh shit, okay. Yep. Now I got it.

I didn't think again after that, my body consumed with growing pleasure until I was hanging on the precipice by my nails. He was sucking on my breasts, and then his hand was between our bodies, grinding his thumb on my clit, and I came on a scream.

"Bobby!"

He grunted, his thrusts getting wilder as he leaned forward to give me a wet kiss.

He pressed his cheek to mine. "Fuck, Carmen. Yes," he groaned as his body slammed into me and he shuddered, collapsing on top of me like I made *him* weak.

"Holy shit," I gasped.

"Holy shit," he agreed.

"A-fucking-men," a voice said from the other side of the paper-thin walls. Oops.

I grinned as I knocked against the wall. "Sorry, Flint."

"Don't be, Sugar Plum. Best spank of my life. Fuck, I need a cigarette," he replied and I laughed as Bobby rolled to his side, chuckling as well.

He kissed the back of my neck. "Okay?" he whispered in my ear.

I snuggled my body back into his. "Perfect."

And it really was.

BOBBY

The shittest part of Carmen being stuck at Eden was that I couldn't see her on the weekends. They closed the gates to day students, probably so there weren't a whole bunch of people roaming around out of uniform while the teachers had their "days off". But that meant she was there, and I was stuck up at Nîso with my parents.

I jogged through the streets of the town that would one day be mine. I nodded at people who would one day be my people, and I knew every person, their families, their favorite form. I knew what worried them, what they excelled at. I knew everything I needed to know to lead one of the largest shapeshifter packs in Canada.

I spotted Lulu coming up the street, her hand

waving to catch my attention. I grinned and slowed my pace.

"Hey Lulu."

She gave me a soft smile. "Hey Bobby. The Alpha is looking for you."

I wiped my forearm across the sweat on my forehead. Lulu was gentle and broken, absolutely petrified of men, but I hardly blamed her. Her dad had been a piece of shit. I also thought she might have a little crush on Carmen, but I would never bring it up with either of them. "Thanks. Wanna run back with me?"

She gave me another half smile and jogged toward me. "How's school? I heard through the grapevine that you and Carmen are finally a thing."

I couldn't help the small smile that curved my lips. I looked over at the girl who'd been my friend since we were kids. She'd been my best friend for years, and when Mouse and her siblings had come along, she'd taken to them completely. I was pretty sure there were bets placed in the Pack that I would end up with Lulu as a mate. But we'd never been that to each other. She was smart as a whip, but damaged. She also flew below the radar and knew all sorts of things about the people of the Pack. I was going to ask her to be one of my Enforcers when I was made Alpha, because your Enforcers were an extension of the Alpha, and it wasn't all brute force. Sometimes, it was just knowing whose ear to whisper into. Lulu, although she'd never admit it and would probably be embarrassed by the praise, excelled at that.

"Can I tell you a secret, Lulu? I mean, it's not a real secret, and if I have my way, it won't be a secret for long."

She raised an eyebrow at me. "What's up?"

"Carmen is my fated mate."

Lulu skidded to a stop, her eyes wide. "Are you shitting me?"

I grinned because Lulu never swore, it was a leftover from her dad beating her anytime she said anything that remotely constituted swearing. So I knew she was surprised.

I spun on my heel, jogging backward and beckoning her along.

Lulu skittered to catch up. "Does she know?"

I winced. "She does now."

Lulu shook her head, jogging to catch up. "But what about the other guys?"

I huffed. "The rumor mill over at the Academy is working overtime."

She shrugged. "You're the future Alpha and she is... Mouse. People watch you. Plus she collected the Djinn and the MC kid? She took two eligible bachelors straight off the market and the Pack girls talk. They aren't happy."

I gave her the side-eye, but she didn't look jealous

or angry about it. More bemused. "Should she expect trouble?"

Lulu laughed. "It's Mouse. She should always expect trouble. But nothing that she can't put down easily, you know?" There was envy in her tone now, and I stopped, reaching out to grab Lulu and pull her into my arms.

I was her Alpha, and Pack was Pack. Touch was comfort, especially if you added in my Alpha vibes. "Lulu, you are one of the strongest women I know. You mightn't throw punches or kick ass, but you have a steel backbone and balls of solid gold. And when I'm Alpha, I'm going to make you one of my Enforcers."

She reared back, her face comically horrified. "Are you fucking insane, Bobby?" She slapped a hand on my chest and shoved me. "I can't be a fucking Enforcer," she hissed.

I bundled her back into my arms and squeezed her tightly before releasing her. "You're my oldest friend, Lulu. Better get used to the idea."

"You need your head examined. Love is making you loopy." She flipped me the bird and started jogging away, and I couldn't help my laughter.

"Just think about it," I yelled after her, and bounded up the steps of the Alpha's office here. Ghost was lazing in the foyer, half asleep on a couch in the sun. I didn't fool myself though—Brody's head

Enforcer would be on his feet with my throat torn out in a second if I was a threat to his Alpha.

I knocked on the office door, and Brody called me in. I bowed my head deferentially. Here, he was all Alpha and not my girlfriend's dad. "Alpha."

"Alpha-Heir," he said, dipping his chin back. He motioned to a chair across from him, and I sat down. "How is my daughter?"

Eesh. I swallowed hard and held his eyes briefly. I wasn't convinced that he didn't know I'd taken her virginity. Maybe he could read it in my body language?

Shit, think of something else.

"Uh, she's good. Chafing at being stuck inside a fence. You know what she's like."

He just hummed his agreement. "There are too many strangers in our Packlands for my liking at the moment. This Rook is elusive, despite X and Lucius being out for blood, and half the members of your little fight ring are still loitering around, including the Wendigo."

I frowned. "Monster's still here?"

Brody nodded. "Lucius picked him up in the outskirts of Dark River last week. Gave chase, but this guy just disappeared into the woods. The former Matriarch was of the old school that believed that Wendigos were bad luck." He lifted a shoulder as he frowned. "The old superstitions are just that, but still, sometimes it's hard to shake these old prejudices. What do you know about this Monster?"

What did I know really? When I took Mouse to those fights, I was solely focused on getting her out of there alive. But I'd picked up a bit from Rat and his guards. "Not much. He's a bit of a legend in the underground circuit apparently. Only takes on the baddest, most brutal fighters. The undefeated ones that were dripping in blood basically. And then he'd toy with them. His thing though, the thing that makes him so infamous, is that he eats the hearts of almost all his opponents."

I mean, we shapeshifters had a pretty brutal history, and I was sure that there was more than one Alpha that had eaten the heart of his enemy. But Wendigos were cannibals, and from folklore, they were sustained only by flesh.

"Where'd he come from? There hasn't been a Wendigo on tribal lands since before our Pack settled here."

I shrugged. "I heard he comes from Nova Scotia, that he just follows the underground fights until he either kills all his opponents or they run him out."

Brody frowned. "We'll keep an eye on him. If he's just passing through, we'll leave him be. Now, we've had a bit of change in suppliers..."

Brody droned on about how to find alternate suppliers for basic goods and I listened intently, but still let my brain drift a little back to the Wendigo. Mouse had said he'd helped them when they'd taken Flint, and for that reason I didn't want to move him along. We kind of owed him one. I wasn't too proud to admit that I didn't want to fight him either. I'd seen him in that slaughter ring and I was not keen to be on the other side of those claws.

I GOT to school a full hour before I normally did, just so I could see my girl. I was so freaking whipped, but after making love to her and then not seeing her for two whole days, I felt like howling at the moon like a lovesick puppy. I threw my dignity to the wind and basically jogged to her door.

I frowned when I found it unlocked, but a person would have to be insane to break into my girlfriend's room. Mouse would say I had an ego the size of Canada, but it was true. I held sway over this Academy, over this area, hell over this country in general. I could make a person's life really, really uncomfortable. I'd proven that when that little fuck Josh had touched her against her will in junior high.

If that wasn't enough? Her family would tip the scales. Not even I would fuck with her family.

I was quiet as I crept into the room, and I was completely unsurprised to see Flint wrapped around my girl. No. Our girl.

The Alpha in me reared its head, poking at me to be a jealous fuck. But what both the Alpha and the man agreed on was that they wanted their mate to be happy. No, more than happy. Deliriously content. If these other guys made her happy, then I was okay with that too. I kicked off my shoes and climbed into the bed beside her, pressing her body between mine and his. Her eyes fluttered open and I stared into their sparkling blue depths. She gave me a sleepy smile and I fell in love all over again. Jesus, I needed her to be my mate so I could wake up to that smile every morning.

"Hey." Her voice was rough and sleepy, and it instantly made my dick hard. "He has nightmares. I couldn't leave him to face them alone," she whispered.

I nodded, leaning in to kiss her, and hoped she could taste my emotions on my lips. As if to prove her point, Flint's face screwed up and he whimpered a little in his sleep. He tossed around in his spot, like he was trying to escape whatever invisible thing haunted him.

Carmen rolled over and pressed her lips to his forehead, murmuring softly. He calmed a little, and when I reached over her, pressing a hand to his shoulder, he eased more. He was wound so tightly I could feel his muscles trembling beneath my palm. What was he dreaming about that made him as scared as a cornered pup? I channelled a little bit of my Alpha power into the room. "Rest, Flint. We'll guard your dreams," I whispered, and his body seemed to let go of all its tension like a marionette with its strings cut. It was so fucking sad.

I stayed where I was, both of them wrapped in my arms, and Mouse wiggled her body back into mine. I bit back a groan as her ass brushed my dick.

But when she looked over at me, her eyes were wide and shining. "You are the best man, Bobby. I love you."

My heart stuttered in my chest. I leaned in and brushed my lips across hers again. "I love you too, Mouse."

She made a happy humming noise as she rested her head back against my chest, her hands running soothing strokes up and down Flint's spine, brushing gently over the raised scars. I knew that some of those long gashes were knife wounds, like someone had taken great pleasure in slicing him open. It made me incredibly angry, but I blew out a breath to release the tension. I was angry, but they both seemed like they needed the rest.

I nuzzled my face back into her hair, breathing the scent of my mate deep into my lungs. "We have time for a bit more sleep. Sleep, baby."

But judging by her soft breaths, she had already dozed. I let my eyes close and slept beside them. My Pack.

CARMEN

I wouldn't admit it to anyone else, but this shit with Rook was really fucking with my head. How easy he could have taken me. How helpless I'd been. I swear I could still feel his eyes on me, and a small part of me worried that he'd make good on his threat, because he had to know I'd blabbed to my parents by now.

The hairs on the back of my neck tingled like I was being watched, and I rubbed my palms over my arms. Sammie had the class outside on the back sports field, doing a combination of archery and throwing daggers. Well, not just daggers. You could throw ninja stars, axes, javelins or even freaking tridents. Where the hell Sammie had gotten a flying fork was beyond me, but you bet your ass I lined up to throw that bastard like I was freaking Aquaman. Cara was beside me, casually throwing daggers at the target, hitting the bullseye every time.

"I think I might murder your brother and bury him in a shallow grave. On a scale of one to ten, how upset would you be?"

I shrugged. "I mean, is it on a day when he's being a pissy bitch, or when he does something really sweet, like make me coffee before school?"

She turned toward me, not looking as she threw her dagger but still hitting the bullseye. This bitch was a freak of nature. "You mean he has a setting that isn't 'pissy bitch'? Huh. I'm yet to see it."

I just laughed, my eyes eating Sammie alive as he corrected Teesha and she fluttered her eyelashes like she was stupid. I wondered if I could accidentally let my flying fork slip and spear her in the thigh?

"Stop eyefucking my brother and listen to me whine about yours," Cara grumbled.

I dragged my eyes back to Cara. "I'm kind of attached to him. We shared a womb, you know. But if you want to just generally fuck with him, I have a mountain of ideas and years of experience. I'm your girl."

She laughed, grabbing a handful of throwing stars and interspersing them perfectly between her dagger strikes.

"Are you like some kind of dagger-throwing savant? What the hell, girl?"

She gave me a crooked smile. "Knives are my thing."

Obviously. Honestly, she kind of gave me a lady-boner, and I was strictly D. But she was all ink-covered attitude, and that was a pretty hot combination. No wonder Christopher was all twisted up about her. Flint was on the other side of the sports field, entertaining the rest of the class as he threw fireballs at clay pigeons, while one of the juniors ran around putting out spot fires with an extinguisher. I wasn't sure that was following the school-assigned safety handbook, but everyone seemed to be enjoying the activity if the laughter and whooping was any indication.

I walked over to grab the daggers, when something beyond the security fencing caught my eye. A shadow or a movement. Something. I grabbed the daggers and drifted closer, though they'd be useless from this side of the fence. The boundary fence had super-special electrified mesh, so if something wanted to cross it, they'd have to be made of rubber and resistant to wards.

Something moved again, and I could hear Cara calling my name. I didn't stop though.

I had to see.

When I reached the wall, I could hear the low hum of its voltage. I looked through the dark undergrowth, but whatever was there was gone. Probably just a bear or deer or something.

I turned back to the group, and Sammie's horrified face made time slow.

"Carmen."

I spun around on my heel and screamed.

In the next second, a flaming body was between me and the fence, Flint in full Ifrit mode, his whole body covered in flames.

Monster the Wendigo flinched away from the dripping flames.

"Get the fuck out of here," Flaming Flint growled. It was kind of hot. My brain was obviously broken because I half smiled at the good alliteration, coupled with a pun. Ten points for Gryffindor.

I stepped around Flint, my knives held loosely in my palms like Cara had shown me. "What are you doing here?" I hissed, but my voice wavered in fear.

I hadn't seen him since the night he fought Flint and almost killed him. He looked gaunter, like he'd been sleeping rough.

His black eyes watched me intently, like he was trying to pick me apart piece by piece, and a shiver ran over my skin. "I need to speak with you."

"Oh, fuck no," Flint shouted, and then suddenly there were two large Lycanthropes there, snarling at the fence, and Sammie was dragging me away from the wall.

I watched Monster shift into his Wendigo, his pink bone antlers jagged, and shook my head. But he never took his eyes from mine, even as they dragged me away. His face was desperately sad and his eyes implored me for... something.

I COULDN'T SLEEP. I was restless.

I slipped from the blankets, shifting a pillow under Flint's arm, and he snuggled it into his chest. I slid his hoodie over my head, and pushed my feet into my boots. Tiptoeing down the hall, I didn't walk normally until I was out the front door of the dorms, and heading toward the field.

I had to find out what Monster wanted. It kept swirling in my brain, until my mind was a jumble. Was it Wendigo magic? I didn't know anything about what Wendigo were, exactly. But I know the Matriarch had paled every time one was mentioned.

"Bobby said you wouldn't be able to help yourself. Said curiosity would be your downfall."

I let out a small scream as Sammie stepped from the shadows, his lips tipped up in a dark smirk.

"Jesus H. Christ, Sammie. You scared the shit out of me." I stepped into his space and let him wrap his arms around me. "Are you here to make me go back to my room?"

He shook his head. "I'm coming with you. If you argue, I'll take you and handcuff you to my headboard. Flint left them when he stayed over."

I quirked an eyebrow at him. "He left his handcuffs on your headboard. Anything you wanna tell me there, Mr. Richards?"

He just kissed me quickly. "Nope. Let's go before Flint wakes up and flames on."

I grabbed his hand and we walked off the path and into the inky darkness. I'd never been scared of the dark, probably because I'd grown up in the darkness. Being raised by the night's scariest creatures had that effect. There were a few of the nocturnal students roaming around, and I knew they had at least one class while everyone else slept. Moon Rituals or something like that.

I stepped on the slightly crispy patches of grass where Flint's fireballs had landed during this afternoon's weapons class.

"What do you think he wants?" Sammie whispered, and I honestly had no idea.

"No clue. I haven't had a single conversation with him in my life. I don't even think I've ever heard him speak before today." I'd seen him fight a little, and heard the stories even more. I didn't know who he associated with, if anyone, and I didn't know where he slept or what he ate. Or who he ate. Wendigo were cannibals, that much I knew. He deserved his moniker. He was a monster in the truest definition of the word.

Sammie frowned, but didn't say anything else. My hand brushed across the gun in its holster under his jacket, and I worried at my lip. I didn't think a bullet could kill a Wendigo. It would probably hurt like a bitch though. Didn't matter. I was confident that he couldn't get across the wards.

I reached the fence, but there was nothing there. I don't know why I thought he would be. I had no doubt that Micah and Alistair had chased him off this afternoon. You didn't fuck with Lycans.

But in the next moment, Monster just appeared. I bit back the scream that burst from my chest.

"What the hell is wrong with you? You can't just appear out of the darkness like that," I hissed, and he cocked his head at me like I was insane. I huffed, glad I couldn't see those abyss eyes in this darkness. I got trapped in those eyes. "You wanted to talk to me? Here I am."

His eyes flicked to Sammie, and then back to me. "I wish to join your Pack."

I wrapped my arms around my body as I frowned. His clothes were shabby, a dark fleece-lined jacket wrapped around his body. But his face was clean, his hair combed, and I think his beard was trimmed since the last time I saw him. He looked like he was making an effort despite how gaunt he looked, as if he was starving.

How did a Wendigo starve?

I shuddered. "You're asking the wrong person. If you want to join the Nîso Pack, you'll have to make an appointment with the Pack Alpha, Brody. But I should warn you, seventy percent of the town is First Nation people, and they still have certain beliefs in regard to, uh, your kind."

He inclined his head. "That I'm cursed by evil spirits. They aren't wrong."

I swallowed hard. "That you're bad luck. That you are a mindless monster in your other form. There is a lot of folklore around your kind."

He didn't dispute any of it, sadness dragging down the lines of his face and my heart broke for him a little. The loneliness hung around him like a cloak, choking me with a darkness that had nothing to do with the moon.

He stepped closer to the fence, and I stepped forward too. I wanted to look into his eyes just once more. Sammie tensed beside me, his hand going to his gun.

Monster looked back at my boyfriend, his lip curling. "I'm not going to hurt her."

Sammie didn't move his hand. Words didn't matter. Shaking his head, Monster looked back toward me. "I don't want to join the Nîso pack. I want to join your Pack."

I threw my hands up. "I'm a part of the Nîso Pack. They are my Pack." I tried saying it slowly in case he'd taken one too many punches to the head. It happened sometimes, though I'd never seen it in a supernatural fighter.

"No. Your Pack. The young Alpha, the broken fighter, the MC outcast." I stepped back like he'd struck me, but he continued. "You are my fated mate, Carmen Baxter, and I've waited a century for you. I'm ready to join your Pack."

I... he what? I shook my head like if I whipped it back and forward fast enough, what he just said would make sense. His eyes implored me to give him a chance, and Sammie had pulled his gun and was pointing it through the fence. Monster didn't even spare him a glance, his face so full of hope yet still tainted with despair. I could feel the weight of it on my chest, crushing me.

"I'm sorry," I whispered, and then turned on my heel and ran all the way back to the dorm rooms. I didn't stop until I was climbing into bed beside Flint. The guilt that I'd left Sammie in the dark with a killer ate at me until I made Flint get up and make sure he got home okay.

And while Flint was gone, I curled up into a ball and cried.

Cried for the man who had nothing.

Cried because he looked at me like I was his savior.

But I was no one's savior, so I let the tears fall down my cheeks until they soaked my pillows.

I watched her flee. I didn't blame her. Her pack mate stood at the fence, his gun pointed at my face, and I wished he'd pull the trigger. End this.

He didn't chase after her, and when I slid my eyes back to him, he hadn't moved, hadn't lowered the gun even an inch.

His eyes ran over my body, and I knew how I looked. Vagrant. Animal. Like the monster that they'd named me after. He shifted his head partially to the side.

He's human, we should kill him and eat his heart, Hew muttered.

Excellent suggestion. Let's eat the lover of our fated mate. I'm sure that will make her love us, Wati shot back. *No wonder you're fucking dead.*

The voices in my head bickered back and forth,

and I dragged a rough hand down my face. When I'd allowed evil spirits to possess me, so that I could become a Wendigo and avenge my sister, I kind of thought they'd be scary evil. Not annoying evil. Guess the definition of evil changed with the times too. After a century, I'd learned to tune them out, mostly.

The guy dropped his gun, which was foolish, but it made something thump in the empty cavity of my chest. "Is it true, what you said? Are you her fated mate?"

I swallowed, but my face remained impassive. "Yes." I mean, I'd always suspected. But that night, the night of the fight when she'd stolen the Djinn, she'd attacked me and gotten me on my back. I'd been so fucking shocked that I'd almost gotten my throat slit. She'd looked down at me, her face fierce even though I could hear the pounding of her heart. She'd fought me for the Ifrit. Me.

She was so damn young. She was right to flee. I shouldn't even be here.

Yeah, except we'll be trapped together for eternity, Wati grumbled and Hew cackled evilly.

The kid through the fence nodded. "I'll talk to her. But ultimately, I won't let her be guilted into shit. But if what I know about fated mates applies to Wendigo, she'll be drawn to you anyway?"

I shrugged. It wasn't the Wendigo that was fated. It was the wolf shifter I'd been before I'd been transformed into a monster. I'd had a name once. I'd forgotten what it was.

No you haven't, Hew taunted. *You're just too guilt-ridden to remember.*

The kid nodded, and walked away, showing bravery or stupidity by showing me his back. He probably thought this electrified wall protected him. It didn't. The spirits that inhabited my body were of this land, threaded through the very energies of the earth. Wards and electricity meant nothing to them or their vessel. They were one with the earth, even if they were troublesome spirits.

I slunk back into the woods before the Lycanthropes came back. The confrontation this morning had been rough, filled with teeth and claws, and punctuated with threats. I could respect that, they had a lot of young to care for. But the spirits had wanted to rend and tear, to snap their necks and then reach in and devour their heart's blood.

You can't blame that all on us, Wati baited. *Some of it is your own bloodthirsty nature. It's why we are all saddled together in the first place.*

I ignored her and strode through the forest like I was the greatest predator in the night. Once upon a time, it might have been true. But now these woods were inhabited by shapeshifters and vampires, Lycans and creatures that had no name. The things that went bump in the night were more plentiful in this little section of the world than any other I'd been in for the last one hundred years.

My bike was in the shadows just off the main road, all my worldly possessions in the saddlebags. Which was basically nothing. I kept everything with any value on my body unless I was fighting. During a fight, I wasn't worried about people stealing my shit. Watching me eat a man's heart was a real good deterrent.

I straddled my bike, kicking it over and feeling the thrum of the motor that ran through my body and drowned out the voices. The open road was the only time I was ever free of Hew and Wati. They had really long traditional names, but I'd long forgotten them.

I rode back through the small town of Dark River, knowing better than to stop. I knew the predators that lived there, and they scared the fuck out of me. I was pretty invincible really, but I'd heard of some of the vampires living in that town. There were a handful of ways for a Wendigo to die, and I bet they knew every single one.

The next town over was slightly bigger, big enough that they didn't look askance at strangers. Well, most of the time. I always drew stares. The night was still, no moon to shed light in the darkness. It was just an unending abyss of blackness outside of the single headlight of my bike.

When I rolled in, I drove to the twenty-four hour

gym. It was still early enough that there would be some eager office worker there, working off that extra bagel rather than be at home with their wife. I pulled my bike around the back, hefting my saddlebag onto my shoulder.

When a man walked out, red-faced and puffing, I didn't even feel satisfied at being correct. I just caught the door before it fully closed and let myself in.

There was another guy pumping iron in the corner, and he stared at me from the corner of his eye like I didn't belong. He wasn't wrong, I didn't belong. I strolled into the changerooms. It was steamy and smelled a little like piss and sweat, but it had a shower and that was all I needed.

I got the stall right at the end, closest to a window, and hung my saddlebag over the partition wall. Switching on the shower, I undressed and tried not to look at myself in the mirror on one of the walls of the stall. Fucking gyms. Everyone wanted to look at themselves in the mirror all the time, even when they were getting undressed to hit the showers.

I purposefully didn't look at the melted skin of my side; it was no longer red and raised, but had the look of melted wax. It ran from just below my armpit, across half of my chest, and down to my thigh. Missed my dick, which was a small mercy I was thankful for every single day.

Not that we get to use it much, you antisocial fuck.

What is the point of being evil if you're going to live like a blushing virgin? Hew grumbled.

Hew and Wati were spirits, and therefore didn't have genders, but I had the vague idea that Hew had been a man in his past life. He was just lecherous, though it didn't matter if the object of his lechery was male or female. Hmm, maybe women more. He was more likely to suggest fighting and then eating a man.

Wati, however, I had no idea. Man or woman, I just called her *she* because she bitched about Hew like she was his wife of twenty years.

I stepped into the steaming water and sighed. I hadn't gotten paid for my last fight, mostly because Carmen had caused a riot saving the Djinn kid and then I'd murdered a whole bunch of guys and eaten their corpses. I was in glut, and consuming two dead men should keep me satiated for a month.

But that was the thing about being a Wendigo; you were never satiated. Always yearning for more, always with that burn of hunger in my stomach. Really. What was I thinking? I couldn't be Carmen's Packmate, tie my soul to hers. She was not going to be okay with me eating people.

I thumped my fist against the tiles of the wall, making one of the cheap subway tiles crack. She was my fated mate. My one chance to die properly, without becoming an evil spirit like Wati and Hew to haunt some other poor fuck.

If she accepted me, mated with me, our souls would become one and when she died, her pure soul would drag my sludgy one to the afterlife. Ending my curse. Hell, ending Wati and Hew's curses too.

I rested my forehead against the tiles as my mind warred with itself. She'd said no. I would just continue to wander until I accidentally, or more likely on purpose, died. And then I'd wander the earth as a malevolent, annoying spirit until some other poor sucker with too much rage and not enough brain cells did dumb shit and I ended up haunting his brain.

So much love. If I had emotions, I'd be offended, Wati grumbled.

I blocked them out and finished my shower. I'd washed and brushed out my hair, and it fell in short, messy waves. I trimmed my beard, not bothering to shave. It would be back in days anyway.

I packed everything up, and cursed a little seeing that the guy lifting weights was still here, his eyes burning into my skin as I walked toward the door.

"Hey, you. This is the YMCA, fuckhead. Keep your vagrant ass out."

I ignored him and pushed through the front door. Too many cameras in this new age.

Once upon a time we'd be on his throat in a second, Hew whined. He was right.

But when the door opened and closed behind me, I

let my lips twitch. I walked into the alley, and the guy stomped behind me.

Five.

Four.

Three.

Two.

He reached my arm and grabbed it, spinning me around. "Hey, you hobo fuck. I'm talking to you. Dirty fucking trash. Keep your bug-infested ass—" He stuttered to a stop, probably due to the creepy ass smile on my face.

He smelled of chemicals, probably steroids, which had obviously made him stupid. He went to backpedal toward the gym, but it was too late for him. I reached out and grabbed his arm, pulling him back toward me and my rapidly growing head. I knew what he was seeing right now—a buck's head, but the more I morphed, the more the flesh peeled from it, until I was left with a bleached deer skull. Plus I had huge pink antlers with viscous strands of flesh and muscle spread between the barbs. I continued to grow, my body curving in on itself, until I was a nightmare with gnarled clawed hands wrapped around his over-pumped forearms.

The dude screamed, but only for a moment. Like the beep of a car alarm when you unlocked it.

It was kind of the same, but instead of opening a car, I was opening a chest cavity.

29

CARMEN

I must have been giving off some seriously stressed out vibes, because Enit was practically curled in my lap trying to soothe me, and Christopher was growling at anyone who even looked at me.

The only people they let past were my guys, and I rested with my back against Bobby's chest even as I ran my hands through Enit's smooth, white hair. I didn't know how to tell Bobby that I had another fated mate. Especially one that had probably murdered more people than he'd eaten hot dinners. Also, he was almost a decade older than me. Hell, maybe he was a century older than me. How did Wendigo age anyway?

Bobby might have been cool with me having other lovers, because he was secure in the fact that we belonged together. But what if I belonged to another man too?

I whined low in my throat, and Enit whined with me. I swallowed down my turmoil, willing myself to be calm.

"What's wrong?" Bobby murmured into my hair. I gave him a tight smile.

"Nothing. Exam stress. And the whole Rook thing, you know?"

It was plausible. I was still stressed as fuck about Flint's former owner.

I didn't think Monster was lying about being my fated mate either. I wished I did. That restlessness I had under my skin, it was worse since Monster had come to visit. The urge to fight, fuck or flee rode me hard, making me anxious. That was what they were all picking up on now. Plus, I hadn't had a fight in a month and the darkness was demanding a tribute.

I hadn't seen Sammie in a couple of nights, but I wonder if I could arrange a couple more combat lessons with him and Flint. We'd either fight or fuck, and I was down for both of those options.

Speaking of Flint, he looked even shittier than I did. He wasn't sleeping, unless he was in bed with me, which was most nights now. But last night, he'd tossed and turned, even with my body wrapped around his.

Fun fact about Flint? He liked to be the little spoon. And I was here for it. I didn't have to worry about what my hair was doing, or whether my head was making his arm dead. It was just skin on skin comfort and I low-key loved it.

Right now, he picked at his food, and I untangled my fingers from my sister's hair to reach over and grab his hand. "Are you okay?"

He gave me a forced smile. "I'm fine."

Oh, so that's what my lie had looked like. Neither of us was fine, but we were both happy to fake it. Uh uh. Not today. I sighed, looking between my siblings.

"I'm skipping today's classes. Can you tell them I got the runs or something?"

Christopher eyed me. Normally he'd be on my ass about what was wrong, but he had his own problems at the moment. That problem was flirting with Kingston the unicorn shifter right now, and I could basically hear Christopher's teeth grinding.

I shifted Enit off my lap gently, and she pouted a little. I hadn't seen as much of her lately, and I knew she was missing the connection. Though, the way the lion Alpha was eyeing her like a juicy steak told me it wouldn't be a problem for long. If that was what Enit wanted. If it wasn't, I was itching to shed some blood, and a pretty blonde Alpha was calling to me to break his face.

"Stop growling at Bohdie," Enit chastised, and I was a little embarrassed that I had been. It was a testament to my emotional unease. But I wouldn't admit it out loud.

Bravado it was. "I don't like how he eyes you," I grumbled, which was true.

She gave me a soft smile. "I like him."

Of course she fucking did. She liked nearly everyone. "Enough to make him your boyfriend? Because anything less than fully committed, and Christopher is going to make him into a rug."

Christopher just grunted. "Might do it anyway."

Enit cocked her head. "I think so. He makes me feel... Omega things."

I had no idea what that meant, and I had enough problems of my own without borrowing Enit's. But if he made her happy... "In that case, you have my blessing. I'll beat the stupid machismo out of Christopher so you can have your happiness."

Christopher gave me a droll expression. "Good luck with that."

I stood up, and Bobby kissed my head. "I'm going to skip with you, if you like?"

He didn't presume. Didn't assume my answer would be yes just because he was my Alpha. I eyed Christopher. "See this? You'd have more success with Cara if you pulled the stick out of your ass."

He scowled back. "Bobby is whipped. No offense, man." Bobby just snorted. "Besides, I don't want anything to do with that annoying, shrill, trouble-making human."

Now it was my turn to snort, and I gave him a condescending pat on the head. "Keep telling yourself that, brother." I grabbed Bobby's hand. "I'd be glad to spend the day with you, if you aren't going to get in trouble for missing classes."

Bobby just shrugged, and pointed to Flint. "You too, Zombie. You look like a reanimated corpse. You need a nap."

"Is that code for listening to you two bang like horny goats again?"

Enit's eyes went wide, and Christopher's jaw dropped. "You fucked my sister?" he growled.

Oh, for fuck's sake.

I stepped into his space. "You better watch your tone, Christopher Baxter, or I am going to superglue your testicles to the toilet seat again. What I do, and with whom, is not any of your business. Plus, he's my freaking fated mate and this isn't the eighteenth century. I will fucking stab you with a damn fork."

I flounced away, grabbing Flint's hand as he grinned. I shook my head at him. "You're trouble, you know that?"

We pushed through the doors of the cafeteria, Bobby a step behind us. Flint darted out in front of me, stopping me in my tracks and making me back up into the body of my fated mate. Then he kissed me. Pressed between them, the plundering tongue of Flint in my mouth and the steadying hands of Bobby on my hips, was a heady experience. One I would happily get used to.

How many times did I have to have sex before I could graduate to orgies? Enquiring minds wished to know.

Bobby clipped Flint upside the head, making him pull back with a grin. "Come on, Romeo. We're making a spectacle and the Academy has a clear 'no foreplay in the hallways' rule. Besides, we are going to nap. Not get naked."

Flint sighed. "I don't think they need to be mutually exclusive."

Me either, Flint. Me either.

APPARENTLY WE ALL napped better in a puppy pile, because by the time there was a knock on my door, the sun was beginning to set. Bobby stretched, and Flint remained completely oblivious to the world, his face smooth and innocent in sleep.

Bobby kissed my temple. "I'll get it."

He stood and stretched, his t-shirt riding up to show the hard lines of his abs. I may have drooled a bit into the pillow.

He pulled the door open, revealing Sammie, who was holding three pizza boxes. I smiled at him and waved him in. Bobby picked up his backpack and wandered back over to me. "I better get home before my mom freaks out, or worse, Miss Pea kicks my ass for being here after hours." He leaned down and kissed me hard. "Love you, Mouse."

He didn't wait for me to say it back, thank god, because the guilt over hiding Monster's claim over me was eating at me. He leaned over and ruffled Flint's hair softly, and my heart melted. This was why he was going to be such an amazing Alpha. He slapped Sammie on the shoulder. "You guys should come to Nîso on the weekend. Come to the family barbeque. You'll be safe from Rook within the wards, and you should really meet the family now there are no explosive secrets between us."

Sammie's eyes shot to mine, and I shook my head minutely. He smiled at Bobby. "I'd like that. Can I bring the kids?"

"And Cara," I added. "Christopher will be there too, and what's a cookout without some fireworks, right?"

Bobby laughed and shook his head. "The more the merrier. I'll pass it by Ghost and the Enforcers. We'll make it a Pack thing." He blew me another kiss and left.

Sammie crept toward me, sitting on the edge of the bed. "You didn't tell him." It wasn't a question, because it was super obvious. I shook my head and pulled him into bed, so I could wrap myself around him.

"I want to say I was waiting for the right time, but the honest answer is that I'm a chickenshit. I don't even know how to approach the conversation." I sighed and raked my hand down my face as Flint softly snored beside me. "I'll do it this weekend. It's better we have this conversation in Nîso anyway."

Sammie shifted me so my head rested on his chest and he could stroke his fingers through my hair. "Just because he's your fated mate, doesn't mean you have to accept the bond. I asked Bohdie about it, and he said that you can have other mates. The love won't be as intense as it is with your fated mate, but you can still have love and be happy. Monster can still be happy."

We both knew it wasn't the same, and judging by Monster's absolute desperation, I couldn't imagine it was as easy as finding a little woman and settling down to have a bunch of other flesh-eating Wendigo.

Ugh. I buried my face in Sammie's neck and took a deep breath of his scent. It was gloriously human, without any supernatural notes. It was like a fresh spring day, clear and full of potential.

I kissed his pulse point, that place that if I broke the skin, would turn him into a wolf shifter. It was an act that was forbidden—you had to petition the Shifter Convocation Member for permission. Fortunately, or perhaps unfortunately, that was my pseudo-great grandfather, Alexander. He was a dragon.

Told you my family was well connected. Rook

didn't understand who he was fucking with. I sounded like a rich kid, lying in my dorm room, in my expensive Academy, thinking about all the power my family had. But I'd never been spoiled, except in regards to safety, I guess. I was the safest person in the world, and I could sleep easily every single night, which was a luxury I'd never take for granted. But despite my family's far-ranging power and general bloodthirsty history, we'd had a reasonably ordinary middle class upbringing. I had to work at the cafe or the diner during the holidays to earn money. I knew how to cook basic meals, though Enit was a much better chef than I would ever be, and we cleaned up after ourselves. We were ordinary. Except my mom and great grandfather sat on the ruling council of all supernaturals. Also, my Uncle Titus.

Monster had really chosen the wrong girl to get fated to.

Sammie's hand roamed down my spine, soothing me with his touch. I kissed the hollow of his throat, and felt his moan beneath my lips. I moved my hands beneath his shirt, pushing it up as I slid my body further down his.

"Mouse..." he breathed, and I wasn't sure if his words were a desperate plea or a warning. I was going to go with a plea.

I pushed his shirt right up until it was tucked under his chin and his torso was exposed to me. I kissed the valley between his pecs, then stroked the flat of my tongue across one of his tight nipples. He sucked in a breath and shuddered, so I took it between my teeth and pulled back gently. His body bucked, and he grabbed my hips, pulling me onto his body so I straddled his hips.

I moved onto his other nipple, sucking it hard and he hissed. "Carmen, fuck," he whispered. Flint was still sound asleep and I grinned wickedly.

"Shh, don't wake Flint. He needs sleep." Oh, this was going to be fun.

I slid down further, until I could feel the hard line of his cock in his sweats. He ground up, and I moaned. I sucked his skin, leaving small love bites down his chest and the top of his stomach. He grabbed my hips and pressed me down again, rolling his hips and hitting my clit. Hoo boy.

I sat up so I could stare down at him, and he was a glorious dark god beneath me. His eyes burned with lust as he stared at me like I was the most beautiful creature he'd ever had on his lap.

I grinned and scooted down his thighs. There was something I wanted to try. I shifted myself between his knees and grabbed the waistband of his sweats.

His fingers wrapped around my wrists, stilling my hands. "What are you doing?" he whispered, his eyes wide.

"Um, I know you aren't a saint, Sammie Richards,

so I'm pretty sure you've gotten a blowjob before. I haven't given one however, so bear with me. I take direction well though," I added, and yanked his pants down, freeing his cock until it bobbed against his lower abs. I stared at it for a second. It was different to Bobby's, shorter but like, as thick as my goddamn wrist. How the hell did that fit anywhere?

But hey, I was no quitter, so I kept yanking his sweats down until he could kick them off. I pushed his thighs further apart so I could fully appreciate what I was working with. I mean, I wasn't sure my jaw opened that wide. Could I just slobber on it like an everlasting gobstopper?

I leaned forward and puffed a breath across the tip, because I liked it when they did that to me. The principles had to be reasonably the same, right? Except one was an innie and one was an outie?

I was going to treat it like a giant clit.

So I flicked my tongue across the tip and watched his abs bunch. I gripped it in my hand, my fingers not even touching, and squeezed gently. Then I lifted the head to my lips and swirled my tongue around the tip. I was rewarded with Sammie's loud groan.

Okay. I had this shit. I sucked the head into my mouth, and Sammie sunk his fingers into my hair. My jaw stretched a little painfully, but it was adjusting. Yay for the human body. I pushed him back in my mouth further, and his hands tightened in my hair. Then I pulled back out, twisting my head as I went.

"Carmen," he groaned, all pretense of silence gone. When I looked up, I realized why. Flint's coal grey eyes stared back down at me, filled with desire so hot, I could feel it scorching my skin.

He had his hand in his shorts, his hair ruffled. I saw him stroking beneath the grey material.

I got wetter knowing I was being watched. Apparently I was a closet voyeur?

I sucked Sammie back into my mouth, pushing him a little deeper every time until my lips bottomed out and he was swearing in Latin. Fucking Latin. I squeezed my fingers around the base and he gripped my hair, shallow thrusting into my mouth as I slid my hands down to squeeze his balls.

"Carmen, baby, I'm going to blow," he panted, his body flushed. I swallowed him deeper, and hummed my readiness.

"Fuck!" he shouted, and I felt the salty hot bursts of his release hit the back of my tongue. I swallowed it down, and released him from my mouth with a pop. He laid back, gasping, looking at me like my tongue was made of solid gold, and I felt powerful as hell.

I climbed back up his body, kissing him with the taste of his release on my lips. His tongue fucked my mouth, his hands wildly roaming my body.

"I want a taste," Flint said, his voice still rough with

sleep. I leaned toward him, and he kissed my lips softly, as if taking a sip, before he pressed a hand to the back of my head and deepened the kiss. His tongue swirled and tasted, like he was chasing the flavor.

When he pulled away, his tongue darted out to run across his bottom lip.

"That's not what I wanted to taste, Sugar Plum." He looked past me to Sammie. "Grab her shorts."

He dragged me from Sammie's chest, and Sammie dutifully grabbed my shorts, peeling me out of them so I straddled Flint's chest completely bare.

Flint's eyes flashed as they ate me up, and then he grabbed two handfuls of my ass and dragged me toward his face. Holy shit.

I stared down at him. "You want me to sit on your face?"

"Yep."

"What if you suffocate and die?" I squeaked, and he laughed.

"Then I'll die happy." He wiggled down until his face was between my thighs and I forgot to breathe. Maybe I would be the one who suffocated.

I didn't have to worry though, because as soon as his tongue flicked against my clit I was done. That flick? It was a starting gun. Flint ate me out with the same ferocity with which he fought. His hand guided my hips until I was riding his face, his tongue thrusting into me like a piston.

I could hear myself making some kind of garbled noise, and then Sammie was on his knees beside me, his shirt gone and his lips ready to catch my moans.

It was too much. I rode Flint's face until I came, and he squeezed my ass tightly as he lapped up all my juices.

Finally, I shifted backwards until I was sitting on his abs, staring at his soaked face with something that was 80% lust and 20% embarrassment.

He grinned at me like the cat who got the cream, and then turned to Sammie.

"I think I've found paradise."

Sammie leaned down, running his tongue over Flint's cheek until he reached his lips. Then he kissed him with the same ferocity as Flint had eaten me out.

He pulled back and they both stared at me with heavy, hot eyes. "Tastes like it."

30

SAMMIE

If I was going to hell for sleeping with my students, I was going to go with a smile on my face. The pizzas were cold and forgotten on the desk as we feasted on each other instead. I stripped the rest of Carmen's clothes off, throwing them over my shoulder. She was made to be naked. Her body was pale and smooth, and I wanted to taste every inch of it.

As I kissed her again, Flint wiggled out of his gym shorts, until he was naked beneath her. Together they were ethereally beautiful. These two pale creatures completely entwined, and I was going to fuck the ever-loving hell out of both of them. I was like a dark prince beside them, my olive skin looking even darker next to their pale flesh.

Mouse reached over to the night stand and grabbed a handful of condoms. "Ever since Bobby and

I, you know, I thought it was best I had some of these lying around. Plus Miss Pea hands them out like suckers."

I breathed a sigh of relief. As much as I'd be honored to be her first, it was right that it had been Bobby. I took one and ripped it open, grabbing Flint's cock and stroking it, before rolling the condom on.

He grunted and thrust up into my hand. "Why does it feel so much dirtier when someone else puts on the rubber?" he moaned, and I laughed. I leaned over, sucking his latex-covered cock into my mouth, and I felt Flint's hands scrabble around for my head. Before he could reach me, I moved away, and ran a hand down Carmen's back. "Ready?"

She nodded and moved down. I reached back, holding Flint's cock for her to lower herself down on. There was something insanely hot about watching him slide inside her, both throwing their heads back, their mouths opened in synchronized moans. It was like watching live porn, that you could touch and taste.

I gripped my cock which was already getting hard again, sitting back on my heels as she rode him slowly.

Flint looked at her like she was everything. I understood the feeling. I got that desperate need to see her in my chest when we were apart too. That willingness to do anything to see her smile or hear her moan my name.

I had it bad.

I reached between them, thumbing her clit and making them both shout as she scraped her fingers down his chest. Judging by the way he fucked her harder, he loved it. I wasn't surprised he liked his pleasure with an edge of pain.

"Flint," she gasped, and I watched her shudder with pleasure as she came around his cock. She collapsed against his chest, and he gripped her hard around the waist as he continued to grind up into her. Soon though, he was roaring his release.

She turned her head to the side, and grinned at me. "We should do that again. Right now."

Oh yeah. This was love. "Not too sore?"

She chuckled, a low sexy sound. "Not human."

I sent up a small thank you to the moon goddess that I knew most shifters revered. Because if she'd created this perfect creature, I owed her everything. "Come here."

She crawled off Flint and towards me. Even in her human form, she was purely predatory. And I was more than happy to be her prey. "On your hands and knees."

As I moved behind her, I stroked my hand down her spine. She was still grinning. "Are you going to do me doggy-style, Sammie? Bit cliché, don't you think?"

In response, I slammed my cock inside her and she screamed out a moan. I drew out of her slowly and then slid back in, and she panted my name. She was so damn tight and wet, I was going to lose it in three strokes.

I bit my lip, pulling back out and thrusting shallowly until her arms were buckling beneath her. I gripped her hips and continued my slow roll inside her, until she was mewling.

Flint slid beneath her, raising his head until he could take her nipple into his mouth. Whatever he did down there had her screaming and slamming back into me.

Oh shit. I was so, so, so screwed. "Flint," I groaned, but he had me. I knew he did.

I curled over her back. "Come on baby, one last time. Come for me," I whispered in her ear, then bit her shoulder hard. Flint reached down, rubbing her swollen clit, and it tipped the balance. She came around my cock on a scream that she muffled in the blankets. I roared after her, collapsing against her back.

I slid out and pulled off the condom, knotting it and throwing it in her trash can. I'd take it out with me when I went home tonight. As I rolled off her, Flint greedily grabbed her into his arms and curled his body along hers.

Make that *if* I went home tonight. I had a feeling it would be hard to drag myself away.

. . .

I WOKE IN THE DARKNESS. We'd eaten dinner naked, watched some comedy movie, made love to our girl once more, and fallen asleep well after midnight. Judging by the darkness, it was still early in the morning.

I frowned as I tried to work out what had woken me. An unease ran over my skin, and I reached toward the nightstand, and the gun I'd left in the drawer. I pulled it out, sitting up, but there was no one in the shadows of the room.

Flint whimpered in his sleep, his arms trying to bundle Mouse closer as if she could shield him from his dreams. I slid my gun away, but I couldn't shake the feeling. Mouse roused a little, rolling over in his arms, and stroking his cheek softly even though she wasn't really awake either. But even her presence didn't seem to help. All of Flint's body bunched like he was prepared to fight or flee.

I reached over them both, putting one hand on his arm in case he came out of his slumber swinging, and shook him awake.

"Flint. Wake up, dude. You're having a nightmare," I whispered, but Mouse woke up anyway.

She blinked groggily. "Bad one." She stroked her fingers across his lips, leaning in to kiss him. "Baby. Wake up. Come on," she cooed softly, and I gave him a couple more rough shakes as his whimpers turned to shouts.

He gasped as he sat straight up in bed, sweat pouring down his body. He panted, his head whipping around.

Mouse sat up with him, rubbing his back. "It's okay. You're safe. You're here with me and Sammie. It's okay."

He was out of the bed and in the corner of the room before she'd even finished speaking. He looked like a cornered animal and my heart fucking broke. I leaned over and turned on the bedside light, and that seemed to help as he took in our faces, including Mouse's big, wet eyes.

The terror receded from his expression as he woke up more, but I could still taste his fear in the air, see his pulse thumping in his throat. Mouse was only wearing my t-shirt as she crawled across the bed toward him, her movements slow and deliberate like he was a wild animal. His eyes tracked her movements, but he was shuffling toward her. She held out her arms and he dived into them.

He held her like he'd never been held in his life. He probably hadn't. I wanted to hug him too, but I didn't know how he'd react, so I sat back on the pillows and ached for him.

"Do you wanna talk about it?" I murmured softly, and he shook his head.

"No. We need to get dressed. I need to talk to Alistair and the others."

I looked at the clock. "You want to wake the

management of Eden Academy at 3:35 in the morning?"

He swallowed hard, his eyes still had that awful blankness about them. I knew that look. Shell shock. "Yes. He's torturing them."

"Who?"

"The other fighters. The ones that take care of the Kindergarten. The kids are scared."

Mouse sucked in a breath between her teeth. "How do you know?"

"One of the trainees, Milo, has the ability to dream walk. He's one of the older trainees, almost ready for the ring. He told me last year when I'd been gutted in the ring, but we kept it from Rook. I hate to think what that psycho would do with him if he knew. Anyway, Milo has been walking in my dreams. He said Rook found out you told your parents, and now he's torturing the older, injured fighters. Then he said he'll move onto the youngest, the ones who he hasn't invested too much time and money into training yet."

Bile rose in my throat, but I wasn't sure what part of that story horrified me most. Flint being gutted? Torture of kids? Fucked if I knew, but I knew one thing with absolute certainty. "We have to rescue them. Where is the Kindergarten?"

Flint clenched his fists. "I don't know. The Kindergarten is Rook's prized possession. He doesn't tell us the location. If we got injured, we were shipped there in the back of a windowless van. Somewhere in upstate New York, maybe?" He swallowed hard. "I just don't know." His voice broke, and I could hear my teeth grinding.

Mouse held him closer. "Don't worry. We are going to find this fucker, you're going to set him on fire and I'll piss on his corpse."

Flint snorted, but at least it wasn't that near panic. "You say the most romantic things, Sugar Plum."

She led him back to the bed and instead of climbing in beside her, I hopped in on the other side of Flint, putting him in the middle. He threw me a grateful look, and I wrapped my arms around both of them.

She leaned forward and kissed him softly. "But nothing can be done about it at four in the morning. I promise, first thing, we'll track down Micah and tell him. I'll call my grandfather and I'll put more pressure on him. We'll fix this, baby, I promise."

31

It took two cars to get us all to Nîso on Saturday afternoon. We'd gotten special permission for us to all be off campus, and Bobby had come by to pick us up. I was pressed in the middle seat between him and Flint, and in the car behind us, Christopher drove Enit, Sammie, Cara, Madoc and little Attica.

Enit's Alpha, uh I mean Bohdie, had elected to stay home, because there was a whole thing about Alphas and territories. Besides, if any of my dads saw how he mooned over Enit, Bohdie would be beaten down so hard into the ground, they'd have to get an excavator to remove his body.

I didn't envy any man that Enit decided to bring home. That didn't mean I wouldn't put them through absolute hell to make sure they were worthy. But I liked both Sammie and Cara, and Bohdie was their friend. I trusted that he wasn't a piece of shit.

I moved my head to Bobby's shoulder, and he pressed his cheek against my hair. I didn't know how to tell him about Monster. Why couldn't I just bury my head in the sand and pretend none of it happened? That nothing else but this mattered?

I sighed heavily. I'd talk to him this afternoon. We'd work it out. "That was a big sigh, Mouse."

He glanced down at me before flicking his eyes back to the road.

"It's just been a wild month. I'm ready to settle into school, focus on my studies and have orgies every other day again. All the fun stuff, you know?"

The truck swerved and Bobby whipped his eyes back to me. "Again? You guys are having orgies?" He shot a glare at Flint. I tensed, but he just shook his head. "Without me? Assholes."

I grinned and squeezed his thigh, sliding my palm further up toward his crotch. He took his hand off the stick and gripped my wrist.

"If I accidentally crash this truck because you had your hot little hand wrapped around my cock, your parents will reanimate me, just to kill me again."

Flint laughed, pulling me from Bobby's side, and into his arms. "I can keep her distracted if you want, Alpha?"

Bobby's eyes flashed, and he licked his bottom lip. I leaned closer to Flint's ear, pretending to whisper a secret even though we all had supernatural hearing. "I think he likes it when you call him Alpha." I leaned forward and nipped Flint's ear, and he growled.

He tried to drag me onto his lap, but my belt kept me in my seat. Flint moved to unclip it, but Bobby batted his hands away.

"No way. She stays strapped in and you keep it in your pants. No distracting the driver, and you fucking our girl? That's like the definition of distraction."

Flint pouted, but it didn't matter because we were crossing the ward into Nîso. I had balls, but not enough to make a spectacle of myself in Pack lands. Instead, I grabbed Flint's face, turning it toward me. I kissed him hard.

"Later, I promise."

It was a promise I was going to make good on, because I hungered. Sex with them was like a drug. The more of them I had, the more I wanted, until even just looking at them made me wet. I had a flash of the other night, pressed between Flint and Sammie, and my whole body went hot, my core clenching.

Bobby groaned loudly. "Mouse, whatever the hell you are thinking, stop. You smell like fucking heaven and I don't want to go to a Pack cookout with a raging hard-on that I can't get rid of until tonight." He looked between us both, and his tongue darted out to wet his bottom lip.

He looked seconds from saying fuck it and driving us to a secluded spot, but he was saved by arriving at the town gardens out the front of the Packhouse.

He parked his truck under a tree. Instead of climbing out though, he fisted the front of my t-shirt and pulled me close. He kissed me like he was physically pained, and when I ran my hand over the front of his jeans, I think I was probably right. Just when I thought my lungs would burst, he tore his lips away. He looked over at Flint, and curled a finger. Flint leaned over me, and Bobby met him halfway. Bobby kissed him softly compared to how he kissed me, and I resisted the urge to squee. When Flint sucked Bobby's lip between his teeth, I actually moaned.

"I like it when you call me Alpha," Bobby growled.

Flint's answering grin promised mischief of the best kind. Then they both climbed out of the car and I panted. Seriously? I wanted to yell for them to come back and kiss again.

Instead, Sammie appeared at the door.

"Hey, Sweetheart. Whatcha doin'?"

I pouted and climbed out of the car toward him. "Bobby and Flint just kissed."

Sammie frowned. "And you're upset because...?"

"They stopped."

Sammie laughed and dragged me the rest of the

way out of the car. Then he kissed me quickly. "I don't blame you. I wanna pout because I missed it. But as much as I'd like to kiss you happy, your parents are here and they scare the fucking shit out of me."

Someone laughed behind us, and I was pretty sure it was one of my parents listening in. I dragged him toward the crowd. The whole Pack was here, and every single one of them was staring at Madoc's wings. Sammie rolled his eyes, twining his fingers in mine and strolled toward his little group with forced ease. I mean, it was a good imitation of ease, and I could only spot his tenseness because I'd seen him truly relaxed.

"Madoc, what did Judas say about your wings?"

The fire-haired kid just huffed. "I should treat my wings like my dick. I might think they're impressive, but it's rude to have them out in mixed company."

I tried to keep a straight face, I swear. But the laughter bubbled up until it was spilling over my lips and I could hardly breathe. That set Attica off, and even Madoc began to giggle. Sammie had said they were both empathic, which made sense. Cara just shook her head, grinning as she slapped the younger girl's back when she started to wheeze.

"Come on, Chuckles. We should go and introduce ourselves to the Alpha."

I wiped my eyes with my palms, and straightened. "I'll introduce you."

Flint was still with Bobby, and I was kind of glad

they were, uh, getting along. It was one thing to be the only girl in a harem of guys, but I only had two hands. I wanted us to be a unit, not just me having three different relationships.

Maybe four, an annoying little voice whispered in the back of my brain.

Monster's words about us being a Pack made more sense. We were all different, but I wanted us to be a Pack within a Pack.

I shook off thoughts of Monster and stopped in front of my dad, Brody, Alpha of Nîso. Up here, he was God. His word was law.

"Dad, you remember Sammie? This is his family, Cara, Madoc and Attica."

Sammie dropped his eyes. "Sir."

Cara and Madoc did the same, but Attica mustn't have been around as many shifters, because she just smiled happily until Madoc tugged on her hand. "He's the Alpha, you gotta drop your eyes in respect," he hissed.

Attica's eyes went wide. "Oh, I'm sorry. You just have such a happy aura and I got all caught up in all the blues, and then your, uh, friend? His is all pretty and purple and yellow, and then they mingle in the middle and—"

"Attica," Sammie grunted, and she dropped her pretty blue eyes quickly, her lip jutting out like she was going to cry.

Brody laughed. "It's fine, little pup. Our customs can be hard to remember. Please, relax. I don't hold to many of those old traditions. This is my packmate, Tex."

Attica bounded over to him. "Oh, you're blind? Madoc, he's blind. I wonder if that's why your aura is so intense. Madoc, can you see it?"

Madoc looked between me and Sammie frantically, like his cousin was one more run-on sentence from being eaten.

I laughed. "Give them hell, Attica. Keeps them on their toes."

"Who's on their toes?" My father, X, did that creepy ass thing where he just appeared behind me, mainly because he knew it annoyed me and he was really a big kid on the inside.

Attica turned to him, her jaw dropping. "You don't have an aura at all. Holy poop. Madoc, he doesn't have one."

Madoc jumped in front of her, covering her mouth with his hand. "He's a vampire, Attica. Shh."

Attica went pale. "Oh no. I'm so sorry," she said in a terrified squeal, and I could see X soften like butter in the sun.

God, he was such a marshmallow. He gave her a fangy smile. "Maybe we have no souls?"

She frowned and looked at him like he was crazy.

Which he was, but she wasn't to know that. "Of course you do."

She said it with such certainty, it made Tex laugh. "I know a couple of the other Pack kids in your grade are over near the benches, pretending to be too cool for family barbeques if you want to go say hello?"

Madoc looked at Sammie, who nodded. "Look after Attica," he said quietly, and I had the feeling that perhaps Attica might need protecting. She reminded me almost of an Omega, and in a Pack of shapeshifters, that wasn't a bad vibe to give off.

They skipped off, and Sammie and Cara watched them go like mother hens.

As if I summoned her with thoughts of Omegas, Enit appeared and grabbed Cara's hand.

"Come on, I want you to meet someone. It'll drive Christopher insane."

Cara laughed, her expression soft when she looked at my sister. "How did you come out of the same womb as the other two? It's like you got all the sweetness and light," she said to Enit, before sliding her eyes to me. "No offense, I totally appreciate the badass ballbreaker vibe you have too. Come on Enit, I'm always down to do anything to piss your brother off."

They flounced off arm in arm and I couldn't help but laugh.

Brody shook his head. "Christopher needs

someone who won't take his shit. I have a feeling that your sister is one of those people."

Sammie snorted. "You have no idea, Alpha."

I grabbed us both a soda, and pulled him into the crowd of people to find Bobby and Flint. I hadn't been to a Nîso event since Bobby had claimed me. I wanted to make sure some of these bitches got the message, with my fists if I had to.

32

BOBBY

ouse sat on my lap, curling her lip at all the females that came within two feet of me. Except Lulu. Lulu was talking animatedly with Sammie about his life in a MC club, like she was thinking about signing up and becoming a patched member.

I snorted at the idea of her driving a Harley, but hey, crazier things had happened.

This was honestly the most peaceful Pack gathering I'd had since I'd come of age. Hell, probably since I'd been named as the Alpha-Heir. There were always girls looking at becoming the next Alpha Mate, or guys jostling for a moment of my time so they could ingratiate themselves, hoping I'd make them Enforcers or some shit.

It was nice, just us and Lulu. Others had come to

say hello, to catch up with me about something or other, and to say hello to Flint and Sammie, but none of them had stayed long.

Just a cold beer and my fated mate in my lap. I couldn't be happier.

I watched the rest of Sammie's family with my Pack, and it made me happy too. If things went how I wanted them to go, eventually they'd be an extension of my family too. I was glad to see Attica and Madoc playing with the other kids, though I noted Madoc had his wings back out and a couple of the pups were patting them. I'd have to watch that kid. I had a feeling he'd break some Pack hearts soon.

They blended seamlessly, and that was honestly down to Mouse's parents. I'd been a kid when Brody had presented Raine, a newly made vampire, to the Pack as his Alpha Mate. It hadn't gone well for that first year, but now they loved her. Until Brody, I'd have been expected to marry a nice shapeshifter girl, and the idea of me marrying a two-natured shifter would have been... insane. Even Ghost, who was a snow leopard shifter, had been frowned upon or outright shunned by the older members of the Pack until Brody had become Alpha and made him an Enforcer. Ha! They'd changed their opinion real quick, or at least kept it to themselves.

But you'd have to be blind or stupid not to realize how much Brody's rule as Alpha had enhanced Nîso and our Pack as a whole. Hopefully he reigned as Alpha for decades to come because I was in no hurry. Ready to lead, but not in any rush.

There was a lull in conversation and Sammie gave Mouse a pointed look. She sighed and tensed in my arms, wiggling off my lap. Her normally crystalline blue eyes were cloudy with worry, and my heart began to thud.

"Bobby, I gotta tell you something."

Jesus, was she pregnant? Fuck, her parents were going to murder me. I mean, we were safe, I would always take care of her, but condoms weren't a hundred percent effective. Oh my god, I was too young to be a parent, but I'd stand by her, and love our cubs.

Lulu stood. "Uh, this sounds private. I'll just be over there." She looked between me and Mouse. "I'll keep everyone away for a bit."

This was why I wanted Lulu as an Enforcer. Though that was a problem for another day; I was too busy in my full-blown panic. "What is it, Mouse? Are you okay?"

She smiled and leaned forward to kiss me. "I'm totally fine. Now, remember you love me, okay? And that I love you."

Sweat broke out across my skin, and for some reason, I began to panic. She took a deep breath.

"So you know how there was a security incident at

the fence the other day?" I nodded. I'd heard about it of course. "Well, it was Monster."

I frowned. A monster? I mean, we were all... Fuck. "Monster the fucking Wendigo?"

She nodded, wincing a little. "He was there to see me. Alistair and Micah ran him off, but that night I couldn't sleep, all restless and stuff, so I went for a walk. And I ended up back at that spot in the fence."

My heart was beginning to thud in my ears. "He was still there? You went out to see the Wendigo by yourself?"

She nodded, her eyes darting to Sammie. "Not on purpose, but Sammie came with me."

I growled low in my throat. "No offense, but you were going to meet a fucking Wendigo. A human is not adequate backup."

Before I could blink, Sammie had his gun pulled and pointed at my head. Almost inhumanly fast. Lulu lurched toward me, but I held up a hand. "Fair point. Sorry. I'm just... shocked. I know you can hold your own against us."

I wanted to scream that a Wendigo wasn't like me or even Flint. He was the specter of death, and a bloody one at that. I looked into Mouse's disapproving face as Sammie sat back down, tucking his gun away.

"He made his point, Mouse. I'm sorry. Please, continue."

She shifted in my lap, and I got the feeling that she

would have moved to Sammie's if she wasn't trying to butter me up. Which made me anxious all over again. There was more to this story.

She chewed on her bottom lip, before speaking again. "He said a lot of things, but I guess the most important thing, um I guess, was that he was my fated mate and he wanted to join our Pack."

I shot to my feet, barely catching Mouse before she slipped to the ground. I gripped her shoulders and spun her to face me. "He said what? You can't be. You're my mate!" I realized I was yelling at her, so I took a deep, steadying breath and loosened my grip. She wrapped her arms around my waist and leaned her head on my chest. The sense of rightness when she was in my arms told me I hadn't been wrong. I knew with every single ounce of my soul that she was my fated mate. I'd known it for years.

"I know, Bobby. I am definitely yours." She took a shuddering breath. "But I think I might be his too."

I kissed the top of her head, and then walked her back into Sammie's waiting arms while I paced around the clearing. I didn't know what to say, what to do. I thought about how I would feel if Carmen denied me —if my Mouse, the girl I had loved forever, said she didn't want to be mine. The pain in my chest was as real as a heart attack just at the thought. Could I do that to another man?

I looked at Mouse and wondered if she'd reject him

if I asked. But even as I thought it, I knew she wouldn't. Her heart was one of the many reasons I loved her so much, and she would never doom a man to a lifetime alone. To the insanity of having your mate, fated by the Moon Goddess or the ancestors or whatever you believed in, reject you to your face.

Yeah, Mouse would never do that.

I took a shuddering breath in. Another fated mate I could deal with, but a Wendigo? "He's steeped in blood, Mouse. The Pack would never accept him."

She shook her head sadly. "He didn't mean Nîso. He meant us. Our Pack of four."

I'd seen Monster fight. On nights when Mouse had fought early, sometimes I'd dropped her home and come back to the fights. It was good for me to know who was attending these fights, what went on in our territory.

All his fights ended in a brutal death, but one time was forever burned into my brain. It was one of his first fights in this area, and I remember Rat's absolute glee. Mouse had KO'ed her opponent early, and I'd driven her home and come back, because I didn't trust Rat even a little.

It had been rowdy, and Monster had sat in the corner, holding a beer. His opponent had been a big, mean motherfucker, a bobcat shifter, I think. Not from Nîso, but close enough that I'd heard rumors of his brutality.

Monster, yeah he'd been Monster even back then, had looked malnourished and I'd almost felt sorry for him. Don't get me wrong, he was still huge. Tall, muscular, with a long reach that marked him as a good fighter, but there was something almost gaunt about him. Anyway, I was kind of worried the reigning champion would just fuck him over and put him in a shallow grave. But that wasn't what happened. Monster had stepped into the ring and fought like a demon. He'd gotten the bobcat shifter onto his back in seconds, and three solid elbows to the guy's temple had dazed him. Then, I'd watched him land blow after punishing blow until the bobcat's cheekbone collapsed. I'd thought Rat would call it or hell, that Monster would just get up and walk away, but instead he grabbed the dude's hand and started breaking every single one of his fingers. And then his wrist. Then his arm.

When the guy was screaming in agony, Monster shifted to Wendigo. I nearly fucking pissed myself. I wasn't proud of myself, but when he shoved his clawed hand into the guy's chest, ripped out his still beating heart and ate it, I fucking turned and ran out of that hellhole faster than I'd ever run in my life.

I sucked in a breath. Could I expose Mouse to that every day? I looked at where she was, snuggled into Sammie's chest. God, they were such a beautiful couple. "Do you want him?"

She shrugged. "I don't even know him."

That wasn't a no. I looked over at Flint, because he had history with Monster too. "Are you okay with this?"

He was frowning, his eyes moving between us. "He is... wrong. When the other fighters, like the meanest assholes in the scene, speak about him, it's with something between fear and disgust. But I don't know much about him other than that he had our backs the night I escaped and that he has a really brutal right hook."

Sammie just shrugged too. It was too much. I'd only just got the girl, it was too soon to have to share this connection, the mate connection, with someone else.

But I wanted her to be happy. And if that meant seeing how this panned out, then so be it. There was only one thing for it. We'd have to meet face to face. I just had to hope we wouldn't regret it.

THE NIGHT WAS moonless behind the heavy cloud. The temperature had dropped again, I wondered if it would snow early this year. I'd dropped off Flint and Mouse safely into Eden, parked my truck up the road a bit, and ran the fenceline, careful to avoid the sentinels that guarded the boundary. I walked to the section of fence that ran behind the sports field, my senses on high alert.

Even so, I was surprised when Monster stepped from the darkness. He moved silently, like he was made of the darkness.

"Little Alpha. It was brave of you to come alone. Or stupid."

His voice was rough, like the smoke damage from being burned alive had permanently injured them. I bared my teeth at his words, but he held up his hands placatingly.

"I wondered when she'd tell you and I'd find you out here."

My whole body was so tense that I nearly vibrated with it, but I kept my face calm, neutral even.

"She's been busy with her Pack."

"She's my fated mate," he grunted. "I didn't mean for it to happen. I understand if you want to challenge me. I... I won't contest it."

He'd just lay down and let me tear out his throat? I really stared at him, the darkness no limitation for me. His whole face seemed to be dragged down in sadness, and maybe a dash of hope, like he wanted me to kill him?

Fuck, I was getting soft. "Do you mean to harm her?"

His face twisted. "Never."

I lifted my chin. "The others? Flint and Sammie? Will you be able to share her with them?"

He was silent for too long, and I shook my head as I

moved away. He wasn't right for Mouse, wasn't right for us. He didn't care that she would be heartbroken without them, even though she hadn't known them that long. She loved hard and fast.

"Wait," he barked out. "Sharing my fated mate doesn't come easy. You must know that, Little Alpha. But I am trying."

"Just Alpha if you really want to be part of our Pack," I snarled, though I tried to tamp it down.

He shook his head. "It's been a long time since I've had an Alpha. I've almost forgotten what to do."

I shook my head and sighed. "I'm not going to lord it over you, man. I just need to know that you'll respect me, respect her and the relationships she's created." I stopped, but the need for honesty in this moment was more important than my pride. "Watching her with them is hard. Watching her with you would be even harder. But this isn't the damn Dark Ages. She's not a prize for us to piss on and claim. She is ours to love, and if that means sharing her with a beast literally soaked in blood, so be it."

He nodded, staring off into the darkness. I shook my head. "We'll meet you at the Morning Glory diner on the highway outside of Pack lands. You know the one?"

He snorted. "Yeah, with a name like that, it's pretty memorable." His mouth tipped up on one side, not a smile, but not the abject blankness of a man who had nothing anymore either.

"We'll meet you there tomorrow at eleven."

He cocked an eyebrow. "Not Dark River? I thought for sure you'd want the backup."

I stifled a chuckle. "Let's just say none of us are ready for that shitshow."

He nodded again. "I'll be there," he murmured softly and disappeared back into the darkness, completely silent like he'd never been.

That was creepy as shit.

33

CARMEN

as it weird to be nervous? I was nervous. I'd had to lie to Enit about where we were going, and I hated doing that. But she wouldn't understand. And then she'd tell Christopher and he *really* wouldn't understand.

I was wearing a pretty dress, which was weird in itself, but for some reason I'd wanted to look nice and sweet today rather than the badass ball buster that I usually portrayed. I wanted to look like someone's fated mate. So I'd borrowed one of Enit's floaty little dresses, and paired it with a pair of high top sneakers.

When I'd knocked on Flint's door, he'd just whispered 'wow' and then kissed me until I'd had to reapply my lipgloss. Then he'd kissed it off again. Now I sat in the backseat of Sammie's SUV, my knee bopping like I was driving to a fight. Flint slid his hand up my thigh and squeezed it gently.

"You know, I could take your mind off it? You in that sweet little dress makes me want to do filthy things to you just to dirty you up."

I flashed a grin before giving him a mock stern look. "Behave. I'm not reapplying my lipstick again."

He just waggled his eyebrows. "The lips I'm thinking of kissing don't have any gloss on them... yet." He winked and my whole body flushed. I'd been so worked up about this whole Monster thing after telling Bobby about it. It didn't seem right to make love with the guys until we sorted the whole thing out. I was kind of regretting my decision now though, because I wanted to climb Flint like a tree in the back of Sammie's car.

"Keep it in your pants, Fireball. We're here," Bobby said, though the tight whine in his voice told me he wasn't impervious to my arousal.

Sammie slid the car into the near empty parking lot, just a couple of beat up cars and a single motorbike making up the diner's clientele. Bobby climbed out and opened my door for me, which made me feel a bit like a princess. It was definitely the dress.

"Hey, do you think if I twirled, this dress would fly out?" I whispered.

Bobby laughed as he spun me in a circle and the skirt fluttered out. I actually giggled as I pushed it down. I don't care how badass you are, a fluttery skirt was still fun to twirl in. Fight me.

Sammie opened the diner door for me, and I kissed his cheek as I went past. Bobby led the way, and Flint pinched my butt as he followed in behind me. Sammie quickly caught up with me, grabbing my hand.

"You're so fucking beautiful. I'm a lucky bastard. You're more than a prize though, remember that."

I squeezed his hand. "Thank you."

He kissed my temple, and we walked to the back of the diner. Monster was in the corner booth, and there was not another diner for six booths. I got it, I really did. He looked intense. His hair was a tad too long and mussed like he hadn't brushed it in ages, and it curled in dark brown waves around his ears. His beard had gone a day or two past five o'clock shadow. His clothes were well-worn and he just had this air of wild danger about him. Strong, dark brows gave him an angry set to his face. His jaw was strong and tight, and the longer I looked at him under the fake fluorescent light of the diner, and out of the shadows of the forest, the more I realized he was actually kind of handsome.

He looked up at us, dipping his chin at Bobby, making my Alpha huff an amused sound. Then his eyes snapped to mine and I felt like I was drowning all over again.

"Carmen," he said softly.

"Hey Monster." I frowned. It didn't seem right to

call him that. "Do you have an actual name?"

He frowned. "I did once, but I don't remember it." He cocked his head, like he heard something outside. "I have been Monster for as long as you've been alive."

I chewed my lip and slid into the booth opposite him. Sammie slid in beside me, and Flint slid in beside Monster. Bobby grabbed a chair and pulled it up at the end.

I shrugged. "Fine. Doesn't seem like a very good name to yell out during sex, but how would I know?"

Bobby's head whipped toward me. "Mouse!"

Flint laughed, staring down at the menu like he was going to order the entire freaking thing. I just grinned.

"As you can see, no one calls me Carmen, except Flint. Everyone calls me Mouse."

Sammie chuckled. "Monster and Mouse. You guys sound like a children's book."

Flint snorted a laugh. "Except when we say the Monster wanted to eat the Mouse, it's definitely not safe for a kid's book."

Bobby reached over and punched Flint, and Monster just looked at us in bewilderment. I cleared my throat. "Uh, sorry. Have you ordered?"

He shook his head. I looked down at the menu, not really seeing it but not knowing what else to do. We were silent for a bit until the waitress came over with a coffee pot.

"Coffee?"

I pushed my mug toward her and she filled it up, eyeing the rest of the guys warily. Flint was wild, and he gave off a pretty intense vibe, and although I knew Sammie was a sweetheart, he was dark and tattooed and looked like he'd just climbed off a Harley after murdering someone in the woods.

Bobby was the most clean-cut of us all, but sensitive humans could find his Alpha aura a little unsettling.

And Monster was, well, Monster.

I gave her a bright smile. "They'll have coffee too, thanks." I looked up, my eyes flicking between Flint and Monster as I tried to act natural. "I think I might have pancakes."

They were basically an institution in my household, along with cheese fries and Beatrice's lasagna.

That seemed to finally kick off everyone ordering, until we got to Monster. "I'll have the steak. Rare." The way he growled it sounded so ominous that the waitress paled and scuttled away.

Flint laughed as he downed half his boiling coffee in one mouthful. "I'll have flesh, bloody," he growled in mock imitation of the man next to him, and I had to admit, Flint had some big brass balls.

Monster narrowed his eyes at Flint, making Sammie tense beside me, but then his lips quirked. "Only meat satisfies the hunger. It's either rare steak or hearts. I can't imagine you're volunteering to be my lunch." He watched him swallow the rest of his coffee. "Doesn't that burn?"

Flint just grinned. "Fire Djinn. Flame resistant."

"But not fist resistant," Monster growled. Or maybe he joked.

Was that a joke?

Bobby leaned back on his chair. "Did the Wendigo just make a joke?" He gave us another small smile. Maybe he could fit in with us.

As if we all just thought the same thing, the mood at the table grew awkward again. I fiddled with my coffee mug, and then sucked in a breath.

I was Carmen fucking Baxter. I would take this situation by the testicles and show it who was boss.

"We should talk about it. About the fact I'm your fated mate."

Monster went so still, I worried he was going to bolt. I watched him blink at me slowly, then nod. "Okay."

Well, way to give me something to work with. "When did you realize that it was me?"

I remembered that connection, when I'd been looking down at him in the ring, staring down into the abyss of his eyes. The absolute sadness that consumed me, but was really just an echo of his own loneliness.

"First time I saw you fight. You were around seventeen, maybe? Not long after I arrived. You were fighting this slimy little fucker who kept hitting you in the breast and taunting you about taking it like a man. I wanted to climb into the ring and rip out his tongue." He shook his head. "An extreme response, even for me."

Bobby growled. "Evan Munch. Fucking slimeball. I heard he got jumped at the back of a bar a few towns over. Snapped his hands in..." Bobby trailed off as it dawned on him.

Monster shrugged. "I tried to tell myself it was because he was hitting a woman. But I knew she could hold her own. No, what I felt was more consuming, more territorial, more everything. I knew she was my fated mate."

Oh for fuck's sake. I had two fated mates, and both of them had known for years before they deigned to tell me. How damn annoying.

"Why now?" Sammie asked, his tone gentle but his eyes suspicious.

Monster was saved from answering by the waitress returning with the food. She hesitantly flitted around us, trying very hard to be unassuming. I couldn't imagine what it would be like to live like that, knowing you were so vulnerable to literally everyone around you. I knew I could defend myself in both my human and wolf forms. But this scared little rabbit? She had no defense.

Unless she was a secret badass. You really couldn't

assume these days.

When she finally ran away, all eyes turned back to Monster.

"They disbanded the fight ring. I left. I made it three towns over before the bond was trying to drag me back. I made it to Calgary until it got overwhelmingly bad and I had to return."

I sat back in my seat. "You were going to run?"

He grunted, stabbing at his steak with his fork. It was nowhere close to rare, and he seemed disappointed. He didn't look up as he muttered. "You deserve better than being tied to a Wendigo. I will dirty your soul with mine."

Well, fuck. Wrap him up and stick a bow on his ass, because I was going to fix this sad, lonely man purely with the force of my sarcasm and vagina magic.

Bobby groaned, because I'm pretty sure he knew my determined look by now. I cocked an eyebrow in his direction as I stuffed pancakes in my mouth, and dared him to protest. We all ate in silence for a bit, because Morning Glory made some pretty decent pancakes, until it got too much for Flint.

"How old are you exactly if you can't even remember your original name?"

Monster shrugged. "About two hundred or so. Give or take. I don't exactly have birthday parties."

I dropped my fork onto my plate. "Holy shit." His eyes were downcast again and I reached out to touch his cheek. "How old were you when you became Wendigo?"

He looked up into my eyes again. I realized his eyes weren't black, but a shade of blue so dark, that there was only the odd flash of blue when the light hit them right. "Twenty-five."

I wanted to ask him all the questions. How much of his story was rumor? How much was fact? Did they really burn him alive? Had he really been alone for two hundred years?

Instead, I cocked my head to the side. I wondered if... "What were you before you were Wendigo?" The legends of the Wendigo were pretty hazy. No one liked to talk about them, because they were considered bad luck. And saying their name would invoke them or some bullshit.

"Wolf shifter."

I sat up like I'd been electrocuted. Bobby whistled through his teeth. "Well, that makes sense, I guess."

Sammie picked up a fry and held it out to me. "Seems kind of mean of your Moon Goddess to put a couple of centuries between you and your fated mate though. Unless you being a Wendigo was the plan all along, and that seems kind of mean on her behalf too."

Monster lifted a shoulder like he was used to the idea that the Moon Goddess hated him.

Well, if she hated him, then she hated me too, and I refused to believe that.

34

MONSTER

I hadn't spent this much time in other people's company in decades. I was shunned by all other packs, other people, even humans avoided me. But not this sunny girl in a bright yellow dress, with three men who would jump in front of my teeth for her.

Fools, Hew grumbled.

Wati had been oddly silent this whole time, but I appreciated it. The human to Carmen's left, Sammie, held out a fry to her and she ate it from his fingers. So casually, like I wouldn't kill to feed her. The Ifrit, fuck Flint, I had to call them by their names, fidgeted beside me. He looked tired, deep bags under his eyes.

Probably from too much fucking with your mate.

I wanted to tell Hew to shut the fuck up, but I knew it would only egg him on. Besides, I didn't want to slip and let her know that I actually spoke to the evil spirits that inhabited my body. If only a good exorcism would get rid of them.

Hew snorted, and Flint shifted beside me again. I poked at my steak, forcing myself to cut and eat it. It tasted like ash in my mouth, but it helped to keep up pretenses. He watched my careful precision with eagle eyes, and I cursed the Moon Goddess for gifting my mate a lover who was purely made from my one true weakness. Fire.

She really did hate me.

If you keep cursing her, you might feel her real wrath, Wati finally piped up, and I clenched my hand beneath the table.

"So how would this work? No offense man, but I can't imagine them letting you into Eden Academy."

"Brody won't let him in Nîso. The elders are still superstitious," Bobby said apologetically, but he didn't need to be. No one knew the old superstitions with as much painful clarity as I did.

My heart, which I'd assumed was long ago turned to dust, thumped heavily in my chest. "You're considering it?" I couldn't keep the hopeful note out of my voice.

Bobby shook his head. "You don't know her yet, but you should know it was never a question. But if you hurt her, or them, I will fucking tear your heart out and send you to hell myself."

I had no doubt the little Alpha could do it too.

Flint just shook his head. "Look at her face. Our girl is a sucker for a hopeless cause, which is why she's saddled with all my bullshit now."

I could scent the guilt, and I frowned. What bullshit?

I didn't get a chance to ask, because she, Carmen—no, Mouse—was reaching across the table to me.

The contact of her fingers on my hand sent tingles buzzing up my arm. The thrill of holding your fated mate. It was more than I'd felt in years. Even fighting didn't make me feel alive anymore. She gripped my fingers. "We'll figure it out. But if you fuck me over, I'll cut you open in your sleep and garrote you with your own entrails." She smiled as she said it, and I mentally apologized to the Moon Goddess.

Maybe she did have a plan after all.

How sweet. The Monster and the Mouse. A love affair coated in blood and pain. Hew sounded bitter as hell, which made me feel a little satisfied.

"I am fine living in the woods outside your Academy."

Bobby nodded. "The Alpha knows you're there, and he's given the order to leave you be. But that may change if he knows you want to mate with his kid. That lot are protective," Bobby warned, and Mouse's face flushed.

I'd heard of them. I was prepared.

Sammie leaned back in the booth. "So now what? It's all well and good that he's your fated mate, but what does that mean for us?" He looked me dead in the eye. "Both Flint and I are bisexual. We fuck each other as well as Carmen."

"Me too," Bobby stated firmly, unashamed of the fact. "I mean, I haven't had sex with them, but if the opportunity ever arose, I wouldn't object," he said quietly, and everyone's eyes were on me, like they were waiting for something. It took me an embarrassingly long time to work out that they thought I'd disapprove.

"Not my thing. But I'm the last person to tell you something isn't socially acceptable," I grunted out. "I ate the heart of my sister's killer and became the supernatural world's most shunned being. I am in no position to judge."

Well, now you've fucked us all, Wati seethed. *Ease into the murderer story, dipshit.*

Flint stared at me, before he began to laugh. "Well, when you put it like that, fucking hot guys seems totally fine. Which it is."

Soon they were all laughing with him, and my face felt tense. I reached up and touched my cheek, and realized I was... smiling.

Mouse squeezed my hand like she could tell I was about to freak out. "We'll get to know each other. You have to understand, it's different for me and Bobby being fated mates. I've known him my entire life. So I, uh we, can't seal the bond for a long while. I don't even want to seal it with Bobby yet."

That made me raise my eyebrows. I looked at the little Alpha, and he looked at her with such intensity, I had no doubt he'd wait for her as long as she wanted. But given their chemistry, I didn't think it would be long before Mouse caved.

I was willing to wait too. I wouldn't rush her. I had an eternity.

"He should stay in Dark River. Being a Wendigo is going to mean jackshit to a town filled with vampires. He wouldn't even stand a chance against their most unskilled fighter. Then you guys can visit on weekends and, I don't know, we can all get to know each other." It seemed like it almost pained Bobby to suggest that, but I appreciated it. I kept waiting for them to protest, for her to turn around and say no, I'd never defile myself by spending time with this filth-crusted creature.

But she'd seen my Wendigo. Knew the story, even if it was the very basics.

She was chewing her bottom lip between her teeth, and I wanted to suck it into my mouth and chew it for her. Though not chew it off like Hew would suggest.

Sammie raised a finger. "Two problems with that. No, three. One, her parents are going to freak. That's the simplest to solve, but probably has some long-lasting consequences. Two, there's the whole Rook thing keeping you trapped inside the Academy."

"Rook?" I asked, and Mouse shook her head.

"What's three, Sammie?"

"Monster eats meat. And if I'm right, mortal flesh."

My stomach sank to my toes. I was fucked again. He was right, of course. The curse of the Wendigo meant I was always starving. Even now, as I ate this butchered steak, the hollow howl of hunger echoed around my stomach.

I waited for her to recoil, to pull her hand from mine in disgust. She didn't. She just frowned pensively. "Well, you're right. That could be a problem. I mean, I assume that's why you did the underground fight rings. A meal and some cash. But no offense, I'm not travelling my ass around North America fighting, no matter how much I enjoy it." She looked at me once more, her crystal blue eyes haunting. I was snared by those eyes, caught tight and unwilling to drag my gaze away. "Is there anything else that satisfies the hunger?"

Shame washed through me, but her eyes were completely non-judgemental. "The flesh of something I've just killed will help for a bit, even if it's not human. But the only thing that truly satisfies the hunger is a human heart, still beating."

She winced a little, though she quickly smoothed it away. *You should tell her the mate bond would ease the hunger,* Wati said, but I ignored her. I wasn't going to guilt trip Carmen into rushing the mate bond.

I found myself wanting her to be happy, and that

wasn't a sensation that I was used to anymore. Being Wendigo meant being inherently selfish, but some things were stronger than curses and spirits, and fated mates was one of them.

Flint stabbed the eggs he was eating with ferocity. "Well, you can start with Rook's, but I'm pretty sure his heart is black and rotten."

I gave him a smile that was probably terrifying, all teeth and no mirth. "They are my favorite kind."

Bobby clapped his hands. "Well, that settles it, right? We're going to have to introduce him to your parents. I feel like he and Lucius might get along well. Nothing like bonding over rending things to cement good feelings with your in-laws."

For the first time, Mouse looked panicked. Her face looked a little pale and her eyes bugged out of her head. "Now?"

I was already shaking my head, not wanting her to be uncomfortable.

Jesus, are you going to be this much of a pussy-whipped bitch your entire mateship? I wonder if I can get a transfer? Hew bitched.

Please, for the sweet love of the Moon Goddess, do it, you fucking waste of celestial matter, Wati snapped back.

"I am fine where I am for now. Think it over." *Change your mind if being tied to a bloodthirsty monster was too much.*

She gave me an unreadable look, and went back to

finishing her pancakes. They were all silent for a while, lost in their own thoughts, and I tried not to shift nervously.

After a moment, Bobby looked up at me. The kid would be a good Alpha; I could feel his power against my skin. "I have to ask something. I saw your first fight here. Against a bobcat shifter. You were..." He seemed at a loss for words, so I nodded.

I was brutal. I was pain, and punishment, and death.

"Why? I get your need for human flesh, but that one fight was, I don't know. It was wrong."

I paused, wondering how I could phrase this so I seemed less of a monster.

"When I came to this ring, Rat had been excited by the idea. As part of our agreement, he would give me the names of my opponents the week before the fight. I won't fight anyone else, even if that person pulls out."

Flint frowned. "So?"

I'd briefly forgotten how young they were. I was crazy. I felt like a fucking pervert or something, chasing around after an eighteen-year-old. I should have left. "So, I use the week beforehand to research a person. I don't have much else to do," I joked, but it fell kind of flat. "To work out if they deserve to die or not. The bobcat shifter? Domestic abuse. Put his wife in hospital fifteen times, once for smashing her cheekbone, and broke every one of his son's fingers. Broke his daughter's arm. It was very bad. I got retribution for them, then I fed the Wendigo."

I looked up into the face of the woman who held my very immortal soul in her hands and said, "I don't regret one moment of his suffering."

She searched my face and I held my breath. Then she squeezed my hand and something inside me relaxed. "Neither do I."

We finished the rest of our meals and Bobby insisted on paying. That made me feel like shit, but with no fights, that meant no money. I actually brought nothing to the Pack except the burden of what I was.

And my claws.

When we stopped at the front of their car, Mouse stepped closer to me. "I had a nice time. You're good company."

Then she hugged me. I stood frozen as she wrapped her arms around my waist, unsure what to do. My soul sang with the feel of my mate so close, and I desperately wanted to hug her back. How long had it been since someone had actually hugged me? I curled one arm around her, petting her back gently, trying to touch her as little as possible so I didn't scare her off.

She stepped away and gave me a soft smile that I knew I didn't deserve. "We'll see you next weekend? I'll talk with the Town Council of Dark River about giving you a place." She hesitated. "But, I wouldn't mind coming to talk to you at the fence?"

My throat suddenly seemed too small so I nodded.

She stepped back and one of the guys opened the car door for her. She slid in, and I got an eyeful of her long, pale legs. My dick twitched in my pants, and I wished I could talk to it the way I talked to the evil spirits that inhabited my body. She turned, looking over her shoulder at me with a grin, the little minx shaking her ass as she climbed the rest of the way in, and I couldn't control my smile or my hard dick.

I didn't think I wanted to.

Every night for the past week, Flint had woken up with nightmares. Instead of soothing him back to sleep, which didn't work most of the time anyway, we'd get up and walk to the back of the school. I'd sit on one side of the fence, leaning back against Flint's chest so he could keep me warm, and Monster would sit on the other.

He wasn't a big talker, but that was okay. We started off talking about the fights, the other competitors. How much we hated Rat. But I slowly got to know him. Little pieces of who he was, what he liked, as well as his history. I wanted to spar with him, though unlike Flint, he'd find it difficult.

Flint, for his part, filled in the quiet, awkward spots, and generally just watched my back in the dark. But he was getting steadily more restless, more guilt-ridden, as the days went on and no one would tell us what was happening with Rook. I knew my parents had passed it onto the Convocation, who would either do something about it or they wouldn't. Alistair had said Azar had stormed what they'd thought was Rook's base of operations, complete with the Kindergarten, but they'd found it frustratingly empty. So either Rook had packed up shop or they hadn't found the right location.

The not knowing was the worst, but it was especially bad for Flint. He could no longer tell if his night terrors were Milo dream walking or his own brain supplying him with one terrifying scenario after another.

His body was tense even now, and I ran my hand up and down his thigh. "What I want to know is would you have eaten my heart that night if Carmen hadn't stepped in?"

Monster snorted. "You're a kid. You haven't been alive for long enough to accrue enough badness to warrant me taking your heart. Your boss is another story," he growled. We'd told Monster the bare minimum about the situation with Flint and Rook, because despite the fact I really liked the guy, I'd only known him a week. I wasn't gambling with Flint's life like that quite just yet.

"He is a shit human being. One day I'll end him," I muttered, and Monster nodded.

"I will eat his heart or maybe stomp on it. Some flesh is too rotten even for me."

I kind of wanted to kiss him. Was it weird to want to kiss him after he talked about stomping someone's heart? Pretty sure it had to be a little weird. I knew he was centuries old, but I was easily distracted by his youthful face. He looked only marginally older than Bobby.

The sun was beginning to lighten the sky, which meant I had three more hours before I had to drag my ass out of bed to go to class.

I stood, and Flint climbed to his feet behind me. "I'm going to talk to my parents tonight, and then hopefully we can move you into Dark River this weekend."

Monster gave a sharp nod. "I'm okay if they don't want me in their town. I'm used to it." He paused, his eyes still drinking in my face. "Besides, I enjoy this."

I couldn't help my smile as I stepped toward the fence, poking my finger through the gaps in the chain link, very carefully not touching the wire. They electrified it at night with enough zap to down an elephant. He reached out and stroked it with one of his own, and I wanted to melt.

He had a crease between his eyebrows, an almost permanent fixture on his face I decided, like he was always perplexed, or listening to something far away. "I'll see you this weekend, either way."

With that, I pulled my hand back through my side of the fence, and watched Monster melt into the trees. Logically, I knew he was probably still out there in the darkness, but it made me feel better that we weren't leaving him behind.

I climbed onto Flint's back and he piggybacked me toward our rooms. And they were our rooms now. Flint always slept in my room, and most of the time we hung out in his. I wound my arms around his neck and kissed his throat, and he hummed happily.

"What do you say we go sneak into Sammie's bed for the rest of the night?" he whispered, and I grinned. That sounded like the best fucking plan ever. He ran back towards the family housing and I laughed softly, my arms and legs tightly wrapped around his body. When we reached Sammie's house, we stepped up to the kitchen window.

But the whole house wasn't asleep like you'd think. The big Alpha lion stood near the front door, shirtless. The glow of the living room lamp cast a shadow, and I could tell he was talking to a girl by his body language. So much for his Omega obsession. Fucking asshole.

But when the girl leaned in, a familiar waterfall of white blond hair fell away from her face as she tilted her head up for a kiss, and I was rooted to the spot in shock.

"Is that your sister sneaking out of a booty call?" Flint hissed, and I was too shocked to even nod. I ducked down as the front door shut, hiding in the shadows as my sister dodged back across the lawn between the house and the dorm building. I stood back up, watching the lion Alpha climb the stairs.

I narrowed my eyes, and tilted my head at Flint. We crept through the side window with the faulty catch, both of us light on our feet in the way only fighters can be. I heard the soft sound of a shower running, and I threw Flint an evil look.

If Enit wanted a booty call, who was I to stop her? But I figured me and loverboy needed to have a little conversation. Lifting my finger to my lips, I kneeled down and grabbed his knives from his boots.

Flint gave me a warning look, but I shrugged him off. The shower was an over the bath one, a curtain pulled across, hiding me from the Alpha in the shower. I could smell the vanilla scent of his shampoo, and I knew I had moments before he scented me over the body products. I mentally judged his size, took a deep breath, and Flint ripped back the curtain. I jumped into the shower, one knife pressed to his throat, and the other to his dick.

"What the fuck!" he roared, and I grinned.

"Move, asshole, and I'll chop off the dick you're using to defile my goddamn sister," I growled, my wolf close to the surface. If I was honest with myself, it was probably the wolf who had inspired this whole thing.

"Carmen?" Bohdie squeaked. "You are fucking

crazy. Put down the knife before you slit my throat." His words were coated with Alpha, and I almost did it involuntarily.

I pressed it a little tighter against his throat. "Bitch, I've been Alphaed my entire life. Now listen. You fucking break my sister's heart, and I won't give you warning. I will slit your fucking throat in your sleep, and console her at your damn funeral. She is not your fuck buddy. She isn't your two a.m. booty call. If you aren't serious, I suggest you run the fucking other way now, or I will be the least of your problems."

The light flashed on in Bohdie's bedroom, and suddenly Sammie was there with a gun. He dropped it when he realized it was me and Flint in the bathroom. Cara was behind him, daggers held loosely in her fingers.

She barked out a laugh. "Told you that your dick was going to get you into trouble, Bo. Though I wouldn't sneeze, or Mouse is gonna rid you of the problem."

Bohdie growled low. "This isn't fucking funny, Cara." I looked over at the mirror, and I was indeed close to his dick. Well, not too close but the dude was hung, so I had a little bit of room for error.

I moved my knives and patted him on the shoulder. "Impressive. Good for Enit. I'm glad we could have this little chat."

Flint lifted me out of the tub, kissing me hard. "I'm

so hard right now, I'd probably let you cut me to get off."

Bohdie let out a snort of disgust. "You are both fucking nuts. How Enit came out of the same womb as you is life's greatest mystery." He grabbed his towel and wrapped it around his waist.

I just grinned. "I get that a lot." I sashayed back out to Sammie. He was in tight boxers that did nothing to hide his semi-hard cock either. I looked over my shoulder at Bohdie. "She got all the sweetness and light for the both of us. All that was left is anger and pain. We'll do anything to protect her from that fate. Best you remember." I looked at Cara. "Sorry for the early morning dramatics. Alphas, am I right?" I rolled my eyes and she grinned.

"I think I might love you, Carmen Baxter."

I winked, and leaned up to kiss Sammie. "Wanna get me out of these wet clothes?"

Cara groaned. "And there goes my lady boner. Keep it down, don't wake up the kids. I'm putting in my damn headphones." With that, she stormed away.

Sammie reached down and lifted me into his arms. I wrapped my legs around his waist and snuggled my face into his neck. We made it back to his room, Flint slipping in behind us and closing the door, before he began stripping me naked and fucking me like I was the best thing since apple pie.

· · ·

I WORE Sammie's shirt to class the next morning, which was how I ended up in the boy's locker room, pressed between the wall and the hard body of my Alpha mate. "I hate that I'm all the way in Nîso, and can't be with you at night like they can," Bobby growled, kissing down the long column of my neck. When he dipped his tongue into the hollow of my throat, I threw my head back as he ran it in one flat, hard stroke back to the point of my chin. He nipped and sucked at my skin like he was starving for just a taste. "Even Monster gets to see you at night." His hand wrapped around my throat, his thumb keeping my chin tilted up so he could sip at my lips like he owned them.

He totally did.

I clawed at his shoulders and he ground his hips into mine. "So move on campus for a while. You're my mate. They'd let you," I gasped, as his hand slid between our bodies and under my skirt. He found my clit quickly, rubbing softly, before rolling his hips again, this time grinding his hips against his hand that was poised perfectly over my fucking happy place.

"Jesus, Bobby. Please." I didn't even care that my words were a desperate whimper, or that anyone could walk in here. He rolled his hips a couple of more times before groaning himself.

"Fuck, baby, you drive me crazy," he says, pulling his hand from my underwear despite my whimper, but thankfully using it to unzip his jeans quickly, pulling out the hard length of his cock. He pushed my panties to the side and slammed into me in one hard thrust, as a small scream burst from my throat.

"Shh, baby. Someone will hear," he cooed, but then slammed into me again. I bit his shoulder, not hard enough to break the skin, but with enough force to muffle my moans as he quickly snapped his hips into mine with short, shallow thrusts.

The concrete wall cooled my back, which was good because the front half of my body was on fire. Bobby's heavy thrusts scraped me up and down the wall, and there was a light sting where the rough surface was scraping my back.

That edge of pain made it so much better. I looked up at Bobby. "Choke me, Alpha," I moaned, and Bobby's whole body shuddered at my words. His hand slipped up from my hips to my throat, and wrapped his long fingers around my neck. He tilted my head back with his hand and kissed me almost savagely. The pressure increasing around my throat seemed to be directly related to the pressure in my lower belly, as an intense pleasure swept down my body.

My nails dug into his shoulders, and too soon I was screaming his name with his flesh between my teeth. My wolf rode me hard, urging me to take our mate, but with willpower I didn't know I had, I turned my head and just breathed in his scent as my orgasm hit me in waves.

Bobby wasn't done though, thrusting into me with ragged strokes. "Fuck, god, I love you. I'm going to come," he groaned, slipping out of me.

I wiggled out of his arms, sliding to my knees and grabbing his cock. He grabbed my head, his moan just as loud as mine. I looked up at him, my grin smug satisfaction. "Shh baby, someone will hear," I teased and then sucked him into my mouth, pushing him back until he was touching the back of my throat. He tangled his hands in my hair, and I was glad I'd gone with a messy bun style today. He only managed a couple of thrusts before he came down the back of my throat, leaning into the wall, gasping. Looking down at me, he cocked an eyebrow. "Been practicing?"

I give him my own cocky look back. "Complaining?"

He pulled me from the ground and back into his arms. He kissed me hard, possessing me, and it was so damn right. I had no idea how I'd missed it for so long. Of course we were mates. This pull in my chest wasn't puppy love. It was my soul reaching out for its other half. And now?

Now it was being pulled in all sorts of directions.

"Never, baby." He nuzzled my hair. "Jealous, hell yeah. Insanely jealous. I'm going to talk to Alistair. See if I can move in because I want in on whatever you guys have going on every night. I don't want you to forget about me when you are being tag-teamed by two hot guys."

I slapped his arm. "As if I could ever forget about you, dumbass." Then I kissed him softly, leaning up to whisper in his ear. "You should see them together, Bobby. They are so fucking beautiful, I swear I could orgasm just watching them."

Bobby groaned again, kissing me once more, his tongue slipping past my teeth to thrust into my mouth. "Soon, baby, I'm going to fuck you while we watch them together. And then we'll swap until we're all sweaty, satisfied messes. We are going to have the most content Pack North America has ever seen."

As one, we thought of Monster. I knew he was thinking of him too, because the shadows chased out the hope in his eyes, and worry replaced them. "When are you seeing your parents?"

I wiggled from his arms and slid back to my feet, straightening my skirt. "Saturday. It's Family Day, so we're going home. I'll bring it up then. Mom will be okay about it, you know what she's like. But Brody is going to shit bricks."

Bobby just nodded, reaching into the front of my bag to grab my hairbrush. He gently untangled my hair from its hair tie, and it flowed messily down my back. He ran the brush down my hair and I resisted the urge to purr. There was something insanely intimate about this act, even though he'd just given me an orgasm, and I'd just had my mouth around his dick.

This little act of service though? It meant something to me. And the more I thought about it, the more I realized he'd been doing these things for me for years.

Making sure I ate first at barbeques. Helping to pick out my prom dress, even though he didn't take me. Making sure I was safe at all my fights. Giving me his hoodie and dressing me in his scent.

He'd been doing these things for as long as I could remember, and now it all made sense. "I'm such an idiot, you know that right? All this time, we've been meant for each other. So many wasted years."

He leaned forward, kissing my shoulder. "Nah, baby. We just had to grow into the people we were destined to become first. We are exactly where we're meant to be."

I wanted to scream. Just scream and scream into the abyss and hope that someone would hear me in time to pull me out.

No, that was unfair. Carmen was there, her arms around my neck, desperately trying to keep me afloat, but with every passing night, I was being dragged deeper. And I would just drag her down with me in the end.

I looked at the big screen across the conference table, and Azar's face was filled with sympathy.

"I'm sorry, Flint. The Council searched all the locations you suggested and came up with nothing. We will keep an eye on the underground, but until he weasels his way back out of his hole, we've got nothing."

They were haunting my dreams, but I couldn't help

them. It was eating me alive. Still, I nodded. "I'll try harder."

Alistair sat beside me, and for the first time, I'd met his wife. Layla. She had a baby in a sling across her body, and it was sound asleep. She was on my other side, and like she could feel me floundering, she reached out and grabbed my hand. She didn't give me false platitudes about how we'd catch him, or how we'd save them. No, she just held me like she was a lifeline I could cling to.

It made me want to cry. That little baby didn't know how lucky it was. At least its mother wouldn't sell it to the highest bidder.

Azar was still talking, but she mustn't have needed much from me, because Alistair seemed to be answering all her questions fine.

The baby woke and started fussing, and Layla removed her hand to free it from the sling. I mourned the loss of her warmth, but the baby needed her more than I did.

But she just handed the baby to me, and I took it instinctively. I mean, if someone thrusts a baby at you, it's not like you can 'Not it!' and let it drop to the ground. I tucked it into my arm like I saw them do in movies.

"Feel his newness. His potential. His life." She looked down at the baby with big golden eyes in my arms. "He doesn't know that the world can be bad. He doesn't know that people like Rook exist. All he knows is that you didn't let him fall. That you caught him when he needed it." She squeezed my arm. "We're your arms. We'll catch you if you fall, Flint."

I swallowed hard, desperate not to cry in front of these people. I nodded, not dragging my eyes from the baby who'd stopped fussing to just stare at me. Layla looked back at the screen, and Azar was staring at me too. Something passed between the two women, and then Azar was signing off.

I handed the baby gently back to Layla. I looked at Alistair, and Locke who was leaning against the wall in the corner. "I, uh, thanks. I better go to class."

I ran out of the room like a chickenshit, tearing from this wing of the building toward the dorms where I could just break down in peace.

I was too caught up in my panic, I ran straight into someone. I bounced off a chest, and I scrabbled to my feet, ready to cut someone to just relieve a bit of this pressure.

Bobby was there, frowning in concern. "Flint. Are you okay?"

His lips were swollen, a bite mark on his neck from our girl. I looked at the big guy who had an aura of such calm assurance, like he knew the way things were going to go, that he made me feel scattered.

"I— Fuck, Bobby, I—" What did I even say? I was sinking. Panic clawed at my gut, and Bobby must have seen it because he grabbed my hand and led me through the school until we were standing outside Carmen's room.

He unlocked it with a key from his pocket, gently guiding me into the room. It smelled of Carmen, and it eased something in me slightly. Bobby took my face into his hands, his thumbs pressing tightly into my cheekbones.

"You are Pack, Flint. You are mine. Tell me what you need."

I shrugged, my eyes burning. "I don't know. I feel so helpless. So fucking tired."

I rubbed my face, my hands coming away damp, and I stared at the moisture on my hand. Tears. As if seeing them broke something in me, I let out a ragged sob. My body curled as the tears just burst out of me. Years and years of tears flooded down my cheeks, and I was dragged into Bobby's arms.

This was so fucking weak, and disgust warred with the need for comfort until I was clawing at his back like I was trying to simultaneously pull him closer and push him away. I just cried out years of injustice. Of being used by evil men for evil purposes. Of violence and violation.

And Bobby held me the whole time, his calm aura keeping away the worst of the demons. Somehow, he slid his shirt off, and tugged my own tear-soaked shirt off too. "Get into the bed, Flint. Skin to skin contact helps the shifters. I promise I'm not trying to come onto you. I just think maybe, after all these years, you might be touch-starved."

I was too wrung out to protest, and as I climbed beneath Carmen's blankets, Bobby hopped in beside me. Her scent wrapped around me, and he pulled me against his body, curling himself around me like he was protecting me from anything that would hurt me ever again. It wasn't sexual, although I'd almost prefer it was. I'd feel less vulnerable.

Instead, it was something more. It was family. It was comfort and protection, which made me feel weak all over again. I had been my own savior for so long, the walls around my heart so strong that I thought nothing could make them crumble. However, the smallest crack had destroyed them like an Achilles heel.

I'd let myself have this moment of weakness. Tomorrow, I would beat someone's face in to remind myself that I was a man if I had to. But today, I soaked in Bobby's strength, and let a decade of pain seep from my soul like bad blood.

He ran his hand over my skin as he whispered something in Cree. I didn't even realize he spoke the language, and while I had no idea what he was saying, I knew that it was a vow. I had nothing to give him back but pain. Monster and I were a lot alike in that way. We came with nothing but baggage. Bobby, Sammie and

Carmen didn't deserve that, but they were the same in that way too. They both had an absolute certainty of their place in this world. And then they'd bundled us to them, the lost and the hopeless, and gave us a place too.

Exhaustion sunk over my skin. I fell into a dreamless sleep, the steady hum of Bobby singing some kind of lullaby. Tomorrow I would be strong. Today, I would sleep.

I woke to soft lips kissing my face. "Flint, wake up."

I lifted my face towards those lips, like a sunflower searching for the sun. A soft touch to my own, as those lips kissed me back, had me sighing happily. "Get up. I've got a surprise."

I stretched and realized Bobby was gone. I didn't know if I was relieved or saddened that he'd left while I slept.

There was a low chuckle from the corner of the room. I rolled over and Bobby was smiling softly at me. "Don't worry, Fireball."

I snorted. "Not worried, just looking for the warm spot."

They both laughed at me, and I had to admit, that was a pretty poor deflection even for me. I pulled back the blankets and searched the floor for my shirt. Before I could put it on, Carmen was in my arms, nuzzling against my skin like she was the one who needed comforting. When she gently bit my nipple as she pulled away, I growled.

"Is my surprise an orgy? Because I'm very sure that would make me feel better."

Bobby laughed and I looked at him, but quickly darted my gaze back to the girl in my arms. I was... embarrassed by my weakness. He'd seen me at my most vulnerable and I wasn't sure how we regained equal footing.

I sighed against her hair when she squeezed me tight. "Nope, not an orgy. I want to say it's better, but really, that would be a lie."

She dragged me out of the room as soon as I had my shirt on, and then out of the dorm wing. She led me through the Academy and into the woods at the back. "If we are going to sacrifice me to the gods of dirty sex, I'm ready," I joked, and she gave me a secret grin.

"We only do that on Saturdays." She pulled me into a clearing, and I was surprised that there were a few dozen Academy seniors hanging around, most chatting in small groups or standing around fire bins that littered the area.

In the middle was the undeniable circle of a ring. "Holy shit, is this Fight Club?"

Bobby laughed. "Well, if it was, the first rule is we can't talk about it." He shook his head and led us toward Carmen's brother, Christopher. He was glaring at Sammie's sister, or maybe it was at the lion shifter, Bohdie.

Given what I saw the other night, I was going with the latter.

Bobby looked around at the crowd. "There are a lot of different supes at this school, each with different hierarchies and structures. Sometimes we have disagreements, so back when the school first started, Micah set up fight night. He oversees it, to step in if something goes wrong. But otherwise, this is where we settle dominance fights, arguments over territory, all that kind of shit. Mouse thought that maybe you'd like to work out some of your tension on the face of someone who'd slighted her this month."

Oh yeah. "The big, ugly fuck with the mouth?"

Carmen grinned. "Yep. I thought I might join you. The couple that fights together stays together, right?"

I laughed, my chest feeling lighter at the thought. Which was probably not a good thing, that physical violence gave me relief. But we were all a little fucked up so I wasn't going to beat myself up over it.

I kissed her hard, and she wrapped her arms around my neck, deepening it. She was so damn perfect. Micah growled and stepped into the ring, a basket of protective equipment at his feet.

"Alright, you guys know the rules, but just in case you're stupid, here they are. You will wear the protective equipment, I don't care how badass you are." He looked directly at us and I grinned. He shook his head. "The fights go until you or your opponent tap out, or I say stop. If you fail to stop, I will shift and tear your fucking head off. Only one fight per night, so make sure you aren't wasting it on something trivial. Lastly, no shifting, no powers. We settle this in our human forms only. You are only as strong as your human form, so learn to fight in it or go home. Any questions? No? Okay, first contenders, step up."

No one spoke, and the nervous energy in the clearing ratcheted up. There was silence, but then Christopher stepped forward into the ring.

He looked at Carmen, his head tilting toward Enit. Carmen rolled her eyes, and grabbed my hand, and we moved around the circle until we were standing beside her sister. Neither of them seemed worried, and given what I knew about Christopher's personality, I doubted this was the first time he'd been in the ring.

"Well, here's a goddamn surprise," Micah grumbled. "Okay, who are you challenging today?"

"Bohdie, the lion Alpha."

Enit gasped, and Micah rolled his eyes. "Shocker. Do you accept?" he asked Bohdie, and of course, the lion Alpha nodded. "Fine, equipment on. I don't want to have to call either of your parents and tell them that you stupidly murdered each other."

With that, he stepped from the ring. I was interested to see how Carmen's brother fought. He had that same coiled violence in him, but I had a feeling he lacked her discipline. Being an Alpha could be a limitation like that sometimes.

The two Alphas shed their shirts, and both put on sparring gloves and headgear. That was it. The extent of the protective gear. Well, fair enough. I could work with that.

Finally, Micah called fight, looking bored but I could tell his senses were attuned to the fight. He was talking to another guy, easily in his forties, tall and dark with a lot of tattoos. Someone leaned close. "He's one of the founders, a human. His packmates funded the building of the Academy."

And now he came out to watch us fight. Interesting.

Enit was basically vibrating with anxiety beside me, despite the fact that Carmen had her arm around her sister's shoulders.

I wrapped my arm around her too, snuggling her between us. I could get used to this Pack thing.

"Don't worry, Little E. I promise that I will dive into the fray and spank both their asses with my fiery hand of fury before shit goes too far. Let them get all their dick waving out of their system. Though, having seen ya' boy naked, I feel like it would be less wavey and more helicopter style, you know? You get it, girl."

She gaped at me, forgetting her nerves for a moment. "I... What? When did you see Bohdie naked?"

She gave me the stink eye, and I had a feeling this little wolfie might have sharp teeth. I leaned in close to her ear.

"The other night after you snuck out of his house, Mouse and I were sneaking in, and let's just say, Mouse wanted to have a little chat with him while he was in the shower. She threatened to cut off his dick." I sighed and stood tall, looking over at Mouse as her eyes danced around the fight, watching her brother as he dodged a punch and landed one on Bohdie's abs. "It was hot as fuck. I think I love her."

Enit choked out a laugh, and then went pale. "Oh shit. She knows?"

I grinned, tugging her tighter against my side. "It's safe to assume that everyone knows that the big, and girl I mean big"—I let out an appreciative whistle—"Alpha has the hots for you. I'm thinking your other littermate might know that he's defiling his baby sister too, judging by the uppercut that's coming in five... four... three... two..."

Christopher slammed his fist into Bohdie's chin, laying the lion out. But despite the force of that hit, he didn't stay down long. He was up, blood dripping from his chin as he climbed to his feet. He wavered a little, but he bared his bloodstained teeth.

"She's worth it, fucker." With that, he charged Christopher, and they went to the ground again. They rolled around, each getting in close range hits, Christopher getting a solid elbow in the nose with enough force that Carmen winced and Enit whimpered. I bundled her closer to my chest, tucking her tight into me.

"Don't look. They'll call it soon. Then you can kick both their asses. I'll hold them for you if you want." Carmen looked over at me holding her sister, and smiled. Yep. Definitely loved her. Not an ounce of jealousy in her expression.

As I predicted, they were too evenly matched, and Micah dived into the ring to call it.

"Enough," he shouted, though they both saw too much red to hear him. He reached down, grabbed the golden hair on the back of Bohdie's head, and yanked him off. Stepping between the two fighters, he eyeballed them both. "I said enough. Fight is done. Fists won't work, so I suggest you try words." He muttered something beneath his breath, and Bohdie stumbled bleeding and dazed toward us, as did Christopher. I felt Bobby tense up behind me, and they were way too close before I realized they were both storming towards me.

Oh yeah. I guess I was kind of hugging Christopher's precious Omega sister, and the big lion Alpha's girlfriend.

"Better let you go, Little E. Though I'm happy to set both sets of their balls on fire, if you want?"

She hiccuped a laugh and then turned toward the

two huge Alphas striding toward us. She held her ground, and when Christopher made it to us first, the trembling girl from the beginning of the fight was gone.

"Enit, let's—"

Smack! Enit whipped out a hand and bitch-slapped her brother into next week. The red handprint on his cheek was so perfect, I could probably see her fingerprints if I looked hard enough.

"How fucking dare you, Christopher? How. Dare. You."

I let out a low whistle. Oh shit.

Bohdie looked smug, until she whirled on him. "Baby..." he cajoled, and she slapped him too.

"I am not a bone to be fought over. Get the hell over yourselves."

She whirled, her white hair swinging out behind her, and strode into the darkness. I looked at Carmen, and Bobby. Someone should go with her.

But it was Sammie's sister, Cara, who went after her. She didn't say anything, but if looks could flay, they'd both be broken and bleeding on the ground right now. Carmen, my beautiful Mouse, looked like she'd happily beat them both. My money was on my girl. She mightn't be Alpha, but she was a 100% badass bitch.

"Fix it," she growled, and I didn't know which one she was talking to, or if she meant them both.

Then she grabbed my hand and dragged me into the ring. I looked over my shoulder at them both. "Good fight, assholes," I grinned, and Christopher gave me the finger. Bohdie went to lunge for me, but both Sammie and Bobby were there holding him back.

I would floor him in an instant, but let him have his illusion of Alpha superiority.

I was going to fight with my girl, and we'd make some bodies hit the floor.

37

Micah looked at me and Flint with narrowed eyes. "No."

I huffed. "Come on, Micah. We'll play nice. I'll even go easy on them, I promise? Hell, they can add like, another two, if it would make them feel better?"

"Yeah, sure. Make *them* feel better. You aren't fooling me, Carmen Baxter. I am not letting semi-professionals fight on school grounds. Layla would kick my ass."

Layla, his mate, was the sweetest person on earth, and probably the only person that could corral two Lycanthropes until they were as docile as corgis. "Naw, you think I'm semi-professional? Stahp."

Micah gave me a bland look.

"I swear. They called me a whore, Micah. A whore,

because I had the audacity to love a man who hadn't had any love in his whole life."

Flint squeezed my hand. "It's all good, baby. Their opinions don't matter."

The sigh that Micah elicited was resigned, and I had to school my features. We had him. He hated misogyny, especially because his kind were polyamorous. "Fine. You stop at first blood. If you go too far, I won't just intervene, I'll straight up expel you. Are we clear?"

I grinned, saluting him jauntily. I turned before he could change his mind. "I challenge Derek, Rex, Justin and Lance."

Someone scoffed. "Four of us? You're out of your mind, trashcan puppy." All four of them stepped in the ring, and while their eyes dismissed me, they caught on Flint like he might be the bigger challenger. That just pissed me off.

Flint pulled on his gloves and headgear, looking kind of disgruntled as he secured the strap under his chin. "Who wears this shit?" he grumbled. I just laughed at him, pulling on my own gear and letting him strap my gloves around my wrists. "How about I take the big guy, because I'd really like to pound his face, and you take the other three."

I frowned at him, tightening his own gloves. "We are out here so you can work out some frustration."

Leaning forward, he kissed me again. "Sugar Plum,

watching you pound the fuck out of bullies is theraputic as hell. Though not going to lie, still holding out for the orgy."

I laughed and turned toward Micah, who was giving us a stern look which basically said, "Don't fuck up."

Micah stepped out of the ring and I let my body relax into the right stance. "Fight."

They all sprang toward Flint as one, obviously not having discussed tactics beforehand. Guess they thought they were just going to to overwhelm us with their numbers and sheer stupidity.

Flint waited til the first guy got inside his reach and then laid a punishing blow to his solar plexus.

First blood meant avoiding the face. Always pay attention to the fine print. Annoyed by these misogynistic assholes, I swung a low kick to Justin's knee, not enough to pop it, but enough to send him plummeting to the earth like the boulder he was.

That made Rex spin on his heel, watching us both. Rex was always the slightly smarter one. He roared and ran at me. I did say only slightly smarter.

I shifted my weight easily, moving out of the way at the last second, then spinning to kick him in the ass.

There was something about good old-fashioned brawling that made me happy. I cast a quick look at Flint, but he seemed almost bored as he easily dodged all of Derek's punches because the guy broadcasted his moves like he was fucking HBO.

The fourth amigo was attempting to creep around behind Flint, and I let him, just to make shit a bit more interesting for Flint.

I landed on top of Rex and laid my fist into his jaw a couple of times. "Now who likes being on their back, big boy?" I growled. "Or maybe you love taking it like a bitch?"

He roared again and by sheer luck, tangled his feet in mine as he bucked, sending me flying off but still all caught up, landing on my back. He was over me in a second, and I got a solid blow to the face for my cockiness. Guess we were playing serious now. So be it.

I reached around and gave him some punishing blows to his kidneys that probably meant he'd be pissing blood for a couple of days, then I headbutted him.

Look, my dad once told me that no one wins in a headbutt, but sometimes it was necessary.

Unfortunately, I broke Rex's nose, and blood began to pour onto my face.

Ew.

"Enough," Micah boomed, and Rex's face went bright red.

I gave him a pouty face. "Aw, I'm sorry, Rexie. Maybe next time?"

He just growled, his fist pulled back until another gripped it. Micah was there, his face so fucking cold it sent shivers down my spine.

"I said enough. Get the fuck out of the ring before I break your arm for being a coward." Rex looked like he wanted to spit in my face, but his buddies were there, dragging him away. Well, they all limped away. Flint was above me in moments, his smile so wide I thought it would crack his face.

"Wasn't that fun?" he crowed, and I grinned back, wincing a bit as some of Rex's blood ran into my eyes. I lifted my shirt, wiping my face and then climbed to my feet.

I shook my head. "Definitely fun."

Micah walked away mumbling about goddamn kids, then called for the next contender. I walked straight into Bobby's arms, even though I wanted to climb into Sammie's too. But we were keeping our relationship a little on the down-low. The schoolboard knew, because they weren't idiots, but we were trying to keep it from the general school grapevine. Still, I snuck him a secret smile, and the heat in his eyes made my skin burn with need.

Bobby kissed me softly. "Are we done here?"

I nodded, and we all walked back toward the dorms. Except, when I looked toward the woods on the other side of the fence, I swear I could almost feel Monster's eyes on me. I smiled brightly, lifting my hand in a wave, although it could totally be my imagination. Still, a small part of me hoped he saw me fight, that my mate was proud of me.

I OPENED MY GIFTS, which were exactly what I wanted, as always. A set of throwing knives from X, a yearly Netflix subscription from Judge, a jumbo box of condoms from Tex because he'd accidentally mated my mom as a teenager so you know, no one knew better than him that 'accidents' happen. Awkward as fuck. I got a cute pair of Converse from Nico, a new phone from Brody, a Swiss Army knife from Walker, cute as fuck ripped jeans from Mom, and a newspaper article that described an unexplained massacre in a Calgary warehouse from Lucius. Apparently, it had been the local meeting place for the black market, including the sale of supes.

It wasn't Rook, but it was close.

I grinned at the craziest of my parents. "Thanks. It's what I've always wanted."

He snorted from where he stood behind Mom, inhaling her scent. "I know."

It was weird to have this anniversary in the middle of the year, just a day that celebrated us as a family, but I'd missed them so much since I'd been boarding at Eden, and I soaked in the warmth.

Well, Enit was still not talking to Christopher, even

though he got her another cute crystal figurine for her collection. She was softening though; it wasn't in her nature to stay mad. The parentals were looking at us strangely, at the obvious frozen tundra between Christopher and Enit, and Nico narrowed his eyes.

"What's going on with you two?" Neither of them answered, but there was no way they were going to let this drop. Not on Family Day.

I leaned over to Enit. "You totally owe me," I muttered, and then I stood.

"Guys, I need to tell you something."

Walker groaned, rubbing his hand down his face. "She's pregnant already. We're failures at parenting."

Judge elbowed him in the ribs. "Let her talk."

I gave them both a narrow-eyed look. "No, I'm not pregnant. Jesus, give me some credit. No, apparently, I have two fated mates, and the other one is a Wendigo."

The silence in the room was... intense. "I think I would have preferred her to be pregnant," Brody muttered, and Tex whacked him in the head. "Watch it, Pup," he growled, but there was no heat in it.

Tex ignored him. "Someone is going to have to explain this to me. What's the big problem with her mate being a Wendigo? Having multiple mates isn't a problem. I mean, look at Raine?"

Everyone was silent again, and it was Brody that answered him. "Wendigo were once shifters, who invited evil spirits into their bodies. They are insatiable beasts that feast on the flesh of humans. They are insane, bad luck, and generally considered evil."

There was silence again. "So, basically Lucius?" X said, and Brody groaned.

"No! Well, yes, kind of, but with like big ass antlers and a need to eat hearts."

Lucius grunted. "I like hearts."

Brody looked like he wanted to thump Lucius, but it was Walker who held my gaze. "Are you sure?"

I nodded, because I was sure he was my fated mate. "I mean, it's new, but the yearning is there."

The silence was drawn out again, and this time it was Mom who spoke. "What do you need? Do you need us to help you break the bond?" A cold sweat broke out over my skin at the thought of Monster being gone forever. He might be a new development, but he was slowly working his way beneath my skin.

I shook my head. "I don't really need anything except, maybe he could stay here, in Dark River? Just for a while until we figure everything out."

Brody hopped up, pacing around the room. Surprisingly, it was Judge that came to Monster's defense.

"We know better than anyone that just because this guy is a Wendigo, doesn't mean shit. Superstitious rumors are no reflection on who he really is. We're going to have to meet him."

Ugh. I was worried it would come to this. I ran my

hand down my face, but I nodded. I didn't think they'd let him live here sight unseen. "The apartment over the diner is still free. I can talk to Beatrice."

My heart thumped in my chest like a staccato drum, and my eyes started to burn. "You guys are really the best, you know that right? I love you so much." I looked at Brody, who was still pacing around. He'd have the most ingrained prejudice, I understood that. Superstitions were hard to shake. "I promise you, Dad, that he's a good guy. I would slit his throat myself if I thought he was any danger to me or the Pack."

Brody raised an eyebrow. "I don't know if I find that statement reassuring or more concerning."

"Makes me so fucking proud," X crowed, moving toward the kitchen. "Now let's have some damn cake. Nico made the one that when you stab it with a knife, its guts gush out and it's been a long time since I've made anyone but your mother gush."

"X!" Mom screeched.

I gagged and Christopher swore, and honestly, we were going to need therapy. Nico just strolled over, shaking his head and taking the knife from X. "One, it's a lava cake and two, now you don't get to stab it because you've traumatised the children."

An hour—and two slices of lava cake, that would never be the same—later, I climbed into the passenger seat of Christopher's SUV.

Enit sat in the back, though she kept sneaking me looks and asking me questions about Monster. I answered what I could, made a note of what she wanted to know that I couldn't answer, and I ignored the fact that Christopher was pissed at me. Again.

"You can pull the stick out of your ass, Christopher. You've been busy."

He slid his eyes towards me. "Maybe. Or maybe you've been cutting us out. You used to tell us everything, Mouse. Now you're running around with a cannibal, and Enit is fucking that stupid lion Alpha on the down-low, and I feel like I'm losing my siblings."

Gah. Guess we were doing this deep and meaningful thing in the car. "Christopher, I love your stubborn ass more than any person on this planet, except Enit. More than I love Bobby, and he's my fated mate. But we aren't kids anymore. We're adults, and that means that we're going to get our own mates, and our own lives, and we won't be as close as we were when we were six. You have to give up a bit of control, brother, or you're going to end up alone, with only Enit visiting you at Christmas because her heart is too big to leave you alone on the holidays even if she thinks you are a stubborn, pigheaded asshole."

Christopher growled. "I've always been the one to protect you guys."

I got it. I did. Christopher had clung to being our

little Alpha, our protector, as a means of not dealing with the shit that happened when we were kids. "We can't be your crutch forever. At some point you are going to have to take a chance that you might get hurt, maybe with a hot little brunette from a motorcyc—"

It happened so fast. Except for the car flipping in the air. That bit was painfully slow motion. I saw the tactical vehicle hit my door, felt the glass cut my skin as it smashed, heard Enit scream. We flipped end over end, my head hitting the dash and my vision going black.

I woke up, looking over at Christopher's prone form, his body twisted wrong. "No, no, no. Christopher. Hey, Christopher. Come on, wake up."

He moaned and I huffed a relieved breath. Where was Enit? I tried to twist, but my neck screamed at me. "Enit! Enit, answer me. Enit?"

My passenger door squeaked open, and a hand reached in, cutting my belt so I fell and landed on the roof of the car. That was the first moment I even realized we were upside down. The hand was back, grabbing me by my hair and dragging me out of the car. I screeched as he dragged me across the broken glass, embedding it in my skin. The hand let me go, but I couldn't move my body.

I was paralyzed. No. Fuck. "Help me," I whispered, and the person who'd dragged me came into view.

Rook.

I tried not to whimper as he squatted down in front of me. "You are either shit at giving messages or bad at following orders. Neither of those are very helpful to me right now. So, I've decided you will be the message."

He picked up my completely limp arm, even though I tried so hard that I cried attempting to pull it away. He took it between his fists and twisted, and the cracking sound of bones breaking echoed around the forest.

"Ahh!" My scream lit up the evening air. Then, he unfurled my hand, and I was helpless to stop him. "Please, don't. Please, please, plea—" he cut off my begging with another scream as he snapped two of my fingers at the knuckle.

He stood up, stomped my knee, and my body went white with pain. My whole body was pain.

"That should be enough of a message, but if not..." He snapped a finger at the car idling on the shoulder of the road. A man hopped out, and he was huge with a permanent snarl on his face. I was crying so hard now my body was shaking with it. The huge man dropped a bundle of wrapped rags beside me.

"If not, I think this should make my point just fine." With that, they strode away back to the car, leaving me lying broken on the road, Christopher alive but injured in the car, and Enit... where the hell was she?

The car roared away and I screamed. "Help me!"

I looked at the bundle of rags, finally able to reach out with my good hand and pull them apart.

I wished I hadn't.

I screamed and screamed until my voice went hoarse.

38

Something was wrong. I could feel it.

You're right, Wati added, and if my gut feeling hadn't been enough, that would have sealed it. Wati was hardly ever wrong.

I was in the woods outside the Academy, but I turned and headed north east. I didn't fight the pull that was dragging me that way.

Carmen. Something was wrong with Carmen. I shifted as I ran, my clothes falling off behind me. I was faster in this form, running like death through the wilderness. I was one with the earth, even if I was decay to its life.

Something inside me twisted, urging me to go faster, and I listened. I moved faster than I'd ever had before, so fast that the trees were merely a blur in my peripheral vision.

Then I smelled it. Burnt rubber and gasoline. The sound of screams made my heart stop.

Mouse. No.

I didn't even remember running that last mile, but I was bursting from the trees onto a car accident. But it wasn't an accident. My mate was in the middle of the road, her body bloodied and broken as she screamed.

I shifted as I got closer, needing my human hands, my human voice. I fell to my knees. "Mouse? Sweetheart?" Her wild blue eyes turned to me, and the relief on her face broke my heart. And then she passed out. I shook her lightly, but she didn't wake up.

I needed help, I needed paramedics or something. Why didn't I have a fucking phone? I got to my feet, sprinting to the car. Her brother was hanging upside down, blood dripping from his face onto the roof of the car. I looked through the other window, and in the back was her sister, the little Omega, bent up and broken like a doll. Beside her was a phone. Thank fuck. I wrenched open the door, checking the Omega's pulse.

Alive. A relieved breath whooshed from my lungs. I didn't move her in case her injuries were severe. Grabbing her phone, I had a moment of indecision. Who the fuck did I call? 911? No.

The Alpha. I'd call the Alpha.

Looking through her phone, I found *Brody (Dad)* in the contacts and called it.

He answered on the third ring. "Enit, baby, did you forget something?"

Oh shit. "This is Monster, the uh, Wendigo. There's been an accident, about five miles out of Dark River. You need to get here fast."

I hung up the phone, and it rang again almost instantly. Bobby's name lit up the phone. I answered.

Bobby's frantic voice came through the phone. "Enit, have you seen Mouse, some—"

"Bobby, it's Monster. There's been an accident and you need to get here. Now."

I gave him the same directions I'd given her parents.

"I'm coming." Then the line went dead. I dropped the phone into my pocket, desperate to get back to my mate, but knowing she'd hate me if I let her brother die of blood loss. I shifted a finger to one of my razor sharp claws, using it to cut through the belt. He dropped suddenly, but I let him down as softly as I could.

And then the vampires were there. A blonde one with ancient tattoos riddling his face hissed at me, backing me away from the boy's prone body. Another one, who looked so exactly like him that they could only be twins, placed a hand on his chest.

"Lucius, this is Carmen's Wendigo. He called us. He's not a threat. Go. Find that fucker and when you do, bring him home so we can rend him limb from limb for what he's done to our young."

The ancient vampire glared at me again, and then he took off down the road so fast that it was almost like he teleported. I looked at the reasonable one. "I found them like this. I knew something was wrong, I could feel it. But I didn't want to move them—" I choked on my words.

The blond vampire nodded. "I'm Nico. Tell me more. Was he still in his belt?"

As I was explaining that I cut him down, another vampire appeared, a huge, tattooed and scarred one, with death for eyes.

"Squeak has been tortured."

My heart fell to the pit of my stomach and all that remained was rage. Someone had tortured my mate?

I growled so low that the sound wasn't even close to human. The big one narrowed his eyes at me, but then he crawled into the back of the car toward the broken little Omega. "Enit, baby, open your eyes," he cooed like he was speaking to a child, and I guess he was. He ran his hand down her arms and legs, checking for breaks. "Enit Baxter, open your feckin' eyes before I ground you for life," he shouted, and it worked.

She stirred but didn't wake, but I could hear both of their exhales of relief, and a third one from the boy Alpha. Nico was with him.

"I've just broken my leg. Hit my head. I'm fine.

Where's Carmen?"

That was all I needed as I ran back toward my mate. I could tell her that they'd be okay now. I skidded to a stop, two more vampires leaning around my girl. Her eyes fluttered open, and she searched the faces around her. "Monster?" I fell to my knees, ignoring her parents. They could take a knife to my throat and I wouldn't leave her.

I grabbed her unmangled hand. "Enit? Christopher?"

"Alive," I murmured softly.

She cried some more. "The kid? Is he dead?"

I frowned, confused, until I worked out that one of the vampires was working on a kid. I could hear his thready heartbeat. "Alive too. We'll get you all to a hospital and you'll be fine, I promise."

Bobby's truck screeched to a halt beside an old Impala, and the man I recognized as the Alpha of Nîso pack barrelled out. A pretty woman who looked all of twenty but I would bet was Mouse's mother climbed out of a van along with the two Lycanthrope founders of Eden Academy. She must have gone directly to the Academy for help.

They ran to the big scarred guy. "X, what have we got?"

I missed whatever the hell he said because Bobby was beside me, reaching down to touch Carmen's face. "Baby, what happened?"

"Rook."

His name was a curse on the wind, and it would be his death knell. Because I was coming for him, and I was going to inflict pain until he begged.

I had no control as I transformed, my body elongating and stretching into my Wendigo form. I roared my pain, my mate's pain, into the wind and hoped that wherever this Rook was, he was close enough to hear it.

A change in the air pressure told me that others were shifting, and the shapeshifter Alpha transformed into a tiger.

A tiger that was snarling at me.

Bobby transformed into a giant grizzly bear, and he reared back on his hind legs and growled at the shapeshifter Alpha, standing between me and what he saw was a threat... My brain kept stuttering around, as I tried to grasp the idea that the little Alpha was going against his own Alpha to protect... me.

The redhead was there, Carmen's mom, and she was glaring at the Alpha. "This solves fucking nothing, so get over yourself, Alpha," she said with scary calm.

The malevolent magic swirled back around me as I shifted back to human. I was fucking this up. "I'm sorry. I didn't..."

Carmen groaned again, and I dropped back to my knees. "Best. Stalker. Ever," she groaned, and I laughed. Actually laughed.

"Sorry I wasn't faster. Mouse, I'm so sorry."

Bobby was still a bear and he roared so loud that my eardrums would have shattered if I hadn't been supernatural.

Then the big scarred vamp was there, checking her over. "Squeak, we're going to move you. I think you might have internal injuries." A hand landed on my shoulder, and I looked up into the golden eyes of one of the Lycanthropes.

"We have to move her. If I could get you to stand back?"

I nodded, scrabbling backwards, holding down my Wendigo as she screamed in pain when they shifted her onto the stretcher. They rushed her to a van where her littermates lay prone. The Lycanthrope looked back at us all. "Stacey is prepping for surgery, but we could use the extra hands," he said to X, and everyone nodded. They loaded my mate into the van and closed the doors, and I wanted to howl in pain.

A hand rested on my shoulder, and I looked over to see that Bobby was human again.

"Let's go. We'll meet them at the Academy."

I climbed into the passenger seat of Bobby's car. I tried not to notice how his hands shook, or how pale he was.

We'd both been so close to losing our heart, and it was a fear I would never forget.

I swear, I thought my heart stopped when Bobby banged on my dorm room door and told me Carmen had been in an accident.

But it hadn't been an accident. It had been a message, one that I heard loud and clear now. I had to go back. I would endure centuries of being bound if it would protect her. He'd broken her slowly, methodically, as well as severely injuring her siblings. She'd never forgive me for the pain I'd brought into her world.

Christopher had a broken leg, a broken collarbone and an acute concussion. Enit, sweet little Enit, was even worse. She hadn't been wearing a seatbelt and the crash had tumbled her around like she'd been in a blender. Her brain had swelled, and a rib had punctured her lung. Both of those had been repaired, but on top of that she'd broken her pelvis, ankle, both wrists and a cheek. Stacey—who was honest to god like sixteen, maybe seventeen at the most but everyone seemed totally okay letting her do brain surgery—had operated for hours, and now Enit was in an induced coma.

And my girl. Carmen had ruptured her spleen, and they'd had to operate to remove it. She had a concussion, but it was hard to tell what injuries had been from the accident and what had been from Rook dragging her from the wreck and *breaking* her. Her arm, fingers and cheekbones were Rook's work. The bruising across her chest was from her seatbelt, and the broken nose and cheekbone could have been from Rook or from the airbag. The glass embedded under her skin.

He'd tortured her.

I leaned to the left, and threw up in the trash can beside me. Sammie wrapped an arm around my shoulders, but I shrugged him off. The waiting room held Monster and Bobby too, as well as Cara and Bohdie. Carmen's parents were in the rooms with them, each by a bedside if they weren't out there hunting Rook.

Layla poked her head around the door. "Flint? They've stabilized the boy. We'd like you to come and identify him if you can?" Her voice was soft, like she didn't want to ask. I wish I didn't have to go.

Another person broken because of me. Because I

needed to be free. How many lives was my freedom worth?

I nodded, standing, and Sammie stood too. I turned to tell him to stay in case Carmen needed him, but he shook his head before I could speak. "I love you. You need me too."

I swallowed hard, building my walls back around myself. I didn't acknowledge him as I followed after Layla, no baby in sight today. She led me back into the hospital wing, pressing a hand to a biometric lock beside the door.

"For his safety," she murmured, but I didn't see how.

We stepped into the room, and my heart sank to my knees. The kid on the bed was a mass of bruises, like he'd been kicked around. But despite the fact his face was swollen and bruised, I knew who he was. I stepped toward him, grabbing his hand gently.

"Milo." His eyes fluttered, but didn't open. "He's been walking my dreams, asking for help. But I couldn't help."

I rested my forehead on the clean white sheets, breathing through the panic and despair gripping my chest. "I couldn't work out where they were, what he was trying to tell me. I'm so fucking sorry, kid."

I gripped his hand, hoping that he could hear me in his induced coma. I could hear Sammie and Layla speaking behind me, and then the door opening and closing. I whispered promises to Milo, about how he was safe now, how this pain will be short-lived and one day, when he was healed and grown, he'd look at this moment like it was the best thing that ever happened to him.

Minutes or hours later, two hands rested on my back, and I expected to see Sammie, but it was the younger members of his family. Madoc was there, his big white and blue wings out, and the little red-haired Attica.

Attica smiled down at me. "We're here to help you both, Flint. To ease his pain, and yours." As she said it, she rested her cheek on my head, and a wave of relief rushed through me. "It's okay to feel angry. He hurt the one person you loved. But do you know what would hurt Carmen more? If you went back. If this was all for nothing."

I tensed beneath her, but she went back to stroking my hair softly. Madoc looked at me, his smile sad, but he rested two hands on Milo's chest until they started to glow. "I'm just easing his pain. My biological father was an Archangel. They're meant to be good, right? But from what I know, he was bad. But his gifts aren't bad. Just because I came from bad blood, doesn't mean I'm a bad person. I can use the gifts I inherited to heal wounds of the soul."

He paused, and the glow got brighter, and some of the tension in Milo's face eased. "The men who raised me, my real dads, are killers and bikers, literally the Four Horsemen of the Apocalypse. The heralds of the End of Days. Bad guys, right? But they loved and protected my mom and me. Adopted Sammie and Cara. Loved us so much that we never wondered if we were wanted. Attica's parents? Fallen Angels. Actual Princes of Hell. And I swear to you that Attica is the purest person I've ever met."

I grunted, and Attica stroked my back, cooing at me like I was a spooked horse, and I had to admit, it kind of did make me feel better. "What are you trying to say, kid?"

"You don't have to suffer for other people's mistakes or decisions. For someone else's evilness. You deserve happiness no matter where you come from. You deserve love."

They were kids, they didn't understand what they were saying really. I was a bad person if I didn't go back. But I took their comfort anyway, and hoped they'd ease something in Milo too.

THREE HOURS LATER, Milo still hadn't woken up, and I had to wonder if he was hiding in his dreams. Attica and Madoc were asleep on either side of the bed, each with a hand touching a sliver of his skin, easing his pain. I crept to my feet, pushing the door open silently. Outside, Sammie rested in a hard plastic chair, his head tipped back, his mouth opened slightly as he slept.

My shoes squeaked against the linoleum and he sat up, his hand going for a gun that wasn't there. "How's the kid?"

I shook my head. "Still unconscious. I don't know if it's medical or if he's hiding in there."

Sammie stood, and before I could move away, dragged me into his arms. I steeled myself to the feelings washing through me, because if I leaned into it, I wouldn't be able to do what I needed to do.

"Carmen is back in recovery." With that, he started to herd me toward a different room, and I let him. Because I needed to see her, needed to know she was okay, even if it did make it harder to leave.

Bobby was still in the waiting room, but Monster was gone. "Where's the big guy?" I asked, sitting beside him.

He wrapped his arm around my shoulders and I let him pull me into his side. "It got too much for him, so he's gone back to the woods. I think he's gone hunting." Bobby's normally congenial face turned vicious. "I hope he finds him and pulls his heart from his chest and then eats it in front of him."

Me too.

Carmen's mom walked out of her hospital room, her eyes rimmed in tears. When she saw us, she forced a watery smile. "She's still unconscious, but you can go in if you'd like."

Bobby was up faster than my eyes could follow, and Sammie and I were close behind him.

She was beaten and battered in the bed, looking small and weak. So unlike my fighter. She was bandaged and basically splinted completely still. Her leg was in an inflated balloon thing, her arm in an apparatus that kept it completely immobile.

"It looks bad, but she's a shifter. She heals fast. She'll be fine," Bobby murmured to us both. Yeah, she'd be fine physically in a few weeks. Mentally though? Who knew how she was. She'd been tortured. She'd seen her siblings broken and hurt. And Milo...

I shuddered, and leaned forward until my forehead touched hers gently. "Love you, Sugar Plum."

I moved away and let Sammie in, watching him stroke his fingers over her hairline so gently that it made it hard for me to breathe. Watching them together, knowing that if my life wasn't such a fuck up that maybe I could have that too, it was like having my heart torn out by Monster.

Bobby hadn't been able to tear his eyes from her. I slapped him on the back. "You're going to be an awesome mate and Alpha," I whispered to him, and he frowned at me.

"Where are you going?"

I smiled softly. "Just to check on Milo again and

then up to bed. I'm exhausted and one of us needs to be fresh for Carmen when the rest of you collapse."

He stared at me for a long time, but then gave me a tight nod. "Sleep tight, Fireball."

I rolled my eyes at the nickname, and slowly crept from the room. I walked out of the medical wing and back towards the dorms. But instead of continuing up the stairs, I walked out the back door. I continued walking until I was walking out the front gates.

I walked until my heart shattered in my chest and headlights bore down on me from the road up ahead. I stopped in the middle of the black asphalt, falling to my knees and hanging my head.

This was for the best. She'd be safe now.

Boots stopped in front of me. A hand grabbed my ear and yanked my head back so I was forced to glare into the face of a demon.

"Flint. I see you got my message."

40

CARMEN

The first thing I became aware of was that every inch of my body hurt. Even my scalp hurt.

I whimpered softly, but then a cool hand ran across my forehead. I tried to take an inventory of my body, what was actually broken and what was just a little banged up. But it all hurt the same, like I was a throbbing ball of screaming nerves. I moaned in pain as I shifted my leg wrong.

"Shh, baby. I'll get someone with some meds to make you feel better." I opened my eyes enough to look up into the liquid chocolate of Bobby's gaze. He looked down at me, dark bags dragging down his face, and worry pinching his features. "Thank god you're awake." Then he disappeared. I tried to call him back but my mouth was cottony.

Something pressed to my lips and my eyes flickered around the room. Sammie was there, holding a straw to my lips. "I've never been more thankful to see your baby blues, Sweetheart. Drink slow."

I sucked down the water greedily until he stole it away and I growled. He chuckled low. "Easy baby. You're just out of surgery and you need to go slow otherwise you'll puke everywhere or something." He gave me the straw back and I sipped at it gently. I was in a light yellow room without windows. It smelled sterile.

I was in a hospital room. It was just taking my brain a while to catch up.

"Enit? Christopher?" I choked out on a still dry throat.

"Alive." I shuddered my relief, a small choked sound crossing my lips. Thank god. Sammie must have known I needed more, because he continued. "Christopher is banged up. A couple of broken bones, but his testy attitude is in one piece. Enit wasn't wearing a seatbelt, and she got real hurt," he said softly. "But Stacey says her surgery went well and she's happy with her condition. They've got her in an induced coma, but they're satisfied with her vitals. They're okay, baby."

The door slid open, and Alistair appeared. His smile was relieved. "It's good to see you awake, Miss Baxter. I'll give you something for the pain, let your body have the time it needs to heal in this form. We'll get you to shift in another couple of days."

I swallowed. I wanted to see Enit and Christopher. No, I needed to see them. Also... "The kid?" I shuddered as I remembered the grey and swollen face of the child wrapped in rags, and tears welled on my cheeks even as my eyes got heavy. He was dead, I'd been sure of it. No one could take that kind of beating and live. I struggled to stay awake as Sammie grabbed my good hand.

"Milo. He's alive too. He's been beaten up pretty badly but he's going to be okay. He hasn't woken up yet though. Madoc and Attica have been in there, so he isn't alone. They made Flint identify him." There was a hint of disapproval in his tone.

"Where's Flint?" My eyes darted around the room but he wasn't here. My heart started to race. I needed to see him, to know he wasn't doing anything stupid.

Sammie made a shushing noise. "He's gone up to his dorm to rest. We've all been here for hours and he was exhausted."

Even as he said the words, the knowledge that Sammie was wrong thudded into my chest. He hadn't gone to his room. No, he was running. Fuck. But before I could tell them, I was sucked back down into a drug-induced darkness.

Flint!

· · ·

I SWAM BACK to the surface of consciousness slowly. I felt like I was fighting it, screaming for Flint even as my eyes opened.

"Flint!"

Bobby was there again, his warm palm on my forehead. "Mouse, it's okay."

"No. Bobby. Flint, I need Flint."

His hand felt good on my sweat-soaked skin. "Sammie's just gone to get him. Monster is gone though, I think he's gone to find Rook. So did Lucius. I'm a little gleeful about what would happen if those two teamed up."

A bloodbath.

Bobby's phone rang, and he grabbed it from the nightstand. "Hey." He frowned, his eyes shooting to mine. "Okay, yeah no, you come back here. I'll be right there." He hit the end button and I knew what he was going to say before the words even left his mouth.

But I asked anyway, that dreadful hope that I was wrong like a bubble in my chest. "He's gone, isn't he?"

With a single nod, that bubble popped. "Doesn't look like he even stepped into his room."

I knew he wouldn't. I knew he'd feel like this shit was his fault and he'd do that noble, stupid thing because thats just the kind of person he was. He'd go back to Rook to save me, because he loved me.

I threw back the blankets, ready to get out of this bed, to go and get my mate back. But Bobby was there, pushing me back against the bed. "Don't be an idiot, Mouse. You have more broken bones than I can count on one hand and you are legit just out of surgery."

He crowded close, his lips brushing mine. He looked me dead in the eye, his brown eyes shining with determination. "Flint is Pack. I will get him back, one way or another."

I sucked in a ragged breath as pain shot through my body. I lowered myself back down to the bed. I picked up a pillow, burying my face in it and screamed. I wanted him back. I wanted Rook dead.

Bobby squeezed my good hand again. "It's hard, I know that baby. I know you want to fucking tear Rook apart with your teeth, to fly in and save your mate, and I know your wolf is riding you. But you have to trust us to get him back."

Sammie burst into the room, his eyes wild. His hair was messy like he'd spent too many hours combing his fingers through them. Beside him was Cara, and I could see the outline of a gun beneath her shirt.

Sammie was across the room, kissing me probably a little bit too hard. "I'll get the self-sacrificing dumbass back for us, okay? Trust me." I sniffed and nodded, because if I tried to speak right now, it would probably come out as a wail. "Cara is going to stay here, mostly so you don't do anything stupid like climb out of bed on a busted knee and come after us."

I huffed out a teary laugh, because he already knew me too well.

Bobby paced, his shoulders rolling. "I want to put my mark on you so bad, but I won't be rushed into it out of fear." He stopped and kissed me again. "I love you so damn much, Mouse."

With that, he strode out of the room, Sammie planted a kiss on my lips and followed him out.

Both Cara and I watched the door for a moment longer, before she turned to me.

"Guess this probably isn't the time to ask you if you want to become my platonic life mate? Men, while delightful, are so fucking stupid."

I huffed out a tortured laugh. Because she wasn't wrong, but I didn't think I'd trade them for anything now. "Too late. I love them."

She sighed in a very put upon way. "Damn." She pulled up a chair and sat right beside me, grabbing my hand and threading her fingers through mine. "Nice girls always finish last."

41

SAMMIE

There were a dozen people on the lawn, and Bobby paced back and forth like he wanted to claw at them all. I understood his frustration, because I felt it too. Flint was out there, probably getting beaten within an inch of his life for his defiance. I'd sugarcoated it for Mouse, but what they'd done to that kid had been horrendous. There wasn't an inch of his body that wasn't bruised, like they'd thrown him from the car.

If I met Rook and his buddies, I was going to send them straight to Hell where they belonged. But the team on the lawn were talking extraction, reconnaissance, and I knew the longer that Flint was there, the worse he would be when we got him back.

Bobby knew it too. He stepped up to Micah, running his hands through his hair. "We are going out to look, see if we can't pick up anything through our bond." What a fucking lie, we weren't bonded, which was something I knew Bobby regretted right now.

Micah eyed him. "You find them, you call us. You don't do anything stupid."

Nodding, Bobby started running toward the car. I stared at Micah, but I didn't want to lie to him too. We all knew that if we found them, we were getting our Packmate back as soon as possible.

We roared out of the gates of the Academy, driving south. We were silent in the cab. "What if he kills him as an example?"

Bobby looked at me, his fingers tightening on the steering wheel. "This is a lot of effort to go to just to kill him." He shook his head. "No, he'll try and break him first. But that's okay because we are going to get him back before that happens."

I had options, but they came with permanent consequences. I was keeping them in reserve. Bobby's phone rang, and he picked it up. He stared at the screen, looking at me. "It says it's Enit, but she's..." He fumbled the phone answering, putting it on loud-speaker. "Monster?"

"I followed Flint."

Relief made my stomach turn. "Do you know where he is?"

There was a murmur on the other end of the line. "Lucius says we are at a warehouse on the corner of

First and East Preston Street, near the park where Mouse threw up after eating too much cotton candy. He said Bobby will know where that is."

Bobby nodded. "I know it. Monster?"

"Yeah?"

"Make them hurt."

The growl that came down the line sent chills down my spine. "He is already dead, he just doesn't know it yet."

There was a laugh from close by, and it wasn't even a little human. When I looked at Bobby, his grin was savage. The line went dead, and Bobby put his foot to the floor, speeding us off into the night.

Rook was as good as dead. I would set fire to his corpse and make sure he went to the very depths of Hell where he belonged.

We were silent all of the way there, each of us lost in our thoughts. Bobby drove with reflexes that weren't even a little bit human, and the car took the corners way too fast, but I didn't tell him to slow down. I wished we could go faster.

An eternity later, Bobby was slowing and pulling into a side street. We climbed out, and I pulled my gun. I looked around, too aware of the shadows. Bobby shed his clothes and transformed into a fucking leopard.

"Holy shit, dude," I hissed, suddenly thankful for those shadows. "How the hell do I explain a leopard at midnight?"

Leopard Bobby just chuffed, slinking into the shadows and blending perfectly. Well, fair enough then. I grabbed my phone, putting it on silent, and shooting Micah a text with our location. I moved toward Bobby, stretching my senses for anything that shouldn't be there. But in the end, I was just human, so I relied on the actual supernatural creature with the jungle hearing.

I wished I had the rest of Damnation with me. Cara had suggested we call in our dads. If it wouldn't have taken them too long to get here, I would have called them in a second to get Flint back. But something in me told me he didn't have twenty-four hours.

We got to the back of a warehouse and it had metal stairs that led up to a door. Bobby chuffed again, bounding up the stairs three at a time. When we got to the landing, the door was locked and bolted with a padlock.

"Score one for the human with the opposable thumbs," I whispered, and the leopard gave me a droll look. I was worried when there were no guards at the back door, but it was locked so I guess that was a deterrent if you hadn't been picking locks since you were eight. I grabbed my kit and picked the padlock on the outside and then the deadbolt. It was slow work, and the leopard swirling around my legs only made it worse.

But eventually, the deadlock popped, and I stuffed

my picks back into my pocket and pulled my gun. It had a silencer attached to the end, making it nearly as long as my forearm. I pushed the door open, my gun in front of me. I was in a hallway, and either there was no power or the lights were out. Fuck, I was blind in here.

But Bobby wasn't. We moved slowly through what I assumed were offices, but they were all empty and quiet. I'd have loved some night vision goggles right about now, but I had to hope that this end was just abandoned. We made it out onto a metal walkway. There were stairs that went directly down into more darkness, or a door at the end of the walkway. I stilled as I heard screams from behind the door.

That way it was. We crept along, each creak of metal under our weight had me holding my breath, but this half of the warehouse seemed abandoned.

I reached the doorway, and light trickled underneath it. I lifted my gun, and pushed it open. A man whirled, his gun raised, but I shot him between the eyes before he could raise the alarm. Leopard Bobby looked up at me and snarled, and I shrugged. "Bullet is quicker than a giant pussy. It's just science, man. Don't take it personally."

He huffed and prowled forward. This side of the door was a mirror of the abandoned warehouse. There were offices, but these ones weren't empty. They were filled with kids.

"What the actual fuck?"

There were dozens, way more than Flint said. They all looked terrified and dirty. What the fuck do we do? "Bobby, we can't leave them here."

Bobby shifted back to human, his eyes taking in all of the children. They seemed to be bunched by age, some as young as four or five, or maybe they were just emaciated. Every single one of them was filthy.

I was at war with myself. I needed to get to Flint, but if I rescued Flint and these guys got taken in exchange, Flint wouldn't forgive me, and I wouldn't forgive myself either. "Let's take them out through the warehouse and down to the truck. Then we'll take them, fuck! I don't know where. We can't just drop them somewhere and come back for them."

I opened the door to one of the rooms, and looked at a bunch of maybe eight-year-olds? No, younger. "Come on, we are here to rescue you."

They all shrank away from me. I made a grab for one of the little ones. A tiny ball of black fur ran at me, launching an attack with claws and teeth. It landed a good bite on my shoulder, before Bobby was there, pulling it off.

"Calm," he growled, and the kitten went limp. It couldn't have been much bigger than a puppy. All the rest looked at me with big eyes. "We aren't here to hurt you, I promise. We can take you somewhere safe, where you'll never be hurt again."

Their eyes were so haunted and hopeful, and it

broke my heart. Then one stepped forward, a little kid with copper hair and huge green eyes. Then another, and another and I breathed a sigh of relief.

Then there was a roar from on the factory floor below and every single one of the kids froze in terror. Shit. Shit fuck shit. There were too many to carry out. I looked at Bobby. "Can you use your Alpha mojo to make them move?"

He shook his head. "Only on the shifters. If any of them are Djinn or any other kind of supe, my call will be useless."

I looked down at the kid, and then at Bobby. "Do you trust me?"

Bobby frowned, still holding the kitten in his hands. "With the life of my mate. Why?"

I squatted down in front of the kid with the bright green eyes. "What's your name?"

He looked at me silently and I could see him gathering his courage. "Sean."

"Okay, Sean, I need you to do something for me. When I leave this room, I need you to say 'Lucifer, I want to make a deal,' okay? But you really need to mean it. Put all your intention behind it. You can save all your friends, if you mean it enough. Do you think you can do that?" Sean nodded, and I smiled, squeezing his shoulder. "Good stuff. Now one or two people will appear, and they'll look scary, but they are really big softies. They'll take you out of here and they won't rest until every single one of you is happy."

Sean nodded, and I stood. "Okay, Sean. You're up." I looked at Bobby, moving toward the door at the end of the end of the hall that must lead down to the warehouse floor. "Let's go."

Bobby looked back at the kids, and I saw him weighing up if I was crazy or not. I pushed open the door, and it was empty on the other side as well. Whatever was going on down on the warehouse floor must be epic. Bobby stepped out after me, and I shut the door.

I paused, waiting. "Come on, Sean," I whispered.

"Lucifer, I want to make a deal," he said in a loud, clear voice. I felt the drop in temperature, and heard surprised screams from the kids.

Then I heard a dark chuckle. "Well played, Sammie. Well played."

I grinned and moved down the stairs. Bobby looked between me and the door. His eyes were wide. "You going to explain that?"

I shrugged. "My parents are the Four Horsemen. Let's just say, I know a few tricks when it comes to Hell and the Devil himself." He just stared. "I'll explain later. Let's go save our packmate."

42

MONSTER

I stood in the shadows of the forest, before the hidden turnoff to the Academy, shrouded in darkness. I was waiting.

I had seen Flint's face when he realized it was Rook that had hurt Mouse so badly, and I knew his expression. It was fear.

Which meant he was doing something noble, but stupid. I wasn't going to stop him, but I was going to use him as bait. And then I would save him and give him back to my mate as proof of my seriousness. Proof that I had the ability to protect her and our Pack.

I was rewarded when Flint walked down the middle of the road, uncaring if he was hurt, unseeing to the threats around him. He was a man walking to death row, and something had twinged in my chest. The headlights speeding down the winding mountains toward him had barely stopped before he was being kicked in the face and stuffed in the back of a car.

I'd followed along behind them, knowing that conceited fuck would lead me right where I needed to go. Oh sure, he trailed us around the damn city for an hour first, but I could be invisible when I needed to be. When he'd finally pulled into the underground parking lot of a warehouse downtown, I knew I was in the right place. The Wendigo had screamed for his heart, and I was going to give it to us both.

He had hurt my mate. Tortured and almost killed her. I would exact my revenge in the most bloody, painful way imaginable. I crept up to the front entrance, shrouded in shadows. I was death, and tonight I would feast.

"His death is mine," a voice said softly from the darkness, sending shivers down my spine. I turned to see the vampire Lucius, his lips pulled back over his fangs in a gruesome snarl.

I shook my head, even though my Wendigo sensed a predator far greater than any we'd ever encountered. They say love is blind, but then again, so is vengeance. And it made me either brave or stupid, because I whirled on him. "She is my mate. I will kill him and present his dead heart on a plate to her as a courting gift."

Lucius tilted his head to the side. "That is a good gift. But she is my child, they are all my children, and it would have broken my mate's heart if one of them had perished due to that dead man."

Now it was my turn to frown. "Rock, paper, scissors?"

Lucius snorted. "First person to touch him gets to kill him. But I'll leave you the heart. My child deserves hearts and roses."

I frowned. I don't think that was what it meant to give someone hearts and roses, but it kind of worked.

This asshole is insane, Hew chimed in, and he wasn't wrong.

I nodded. "Thank you."

I pulled the little Omega's phone out of my pocket, and dialled Bobby, telling him where we were, as per Lucius' bizarre instructions. If the near impossible happened and someone ended my long, cursed life, I didn't want to take Flint down with me. That kid deserved a little happiness, far more than I did.

Hanging up, I prowled to an outside window, sticking to the shadows yet again. I smashed the window, uncaring if they heard. Let them hear. Let them know that death and pain stalked their halls, and it was coming for every single one of them.

I climbed through the shattered glass window, ignoring the cuts that scraped along my body. I dropped down into the hallway at the back of the factory, in what I assumed was some kind of storeroom.

I took the moment to shift into my Wendigo, and for the first time in a century, I was happy to have it. This time, I didn't try to halt the change halfway. I let it consume me until it was stretching my body long, the antlers growing and my face elongating into that of a buck.

I couldn't talk in this form, but that didn't matter. I wasn't here to chat. I was here to kill.

In this form, the spirits I shared my body with were quiet, as we were all consumed with the hunt.

It wasn't long until I found my first feast. I scraped my long nail along the metal railing, moving softly to stand behind my victim in the darkness. The guard spun on his heel, and the look on his face was comical. He didn't even lift his gun as I grabbed his face between my hands and broke his neck.

The Wendigo wanted to eat his heart, but no matter how hungry I was—and I was always starving to the point of delirium in this form—both the Wendigo and I knew that we were here to defend our mate, and there was only one heart we wanted.

I threw down the body of the guard like a broken toy and continued prowling further and further into the building. I wanted to get there before that crazy vamp, but logically, I knew that was almost impossible. They didn't look like they were carrying weapons that could cut down an enraged ancient vampire; in reality there were very few things that could do that, and he would be like a whirlwind of pain and suffering.

I could hear the steady thud of flesh on flesh, and knew that it was Flint being beaten. I growled, pushing down my need for vengeance, instead choosing to save my Packmate. Mouse didn't want a heart. She wanted her mate.

I could do that. And if the two actions overlapped and I got to kill Rook at the same time, so be it. I moved toward that sound, and the stench of fear that hung heavily in the air. There was less protection than I thought there would be, but it made sense. Rook wasn't the head of an underground crime family or anything like that. No, he was a businessman who bought flesh and then made it fight until it was broken. He didn't need to worry about people attacking him. He only had to worry about his toys escaping.

Until today.

Today he was going to wish he had more men. Or that he was dead. Only time would tell which it would be first. I stood in the darkness of the doorway, blending into the shadows like a ghost. The room beyond me made my stomach turn. It appeared to be a holding area of some kind, and there were cages along one side holding people.

None of them were crying or screaming, so they were probably not new acquisitions. They just seemed... dead. At least on the inside.

The beast in me rebelled at the idea of being chained and caged like some junkyard dog, and for once, I had to agree with the Wendigo. I would rather be dead than be some psychopath's pet.

In the middle of the room, they had Flint chained to the ceiling, his body black and blue from the heavy fists of the large man hitting him. It wasn't Rook though. No, he was sitting a little away on a folding chair like it was a throne.

I wanted him to be rodent-faced, but he wasn't. He was a big guy, and if I didn't miss my mark, a former fighter. But I knew his type. He was in it for the pain. The type you inflicted on others, and the type you received. He didn't care about his opponents, they were just useless commodities standing in the way of him and his high.

The big guy laid his fist into Flint's stomach again, and Flint just hung there like a side of beef. I remembered what everyone said about Rook's abilities to paralyze you, and I wondered if he could do it from a distance. Or maybe all the fight had just gone out of Flint.

I moved into the room, killing the first guard by stepping up behind him, covering his mouth with one hand and punching my claw through his eye with the other. He died silently and pitifully in the shadows. No one noticed, except a man in the cages. He was crammed in there and I knew his muscles must ache with excruciating pain at being folded up like that.

He watched me as I moved to the next guard and twisted his head around like a demented barn owl, without the flexibility. Unfortunately, despite what Hollywood would tell you, that isn't a quiet way to kill people. I had seconds to make it to the man throwing punches at the already battered body of Flint before there was a gun out and pointed at my future Packmate.

I pressed my claws to the throat of the torturer. "Drop it or I'll kill him," I growled from a mouth that wasn't made for words. It was made for rending and tearing and howling at the moon.

Rook laughed, a cold, humorless sound. "Do it. I couldn't give a fuck."

The guy in my arms was dead already, we all knew it. Still, he made a half-decent shield so I'd keep him alive for now. I edged closer to Flint, and Rook shot at the ground by his feet, making the bullet ricochet wildly off the concrete.

Rook sneered, and I decided I was going to tear his head clean off his body, just for fun. "I'll tell you what, Wendigo. I'll exchange you for him. He can go back to the little bitch, and I get myself a Wendigo. Seems like a fair trade."

I mean, I considered it for half a second. There was no doubt in my mind that Flint's life was more valuable than mine. If I was a selfless person, I would take Rook up on his offer and send Flint back to Mouse. Would travelling around being Rook's pet sideshow freak really be that different to the life I was already living?

But I wasn't a selfless person; we'd already established that. I selfishly wanted both Carmen and her happiness. And that meant getting this Djinn back to our Pack, and getting back there too, to enjoy the look on her face.

I saw a shadow across the room, so I grinned. Well, kind of. Wendigo had no flesh on their face to grin, so basically I just bared my teeth even more. "Never."

Rook raised his gun and pointed it at Flint. He had been quiet up until now, but when he turned his battered face to me with such desolation on his face and wheezed, "Run", I realized they'd done some kind of internal damage. I spared him a quick look, then I snapped the neck of the guard I was absently holding and flung him toward Rook, moving across to put my body in front of Flint's. Mine could take some damage, but looking at Flint and not knowing how well he healed, I was unsure he'd survive a bullet wound.

The gun went off, and everything slowed down as it usually did in those monumental moments in your life. The bullet hit my chest, and I roared, but then Lucius appeared from the darkness like the specter of death, doing something complicated around Rook's neck and then dropping him to the ground.

I sucked in a breath, though it was hard to breathe around the pain in my chest, and I watched Rook open and close his mouth like a fish on the floor. I looked at Lucius. "You're not going to kill him?"

The look the ancient vampire sent back at me was so terrifying, even the Wendigo shivered. "He will wish he died this quickly. I shall send you his heart."

With that, he hefted Rook into his arms and disappeared. I roared, the Wendigo upset at the loss of its prey, but I knew that I would have obliterated him with a level of ferocity that I couldn't come back from. Blood poured from my chest, and I wondered if he'd hit something vital as I gasped for air.

I turned to Flint, unhooking him from the chain, and recognizing the cuffs on his wrists. Slave cuffs. I'd heard the story from Mouse, how he'd been wearing a pair when he'd been rescued and they had them removed. These things were meant to be destroyed, how did a petty criminal like Rook have so many pairs lying around?

I held Flint close to my body as I released him from the chains, not wanting to worsen any of his injuries. I was gasping for air too now, so I laid him on the concrete beneath the chains. I shifted my face back to human enough that I could speak without the hissing grunts. "Your Packmates are here somewhere. They will save you soon. But I must feed." I waved a hand in the general vicinity of my bullet wound.

Flint's hand gripped my wrist. "You are my Packmate," he gasped.

I felt like I'd been hit in the chest with another bullet, the force of the emotions I thought long dead consuming me. I laid my hand on his chest, and nodded. "Close your eyes, I do not wish you to see this."

Flint closed his eyes, either from his injuries or because I asked, and I went to the guard I had killed and cracked open his chest.

I was a monster, and even monsters must eat.

43

BOBBY

I drove carefully through the back roads that climbed the mountains toward Eden. Flint was laid out between us, his head on Sammie's lap and his feet on mine. He was in rough shape, but he was alive. The rest of the Eden crew had arrived just as we were loading Flint into the truck, and we'd insisted, well I'd insisted, that we be the ones to take him back to Eden. I couldn't let him out of my sight again.

When we'd stumbled into that hellhole and found a brutally beaten Flint and a giant fucking Wendigo moving around the room eating hearts, my stomach had dropped to my ass. There was something about the Wendigo that just created a primal fear response, which aggravated the Alpha in me. But when Monster had seen us, he'd shifted back to his human form, and

I could see the perfectly round hole of where he'd been shot.

He'd given us the quick version, insisted that he was fine and we should take Flint. Then he'd disappeared, but not before telling us he'd be back with Rook's heart. It was some medieval Dark Ages shit, but I could appreciate the visceral nature of that kind of revenge. Flint groaned as I eased into the driveway of the Academy, driving my truck right up to the doors. It was still the middle of the night, but the first light of dawn was touching the horizon.

As soon as the car was stopped, the door was wrenched open. Stacey began checking Flint's vitals right there on Sammie's lap. "What are his injuries?" she said in that no-nonsense way she had.

"Severely beaten. I think there might be a rib or two broken, and probably some internal damage."

She nodded, a stethoscope in her ears as she listened to his chest and then his abdomen. She frowned, but I didn't really know if that was a good or bad thing.

"Get him on the stretcher."

Sammie slid from the truck, and two seniors pulled Flint as gently as they could from the front of the truck. They lifted him straight onto the stretcher, but still, Flint moaned raggedly. "Move," Stacey barked at them, and the guys moved towards the door of the Academy as quick as they confidently could.

She stopped, looking over at Sammie. "What are your injuries?"

"I'm fine. Go help Flint," Sammie growled, and she put her hands on her hips and glared. She didn't ask again.

Sammie grunted. "One of the kids bit me."

Stacey stomped over, pulling his shirt to the side. There was a small, bloody bite mark on his shoulder, and I cursed myself for not noticing. I stared at Sammie now, noting he was a little pale and shaky.

I'd been so focused on Flint that I hadn't noticed the signs. "He's been bitten by a panther." I glared at Sammie. "Why didn't you tell me?" I growled at him, the Alpha in my voice finally affecting him.

He let out a shuddering breath. "We were busy. It was just a tiny bite."

I wanted to shake him. It was never just a bite with a shifter. Stacey pointed a finger at my chest. "Get him down to the isolation ward and coax him through it. I have enough on my plate. A fucking Angel popped in from nowhere and dropped off like twenty kids."

Sammie huffed. "Not an Angel. The Devil himself."

That shook Stacey's normally stoic demeanor, but it only lasted a second as she shook her head and started jogging back into the building.

I jammed my shoulder under Sammie's arm and helped him into the building. "I'm so sorry, man. This is my fault."

Sammie's knees shook. "Not sorry. Can spend longer with Mouse and Flint." He gave me a half smile. "You."

I shook my head. He didn't understand. Being turned wasn't a guarantee. There was also the chance of just straight up dying. I needed to find that kid. Work out if he was Alpha or not. The bite of an Alpha was more likely to result in a turned shifter. I also needed to find an Alpha to feed him their blood to finish the change. Again, an Alpha's blood was better. I was a shapeshifter. Our DNA wasn't the same or I'd do it myself.

I knew who. I just had to get Sammie situated first. The change was rough, even for the strongest of humans.

We took the elevator down to the medical wing, and by the time we hit the right floor, Sammie was beginning to sweat.

I needed to check on Flint. Find Monster, and make sure that the bullet wound was healing. I needed to check on the love of my fucking life before I went insane. But first I had to find Bohdie and ask him to essentially tie himself to Sammie forever.

For the first time in my life, I wished I was a two-natured shifter. I could take care of my Pack properly then. I half carried, half dragged him to the isolation ward, and laid him down on the bed.

"Jesus, you weigh a fucking ton for a human," I groaned as I lifted him onto the bed.

He moaned as he curled into a ball. Yeah, here came the muscle cramps. I didn't know much about the process of turning humans into two-natured shifters, but I'd heard about the muscle cramps.

"Not human for much longer," he gasped out.

I stroked his curly brown hair back from his forehead. I leaned forward and kissed it softly. "No. I swear to you, as your Packmate, that I will get you through this. You're going to live a long and happy life with our mate."

His eyes went wide with panic. "What if she isn't my fated mate? What if someone comes along and steals me from her? I love her, I can't..."

I petted his hand. "Don't stress it. Turned shifters don't get fated mates, and even if they did, Carmen is the perfect woman for you. The ancestors or the Moon Goddess wouldn't be that cruel, I promise. Now stay here. I have to go find a kitty cat to make you feel better."

Once I was out of sight of the isolation room, I sprinted. The sooner I got him an Alpha, the better his chances of changing painlessly. I had a feeling I knew where Bohdie would be. I stopped the front of the ICU room, and my chest felt tight at the sight of Enit hooked up to so many machines. I'd known her forever, and we'd been friends just as long. Seeing her like that hurt my heart.

And as I'd guessed, Bohdie was by her bedside. I knocked on the glass and waved him out. He frowned, standing but not before kissing Enit's cheek. She didn't even stir, and I panicked. What if she never woke up?

I shook my head. Enit was tougher than anyone gave her credit for. Bohdie pushed through the door. "Did you get that fucker?" he snarled, and I nodded.

"Lucius has him. And if he isn't already dead, he was definitely wishing he was at this point."

Bohdie nodded, and I could tell the lion was real close to the surface.

I swallowed hard. "There's been an accident. Sammie needs you."

Bohdie reared back, shock contorting his features as he tried to work out why I would need him. I spotted the moment he figured it out. "No," he gasped, and I shook my head.

"There were kids. They were scared and we couldn't just leave them."

Bohdie just strode past me. "Sounds like Sammie. Let's go. The longer this goes on, the worse it is for him. But first, we have to find Cara."

I nodded. That worked for me, because she was in the direction my heart was leading anyway. I had to tell Mouse that her mate was now going to be a cat.

When I pushed open the door, Mouse tried to fly

out of bed and into my arms. Only the strong hands of Cara held her down, coupled with her own frailty from her injuries.

"Thank fuck you're back, I was so worried." She paused and studied my face. "Is Flint okay? Did you get him? Fuck, Bobby tell me. I'm going out of my mind."

I reached her in three long strides, kissing her softly. "We got him, baby. He was a bit banged up, but Stacey is looking after him."

"Then why does your face look like that?" Damn the girl for knowing me too well. "Where's Sammie? Bobby, where is Sammie?"

I swallowed hard and stood up. "Sammie is fine. But there's been a bit of a problem. He was bitten, and it seems to have taken. He's going to shift."

Cara paled, and Bohdie was there, wrapping her in his arms. I couldn't drag my eyes from Mouse. I watched the emotions race through her eyes. The fear that he wouldn't make the change. The happiness that he was now long-lived, like us. The guilt that chased that happiness, because we'd stolen his human life from him. Finally, she swallowed, and pushed up on her elbows. "Bohdie will complete the change?"

I nodded, and Bohdie whispered into Cara's hair, "I won't let anything happen to him."

She shifted her body around. "I wanna be there."

"Mouse—"

"I wanna be there, Bobby. Now find me a wheelchair or carry me like a fucking invalid, I don't care. But I'll be there when my mate changes even if I have to commando crawl my way there myself."

I believed her too. "Dammit. Why are you so damn stubborn?" I growled as I unhooked her from her splints and slings. I hoped she'd healed enough that this wouldn't do damage to her already mangled bones.

I was careful of her bad arm and leg, but by the gritted teeth I knew she was hurting. She didn't let out a single hiss of pain though. Stubborn and brave. I carried her down toward Sammie's room, but I stopped at Enit's first. Finally, Mouse let out a moan of pain.

I nuzzled her head, wrapping her in my arms and my warmth. "She'll be okay. Stacey won't let anything bad happen to her, and Bohdie has been with her this whole time. She's not alone."

She choked back a sob. Cara reached out and grabbed her good hand. "I was sitting with your stubborn as fuck brother too before these guys dragged me in to babysit your stubborn ass. Family trait, for sure. But we've got you, girl."

Mouse's lip wobbled, and I could see her fighting it back. I walked her into Enit's room and angled her so she could touch her littermate. A small sigh passed Enit's lips, like she was comforted by the touch, by knowing that Carmen was safe. "Love you, E. Wake up soon, okay?"

I didn't miss Bohdie touching Enit's foot like he couldn't help himself. There was more than booty between these two, but I'd been too caught up in my own relationship drama to pay attention. Still, Bohdie followed us out as we walked to the last isolation room. I keyed in the code to open the doors, and when Sammie saw Mouse, he struggled to his feet.

"Put her on the bed," he gasped out.

I did what he said, and then pointed to the bed. "There's room for two on there."

He gave me a crooked grin, but he was weaving on his feet. He looked past me at his sister, and his face softened.

"Hey, Sis."

Cara's face went through a comical range of emotions, before she settled on anger. "How could you get yourself turned?" She shouted, her hands on her hips. "What if you die?" She whispered the last bit, like she didn't want to tempt fate.

He held out his arms, and she ran into them. "Not gonna happen. I'm Damnation, you know we're impossible to kill," he laughed, and she punched him in the shoulder.

I didn't get it, but it made her smile. "You better fucking be, or I'm calling Judas and you can explain why you died to him."

She stepped back and he swayed a bit more

violently. I put my hand on his elbow, ready to catch him in case he face planted. "Into bed, big guy."

He laid down gently around Mouse, and kissed her uninjured cheek. "Love you."

She closed her eyes as she soaked in his words. "Love you too."

I stepped back, and let Bohdie in to do his thing. "Have you ever seen this done before?"

He nodded. "Yeah, I accidentally bit my adopted mom as a kid, and my Pride turned her. I've got this, Alpha."

I let out a deep sigh, and stepped toward my Pack-mates wrapped around each other on the bed. All I wanted to do was climb onto the bed with them and keep them both safe. But I couldn't just yet. Soon.

Instead, I kissed both of them gently. "I have to check on Flint and track down Monster, then I'll be back. Be good."

My future stared back at me from the pillows, but I still managed to drag myself away. Stepping into the hallway, I knew it was time to be a real Alpha, and that meant make sure my whole Pack was fine, even though my heart screamed to be back in that room.

Flint first.

y whole body screamed in pain, but not even close to the pain in my chest. Seeing Enit like that, like a broken porcelain doll, had carved a ragged wound through my heart. Now, the anxiety was going to eat me alive as Bohdie stepped toward the bed.

He looked down at us both, his normal cockiness disappearing in the face of the last twenty-four hours. Cara hovered behind him, valiantly trying to hide her fear but I could smell it on the air like arsenic.

"So, I'm just going to give you some of my blood. It's a pretty simple process really, but don't tell your sister. She's been trying to become a pretty lion since she saw my parents in the woods."

Cara punched him in the bicep again. "Shut your face, Simba."

Sammie's mouth curled a little at their antics, then he frowned. "Am I going to be a lion shifter too?"

Bohdie shrugged. "I don't know. Normally you'd take the blood of the breed of shifter that bit you. But you can't take it from a kid and I don't know any other panthers so...?"

Sammie nodded, and Bohdie grabbed a scalpel from the trolley beside the bed. He sliced a line across his wrist, tilting it slightly so blood welled to the surface. He held it to Sammie's lips, but then the door slammed open and Stacey rushed in.

"Stop! For the love of Socrates, did none of you listen in shifter biology class?"

Bohdie pulled his wrist to his chest and stared at the tiny girl who was scowling in front of him. "Shifter what class?"

She hefted a bag of blood by her side and huffed. "I forgot you guys were new." Her eyes slid to me. "You and Bobby should have known better. You don't just give a turning shifter any old blood unless you want him to get super sick, as the different venoms would war inside his bloodstream for supremacy. He needs the blood of the shifter who bit him, or at least someone of the same genus."

She strode to the side of the bed, still mumbling to herself. "I had to find the kid that bit him, work out if he was a jaguar panther or a leopard panther. Panther isn't a breed, you know, it's a melanistic variation of the different species. So congratulations, Samuel, you're a jaguar." She began hooking up the bags of blood beside the bed. "You'll also be happy to know that Flint is fine. Banged up to all hell, and probably pretty sore and sorry for himself, but judging by the old scars and x-rays, it wasn't his first beating, and probably not even his worst."

She said it completely emotionlessly, like she was stating a fact that Flint had been so abused, that being beaten nearly to death wasn't a new experience for him. If you didn't know her, you'd think she didn't care, but I'd known Stacey since kindergarten. She cared, but all her emotions were filtered through logic. She didn't need to be sad for him anymore because he was free. He'd never be beaten again. Feeling sad for the man in the past was a waste of energy, that kind of thing.

She opened a cannula and grabbed the back of Sammie's hand, pushing it in with expert precision. Then she connected it all together, and the blood flowed down the tube and into Sammie. "Because we are a school filled with shifters and other supernaturals and sometimes one of you has a little oopsie and bites a human, we keep the blood of a lot of the different shifter genuses here in the medical wing, in a charmed refrigeration unit to maintain the magic." She frowned as she moved away from the bed. Grabbing her stethoscope, she checked his vitals once more. "So we had some jaguar Alpha blood on hand, though most big cats don't adhere to social group structures, so there's really no such thing as a jaguar Alpha per se. I hear that sometimes getting the transitional blood from the bag and not directly from a living being can make the transition rougher, so I apologize for that. Every transition is different, some can take minutes and some can take hours, so I'll leave you to it. Once you've had the full transfusion, I'll return to check on you. Now, Alistair needs me to do the observations on the rest of the patients, and if I see your shapeshifter Alpha I'll send him back, after I give him an earful."

I lifted a hand to stop her. "Can you put Flint in here too? We'd both feel better with our Pack around."

Stacey nodded. "I'll get your bed sent in here too. You need to get back into traction."

I swallowed hard. "Stacey." The girl stopped beside the door and looked at me. "Enit...?" I whispered.

The first hint of true emotion crossed her face. I saw the fear and the worry, and it softened her face until she looked like an entirely different person. "The surgery went textbook perfect. The rest is up to her. But she will be okay, Carmen. I refuse to let her be anything else."

With that, she strode out the door.

I looked back at Sammie, watching his face for changes. But he looked just the same, his hair a little floppier, his cheeks flushed with fever. He reached over and stroked my cheek, and it was hard to miss the tube coming from his arm. "It's going to be okay, Sweetheart."

I rubbed my face against his head, my nose twitching at how much his scent was changing already.

True to Stacey's word, one of the seniors appeared with my hospital bed. I snarled when they tried to lift me from Sammie's bed, but the wolf seemed okay with Bohdie doing it, like it recognized Enit's scent all over him. I got them to push the bed right up against Sammie's, and I could tell the change was beginning to ride him hard.

He had gone pale, and the sweat was starting to bead on his brow. He shook, and I reached out and gripped his hand.

What felt like hours but was probably only minutes later, the door slid open and Bobby walked in, Flint in front of him in a wheelchair.

Something in my chest relaxed with all three of them in the room with me. I still needed Monster, but my wolf was content with three of her mates in one room.

Bohdie squeezed Cara tight. "I'm going to sit with Enit. I don't want her to be alone."

Tears welled up in my eyes and I blinked them back rapidly. "Thank you, Bohdie. I promise not to cut your dick off."

He gave me his brilliant grin, and I saw briefly what

had Enit so enamored. He was a bit too shiny for me, but still, there was something about him. He shook his head. "Crazy bitch. I'm going to hold you to that." He slipped from the room, slapping Bobby on the back as he walked past them.

I saw Flint, his face an absolute mess, and I burst into tears. It was too fucking much. Too much.

"Sugar Plum, Carmen baby, it's okay, don't cry," he said in a raspy pained voice that just made me cry harder. He struggled to his feet and lurched toward me. He climbed onto Sammie's bed, and I could tell every movement was painful. But eventually, he was situated between us, able to touch us both.

We soaked in each other's warmth, Cara on the other side of Sammie, and Bobby sitting beside me. We were crammed into that tiny room, but I needed everyone. Like a switch, being nestled amongst my mates, my body finally gave up to a healing rest.

WHEN I WOKE AGAIN, the deep even breaths of the men beside me told me that everyone was asleep. My eyes flew open, drifting over a sleeping Flint. Sammie looked okay. I watched his chest rise and fall, assuring myself that he was still alive. I cataloged his body parts, and he looked like average old Sammie. Maybe the bite didn't take after all?

I tried to squash down the disappointment at the

idea, guilt riding the feelings heels. I should be happy he hadn't lost his humanity, that he was the same man I'd fallen in love with. I left him sleeping, looking over at a dozing Bobby.

I tried to work out what had woken me, and then Monster stepped from the shadows. Months ago, that would have scared the shit out of me, but right now, all I felt was relief that he was okay too.

"Bobby said you were shot."

He shook his head. "Just a bullet. It takes more to kill a Wendigo."

I smiled softly at him, wishing I could pull him into my arms. "I'm glad you're here. That you're okay," I whispered softly.

He nodded, and his face was achingly tender as he stared at me all trussed up in bandages and traction. He stepped closer, and my nose twitched again at a familiar scent. Blood.

I frowned. "Are you sure you've healed?"

He nodded. "You're smelling this." He produced a red cloth-wrapped bundle. No, not red cloth. Blood-soaked cloth. He handed it to me and as I unwrapped it, part of me already knew what it was.

Inside the cloth was a heart. It wasn't black like I'd imagined.

"The heart of your enemy. He isn't a threat to our—I mean, your Pack anymore."

There was a low rumble beside me, and I realized

everyone was awake except Cara. "Our Pack, Monster. You have more than earned your place in our Pack," Bobby corrected softly.

I looked at the body part in my hand, and I knew it meant more to Monster than just a piece of our enemy. It was a declaration. Unlike most shifters, there were three parts to Monster. There was the human, the Wendigo and the wolf shifter he used to be. I was the wolf's fated mate, but this heart was proof that his Wendigo considered me his mate also. A creature that was perpetually starving had just handed me its primary food source, gift-wrapped at that.

It was romantic as hell, and I smiled at Monster with watery eyes.

"Thank you, mate. You've protected our Pack well." The words were more formal than our normal interactions, but this was important.

I handed the heart to Flint, who was wide awake and staring at the heart like it was going to grow limbs and come back from the dead.

"It's time to end this once and for all. Turn it to ash, and then the last of the psycho will be gone from our lives forever."

Flint nodded at my words and cupped the blood-soaked package in his hands. Within seconds, it went up in a fireball until not even ash was left. I looked past him to Sammie, and yellow-green eyes stared back at me. The eyes of the jaguar.

Seconds later, they melted back into Sammie's normal dark brown and I shook my head. "You've turned. Do you feel different?" I asked softly, and Sammie nodded but didn't elaborate. I reached across Flint and held out a hand. Our fingers curled together on Flint's chest, and I felt our magics intertwining, trying to work out who was more dominant.

I turned back to Monster, who was standing there awkwardly, the longing on his face so damn painful. I smiled and waved him forward.

"Come here. My wolf wants to scent her mate."

I swear, I saw his whole body ripple with desire. Not sexual desire. Surprisingly my broken, swollen face wasn't overly appealing. No, the desire to be loved or held or something emanated from Monster in waves. This I could give him.

Bobby scooted back, and Monster filled his space. He folded his huge body into the hard molded plastic seat.

"Closer." He leaned forward, but he was still too far away. "Closer, Monster. I promise I don't bite. Well, I do, but you'd like it." I grinned at him and he looked at me bamboozled, but still, he leaned closer. He wasn't even breathing. I lifted my face up and captured his lips with mine, and they were surprisingly soft.

The kiss was gentle and brief, and he closed his eyes reverently for a moment. When he lifted those midnight eyes to mine again, I was trapped in his stare once again. "Thank you for bringing my mate back to me. Thank you for returning to me. I can't wait to be your bonded mate."

He reared back like I'd punched him in the chest. I frowned, making grabby hands, until he was close again, then I pulled his head down to my chest, right over my heart. I stroked his hair, and let our proximity ease us both. His body went loose as tension escaped his body, and I looked over his head and met Bobby's eyes as he took me in with my other fated mate. "I love you," I mouthed and he mouthed it back.

I didn't deserve that man.

In a room filled with the men who I would one day call mine with irreversible bond marks, and the threats to our Pack nothing more than ash, I finally let myself go to sleep again.

I watched Mouse from the side mirror of Sammie's car as she all but hung her head out the window, the passing wind picking up her long, dark hair like streamers. For a second, I forgot how to breathe.

She was so fucking perfect.

Way too good for you, but the fates always had a funny sense of humor, Hew snarked, but not even the voices in my head could bring down my mood.

The medical staff had kept her in the hospital for five days, long enough for her shifter healing to mend her bones enough that she could walk around in a full leg cast, and an arm cast. They wouldn't have been able to keep her a day longer. She was bouncing off the walls, giving Alistair hell, and refused to let Flint out of her sight even after he'd healed enough to leave.

So they'd strapped and plastered her body, and she didn't complain for a moment. We were driving her home, back to Dark River, and she'd insisted that I come too. She'd talked to her parents about giving me an apartment before the accident, and someone had made that happen.

I was... nervous. It was the first home I'd had in nearly a century. It didn't even matter that it was in a town filled with vampires and basically run by my fated mate's parents. An innocent kind of anxiety welled up. I hadn't seen her parents since that night, and I was freaking out.

So you can rend someone limb from limb, but you can't meet the parents? Wati scoffed. That was another problem. I'd have to tell Mouse about Hew and Wati, and what if she thought I was crazy? Not Wendigo crazy, but actually insane?

One of the voices snorted, but I couldn't be sure which one.

"Just go straight to the diner, Sammie. They're giving Monster the apartment above the diner that used to belong to my dad," Mouse said, and I swear, she sounded excited. Actually excited.

Flint was beside her, curled at her side, and when she wasn't looking he stared at her like she was the reason the sun rose. He was devoted to her, and I wasn't sure she understood the extent of that devotion yet, but she would one day.

When Rook had died—which had taken hours because Lucius was a master of his craft—Flint's slave cuffs had fallen off, and had been quickly taken away by the Lycanthropes of Eden Academy to be locked in a safe somewhere. They seemed like good people, but still, I watched them. Having something like that was an incredibly powerful tool.

But neither Flint nor Mouse seemed worried so I kept it to myself, but I would watch. I would always watch over them both. Because despite my connection to the group being through Mouse, I felt quite... fond of the rest of the Pack. Bobby with his Alpha dependability had taken a little while to adjust to, because I'd been without those structures for so fucking long. But he didn't try to make me submit for fun, and I deferred to his judgement on most things. What did I know about what a woman needed? Or how to run a Pack?

Fucking nothing and then some.

Sammie was steady and dependable too, and it made sense. Flint and Mouse were wild and unpredictable, and they needed that balance. Sammie was quickly coming to terms with being a panther shifter, and I was glad that my mate's heart wouldn't be broken in sixty years when he would have died of human frailties. He accepted me without reservation. It didn't matter what I was, or even what I'd done to become Wendigo, he was so sure I deserved to be loved that he'd stepped in for me. For that he had my loyalty for life.

Flint I was more in tune with. That wild violence. The unpredictable nature of his moods. He was both deadly and innocent in ways I didn't think possible. He could fight and kill, knew how to drop a man into the dirt in seconds. But when Mouse had suggested we camp out one day and make s'mores, his eyes had gotten so wide and hopeful that it'd almost broken my newly rediscovered heart. He'd missed so much, and the anger I felt at that made me want to raise Rook from the dead and shred his chest all over again.

"Do you not wish to go home first?" I said softly, and she shook her head.

"No, they'll all be at the diner anyway, and maybe, eventually, the apartment with you would be our home too."

The whole car went silent. "What do you mean, Mouse?" Bobby asked softly from her other side.

She shrugged, which looked weird with her cast. "I mean, we're a Pack right? You're my mates. Eventually, we are going to live together in a big Pack house and maybe, you know, after a year or so, we'll bond."

My heart beat so loud in my chest, I was pretty sure it would explode. As if seeing the hopeful panic on my face, she smiled. "Not yet though. We need to get to know each other more, work out if we can actually live together. Because I leave towels on the floor, and it drives my siblings crazy. Gotta know what you're saddling yourself with for the next century or so."

I shook my head in amazement, and Bobby snorted. "Mouse, you're my fated mate. I don't know if Monster feels the same way, but you could throw every towel on the floor every day and roll around on them like a pig in mud, and I'd still love the hell out of you."

I wet my suddenly dry lips with my tongue. "I do."

She gave us both the most radiant smile I'd ever seen. "We'll see."

She was saved from saying anything else by Sammie pulling the car into a spot at the front of a diner. It looked straight out of a retro painting with its red and white striped awnings. I unfolded myself from the car and stretched. I could feel eyes on me from everywhere, and I kind of wanted to find a shadow to hide in. But this was a town of vampires, and shadows wouldn't save me.

Bobby climbed out from the backseat, and Mouse reached out her good arm to stop him. "I think it's probably best if Monster carries me in."

Bobby raised an eyebrow, but nodded. He slapped me on the back. "You get the lumpy cargo. I swear all that plaster is made from lead."

Mouse scowled at him. "Are you calling me fat? Because I could still kick your ass with only one arm and one leg."

I chuckled beneath my breath as I reached in and

she wrapped an arm around my neck. I managed to maneuver her into my arms so I was supporting her weight and not jostling anything that was still sore. It wasn't an easy task, but I'd rather take an hour to extract her from the car than cause her pain. When I stood, she was only inches from my face, and her scent was all over me. I wanted to kiss her, but I hadn't earned the right yet. I would soon though.

I should have known better than to think I had any say in the matter.

Using the hand she had around my neck, she pulled me closer and kissed me softly on the lips. Her lips tasted like strawberries and were so unbelievably soft. Did women always have lips that soft? I pulled back and stared down at her.

You're staring at her like a dumbass, stop it, Wati coached.

Hew muttered something derogatory, but I wasn't paying attention. I swallowed hard and blurted, "I hear voices in my head. The evil spirits that make me Wendigo."

She went stiff in my arms as she pulled back in shock. "What?"

I swallowed hard and felt like beating myself up. It was out now though. "I felt like we should go in there with complete honesty."

Nice save, Douche Canoe, Hew sneered. Well, he would have sneered if he had a face.

"Their names are Hew and Wati. They have long traditional names, but we all separated from the people we used to be a long time ago. They are the evil spirits that possessed me when I asked for the Wendigo. They are... not terrible. Our definitions of good and evil have changed a lot."

Eh, I'll take it, Wati said, always the more even-tempered of the two.

Mouse frowned, and I went to pass her to Bobby, but she clung to my neck. "Wait, we aren't done here. What does that mean for you?"

I shrugged. "Mostly, they are like having an annoying commentary track running all the time, except when I'm Wendigo."

She nodded once. "Are they a danger to our Pack?" What she meant was, would I be a danger to our Pack?

I shook my head. "No, you're their last chance at salvation too."

More frowning and I was pretty sure I was fucking this up. This wasn't conversation for the sidewalk, but it was too late now. "You better explain that comment, Monster."

I gripped her tighter. "Wati and Hew are attached to my soul, like a symbiote. When, I mean if, we bond and our souls join, then by extension, so do theirs. I'm immortal until I find my fated mate, and then when we bond, my immortality is tied to your mortality. When you pass on, I will too. And so will Wati and Hew. They have been around a hell of a lot longer than either of us. They've been waiting." I looked at the guys, who were all listening intently with various degrees of frowning.

Bobby chewed his lip. "So we are all safe, because they won't want to piss off Mouse since she's their only chance at an afterlife?"

I nodded. "That, plus they aren't bad really. Do they like eating hearts? Yes. But they don't make me do anything and we don't kill indiscriminately. They were happy to starve until we found an opponent that really needed to be ended."

I didn't think about the guy from the gym the other day. I mightn't have done my research, but I was pretty sure he wasn't a boy scout.

Mouse cocked her head to the side. "Do they like me?"

I stared at her, blinking rapidly. "What?"

"Hew and Wati, do they like me? What do they like to do? Do they have a bucket list that doesn't involve killing people?"

I'd like to fuck again, even vicariously through you, Hew jeered.

I'd like to swim beneath a waterfall one more time, Wati answered, and I relayed that one to Mouse.

"We can do that, once the casts are off."

I like her more than you already, Wati snarked and I couldn't help my smile as I looked down into the sparkling blue eyes of my mate. I apologized to every deity I'd cursed for giving me this half-life. If this was the kind of person I was waiting for, well, it was all worth it.

I leaned forward and kissed her, because now I'd started I wasn't sure I could stop. But I was still extremely conscious that we were out in the open and her parents, as well as half of Dark River, were probably watching. "Thank you."

She winked at me. "No, thank you. Now stop procrastinating. It's time to meet the firing line."

Flint laughed, probably more in empathy than anything else. Sammie grabbed the door and held it open as I sidestepped into the diner, careful not to bump so much as a single hair on Mouse's head.

I was concentrating so hard on my task, that the lack of noise didn't register until I was standing halfway into the room, Bobby beside me, Flint and Sammie flanking us.

Everyone stared. I didn't know if they were staring at me, or at the beaten up Mouse, or the equally beaten up Flint.

We probably made an interesting group.

I recognized the vampire that appeared in front of us. The Not-Lucius. The other twin, and according to Bobby's coaching, that was Nico. He reached out and touched Mouse's cheek, and I saw the primal rage behind his eyes, but he kept a better lid on it than his twin.

"How are you feeling, Squeak?"

She rested her cheek in his palm. "Good. Annoyed by these damn casts though."

He gave her a crooked grin. "I bet. But X says you have another three weeks of them, so try to take it easy okay? No 'accidentally' breaking the plaster."

She gave him a mock innocent look, and he scoffed. He looked at me then. "I am Nico, you must be Monster. It is nice to see you under better circumstances."

I inclined my head. He was ancient, this vampire. As old as Wati and Hew, that was for sure, even if this wasn't his native soil. "Nice to meet you."

He shook hands with Bobby, Flint and Sammie. "It's good to see you all in one piece as well." Nico looked back at Mouse. "Raine and Tex are with Enit. X is with Christopher at home, because he is such a terrible patient. I kind of want to accidentally break his cast for him, just so he can run off some of that aggression." He turned and walked human-slow toward the back of the diner.

We only made it another few feet before a round woman with ruddy cheeks was accosting us. "Oh my poor sweet *bairn,* are ye better?"

Mouse accepted the woman's kisses and fussing with a fond smile. "Much better, Beatrice."

Beatrice raised an eyebrow, taking me in with appraising eyes. "I ken see that, lass. I tell you, they didn't have such handsome nurses when I was young." She waggled her eyebrows at me.

Mouse held me a little tighter. "Beatrice, this is Monster. He is moving into the upstairs apartment. He's also one of my fated mates." You could hear the rapid inhale of breaths around the room. She craned her neck so she could see over my shoulder. "The sexy redhead is Flint. And the handsome brunette is Sammie."

"Well, there's more of Raine in you than you'd think," Beatrice said with a wink. "Go on back, I'll bring you the key and something to eat as well."

She disappeared back into the kitchen and I carried Mouse to the table that currently had a Sheriff, a third brooding vampire and if I wasn't mistaken, the shapeshifter Alpha.

The latter eyeballed me, like he was trying to decide if I was going to go feral and eat the hearts of everyone in this room.

The Sheriff stood up, and moved toward us. He leaned down and kissed Mouse's forehead. "I have to get back to the station. Eugene stole Ruby's gnomes and decapitated them, so she wants to file a report. I wanted to stay and say hi first though. I'm glad you're home, baby girl." He looked at me. "I'm always watching."

He said it pleasantly, but there was an undertone of threat, and I could respect that. The Alpha stood up and swaggered toward us with that air of someone who was confident of his power and his station in life. He held Mouse's hand.

"I need to go too, but I wanted to say welcome home." His eyes met mine, and I dropped my own gaze instinctively. "I also wanted to say welcome to the family. I'm sorry our first meeting was so... rough."

I shrugged. "It's understandable."

The other vampire, Bobby had told me that his name was Judge, laughed. "You made quite the impression on Lucius though. He really likes you."

Brody shook his head. "That's a worry." He kissed Mouse's cheek. "Be good, Mouse. I'm getting old and my heart can't take all the worry."

Mouse snorted it. "You're fitter than a man half your age. Don't pull that shit on me."

He just grinned, said his goodbyes, and left. Beatrice bustled up with a plastic carry-out bag of sandwiches and a shiny red key. "You go right up. It's probably going to need a good airing out, it's been closed up since this one moved out all those years ago." She lifted her chin at Judge. "But it should be clean and furnished. Just let us know if you need anything."

Mouse was wiggling in my arms. "Mush, mush, let's go." She pointed to a door at the back of the diner. She looked past me at her dads. "Are you guys coming?"

It was Judge who shook his head. "No, you should go and check it out as a Pack."

I swallowed hard, my heart doing that weird flip-flopping it always did when someone called us a Pack. I was back in a Pack.

We walked up the stairs together, and Flint grabbed the key from Mouse, opening the front door to the apartment. I didn't really care what it looked like, all I knew was that with a roof and these four people, it was the closest thing to a home I'd had in a century.

As if she sensed my thoughts, Mouse grabbed my chin gently and turned my face to hers. "Welcome home, Monster."

Home was in my arms, but this was close.

EPILOGUE

I danced around Monster's living room to the Arctic Monkeys telling me I'd look good on the dance floor. Fuck yeah, I would, especially now I was out of my cast and I could move properly. I didn't need a lot of rehab because, well I was a wolf shifter and that kind of stopped processes such as muscle wastage.

Jumping around to the music, I turned to look at Monster where he was sitting on his couch. The town had accepted his presence here reasonably easily. I guess they weren't mired with the superstitions of the Pack, and he wasn't really a threat to them. Well, at least they didn't think so. They'd given him a job at the gas station during the day, because his Resting Dick Face was so epic, the rare tourists who came through here during the day wouldn't even consider stopping.

He said all he did was read for most of the day, but he seemed content. We could worry about the rest later, after we all found our feet. I smiled at him and he opened his arms wide.

I was helpless to resist. Like I was magnetized, I walked toward him and sat down in his lap, rubbing my cheek all over his like I was a cat. We were waiting for the rest of the guys to arrive so we could go for our very first run as a Pack. I was almost giddy, I was that excited. Today felt just as important as the first time I spoke with Monster, or the first time I fought Flint. It seemed like an age ago, because they were already so ingrained in my life, but it had been only months.

Monster was waiting patiently for me to make my move, so I leaned over and kissed him. It was quite addictive, kissing my Wendigo. He kissed me back gently, but as I deepened the kiss so did he. His beard scratched at my chin, and it felt delicious.

We'd been taking it slow, because the guy was like ancient, and as much as I'd been through, I was still nineteen. My birthday had come and gone, unremarked because Enit had still been in a coma and no one had felt like celebrating. But Monster, he might have been in his twenties when he was turned, but he was centuries old. And that was kind of weird if you thought about it for too long. So he let me take the reins completely, and quite frankly, I was enjoying the slow, teasing build.

I straddled his lap and his hands gripped my hips with a groan. My fingers threaded in his hair, gripping it tightly as I held him to me. He growled as my tongue slipped past his lips, and I could feel the growing bulge of his dick beneath me.

"Mouse," he groaned, and I grinned against his lips.

Then Flint barreled through the front door, a wide smile on his face. "Should we come back?" he said, but his voice was pure mischievousness. But both Sammie and Bobby were close behind him.

I groaned, "Yes!" at the same time Monster grunted, "No."

I could feel his low chuckles against my chest. "Soon, Mouse."

I huffed and climbed off his lap, and while I scowled at the guys, I was so damn happy to see them. Sure, it had only been like four hours since I saw them all at school, but I'd missed them.

I ran and jumped into Sammie's arms, and he kissed me like he'd felt our time apart just as acutely.

"Hey, share!" Flint grumbled, dragging me into his arms and kissing me until my back was arched and I felt completely plundered.

He dropped me to my feet, and I swayed over to Bobby. His eyes ate me up, like he was the big bad wolf and not me. I stopped in front of him, looking up into his brooding face. "You look so happy," he murmured softly.

I couldn't help the smile on my face, and I didn't try to. "Why wouldn't I be happy?" I had four mates. Enit was finally out of the hospital. The true villain of our story was dead, and according to Lucius, chopped into 217 pieces and then each piece burnt and buried in the earth.

Bobby bundled me to his chest and kissed the ever-loving crap out of me, his mouth branding me as his until I had to drag myself away to breathe.

He pulled me into his arms and pressed his face into the crook of my neck. "Are you ready to run with your Pack, mate?"

I felt like my chest would explode. "So damn ready."

I raced out of the apartment, and I could feel my Packmates behind me as I raced out through the back entrance of the diner and into the woods outside Dark River. As soon as I hit the tree line, I stripped and shifted.

It was like being free. I sat down on my haunches and yipped as the other guys stripped off too. Flint walked over, running his hand down my brownish-gold fur. It was average in coloring, with Christopher being entirely black, and Enit being completely white, but I was still vain about how soft I was. I licked at his hand and he tasted like smoke and mate. "Sugar Plum, you're gorgeous."

I gave him a toothy wolf grin, and we both watched as Sammie shifted to his panther. The shift was slower, but not his first. He'd shifted the first couple of times at the Academy under the watchful eyes of the administration.

But soon enough, a glorious black big cat stood in front of me, and I judged the response of my wolf. I mean, it was a cat and dog thing, but my wolf just seemed excited to run with her mate.

I ran around him in circles, yipping excitedly, and he chuffed a happy laugh. I leaned down, wanting to play, and he seemed to work out that was what I wanted because he half-heartedly booped me with his paw, which sent me rolling. Jesus, he was strong.

Oh yeah, it was on now.

I chased him around and he prowled after me, making Flint and Monster laugh. I bounded up to Monster, yipping my question. "No, Sweetheart. There's no place for the Wendigo here. Go and play with our Pack."

Naw. Our Pack. I made a sickly sweet cooing noise, but it just came out as a weird squawk in my wolf form.

Then Bobby shifted into his bear, and it was on. We chased each other around the woods, always ducking back to see Monster and Flint. Flint hadn't changed either, though he did ride around on Bobby's back for a bit, more than happy to wrestle with us completely human. Crazy bastard.

Honestly, it was just one wonderful afternoon in what I was sure would be decades of many wonderful afternoons. Finally, as the sun was beginning to set, I shifted back to human.

We stood around, all entirely naked except for Monster and Flint.

Flint looked between us. "You know, now would be a good time for group se—"

"CARMEN!"

I whipped my head toward the panicked sound of Christopher's voice. Before I even recognized the need, I was running toward my brother. I could see him, blurred by the trees, standing at the back of the diner. He better not have been carrying on just because I was about to boink my pack in the woods like some kind of heathen ritual.

Bobby threw me his shirt and I jammed it over my head as I ran. I skidded to a stop, and the look on Christopher's face made panic burn in my chest.

"What's wrong?" I gasped out as everyone came to a stop behind me.

He was pale, his eyes too wide. "Enit's gone."

I frowned. "What? No, she's still at the Academy with Bohdie."

Christopher was shaking his head furiously. "Bohdie just called. She's completely disappeared. They were shifted, out beyond the Academy fence, and then she was gone. He thinks she's been taken."

Ice flooded my veins. Enit was gone.

ABOUT THE AUTHOR

Grace McGinty is eclectic. She has worked as a chocolatier, a librarian, a forensic accountant and finally a writer. Like her professional career, the genres she writes are also eclectic. She writes romance, reverse harem romance, fantasy, contemporary young adult and new adult books.

She lives in rural Australia with her crazy family, an entire menagerie of pets, and will one day be crushed by her giant piles of books that litter every room.

Head over to www.gracemcginty.com and join my mailing list for sneak previews into what I am working on and to stay up-to-date with new releases and giveaways!

Not ready to leave Eden Academy yet? You can preorder book 2, SWEETHEARTS AND SAVAGES, here: www.books2read.com/eden2

Turn the page for a sneak peek at the prologue of SWEETHEARTS AND SAVAGES (EDEN ACADEMY #2).

SWEETHEARTS AND SAVAGES (EDEN ACADEMY #2)

PROLOGUE - ENIT

3 years ago

"I've written you your final essay. I know you wanted to do it on the French Revolution, but the Russian Revolution is more relevant in today's social context."

I stared at the pretty girl in front of me, my eyebrows drawn together as I took the manilla folder she was thrusting at me.

"Stacey, I don't need you to write my essays for me," I said softly, not wanting to injure her feelings. Stacey was a genius. I don't just use that in the casual, pop-culture sense either. She was like, legit a genius. Just a human whose brain was different, so unusual that she learned things at a rate that blew my mind.

She frowned. "I dumbed it down to the correct learning level. No one will know that you haven't written it yourself. You said you were worried about this essay. I've helped you."

Hell. How did I explain to her that just because I said I was worried, didn't mean I wanted her to do it for me. "Its cheating. I don't like to cheat, Stace."

She chewed her lip, one of the few unconscious habits she had. Stacey was intense. She thought and behaved like someone three times her age, but she didn't really understand social norms outside of what books told her. Some of that was the fact she was rescued from an actual laboratory, the mean kids, stupid Teesha , whispered about it whenever she was around. But most of it was that her brain wasn't thinking like yours and mine. If a conversation were like playing chess, she wasn't thinking about the next move; she had already won this conversation and was onto the next.

It made it hard for her to make friends. But I was an Omega, which meant I could, I don't know, sense things. And she radiated so much goodness, that I'd decided I would be her friend. Plus, with me always came Carmen and Christopher, my littermates. Ever present shadows, snapping and snarling at people who looked at me the wrong way.

Somehow though, despite the fact she inadvertently insulted them at least five times a conversation, they liked Stacey. Carmen thought she was funny as hell, and Christopher just added her into his tiny little flock that needed protection by the big, bad Alpha wolf.

I was still walking toward my History class, my feet dragging as I tried to figure out a way to not hurt my friends feelings. If Carmen and Christopher felt protective of me, I felt that way about Stacey, whether she needed it or not. The only reason they let me walk to History by myself was because they both had P.E. this period. I did not do sports. Gross. Plus Stacey was with me, and no one was stupid enough to tangle with the daughter of the Lycanthropes who ran Eden Academy.

I herded Stacey into an alcove of lockers near the girls bathroom, and turned my softest smile in her direction, passing back the manilla folder. "Thank you, Stacey. I really appreciate you trying to help me, but some things I have to do myself in order to feel satisfaction in the achievement, you know?"

Stacey just stared at me, her face screwed up like she did when she was trying to figure out an extremely complex math problem. And I mean, this was PHD level mathematics.

Then she leaned forward and kissed me.

I stood so still, I was basically frozen. Her lips were soft, and tasted a little like the watermelon chapstick she used sometimes. I flicked my tongue out to taste it, like I couldn't help myself and then I drew away.

I was across the hall in front of the girls bathroom in a flash."Stacey, I- what?"

Stacey was still frowning, but there was a flush to her cheeks now. "I think I might love you, Enit."

She said it like she was coming up with a scientific hypothesis, like it was a problem she wanted to figure out. Like *I* was a problem she needed to figure out.

I was shaking my head repeatedly, and a small voice in my head wondered if I was going to shake my brains up like a milkshake.

"It's just the Omega pheromones."

Stacey was shaking her head now too. "No it's not. We don't have the same physiology."

"You're too young. I'm an Omega," I said again, like it was an excuse for what just happened. It was the only excuse I had for why I'd enjoyed it. "I'm sorry, I have to pee."

Then I pushed open the bathroom door and slammed it close, resting my back against the door. I listened intently, and after a minute, I heard the clip-clip of her shiny blue brogues. They were the only shoes she would wear, not matter if she was wearing a summer dress or jeans and a duffle. She argued they were the perfect shoe and she had at least fifteen pairs for when they wore out.

I let out a shuddering breath and stepped further into the bathroom, stumbling over to the sinks. I stared at myself in the mirror above the sink. My cheeks were flushed and I swear, I could still see the shine of her chapstick on my lips. Holy hell, how did I look her in the face now?

How did I tell her that I couldn't return her feelings?

How did I tell her that she probably didn't even have those feelings, that she was confusing my kindness with something like love?

How did I tell her that maybe I liked the kiss anyway?

I turned on the tap, splashing water on my face as I ignored the opening and closing of the bathroom door. I was sure, that if I turned to look, whoever it was would read what just happened all over my face.

My hands stilled though as an unmistakable scent hit my nose.

Alpha. And not Christopher or Bobby, the safe Alphas.

I straightened, my heart starting to pound. *Be calm, Enit. This means nothing. Don't overreact. He might just be here to...* To fucking what? What logical reason would he have to be in the girls bathroom?

I looked up, not meeting the Alpha's eyes. I knew him, of course, I knew all the Alpha's here by scent and sight, even if I avoided all of them. Todd. Wolf Alpha, from the grade above mine. He was huge and mean, and was from the school of thought that Omega were made for Alpha's to kick around, so they could get out their aggression and better lead their pack.

Carmen had called it bullshit, but with a few more f-words involved. Even suggesting such a thing made Christopher go into a rage.

I skittered around him. "Excuse me," I whispered, dashing toward the door. But his hand whipped out, grabbing my arm, and throwing me against the wall.

"Where are you going, Omega?" he growled, and a primal fear ran over my skin as I froze. I couldn't move, except to shake.

No. I needed to run. I kept imagining Christopher's voice telling me to get out of there. Never be trapped in a room with an unknown or untrusted Alpha. And I definitely didn't trust Todd.

"History class," I whispered, and his other hand came up to wrap around my throat.

He chuckled darkly, and no seventeen year old guy should sound so evil. But still, I couldn't move. Couldn't shout for help.

Couldn't be anything but helpless.

Todd inhaled in a lungful of my scent, the acrid stench of my fear. Then he slapped me. My head whipped to the side, and he laughed.

"Fuck, Omegas really are as pathetic as my Alpha said. Weak. You aren't even going to fight back, are you, little Omega? Not even if I do this?" He slid his hand from my neck down to my boob and squeezed.

I whimpered, screamed in my head to move, but still, I did nothing. He was right, I was pathetic. His hand slid lower, his fingers slipping beneath my shirt, the rough callouses on his fingers stroking my skin.

Then the door slammed open and there was a whirl of anger and fists barrelling through it.

Carmen was here.

I let the tears fall down my cheeks with relief. Carmen was on top of Todd, slamming her elbow into his face repeatedly. Todd growled, rolling out from under Carmen's furious form even as she pounded her fist into his face over and over.

Todd threw a punch, connecting with her cheek in a sickening crack, and her head whipped back. But Carmen was feral, just scrabbling backwards until she had her feet back under her and launching at him again. I don't know where she learned to fight like that, but she was holding her own against the Alpha. She gave him a quick jab to the throat, and he began to choke as she smashed his windpipe. She didn't stop though, oh no, she was way past that.

She knocked him backwards as he grabbed at his throat, and once he was down, she lifted her foot and stomped his dick.

I swear, I heard something crack beneath his howl of pain, his body curling like an armadillo in pain. Carmen pulled back her foot and kicked him in the head, and then he was lights out. The door slammed back open, and Christopher was there.

His eyes took in Carmen and the unconscious Alpha on the floor, and me still shaking like a leaf, the wall the only reason I remained on my feet. He was across to me in two strides, and he wrapped me in his arms, his Alpha presence slid over me like a blanket and I could finally breathe again.

"We've got you, E. We always have you," he cooed and I cried.

Eventually he passed me into Carmen's waiting arms, and she was still blood spattered. She murmured reassurances and kissed my head, echoing Christopher's words about always protecting me.

But I knew they couldn't always protect me. I was weak, powerless, and one day, I would be dead.